SKY PIRATES!

DOCTOR WHO – THE NEW ADVENTURES

Messrs. Levene, Bodle & Darvill-Evans of the fine *Virgin Publishing* Limited Liability Company are Proud, nay, Honoured to Present the First Ever Commonplace Publication of:

SKY PIRATES!

or

The Eyes of the Schirron

Being a most Excellent and Perspicacious Luminiferous Aether Opera by Noted Biographer, Tap-Dancer and Aerialist, Mr

DAVE STONE

and Detailing the Strange and Very Exciting Adventures of *The Doctor* and His Trusty *Companions* amidst the Multifarious Perils of a System caught in the Foul Grip of the Hideous *Sloathes*!

Mind-shattering Spectacle! Heart-stopping Cliffhangers! Fiendish *Villains* of Slithering Unmitigated Evil! Daring Rescues! *Lovers'* Misunderstandings! Foul and Cowardly Betrayals! All Manner of Improving Moral Examples! Incredibly Bad Jokes! All These may be Discovered by the *Discerning Reader* upon the Opening of these *Quite Reasonably Priced Pages*, with Full Hypnagogic Orchestral Accompaniment. No Monies Return'd.

———

Mr Stone tells us that he was Vouchsafed the True and Undeniable *Facts* of this History in a Vision whilst under the *Fiendish Influence* of Laudanum, 3-methoxyl-4.5-methylene-dioxyamphetamine, hash toasties and a Steaming Cup of Bovril. When he Came, however, to Transcribe his Vision he was Cruelly Interrupted by *Fate* in the Unassuming Guise of a Medicated Goitre Salesman named Aiden, from Peckham, and was Forced to Make the Rest of it Up. Sorry.

First published in Great Britain in 1995 by
Doctor Who Books
an imprint of Virgin Publishing Ltd
332 Ladbroke Grove
London W10 5AH

Cover illustration by Jeff Cummins
Internal illustrations by Roger Langridge

ISBN 0 426 20446 8

Typeset by Galleon Typesetting, Ipswich
Printed and bound in Great Britain by
Cox & Wyman Ltd, Reading, Berks

The Dedication

This one's for Manuela, Fillip, Marcus Morgan, Tanya, Derek, David Bishop, Dave Taylor, Wendy, Andy Lane, Charlie 'the man with no name' Stross, Karen, Neil, Kevin, Kevin, Trish and Daniel, Beth, Rebecca, Peter, everybody at the LBG, Charlie 'X-file' Adlard, Giles and Liz and Ben, the Crimson Pirate, Hector, Julie, Jon and Caroline, little Amy, Paul Cornell, Charlie 'sad male fantasy' Gillespie, Sharon, Kim, Lush, Jeff Cummins, the nice people at *Bifrost*, the other nice people at Off-Pink, the rather less nice pack of money-grubbing jackals of the British comic-book industry, Fritz Leiber, Anna Maria and John, Erroll Flynn, the memory of 'Susan', Roger Langridge, Claire, the other Claire, Steve Marley, Mum, Dad, Andy Bodle, Caspar, the Lemonheads, any number of Simons, Harry Harrison's *Star Smashers of the Galaxy Rangers*, Gerard, Clive, Andrew Cartmel, Michelle Shocked, Mo, Richard, Vince and all those many unsung others for variously, sometimes simultaneously and in no related order whatsoever giving me inspiration, information, undeserved love, a sofa to sleep on, a shoulder to cry on, jokes, more jokes, a sounding-board for *my* jokes, mutual massage, pause for thought, an outlet for otherwise unpublishable venomous rants, paying work, unconditional support and the crawling pain of grief and loss that never ends; for providing models to aim for, template skeletons for heroes and villains to infest and animate, unending helpful suggestions, sporadic sex, a soundtrack, beautiful art in a variety of contexts, free money and, just when I needed it, a reason to live; for reducing me to an incoherent spitting fury, for stroking my hair, for wilfully misunderstanding every word I say, for cooking me breakfast, for being drop-dead gnaw-ya-knuckle gorgeous; for the heat of you, the odd cheap thrill, your friendship, talent, pint of semi-skimmed milk, understanding, asinine spite and all those tempestuous nights under the stairs with the tub of Swarfega and the bullwhip.

Stuff. Thing. Anyhow.

D.S.

All the world's a stage,
And all the men and women merely players.
William Shakespeare,
As You Like It

Away, then, with these Lewd, Ungodly Diversions,
and which are but Impertinence at the best. What part
of Impudence either in Words or Practice, is omitted
by the Stage? Don't the Buffoons take almost all
manner of Liberties, and plunge through Thick and
Thin, to make a Jest?
St Clement of Alexandria, *Works*

As I was going up the stair,
I met a man who wasn't there.
He wasn't there again today;
I wish to God he'd go away.
Trad.

The Prologue

The System, in circumference, circumscribes some fifty-thousand leagues, and all of it on the inside: a perfect gaseous globe, encapsulated by an electrostatic Möbeus bubble-shell, through which the four high-density Wanderers spin around the Sun.

And at the edge of that inverted globe hangs Planet X: a black ball of basalt caked with ash and slag, cracked like perished rubber, pocked with volcanic craters weeping red and yellow magma like so many open and infected sores.

An interloper, this planet: flung from its original orbit millennia ago by some long-forgotten catastrophe. The energy field thrashes and flares about it; wounded, possibly mortally, retching upon this fatal irritant in a vain and palsied attempt to spit it out.

The wind is strong here; ash-laden and abrasive. If a man were to stand upon the surface of Planet X he would be scoured to the bones and the bones scattered within seconds. In only one place is the wind still and this, paradoxically perhaps, is a point upon the equator where the prevailing wind is strongest − where a mile-wide ring of vanes and turbines catch and redirect it into an artificial cyclone, a shrieking, spinning maelstrom of ash, the eye of which is a perfect vacuum.

And protruding into this vacuum, the twisting and segmented brass towers of telescopes.

Sloathes live underground.

Beneath the surface, cutting through the substrata and sealed with makeshift rubber airlocks, the shafts of the telescopes descend to a chamber. This is merely one of a vast warren of tunnels and caverns that riddle the little planet's core.

Sloathes are rabidly acquisitive.

Millennia between the stars, with nothing but blank basalt walls to draw the eye, have instilled in them a rabid desire for *things*. Over the years since their arrival in this diminutive system they have looted its various Wanderers with a total lack of discrimination – have acquired so much, in fact, that there is now little room for anything else. Tapestries of Anean silk hang from the walls, depicting the winged god *Kloi Kloi Seki* and its hideous if ingenious death at the appropriate manipulatory appendages of its four billion young. Intricate rugs of Promethean horsehair cover the floors, clashing horribly with the tapestries (Sloathes have no taste). Piled on the rugs a vast and priceless collection of objects and artifacts – even including vestigial and antique specimens from Dirt, that mythical, lost and long-eradicated cradle of humankind. A freestanding barometer with its dial set permanently on 'blustery'. An occasional table inlaid with feathers of peacock and partridge. A tea-chest filled with wire-framed spectacles. A Bakelite radiogram with the majority of its innards missing . . . And all arranged with the cargo-cult misplacement of those who have seen such objects arranged approximately thus but do not have the faintest idea of exactly why.

And all is clotted with the foul ichor that Sloathes exude constantly: running from the walls, radiating in viscous fans across flat surfaces. Drying to a thick and brittle crust.

Food.

For this chamber is *alive*: a seething mass of creatures of various sizes and states of development. The inhabitants of Planet X begin life as spores and exist in a continual state of growth, feeding upon the slime exuded by the larger and, voraciously, upon the bodies of the smaller.

Sloathes are metamorphic; their skeletons telescopic, enclosed by unstable flesh the consistency of boiling mud, skinned by muscle and chitinous platelets. In repose they resemble soft and scaly obloids, but each carries within it a wide assortment of limbs, sensory organs and manipulatory appendages, and can assume a multiplicity of forms more or less at will.

In a corner of the chamber, from the excellent vantage point of a slightly battered vitrine, a creature the size and approximate shape of a lobster watched a scaly pseudo-rat as it munched its way through a particularly crispy bit of slime. As the rat-thing passed below it, the 'lobster' planted suckers to secure itself firmly to the vitrine and detached a section of head and torso from its main mass, lowering it on a string of ligament.

As it descended, the head split open, folded in upon itself and transformed into a hooked and gaping set of jaws.

The rat-thing seemed to be enjoying its meal tremendously, so much so that it absolutely failed to notice the threat from above – until it was engulfed with a *snap*. The jaws ascended on their ligament string to be enveloped by the 'lobster', which in turn collapsed into a flaccid globe.

The globe rippled, then constricted with a wet and slightly muffled crunch. Acidic vapour shot from sphincter-vents with a hiss, raising bubbles on the varnish of the vitrine and scorching the wood. The Sloathe belched. The whole process had taken slightly under three seconds.

Events of this sort were taking place throughout the entire chamber. Quasi-cobras struck at pseudo-gila, swallowing them whole. A 'mantis' the size of a large rat tore the analogue of a throat out of something approximately lupine. A kind of animated mantrap with a wet, lolling tongue struck at a swarm of small flying creatures connected by fleshy tubes as they methodically pecked it to pieces.

None of this was particularly noted by the three hulking forms gathered around the eyepieces of the telescopes. Sloathes only become self-aware at the size of a large dog. It is only at this point that they achieve some form of status amongst themselves – and to these larger Sloathes, the creatures eating and being eaten around them were no more worthy of attention than an insect is to a man.

Sloathes are mimics by nature, entirely lacking in a sense of generative creativity. Their assumed shapes and forms of expression tend to derive from cursory and rather inept observation. The smallest of the three around the telescope had currently taken the form of a monstrous scorpion with a head like the skull of a crow. This was Lokar Pan, who in human terms would be regarded as chief of staff and commander of the Sloathe fleets.

3

Squatting beside it was the Sekor Dom Sloathe: a decomposing humanoid brain the size of an elephant, a single eye on a stalk swinging back and forth.

The largest of them all, the leader of them all, slopped with nine of its eyes pressed to the eyepieces of the telescope, manipulating focus verniers with a thousand fibrillating cilia-appendages.

Ostensibly slightly smaller than the others, the thing in this chamber was merely one small segment of its being. Tubes of extruded tissue snaked from it to other chambers – chambers full to bursting with alien flesh and scale. This was, in short, the Most Elevated and Puissant Kraator Xem – supreme ruler of the basalt planet and thus, in the minds of Sloathes the whole planet over, the absolute and supreme ruler of the entire universe.

The Most Elevated and Puissant Kraator Xem flicked its attention between the eyepieces, focusing upon each of the indigenous Wanderers in turn. The desert world. The jungle world. The water world. The ice world . . .

Even from this distance they were blemished. None were free from the cankers and welts of Sloathe incursion – but the underlying pattern spoke of some more serious disruption. In the solar years since the arrival of the basalt planet, there was a discontinuity in their relative orbits. Slight, admittedly, but building. The system was blowing itself apart in astral time.

This annoyed Kraator Xem – although *annoyed* could not even begin to encompass the sheer scale of the emotion. The nearest way of expressing it, in human terms, would be a small child's temper tantrum in which said child suddenly picked up a knife and slit its mother's throat. And then mutilated the body in a vicious gibbering frenzy.

As it scanned the spinning jewels of the System the surface of Kraator Xem's mind was cold: crystalline, coolly formulating strategies and options. But under the surface, under the skin, under this fragile patina of quasi-identity, something hot and dark shrieked over and over again:

It's mine.

I *want* it.

Make it do what I want it to.

The Most Elevated and Puissant Kraator Xem retracted several eyes from the telescope, and swung them round to

4

peer at the commander of the fleet. Platelets slid back over each other. An approximation of human lips and tongue and vocal cords formed in its soft flesh.

'Report, Lokar Pan,' it said in clotted, glottal tones, like gas bubbling through semi-solidified fat.

The scorpion thing scuttled forward and warped its avine beak into a frame, over which was stretched a membrane.

'Okey-dokey, matey,' it said. 'Expedition to green world satellite is success. Gone now, polymorphous infestation of satellite. Chop-chop. All same. Total dead, yes? Water world goin' likewise. We's a-knockin' 'em on the heads and a-haulin' 'em into the brig tanks like the poxy dogs they are. Bugger-me-bosun. Avast behind.'

The voice from the membrane crackled with static. It shifted in pitch and accent as it acquired the resonances of the locations to which it referred. It was as though the Sloathe commander were running edited excerpts directly from received transmissions.

The brain-thing, the Sekor Dom Sloathe – who up until now had been silent – slithered forward. The nearest human equivalent of its function would be that of seneschal or Grand Vizier – and while obviously lacking in the pointy slippers and twirly moustachio department, there was a marked sense of oiliness about it. The constant search for a propitious couple of rib-analogues between which to stick and turn the knife.

What of this aboriginal Sun cult? it said. There was no sound. Its words simply resonated in the analogues of their brains. *Correct me if I am wrong, but I seem to remember that they have a particularly impenetrable stronghold upon the Green world. Does this situation still obtain?*

The Most Elevated and Puissant Kraator Xem, inwardly, quasi-winced. Sloathes have an innate inability to comprehend the symbolism that other species attach to images – and a major stumbling block to their complete occupation of the System had been the tendency of the aboriginals to rally behind, as it were, a flag. Anything, it seemed, would do: a clump of feathers tied to a pole, a hominid nailed to a tree a couple of thousand years before . . . it seemed to be something inbuilt.

The cult on the jungle planet – or, more properly, in the

5

vestigial network of cities that floated over the planet – appeared to worship the image of a stylized Sun inset with four crude representations of eyes. They had held out against Sloathe incursion for more than ten solar years – and the Sekor Dom Sloathe never missed an opportunity to rub this small fact in.

'The stronghold of the Sun cult is still under siege,' Lokar Pan reported. 'Acceptable losses of our own forces. They are safely contained.'

'They are still pretending to move?' the Most Elevated and Puissant Kraator Xem said. Sloathes do not conceive of anything other than themselves as truly alive, and consider it presumptuous that certain things in the universe go around walking and talking as if they are.

'Pending most explicit orders from myself,' Lokar Pan said.

'Make them stop,' the Most Elevated and Puissant Kraator Xem said. 'Don't want them to do it any more. Make them stop it *now*.'

The scorpion-form of Lokar Pan collapsed in upon itself, then warped into a complex cluster of planes designed to transmit the resonances of thought across thousands of leagues. The Most Elevated and Puissant Kraator Xem watched it absently for a moment, then turned its attention to a corner where something small and viscid and vaguely resembling a lobster squatted smugly digesting on a battered vitrine.

Idly, the Most Elevated and Puissant Kraator Xem shot out a chitinous harpoon on a length of tendon. The speared lobster-thing squealed and planted a sucker and the vitrine fell over with a spray of sludge. The lobster-thing was dragged, vitrine and all, into the slavering mouth the Most Elevated and Puissant Kraator Xem had dilated especially for the purpose.

Canto First:
A Sudden Arrival

We must constantly beware of the 'just-like' fallacy. The existence of a watch might imply a watchmaker – but to relocate this argument wholesale as a Creationist rationale, for example, tends to miss that point that unless we know far less about the fundamental nature of the universe than we think we do, it doesn't run on clockwork.

Down Among the Dead Men
Professor Bernice Summerfield, 2466

'Typical. You wait a couple of millennia for the End of the World to arrive and then three of the buggers turn up at once.'

Roslyn Forrester (attr.)

The First Chapter

Below is the mighty Anacon river, major tributary of a network of waterways entwining the jungle-surface of the Aneas Top. An almost vascular maze of runnels and canals and courses, trenches and ditches and dykes – although, if this is a vascular system, it's a vascular system in a coronary. At some point, some pumping mechanism, some geological equivalent of a massive heart, must have kept it flowing.

Now the waters of Aneas lie still and black in their channels – and over the course of centuries the jungle has taken over entirely: fetid and primordial and crawling with more long-lost species, civilizations and Shaman-tribes than you can shake a dinosaur-gnawed, ceremonial obi-stick at.

And above the jungle, the remains of the Dirigible Cities, their bejewelled spires and minarets fractured and hollow like rotting teeth, the massive gasbags that once supported them leaking in a thousand places, their deserted streets and their derelict twitterns and wynds erupting under Sloathe bombardment.

~~~

The sky was thick with a ragtag swarm of ornithopters and biplanes, banking and wheeling and going down in flames as they harried the pulsing bulks of Sloathe gunships. The Dirigible Cities were vestigial now: one by one they had been reduced to ruins, their inhabitants slaughtered or taken prisoner. Only one segment now held out: the sub-City of Rakath. Home of the fanatical Sun Samurai cult,* who had

---

* A note upon translation is perhaps apposite here. The *lingua franca*, as it were, of the System is almost impossible to convey phonetically, consisting as it does almost entirely of dentation,

sworn to fight on to the last hominid. The sheer determination and viciousness of its Warrior-castes had over the years achieved an uneasy stalemate: the Sun Samurai weren't going anywhere, and the Sloathe blockade around Aneas saw to it that they didn't.

But now the situation had changed. Now the Sloathes were making an active and concerted effort to eradicate this trouble-spot once and for all. Time for the Sun-cult was running out.

In a cavernous chamber, its white ceramic walls inlaid with arabesques of brass and hung with ancient tapestries of surpassing and exquisite complexity, those not actively resisting the Sloathe forces were assembled: the very old, the very young and the sick. The halt and the lame. Although made up predominantly of the Saurian humanoids indigenous to Aneas, there were a fair scattering of others.

Indeed, the high priest himself was human in appearance: an elderly Promethean originally of the nomad-caste. His skin was gnarled and blackened by the sunlight of that desert world so that it seemed to be of the same stuff as his cracked and ancient leather robes. A thousand tiny scars disfigured his face and his eyes were permanently slitted against a nonexistent wind. His white hair was pulled back in the brittle remains of a traditional Anean topknot.

His name was Kimon, and like his predecessors his life had been long given over to the Waiting – watching for the Chosen who would appear amongst the cult. The female Saviour who would undertake the Search, as had been Foretold from Time out of Mind by some unnamed but apparently all-powerful force with an unfortunate predilection for overcapitalization.

---

glottal stops and eructation. Wherever possible we have attempted to translate actual names directly, as in the self-evident 'Dirigible Cities' (lit. *Cities-on-Dirigibles*), or to convey a general sense of meaning from such direct translations – as in 'Sun Samurai' (lit. *Mad-Bastard-Ritual-Worship-Big-Hot-Thing-and-Cut-You-Up-with-Big-Knife-Thing*). Names with no apparent associative value have been simply labelled arbitrarily, as in 'Rakath', which in its original form sounds like a fart in a maraca factory.

The Waiting had taken millennia thus far – the Sun Samurai were extremely ritualistic and the signs by which the Chosen would be known had been scrupulously detailed. Over the centuries a girl-child might be found possessing certain of the attributes required: she might be born with a caul, or the fourth daughter of a thirteenth son, or radiantly beautiful and fleet of foot with a star-shaped birthmark in a highly embarrassing anatomical area – but none fulfilled these requirements precisely.

This had not particularly been a problem. The Sun Samurai had the time. They could wait. It was not as if, say, the entire System was under attack by villainous evil cannibalistic slimy shapeshifting monsters and the Sun-cult was in danger of suddenly being stamped out in its –

So now the old man stood before the assembled congregation of the very young, the very old and the sick. His eyes were closed, and a sacred cloth was bound around them, and he was chanting: 'Thirty-six . . . Thirty-seven . . . Thirty-eight . . . Thirty-nine . . .'

There had been any number of fourth daughters of thirteenth sons born over the years, a surprising number of them born with cauls and the aforementioned and suitably embarrassing birthmark. Radiantly beautiful? But of course. Fleet of foot? No problem there.

' . . . Forty-two . . . Forty-three . . . Forty-four . . .' Kimon chanted.

The problem was that there was also the matter of an extensively prophesied and amazingly detailed sequence of events in the Chosen One's life that must be fulfilled – and while the language of the prophesies allowed for a fair degree of interpretation, a large number of them had, over the natural course of things, simply never happened to anyone.

Outside the concussive detonation of a Sloathe bombshell. The temple-chamber shook.

'Forty-five . . .' Kimon continued. 'Forty-six . . . Forty-seven . . . Forty-eight . . .'

The most important, the most basic prophesy, for example, read more or less as follows: 'She shall be Lost and then She shall be Found, by way of a most Arduous and Magickal Quest. And she shall be garbed in most Exquisite Raiment, Wrap'd and Swaddled in Cloth-of-Gold and playing Dulcet and most Soothing tones upon a Flageolet. Her head it shall Rest on milk-white Marshwort and the Fish of the Stream and the Birds of the Air shall be Her Friends.'

' . . . Forty-nine . . . *Fifty*.' Kimon pulled the cloth from his face. 'Coming, ready or not.'

He cast about vaguely, taking in the altar and the Book in which the Prophesy was writ. 'How am I doing?' he asked the congregation.

'You're *incredibly* cold,' the congregation called back.

Kimon wandered over to a tapestry and, experimentally, twitched one of them aside.

'You're getting colder!' the congregation shouted happily. Kimon wondered if they were taking this Most Solemn and Historick Occasion in quite the right spirit.

He peered about himself again. Eventually his eyes alighted upon the ironwood chest in which, over the years, the various high priests of the cult had stored their missals while the extensive theological research went on into the question of what it was a missal actually did. Kimon strode purposefully toward the chest and, with a grunt of effort, heaved the lid off with a crash.

Nobody had actually said at what *age* the Chosen One had to be found wrap'd and swaddled and being friends with the birds and so forth. The woman in the chest was in her eighteenth year, slim and supple in the manner of a gymnast, her skin comprised of soft scales which shimmered like a spill of oil on water. Her eyes were a pale orange, with vertical pupils, like those of a cat. She was hairless, the scales on her head feathering into a soft down. A short leather kilt was wrapped about her waist and around her midriff was a corslet of some silver-grey and strangely liquid-looking metal.

The shreds of Cloth-of-Gold thrown in with her had been ripped from the tapestries. A hurried search of the more elderly of the temple's congregation had produced a number of medicinal pomanders, commonly used to guard against agues and grippes, and which doubtless contained marsh-wort somewhere amidst the various floral matter.

Certain other elements had proved slightly more difficult to acquire in a floating city starving and under siege, but a small tin toy trumpet had been taken from one of the children (who was still, somewhere in the back of the crowd, loudly wanting it *back*), and she was doing her level best to be friends with the half-eaten chicken leg and the fishbones.

She played a half-hearted toot on the trumpet and put it down. 'That's it, now, is it?' she said.

'Um . . .' Kimon crossed hurriedly back to the altar and the lead-bound book, flipped hastily through the thick vellum pages. 'Have you wept Bitter Tears at the Endless Futility of Being?' he said.

'We already did that.' The woman climbed out of the chest and pulled off sorry tatters of ex-tapestorial Cloth-of-Gold. 'With the onions, remember?'

'Did you heal a Sick Man that he picked up his Bed and Walked?' Kimon asked worriedly.

The young woman silently pointed to a frail and pale-looking human standing unsteadily in the crowd and clutching a sheet, who waved back at her and, in accordance with the universal laws of comedy, chose this moment to fall over again.

'Have you been Most Tragickally and Cruelly Deflowered by *Glog Shabàbabaréd*, the Bloody Humpback, the Black Despoiler of the Many-Sundered Worlds whose Hands Run Red with the Blood of Innocents, a Foul Usage that will put a vary Bane upon your Heart until – '

'Where the hell are we supposed to get a *Glog Shabàbabaréd* from?' the woman said indignantly.

'This is, ah, generally held to be one of the more metaphorical passages,' Kimon said uneasily, blushing to his ears under his leathery skin. 'It just means have you ever . . . well, um, sort of, you know . . .'

As he trailed off desperately another detonation shook the chamber, blowing in a number of stained-glass windows. The congregation milled around, chattering and shrieking with alarm.

'I shall take especial care to take advantage of the very first opportunity that presents itself,' the young woman said primly. 'Have we *done* now, Kimon?'

'Yes, I . . . ah . . .' The high priest shut the Book and turned to the congregation, raising his hands in benediction. 'Behold! The Chosen is amongst us! Long have we Waited for this Great Time, the Time of the Search; long have we – '

13

'Yes, quite.' The woman grabbed him firmly by the scruff of the neck and frogmarched him, despite his protests, towards the door.

———∞∞∞———

Leetha T'Zhan shoved the high priest through the erupting streets. In the sky the biplanes banked and wheeled. More than once they were forced to skirt an area of fighting where Samurai ground forces attempted to prevent a Sloathe landing becoming an actual beachhead until, eventually, they came to a large and domelike construction guarded by a couple of *Seku*,* glowering about themselves with barely

---

* The Sun Samurai, as has been noted, consisted predominantly of native Aneans (saurians evolved into warm-blooded humanoids) with a minority of humans. These species interbred freely, but such progeny would appear physically, and more or less at random, to be entirely human or Anean rather than any graduated blending of the two.

Centuries of ritualized Waiting had produced an interesting social structure, based largely upon the numbers four and thirteen. Every thirteenth male-child was considered semi-sacred breeding stock and protected and pampered until he had fathered four daughters. Then he was summarily ejected to fend for himself for the rest of his life – which, given how he had been weakened by a life of inordinate overindulgence and luxury since birth, was generally quite short. And this was considered only right and proper by the other males, the Warrior caste, who spent their lives fighting vicious tooth-and-claw over the disproportionately few women available in an attempt to establish their own dynasties from scratch – and who tended to be not a little short-tempered with those who had, as it were, had it handed to them repeatedly on a number of plates.

Females themselves were regarded merely as breeding-stock – albeit *precious* breeding stock, as *prizes* – and were kept in a state of isolated and objectified near-slavery that would have any twentieth-century feminist apoplectic and any twentieth-century New Man patronizing them rigid.

The exceptions were of course the *Seku* – every fourth daughter of a thirteenth son. Since any one of these might be Chosen, and might thus have to undergo the many and varied perils of the Search, they were trained from birth in the Ways of the Warrior and every Sun Samurai male clutched his groin in fright when they went past.

Leetha, of course, before she became the Chosen, was a *Seku*.

14

contained belligerence and obviously wishing they were where the fighting was thickest.

Inside, tethered to iron rings sunk into huge blocks of granite and bobbing gently to the shaking of the cities, was a battered scow of the sort used to ferry supplies within the Anean atmosphere, its cabin hastily sealed with pitchblende. Big internal combustion engines, capable of dealing with interWanderary distances had been lashed to the frame, rotor-blades ratcheted around slowly on their bearings.

Leetha turned a handle sunk into the wall of the chamber. Slowly, with a groan and scrape of metal, the dome above them split open into eight interlocking sections and retracted into the vertical walls.

'You have your notes?' she said to Kimon.

The high priest put a hand into his robe and pulled out a thick sheaf of mismatched papers and a slim and slightly worn *livre de poche* – a cheap and mechanically printed copy of the original Book of the Chosen, used by the Priest caste in the instruction of children. This had eventually been compromised upon because, while the prophesies were clear that the Book would be carried by the Chosen at all times and she would derive Much Inspiration and Succour from It, they were remarkably unclear about exactly how far the Chosen would actually get if she had to hump around twenty pounds of vellum cased in jewel-encrusted lead.

Kimon handed her the book and sorted hurriedly through the sheaf of papers. 'The distillation of millennia of scholarly research,' he said. 'There have been several interpretations, of course, over the years – the High Priest Lorcas VII, for example, held that –'

'I look forward immensely to learning what he held,' Leetha said. 'But not just at the moment, yes?' She planted a foot against the side of a massive engine and hauled on the lanyard of the starter-motor.

After the obligatory couple of false starts, the starter-motor whirred to life. There was a series of coughing detonations as the engines themselves caught. The rotors juddered and lurched, and then accelerated.

In the sky above, Sun Samurai aircraft were regrouping for the suicide manoeuvres that would divert the attention of the Sloathe forces; opening a window of escape for the scow.

Leetha said a silent prayer for them, and hoped to the gods that their deaths would not be in vain.

She thought of the perils of a System under siege – and of perils that were worse: the privateer fleets that even now lurked in the traverses between the Wanderers, the slave-traders and the freebooters, the hideous and literally gut-wrenching excesses of these brigands, like the villainous Nathan Li Shao . . .

The engines were firing on all cylinders; the scow strained against its tethers. Leetha swung herself up through the hatch and hauled Kimon up behind her.

'We'll find them,' she said, closing and dogging the hatch. 'We'll find the Eyes.'

———∞———

And as the scow rose through the stratosphere to the thin and chilly interWanderary air beyond, the Dirigible cities finally split open and went down in flames. Watched by the fiendish segmented telescopes of Planet X.

And something somewhere else entirely watched them, too.

The Second Chapter

In an improbable jungle outside space and time, a marmoset launches itself across a gap in the canopy, grabbing hold of and swinging from a banyan branch with its bearlike paws. Startled, a small flock of iridescent green-gold parrots scatter, flapping and squawking indignantly, and then re-form.

In the clearing a structure rises from the forest floor: twice the height of a man and built of crude and sun-baked brick, a flight of steps leading up its wall: a ziggurat in miniature.

On the steps, intently examining the markings on the wall, is a dark woman in her early thirties, in khaki shirt and khaki shorts and lace-up Chukka boots, a sweatband of rag wrapped around her cropped head and a machete in her belt – every inch the intrepid explorer, though there is something curiously affected about this, as though it is merely a costume worn for some impromptu masquerade.

By the ziggurat, catching the sun through a gap in the jungle canopy, is a picnic table and three stripy deckchairs. Reclining in one of these, seemingly asleep, a limp fedora with a paisley band tilted forward over his face, is a small and slightly portly man in linen and raw silk and two-tone brogues. In the manner of the Englishman Abroad the whole world over, this man has divested himself of nothing but his jacket, which hangs on the back of the chair, a yellow smiley-faced button affixed to the lapel. Similarly – and no doubt with said Englishman Abroad's instinctive distrust for the weather – hangs a furled umbrella with a handle in the form of a slightly overelaborate question-mark.

The fedora vibrates to happy and vaguely theatrical snores. Despite the heat, the man's apparel seems well-laundered and utterly pristine, as though perspiration is merely something that happens to other people. Near by, a hand-cranked

Victrola plays the tinny refrains of one Mr George Formby, relating a number of surprising adventures involving his little stick of Blackpool rock.

———⁓⁓⁓———

Benny Summerfield wandered down the steps and flopped into a deckchair. Beside her the Doctor stopped snoring.

'Did you find anything of interest?' he said from under his fedora.

Benny shrugged. 'The markings seem to be Navaho. Sky spirits. Nayenezgani in particular – "slayer of evil gods", you know? The chap who protected the world from the forces of destruction?'

'Somebody has to do it.' The Doctor flipped his hat from his face and sat forward, an eyebrow raised with idle concern. From the Victrola, dubious confectionery was supplanted by the improbable joys of grandad's flannelette shirt. 'At least till someone better comes along. You seem a little ill at ease with the surroundings, Benny.'

'Not really. It's just a little disorientating.' Benny waved a hand, encompassing the scene. 'I mean, plains-dweller markings on Assyrian architecture and stuck in the jungle; banyans and whatnot and Madagascan wildlife . . . It's all over the place. It jars.'

The Doctor smiled. 'Always the empirical archaeologist, eh? Examining and codifying, dusting off little bits of actuality and sticking them in a hermetic and carefully labelled display case? Why not just let the spring-cleaning go hang for a while, and simply enjoy the ambiance of it all? A little ambiguity is good for the soul. Some more wine?' He gestured to the bottle in the Georgian silver cooler. 'A tart little vintage, but I'm sure you'll appreciate its bare-faced cheek.'

Bernice fell in with his mood. She poured herself a glass and swilled it around her mouth with the arch and exaggerated air of one whose ethanolic tastes were formed on spaceport hinterland boilermakers, but has seen the historical recordings of poncy wine tasters.

'The finish is all one would expect?' the Doctor enquired, eyes a-mischievous-twinkle.

'One detects the zest of lime,' Bernice said. 'The hint of

18

fresh-mown grass and a touch of the Auntie Fanny's clock under the stairs.' She grinned. 'Blimey, but this is some rough old stuff. Do they get it out of cats? The urge to spit hurtles even now toward the palate as we speak.'

'Ah yes,' the Time Lord beamed. 'The good old expectorative impulse. As with coffee and brandy and Gallifreyan bog-truffle tincture, it's the acid test of good from bad. Cucumber sandwich?' He proffered a Wedgwood plate.

'I'll just have a refill, thanks.'

'Quite right, too.' The Doctor tossed the plate over his shoulder in a small spray of decrusted bread and legume. 'Can't abide the things myself.'

The plate frisbeed off into the undergrowth. There was a squawk and a subsequent thud as it stunned a parrot.

The Doctor topped her up with what was in fact a perfectly chilled basic Frascati, filled his own glass and sat back with a small and happy sigh (he was unable to metabolize ethanol but, he averred, found certain trace impurities attendant to the fermenting process quite delightful). Benny was struck by the fact that the Time Lord seemed not younger, exactly – the sheer weight of his thousand odd years tended to overload the subliminal senses by which the human mind perceives such things, making terms of 'age' irrelevant – not younger exactly, but less careworn than of late. It was as though several of the upheavals and sea-changes of the past few subjective months had been finally put behind him; as though some crushing weight, only now noticeable by its absence, had lifted. Benny, who had at times found herself actively *loathing* this coldly calculating, cruelly manipulative and fundamentally inhuman being, was once again slightly surprised at the depth of affection she felt for this small, lively and somewhat clownish man.

But it was an edgy feeling, she realized. The sense of something other and alien was always there, amongst other things – indeed, she thought, the Doctor's myriad aspects and attributes seemed almost infinitely malleable, some receding into the background while others came to the fore to deal with whatever circumstance required them. The man who sat now, regarding the world in general with good-humoured interest, seemed, as it were, to be a kind of personality default-setting – but just how much of this was artifice? To what extent did he actively control the perceptions of those around him? What crawling and gut-wrenching horrors would you actually *see* if you stripped away the levels of deception and misdirection and looked at him with a . . .?

(And just what exactly had she been thinking about just now? Oh well. Probably nothing important.)

'This is all very pleasant,' the Doctor said thoughtfully 'but do you know what we really need? What we need, think, is a proper break. No involvement, no meddling, no saving the universe from the fetid and unending night. The Fate of the Universe can damn well look out for itself for a change. It's big enough and old enough, after all . . .'

As though resolving upon a sudden, the Time Lord waved a pontificatory finger. '*Carpe diem*, I cry. For the moment anyway. Wherever we take the TARDIS next, I say *hang* the spring-cleaning! We could all of us do with a little messing around in boats.'

———

Roslyn Forrester, Adjudicator ex-Century Thirty and currently having several fundamental problems with her jurisdiction, sat on the raft and stared moodily into the depths of a pool where piebald, luminescent goldfish swam.

From somewhere behind her, through ferrangeous mismatched jungle vegetation, wafted the sounds of muted conversation and the scratchy, phonetically recorded strains of some congenitally endocephalic inbred deviant – strumming frantically on some stringed instrument and gurgling happily about how he derived a great deal of pleasure from riding in something called the TT Race ('I had a friend who tried to enter Douglas once, but apparently it's illegal. *Incredibly Bad Jokes from the Twentieth Century*, ed. Professor Bernice Summerfield. No. 15,457) and there didn' seem to be any way of stopping him.

She sighed and tapped ash from her small black blended Cuban-leaf and Lebanese Gold cigar into the crystal-clear water, where it was promptly eaten by a fish entwined with a purple tracery like flashing neon, and which would have been quite beautiful had the tracery not in fact spelt out: EAT

20

The fish spluttered violently, spat out a small subaquatic cloud of partially dissolved ash and looked up at her with the sort of pained expression Roz had already come to associate with the Doctor, just before the delivery of a tart and pointed lecture upon the perils of emphysema, heart failure and lung cancer and the proffering of a small fruit-flavoured lollipop as an alternative should she ever again feel the overwhelming need for something to suck.

'Who loves ya, babe,' she said miserably to the fish, which stared up at her with utter astonishment for a moment and then flipped itself away with a contemptuous flick of its dorsals.

How the Sheol did I ever get into this, she wondered – before stopping herself to point out that in fact she knew damn *well* how she had got into this.

She'd know better next time. Vast nefarious conspiracy stretching its fiendish nebulous tentacles to the very highest echelons of the power-structure? Never met the fella. Menacing alien starship lurking derelict in hyperspace and affecting innocent souls with psychosis-inducing tachyons of the slightly implausible Iracon breed? Wouldn't let the bugger in the house.

The nefarious conspiracy in question had wrecked one glittering career in the Guild of Adjudicators – hers – nipped one career slightly less coruscating in the bud – that of one Christopher Rodonanté Cwej, her partner of a matter of days but it seemed longer – and had left half of the 30th century Adjudication Guild busily arranging tragic accidents for either her, or Cwej, or both of them should they ever show their faces again.

And when the time-travelling alien, the Doctor, had offered to take them along with him in his ship – for want of a better word – Cwej's instant and automatic reaction had been: 'What, travel the whole vast panoply of space and time, righting what once went wrong and confronting hideous beings of slithering, inutterable and unmitigated evil on their home turf? Yeah, *boys*!' While Detective Adjudicator Roslyn Forrester stood somewhere in the background with a hand over her eyes.

21

Roz had gone along, simply, because she couldn't think of anywhere else to go – and on the basis that at least this wa she might live to regret it.

She had.

The first shock had been how big the inside of the TARDI was as compared to the outside. The second shock was ho incredibly humungously *sodding* big it was. For forty-eig hours she had merely shuffled to and fro from the spaciou bedchamber that the Doctor had opened up for her, to a ornate brass and marble bathroom-chamber, groaning faintl keeping her eyes tightly shut and feeling a little wan.

Then she had pulled herself together, and gone to th Doctor for some sort of proper explanation, to find hi floating three feet off the floor, juggling four variecoloure balls of blinding plasma and singing to himself an insan little song about a grackle, in three voices, simultaneously.

After that, Cwej had kept bounding up to her, eyes aligh with the wonder of it all and offering her solicitous cups o hot sweet tea, until Roz had forcibly suggested he administe it to himself via an alternative available orifice.

In the end Benny – and more or less, Roz suspected, in a attempt to apply some form of basic homeopathic remedy had produced a large wicker hamper, pronounced that the were all going on a picnic and dragged Roz along despite a the powers of protest at her command.

They had trekked through the TARDIS for maybe four o five kilometres, moving ever away from the control centre if a potentially infinite sheaf of supplementary dimension can be said to *have* a centre. A hothouse full of Proxima flesh-flensers, each fed with little rubber tubes from tanks o blood, devolved into a series of progressively weirder varia tions upon the theme of Cargo-hold in a Space Station, whic in turn became a cavernous attic packed full of dusty toy and suchlike junk, all at least ten times actual life-size.

After that things got a little strange.

'I think these are like its memory-banks,' Benny ha said as they went through yawning porticoes and rustlin arboreta, around muttering cornices and swooping buttresse through halls with chequer-board floors a'crawl with chee fully whistling spiders, and through cavernous chambe filled with burning kites and up through cracks in the ceilin

22

'I think the TARDIS sort of extrapolates the universe from them. It's like we're walking through its *mind*.'

The Doctor had simply beamed and said nothing. This seemed to be something of a defining characteristic with him, and was starting to get on Roz's nerves not a little.

At length, they had come to this little simulated pocket of quasi-jungle environment, where the Doctor had bustled around unpacking deckchairs and picnic tables and various potables and victuals from the hamper as though it were some Chinese-box TARDIS in microcosm, while Benny disinterred ancient and increasingly asinine jokes ('I don't like the sound of those drums/I don't like the sound of those drums/He's not our regular drummer'), and Roz had taken the chance to slip away quietly and let them get on with it.

And so now she sat on the makeshift raft she had found, built from slatted orange boxes and tethered to the edge of a jungle pool, staring miserably into the waters. It was the feeling of rootlessness that was getting to her, she thought. For slightly more than forty years, for every waking moment, she had known exactly and precisely where she fitted into the world – even if every waking moment had actually been spent kicking violently against it. She had thrown over the privileges of being born into an ultra-rich, hi-level Overcity family to join the Adjudicators, knowing exactly what she was gaining and precisely what she was giving up. She'd fought crime on the Undertown streets and fought her superior officers in the Service over procedure, knowing exactly what she was fighting against and precisely whom, and what, she could ultimately trust.

And then it had all come crashing down. Her own partner of fifteen years had betrayed her, her own *memories* of him had betrayed her; the apparently rock-solid foundations of her world had dropped from under her and now she found herself completely lost, cut loose even from space and time. She didn't know anyone and she didn't know the score.

It was at this point that, on the far edge of the pool, a bank of rushes rustled and then began to thrash violently. A number of neon-arabesqued fish shot away from the bank in surprise.

'Oh, bugger . . .' said Roslyn Forrester nervously. She was a city girl to the core and that might be what bullrushes naturally *did* for all she knew, but she wasn't going to bet on it. She grabbed for the rope tethering the raft and started to haul herself towards the side, cursing as the wet hemp slipped repeatedly through her fingers.

And then a creature burst from the rushes with a roar; vaguely humanoid and almost two metres tall. Its teeth were like rotted knives and its reptile skin glistened and coruscated like oil swirling on water. Its eyes blazed with a sickly pulsing and murderous light.

The Third Chapter

Between the orbits of the jungle Wanderer of Aneas and the water Wanderer of Elysium, the air shimmers with a bright and coruscating light: a billion shards of fractured silicate – some smaller than a mote of dust, others larger than a moon – spin in a Ring tens of thousands of leagues across, catching and diffracting the sunlight in waves of primary and secondary colour.

Though the air here is oxygenated, ships traversing this Ring must remain air-tight: exposure to the suspended particles would rip the soft tissues of organic gaseous exchange systems to shreds.

The air also contains massive quantities of lysergic acid diethylamide (the effects of which are known and feared by outer-mariners the System over as Mister White Man Fingers), and in the early years of flight the Ring was seen as impassable due to the number of pilots who would crash headlong into large lumps of revolving glass whilst shrieking about the spiders bursting from their eyes.

Thus, even now, the Ring remains largely unexplored; those who make their way through it, make their way as quickly as they can. And as a result the flotsam and jetsam of the system have gravitated here: fugitives escaping the justice of their native worlds, refugees from Sloathe incursion, traders mining the Ring itself for its hallucinogens.

There are pirates here.

———

A pulsing and apparently solid mass of magenta light congealed around the prow of the Sloathe freighter,* rippled

---

* As with the discrete components of almost any biological system, a certain number of Sloathe organisms are born deformed: some, maybe, without pigment, pale as frosted glass; some, possibly, with

and eddied, swirling out past the outriding destroyers darkening to purple and then fading to blue. Galvanistical discharge arced between the larger suspended glass shards occasionally shattering one with a sound like the exploding of a glass bell.

Inside, the vessel was partitioned into vast holds packed with the spoils of half a year of forays into the inner worlds Strung through these caverns of membrane, ribbed with polished bone and secured to the skeleton frame of the ship itself with ligament, were strings of pickled digestive tract serving as companionways. And swelling from these, the leathery polyps that served as cabins.

The polyps to the stern were devoted to the transport of livestock: slum dwellers from the stilt-walking manufactory city-states of Prometheus in their grimy suits and stovepipe hats; nomads from the deserts that surrounded the cities. A razor-toad from the bayous of Aneas slithered around its polyp, stomach distended with the weakly flopping remains of an entire lost tribe of pigmies that the Sloathes (who could only dimly comprehend the distinction between aboriginal life-forms) had shut in with it.

A smaller polyp, lit by phosphorescent decay in the walls contained two prisoners, one male and human, one female and humanoid.

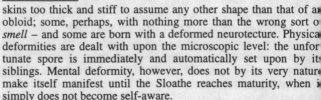

skins too thick and stiff to assume any other shape than that of an obloid; some, perhaps, with nothing more than the wrong sort of *smell* – and some are born with a deformed neurotecture. Physical deformities are dealt with upon the microscopic level: the unfortunate spore is immediately and automatically set upon by its siblings. Mental deformity, however, does not by its very nature make itself manifest until the Sloathe reaches maturity, when it simply does not become self-aware.

When a Sloathe of this sort is noted, far from being killed it is nurtured and cherished and fed upon the crispiest dried slime until it assumes massive proportions. Then it is killed.

The innards are removed and eaten and the corpse is embalmed. Lengths of internal membrane are tied off to serve as gasbags, or stitched together to serve as sails. The skeletal structure is moulded and fixed with ichor to produce masts and rudders and ailerons. The remains are then ready to take their place in the Sloathe fleet.

All vitality seemed to have fled Kimon now: he sat against the fleshy wall of the polyp, knees drawn up to his chest, an air about him of utter defeat. Leetha was slightly more active: moving about the polyp, carefully and minutely examining the seams in the membrane with her fingers.

Shoving through slick and greasy membrane folds, she found the sphincter-valve that shut them off from the intestinal passageway outside. She tried to shove a finger through and failed. She glanced over her shoulder to where the old man still sat immobile. 'You could give me some help here, Kimon.'

Kimon remained motionless.

'You're really helping to keep my spirits up, you know that?' Leetha T'Zhan stroked the side of her living armour and it rippled with pleasure. 'Make me a blade,' she said.

'*Yeah!*' The armour rippled and disgorged a silver-grey knifeblade. For a while Leetha probed at the valve. She had gone through this ritual a hundred times before, and only did it now for the sake of something to do.

The Sloathe destroyer had been waiting for them as they hit Aneas orbit; there had been no time for evasive action. Their battered scow had simply been hauled in on grappling lines, cocooned in solidified slime.

For weeks, so far as the passage of time could be intimated, they had simply been left there in the perpetual darkness, dimly aware that their host-vessel was manoeuvring and that it was under weigh. They had nearly starved to death.

Since their transfer to this cargo vessel, however, their captors had occasionally attempted to feed them – though this was at best a hit or miss affair as the 'food' tended to consist of anything from half a dead calf to a nesting set of ococo occasional tables. The remains of the calf now resided against the polyp wall, as far away as possible from Leetha and Kimon and long since past the point where it would be preferable to any conceivable malnutritious emergency whatsoever. Together with it were containers they had improvised from the more inedible Sloathe offerings for waste matter.

Since their transferral, since it had become clear that they were embarked upon a traverse for the edge of the System and Planet X, Kimon had grown steadily more morose and then had simply stopped talking and moving. Leetha had tried to snap him out of it: talking to him constantly, shaking him, slapping him hard enough to raise bruises under the leathery skin, but to no avail. The only animation he now showed was to swallow whatever edible matter Leetha shoved in his mouth, but this was mechanical, automatic: it was as if there was simply nothing inside him any more.

Now Leetha gave up her investigation of the valve and pressed the blade against her side to be reabsorbed. Then she hauled herself across the polyp and came to rest beside her one-time mentor to wait for someone to bring in something incredibly stupid.

Sometime later the valve dilated and a Sloathe in the aspect of a three-foot-wide leech floated into the polyp.

'Most Supreme Captain will see you now for audience,' it said through a circular mouth with irregularly spaced human teeth as thin and fragile as fingernails. 'Must go now. Chop chop.'

'What?' Leetha, whose initial starved and feeble attempt to overpower her gaolers had long since subsided into a sullen disinterest while she waited for them to go away again, was startled.

'Most Supreme Captain Trenkor Lep is waiting.' The Sloathe undulated meaningfully. 'Will be angry. Must go.'

Beside her, possibly as a result of this break in the routine, Kimon stirred briefly, and then lapsed back into catatonia. Leetha tried to shake some life into him. 'Kimon? We have to go somewhere. Wake *up*, Kimon!' She looked up at the leech-thing. 'I can't get him to move.'

'Must go! Chop-chop!'

No chance of assistance from that quarter then, obviously. Leetha grabbed the old man by the scruff of the neck and hauled at him. He moved easily enough.

The Sloathe convoy tacked to port. Grey humps slithered over the skin of the freighter, erecting the calcine masts that later, when they hit the Outer Slipstream, would be hung with membrane sheets for the outer traverse.

And behind them, just out of observational range, something was stalking.

28

Although a distinct improvement upon the Sloathe vessels in that its mere aspect would not cause immediate nausea in all but the most sensitive of souls, this other ship had little else to recommend it. It was by no stretch of the imagination graceful. The oiled canvas stretched over its warped aluminium frame was piebald with patches, had indeed rotted beyond even these apathetic attempts at repair in places, so that the perished rubber bulks of gasbags could be clearly seen within. Three large internal combustion engines projected from the stern, all in a state of utter disrepair, pitted and blackened from decades of heavy use, slathered with oil from burst gaskets and one was missing its propellers. The majority of motive force was in fact supplied by a stained and billowing parachute sail.

Bolted to the frame of the ship was a latticelike superstructure of untreated bamboo and tarpaulin forming a gangway of sorts, running from the makeshift wooden box that served as the bridge to the gondola; through this a big man hauled himself hand-over-hand. He wore heavy wool and leather stained the colour of blood, reinforced across the shoulders and kidneys by riveted steel plate. A revolver was stuck in his belt, and slung across his back in the manner of a Promethean nomad was a sword curved scimitar-like in its graphite-oiled scabbard. A small brass stud was countersunk into its anacon-skin grip.

The hair of this man was cropped short, his high forehead encircled by a silver band comprising a self-swallowing and highly stylized Ouroboros. His eyes, under clear glass discs sunk into the rubber of his respirator mask, were of different colours: one brown, the other pale green. His name was Nathan Li Shao, and his name was known and feared throughout the System.

Around him the gasbags rippled. He heard the rattle of canvas and the creaking of hawsers. Nathan Li Shao worked his way through the frame of the ship until, at length, he came to the gondola affixed to its underside. He passed through a makeshift airlock, pulled off his gasmask to reveal blocky but intelligent features and instantly regretted it.

The air was fetid here. Sixty or more unwashed bodies – a ferrangeous collection of humanoids and other beings from every Wanderer of the System. A scaly male in the shredded, whimpering remains of living armour jostled a renegade degenomancer from the Rubri methane boglands: animated meat wrapped around a bloodshot eye four feet across. A Reklonian hunter-gatherer, red eyes set deep in albino fur, played knucklebones with a thin human in shabby black and stovepipe hat. In a corner what seemed to be abstract constructions of twigs and rope and pulleys chattered animatedly together in a ratcheting language of ticks and clatters . . .

Hardly a one of those gathered here was whole; hands were replaced by complicated mechanisms of clamps and hooks, eyes replaced by glassy beads or discreetly covered with long-soiled bandage. These, then, were the pariahs of the System, outcasts even in that society of fugitives that inhabited Sere (the largest single body of the Ring), reduced to hanging around its wharfside hinterlands, waiting for a ship desperate or foolhardy enough to take them on.

As Li Shao worked his way through them the multilingual buzz and gabble of conversation died. Some regarded him with dull nonchalance, some warily, some with outright malice.

Li Shao waited calmly until he had their full attention.

'I want to satisfy myself that you know precisely what's expected of you,' he said, his quiet voice ringing throughout the cabin. 'I want this quick and clean – we go in, we take what we can use, we get out. You do your job and you'll get your share. Anyone found personally looting can arrange their own way home without a respirator, you get me?'

Li Shao paused for a moment in the hope that this might sink in, then continued. 'The Sloathes may have prisoners. I want them kept alive. Boarding parties will carry spare respirators, and if women and children are located your first priority is to get them to safety. And there is to be no interference – do I make myself clear, Pelt?' This last addressed to the human in the stovepipe hat.

'Why, Captain,' the good Mr Pelt returned Li Shao's glare levelly with amused and twinkling eyes. His face was pale, his mouth was very red. 'Can you really be referring to *me*?'

'I mean you,' Li Shao said. 'I know something of your . . . habits. You lay one hand on anyone and I'll string your guts round the hull and keelhaul you with them. Do I make myself clear?'

The thin man shrugged. 'As finely cut diamond, Captain. As a crisp winter's day.'

'Don' like this,' the albino Reklonian said as they headed for a boarding party waiting by a lateral hatch. 'No looting for us? No women? What he think we are?'

Beside him, Pelt smiled sardonically, toying idly with the hilt of one of the many little knives hung at his side. 'You take these things *far* too seriously. The good captain expects us to act like the fresh-faced angels that, barring certain unfortunate circumstances of life, we undoubtedly are – and I for one intend to follow his instruction to the very letter.'

The Sloathe took Leetha and catatonic Kimon through the greasy insides of the freighter. Though effectively weightless, Kimon's supine body had a distressing tendency to run away with its own inertia, and Leetha was panting by the time they went through a series of valve-like airlocks and found themselves in a chamber. Leetha planted her heels in the membrane and threw her weight back to prevent Kimon hurtling out into this open space.

The leech-thing was floating towards a mass which was something like an awful parody of a humanoid: a limp and atrophied body, hanging by a string of vertebrae from a swollen head fully six feet across. A splintered jut of bone protruded where its nose should have been. Its eyes were merely holes, from which thick ropes of gelid slime floated to end in viscid gobs. A number of fleshy, pulsing tubes sprouted from it, trailing to sink into the chamber's walls.

Beside this, almost incidentally, she noticed a large wooden tub, fixed to the floor with ichor and covered with tarpaulin.

The leech-thing rotated in the air to regard her. 'Most Supreme Captain will ejaculate now.'

31

The monstrosity opened its grinning mouth.

'Shalom, excrescent hominids,' it said glutinously. 'Make big studies of your kind, me. Is hobby. Pontificate in your idiom pretty good me, yeh? Most Supreme Captain Trenkor Lep I am.'

Leetha shrugged disinterestedly. In another place and time a Sloathe's tendency towards misnomer might have seemed faintly amusing – at least until those actually around to be amused had learnt something of their true nature. Here and now, the distinctive speech-forms merely inspired sullen loathing.*

'Have something for you. Is for you to see.' The Most Supreme Captain Trenkor Lep opened a hole in the side of its head and pulled out a thick and somewhat stained sheaf of papers: mismatched and crawling with notes and spidery diagrams, obviously accumulated over some considerable length of time.

'Make studies,' the Most Supreme Captain Trenkor Lep said, 'like me talk. Know hominids make talking marks. Talk to each other cross space and time.' Its arm extended telescopically, rattling the papers before Leetha's face. 'What talk they say? Make them talk!'

Leetha regarded them impassively. 'I don't know what they say. We found them stuffed in the back of a locker when we took the scow. We couldn't read them.'

'Is prevarication!' The Sloathe captain prodded agitatedly with a talon at the designs upon the topmost sheet: a simplified diagram of the System, wanderers and satellites

---

* Response to external stimuli, in the end, is almost entirely dependent upon context. If, for example, some hideously vicious extraterrestrial force adopted the aspect of stuffed toy bears, the sight of something bright-eyed and fluffy having a picnic would become horrifying. Indeed, and long before the events to be detailed in this history, upon the distant world of Praxis IV, where the dominant predator took a form more or less analogous to a perambulatory radio-telescope, the crystal jungle was alive with its indigenous prey (a kind of pale-blue frogskinned rabbit on wheels, propelling themselves in shrieking terror and a squeal of rubber from the distinctive hunting-cry of: 'This is the BBC Home Service. And now, Gardener's Question Time with . . .'

nd the asteroids of the Ring orbiting a stylized Sun. 'This ou know. This you use to make you *fight* and . . .'

For the first time, the Sloathe seemed to notice Kimon. A limy eye on a line burst from its mouth and peered at him uspiciously. 'Why it not pretend to move? Why it not say aing?'

'He's asleep,' Leetha said.

'Ah.' The eye retracted. Then a grappling claw shot from ae mouth, fastened on to Kimon's left ear and ripped it from is head. Kimon screamed, briefly, voice hoarse and rattling rith disuse. Automatically he clapped a hand to the blood elling from his head.

'Now it awake,' the Most Supreme Captain Trenkor Lep aid smugly.

33

The Fourth Chapter

Back at the ziggurat and at a wrong angle to reality,
desultory conversation was in progress:

' . . . and then there's She-of-the-Wide-Mouth runnin
around like a demented sacred cat in heat and scaring t
ibises,' the Doctor said. 'You couldn't turn your back on h
for a minute.' He shuddered. '*Never* again.'

'So what about Olympus?' Benny suggested.

'Have you ever smelt a god up close?' said the Docto
'Present company excepted, of course.'

Further suchlike desultory conversation was cut short by
rustle in the undergrowth, from which appeared a bedraggl
and dripping Roslyn Forrester and a slightly shameface
hideous reptilian humanoid monster.

'You made me fall in, you bastard,' Forrester was sayi
angrily.

'Look I'm sorry, OK?' the reptile-creature muttered.
pulled you out again, right? It's not as if I actually push
you or anything . . .'

'Yeah, right,' Forrester snorted. She wrung out a sodd
sleeve of her tunic; half a pint of water and a couple of sm
and frantically strobing fish hit the ground with a vague
piscoluminescent splat.

'Wotcha, Roz,' said Benny.

'And hello, Chris,' said the Doctor. 'We were wonderi
where you'd got to.'

Roz Forrester vaguely wondered exactly *how* the Doct
had identified her partner Cwej so readily. Some strange alie
multidimensional perception that could see into the depths
one's very soul? Probably not. More likely it was simp
because the pair of them had been bickering together like
couple of bloody kids.

34

'Love the body,' Benny said to Cwej, equally unconcerned. 'Does it still have the vestigial bone?'

'Um.' The reptile-thing looked down glumly at its jagged manipulatory claws. 'I just woke up and I was like this. I mean it doesn't hurt or anything, but . . .' It turned its evil, pulsing and extremely worried eyes to the Doctor – and Benny, for her part, suddenly realized how truly frightened it was and desperately trying to be brave about it. She felt a bit of a rat about that. Ah well, she thought, he'd get over it.

'Don't you worry about it,' the Doctor said firmly, bouncing up from his deckchair. 'Never, Christopher, fear. The effects of your recent exposure to the Hithis ship were on the point of reacting catastrophically with your genetically restructured tissues, so I asked the TARDIS to do a little work on your biomorphic pattern-signature. Did I forget to mention that? Sorry. Still needs a little fine-tuning though, I think.' He wandered over to the miniature ziggurat and gave it a couple of hefty kicks.

The reptile-thing appeared to shimmer and strobe, like a holographic monitor hunting between channels – and then Chris Cwej stood there in human form: a blond and golden-skinned and friendly faced man of maybe twenty, his teeth and fingernails strangely sharp, heavily muscled shoulders and chest devolving to a washboard stomach and a – Roslyn Forrester nearly bit through her lip and suddenly didn't know where to look.

'Blimey,' Benny said with an evil grin, looking him up and down as he tried ineffectually to cover his embarrassment. 'Bet you don't get many of *them* to the kilo. I was only joking about the vestigial bone, you know.'

Roz started to splutter apoplectically. A furiously blushing Chris Cwej tried to put his hands over his face and realized he'd completely run out of hands.

'Talk about swinging in the wind,' said Benny to the world in general, which only made matters worse. 'I never knew the boy had him in it, as it were.'

The Doctor, meanwhile, had been busy rummaging cheerfully in the wicker picnic hamper to unearth a small bundle of clothing. Cwej snatched it from him with a choked and harassed squeak and darted into the jungle with a crash of trampled undergrowth.

Benny hugged Roz and patted her on the back until she had stopped laughing. 'I think you did that to him on purpose,' she said sternly to the Doctor. 'I think that was very cruel.'

The Doctor merely beamed and sat down again. And it was at this point, Roz realized, later on and with hindsight, that the crawling sense of dislocation that had threatened to tear her head apart simply dissipated and left her. It was no big deal: the wheels in her head just suddenly started to mesh again.

It had been, she realized later, an extremely blatant bit of bog-psychology – and she made a small mental note to kick herself at some convenient moment for not having noticed it at the time.

Now, she simply flopped into the vacant deckchair and helped herself to the remaining vacant wine. 'So what's up?'

'The Doctor,' Benny said with an exaggerated sigh, 'has decided that we all need a holiday. Bags of relaxation, ducky, no excitement – which leaves whole humungous lumps of history like the various Dalek, Draconian, Solarian, Trigorian, Chlamedian, Cyberman and Altairian XIV Bog-woppet expansions out for a start.'

'And quite right, too,' said the Time Lord. 'That sort of thing is exactly what we want to get away from.'

'So now he doesn't like the idea of the interesting stuff,' Bernice said. 'Ptolemaic Egypt, Hellenic Greece, Centauri IV during terraformation . . .'

'The thing you have to remember,' the Doctor said, a trifle stuffily Roz thought, 'is that most of these "interesting" eras are only interesting if you look back, or forward, or indeed sideways at them. If you actually have to live through them you live through unmitigated misery, brutality and squalor. Trust me, I know whereof I speak.'

And it was at this point, from the Victrola, that George Formby, who had all this while been detailing several extraordinary sights available to those who cleaned windows for a living, suddenly stopped strumming on his ukulele and began to speak.

'By 'eck,' he said. 'I'm intercepting a distress signal. SOS. SOS. Turned out nice again. *I'd rather have his job than mine, when I'm cleaning windows . . .*'

36

'Ah well,' Benny said. 'Bang goes our holiday.'

In the control room of the TARDIS (in which they had suddenly found themselves when, after a moment's thought, the Doctor had simply opened a small and previously unnoticed door in the side of the ziggurat and darted through) Chris Cwej squirmed uncomfortably in his jungle-shorts and vest and watched the Doctor's hands as they flew over the levers and switches of the central console. He had yet to discern any repeated or indeed logical sequence to this, and had the uneasy feeling that the Time Lord was making it all up as he went along.

Off to one side, Roz and Benny kept looking at him and then going into a snorting huddle. Cwej affected a lofty *hauteur* and tried to pretend his ears weren't red and pulsing like a couple of flare-beacons. He hadn't felt this embarrassed since an unfortunate incident involving a compound fracture with complications that kept him flat on his back for a week, an industrial-strength chocolate-flavoured laxative and fifteen fresh-faced student nurses being led around the fracture ward.

'There are millions of signals like this,' the Doctor was saying absently as he pulled this, pushed that and twisted the other, 'from millions upon millions of disasters, shot through the Implicate like spiderstrands. The difference is that, here and now, this is the one we've intercepted. This is the one we can't . . . and there it is.'

A circular screen irised to life. Upon it, Cwej saw a desperate face awash with static – saw with a small start the flaring overlays of TerraFed Spacefleet call-codes.

'This is TerraFed class VII destroyer *Black Wednesday*,' a voice crackled. 'Geostat Terminus, grid four niner one. Half our personnel are down. Dean Drive is cycling to critical – four hours, maybe five hours tops. We have massive Biot infiltration, cyborg in nature but unclassified. They're taking us *apart* in –'

Then the face exploded. A lot of it, presumably, hit the photo-optics of whatever was transmitting the signal, which pulled back the focus to show it clearly – and Cwej instantly wished it hadn't. Partially obscured by this gruesome mess were indistinct, dark, bulky shapes.

And Cwej heard the distinctive, grating tones of the Daleks.

When he was a child, Christopher Rodonanté Cwej had been absolutely and irrationally terrified by a holo-vid series entitled *EarthDoom XV*, his favourite viewing position of which – like that of most of his generation – had been from behind the sofa with his hands over his eyes. It had been a highly fictionalized account of the Third Dalek Wars with incredibly low production values – but Cwej would wake up in a cold sweat for night after night after seeing it.

This, on the screen, was the epitome of all those childhood associations and fears.

'Oh, Siva,' he said weakly.

'I've got a fix,' the Doctor said from the control console. 'I'm taking us to point of origin.'

The central column of the console flared. Cwej felt the intangible wrenching he had only ever felt once before in his life, when the TARDIS had dematerialized, and that was utterly unconnected with any primary and secondary human sense.

Benny was still watching the wall screen, thin-lipped and pale with shock. 'Oh, those poor colonists,' she said quietly. 'What they had to do. Children and –'

'What colonists, Benny?' Roz said. She was frantically checking the power-systems on her flenser-gun to see if they had been affected by their recent dunking. 'That was a passenger liner, sub-Infra. They're being boarded by the bastard *Falardi*.'

'What are you talking about?' Benny was suddenly looking at Roz like she had started crawling the walls. 'That SOS was from an archaeological dig on Ramos. They unearthed bioweapons: mutagen bombs and –'

Cwej suddenly became aware of a horrified silence from the direction of the central console.

'Oh dear,' the Doctor said. 'I thought –'

Nobody ever discovered, exactly, what the Doctor had thought because the next thing they knew he was diving for the console and hammering desperately on a control switch.

But it was far too late by half.

Aeons ago – the birth, life and death of suns and systems from the subjective *now* – the humanoid race of Gallifreyans achieved some degree of mastery over space and time. These Time Lords, as they styled themselves with some accuracy if not exactly humility, had the innate advantage of being the first sentient beings (so far as sentience can be recognized in humanoid terms) to do so. From their point of view – from their *now* – the whole vast panoply of galactic history insofar as it applied to organic life was malleable. They could bend it to their will.

Any emergent race that might evolve a similar mastery of space-time was judiciously nipped in the bud – not through any sense of cruelty, the Time Lords assured themselves, but for the simple, pragmatic reason that by definition there could be but a single Supreme Power in any one universe. This era of Gallifreyan history became retroactively known as the Time Wars, and during that segment of subjective Gallifreyan timeline entire future species and whole orders of species were eradicated.

Not even the names come down to us. All that remain are certain artifacts, scattered at random through space-time: tools, building materials, fossilized remains of corporal bodies so utterly at odds with anything alive that they cannot be recognized as such.

Weapons.

Some nameless race, for example, in a last-ditch attempt to counter metatemporal Gallifreyan forces, constructed what we must through paucity of imagination and language conceive of as 'reality bombs'.

These bombs, the main mass of which resided in physical reality, would sink tendrils into the meta-dimensional space through which the Time Lords travelled and corrupt the control systems of any construct they found there, causing them to project a hypnogenic signal.

The signal – a purely visual codified pattern – would be interpreted by any basically humanoid brain into a cry for help, originating from some source to which the recipient would unthinkingly rush to render aid. The recipient would promptly attempt to interface with the real – and find itself slap-bang in the centre of a huge ring of matter-disruptors.

In the crucial nanosecond before materialization was

complete, the reality bomb would detonate, tearing the destabilized interface apart.

The Time Lords had long-excised the vast majority of these bombs from space-time, but some small few remained. One, for example, sculled the immensity of the Horsehead Nebula, like some gargantuan and abstract Nautilus, for a period of some fifty billion years, cloaked from detection by dark matter, fully operational.

And the TARDIS materialized slap-bang in the middle of it.

The Fifth Chapter

In the bowels of the Sloathe vessel Kimon was moaning, blood seeping through the fingers pressed to his head and hanging in the air in viscous liquid tendrils.

Leetha glared at the Sloathe captain with utter loathing. 'You can do what you want to usss.' Her voice had roughened, sibilants extending into a vicious reptile hiss. 'You can do what you like. We'll tell you nothing. You might as well kill usss now.'

'Oh, no!' The Most Supreme Captain Trenkor Lep seemed shocked more than anything else, as though Leetha had made a remark in the worst possible taste. 'Must not die now. Must be interrogated by Most Elevated and Puissant Emperor, Kraator Xem. Must not die now or Kraator Xem be *peeved*.'

It appeared to consider for a moment. 'Then again . . .' The eye on a stalk shot from its mouth and regarded Kimon critically. 'This one not much use, eh? Sleep all the bleeding time and when it wake up it just go moan-moan. Is maybe dispensable, yes?'

Tentacles burst from its eyes in a spray of ichor. One of them grasped the tarpaulin draped over the tub and pulled it back with a flourish: a frenzied, squirming mass of Sloathe young. The tub seethed. Leetha felt her last meal (beeswax scraped with fingernails from a small set of nesting occasional tables) rise in her throat.

A tentacle whipsawed for Kimon.

'Is very dispensable,' said the Most Supreme Captain Trenkor Lep happily.

~~~~~

And the privateer stalked the Sloathe convoy, operating almost entirely upon instrumentation. In the makeshift bridge, sheets of gauze were tacked over the ports to soften the cumulative visual effect of the Ring, over-exposure to which could result in hypnoleptic fugues and fits. Here, mostly, the illumination was provided by the screen of a battered electrical radar set, flashing with an almost solid mass of green blips.

Floating by the set, undulating slightly, was a black and ragged bundle from within which three eyes on stalks followed the sweep of the display. To one side, one foot looped in a leather strap affixed to the deck, a slim man in intricate, embroidered red and yellow silk watched the swirling pastel shades through the ports.

Of dark and faintly golden complexion, this man had jet black hair pleated and interwoven with tarnished silver wire and cracked ceramic beads. At first glance he might have seemed vaguely and permanently amused: the left side of his mouth inclined in a faint smile – but this was utterly unreflected in his slanting, sardonic, yellow-irised eyes.

He turned these eyes to Li Shao as he hauled himself up through the hatch in the deck, raised an eyebrow. 'Problems?'

'I don't think so, Kiru.' Li Shao hung his respirator on a tack. 'They're like a dogpack with no leader. I can keep my thumb on them.'

'*Peh!*' The black bundle before the radar set produced the sound of a wad of chewing tobacco hitting a spittoon. 'Total scumbags one and every all, say we. Cut you up in bits as soon as see you, yes?'

'Six is right, Nathan,' Kiru said. 'I still say it was a mistake to hire mercenaries off the Sere wharf. You just watch your back when the fighting starts.'

'Wharfside mercenaries were all we could afford,' the big man said. 'Don't worry about it, Kiru. I can keep a rein on them well enough for long enough – and it's only for this one time. One decent haul, we're out of hock with Solan and we have a decent ship again.'

Kiru shrugged. 'We'd better. Never mind the last legs, this pig of a boat's on its *knees*.'

Li Shao nodded, and crossed to peer through a small smoked-glass exterior viewing port sunk into the side of the cabin. On the superstructure outside, their forms blurred by the gauze over the ports, yellow oilskinned figures were

42

hauling in the parachute sail. Over their eyes they wore goggles of solid amber resin. Gasmasks over nose and mouth were connected to filter boxes strapped to their chests and stuffed with frayed hemp.

He turned back to the thing before the radar set. 'Changes, Six?'

'Slowing,' the bundle said. 'Changing tack. Making ready to segue into Slipstream, judge we.'

'Then I think it's time we made our move.' Li Shao took the helm, depressed a pair of worn rocker-switches.

There was a juddering as the two working engines at the stern coughed explosively and then spluttered to life. In the view through an exterior port, oil spurted from a loose pipe to hang in viscous and elongating globules as the ship surged forward.

Li Shao hit the galvanistical switch of an intercom that would send his voice ringing around the ship. 'We're going in, lads. Let's slice some mucus.'

A tentacle whipsawed for Kimon – who suddenly wasn't there any more. It was almost a second before Leetha, who had been caught quite as much by surprise as had the Sloathe captain, realized quite where he had gone.

Now he was hitting the curved and slimy membrane wall, flipping himself over to absorb the momentum in a crouch and casting about himself with a predatory, soulless and perfectly controlled intensity. Now Leetha recalled his Promethean descent and mentally kicked herself: she should have remembered it and recognized it *before*.

The desiccated world of Prometheus was an environment of extremes, of burning days and freezing nights, of deserts, and the Promethean nomads had over the millennia evolved a metabolism to cope: a metabolism itself of extremes. A Promethean was capable of suppressing higher bodily functions and going effectively dormant when the need arose, such as when one might find oneself hiding in a hole for a week-long sandstorm – switching instantly to a burst of activity upon the very limit of their powers, such as when one might find oneself sharing the hole with a sudden and slightly annoyed desert lion.

43

In his youth Kimon had been one of those dispossessed by the constant wars between the various Promethean nomad K'ans, and he had joined the Anean Sun Samurai relatively late in life. Such converts were the bulwark of the Sun Cult's priest caste, being effectively out of the game so far as its own complicated millennia of internal rivalries and vendettas were concerned and, in the manner of converts the entire universe over, fanatically devoted to the letter of the Ritual, no matter what the actual Ritual in fact was.

Now, filled with the burning purpose of the Search, his very being committed to it, his most basic Promethean attributes had come to the fore. What Leetha had dismissed as the near-catatonia of defeat had merely been the dormant phase; Kimon had simply conserved his energy until it was required. Until now.

And now he sprang. He hit the monstrosity that was the Sloathe captain head-on and, for an instant, Leetha actually thought he was going to *achieve* something – but then a tentacle wrapped itself around him with a sound like a whipcrack, and he was drawn towards the clutching manipulatory appendages drooling from the Most Supreme Captain Trenkor Lep's yawning mouth.

And still he struggled. A hand shot out and wrenched the sheaf of papers from the Sloathe. With the last of his strength he flung them at Leetha.

'Take them!' he screamed, desperately. 'Take them and *go*!'

For the rest of her life – and she went over and over it again for the rest of her life – Leetha never quite understood why she acted at this point as she did. Possibly the fact of being Chosen had in some way instilled her with some overriding sense of destiny that made the lives and deaths of individuals suddenly unimportant, or possibly the high priest's very tone would have had a small rock jumping to obey it – but in any event, she found herself snagging the papers out of the air and launching herself for an exit hole before she realized quite what she was doing.

Thus she merely heard the Most Supreme Captain Trenkor ululating Lep's shriek of rage, the plunging, the slithering and squirming and chomping of a thousand little semi-embryonic Sloathes.

She wished she had seen it, later. There was no way it could be worse than the images of it in her head that would haunt her for the rest of her days.

When she finally came to her senses and turned back in a belated attempt to assist the priest, all she saw was the Most Supreme Captain Trenkor Lep bending over the tub, tentacles and manipulatory appendages half-buried in it in a manner reminiscent of a slave-caste female washing her smalls.

And then a thousand little voices went '*Yuk!*', and a thousand little pieces of Kimon were spat out of the tank. Quite a lot of them hit the membrane walls of the chamber and rebounded.

The Most Supreme Captain Trenkor Lep straightened up and for a moment regarded the stumps of its appendages that the Sloathe young had eaten off. Then it shrugged with an almost human air of unconcern, and turned its monstrous and misshapen head to regard Leetha.

On the periphery, she was aware of the smaller, sluglike masses of Sloathe guards quietly closing in on her, sliding silently through the fetid air like leeches through water.

'Your sneaky ruse did not fool me,' Trenkor Lep said. 'Give me. Give me back now.'

Suddenly, without warning, an almost human look of surprise crossed its semi-human features. It cast about itself with astonishment – astonishment at something only it, apparently, could see.

'Something coming?' it spat incredulously. 'Something *here*?'

And then the Sloathe ship lurched.

The sudden arrival of Planet X, years before, had disrupted the System in a number of abstruse and cumulative ways as it threw the forces that had held it together out of balance, causing a series of catastrophic geological tremors and quakes from which none of the Wanderers had escaped. On the water-world of Elysium, for example, due to a localized aqua-gravitational effect, a series of tubular waterspouts now circumnavigated that watery globe upon a daily basis – a freak of their internal airflow producing a sonic effect remarkably similar to a set of organ pipes. Playing a snatch of some tune that had hitherto remained unrecognized by anybody. Over and over again.

And the skies of the Aneas rained frogs and twinkly meteors. And strange lights were seen moving under the Promethean earth, shining upward through the sandstrewn rocky crust as though it had become temporarily and limitedly transparent at their passing.

And in the middle of an ice-desert of Reklon a vast fissure opened up with a deafening *crack*, tipping half a village of ice-whale hunters into it. And as the frozen wind howled through this jagged fissure it produced a structured and sequential tinkling sound – a sound that as the surviving hunters shivered in the remains of their yurts and mourned their dead instilled in them strange humours, stranger visions and a sudden urge for frozen polar-bear milk in a little tub.

And on a larger and more System-wide scale these disruptions had produced what had come to be known as the Great Outer Slipstream: a vast and debris-strewn elliptical maelstrom, intersecting the orbits of the various Wanderers and extending to the System Edge and back again. In other circumstances this might have been an invaluable aid to navigation for any vessel capable of taking the strain – but since anything entering it tended to end up being spat out on the planet of the Sloathes, it wasn't.

For the Sloathes themselves, of course, it was extremely convenient – had indeed been the single most important factor in their subjugation of the System, in much the same way that elsewhere, in other millennia, the Trade Winds had made it possible for a miserable rain-soaked flyspeck of an island to subjugate entire continents.

Now the privateers intended to make use of this factor for themselves.

The vanguard of the Sloathe convoy hit the Slipstream and fully half the fighter escort was whisked away. At this precise point the pirate ship barrelled in on all engines, jettisoning clusters of clockwork-detonated incendiary mines, which took out the remainder of the escort before it knew what was happening and leaving only the freighter itself intact.

The Most Supreme Captain Trenkor Lep and his crew, who existed to some degree in symbiosis with the dead mass that was their ship, had sensed the pirate's presence long before – but not unnaturally, given the general condition of the vessel, had assumed it to be merely some free-floating lump of debris. They had been caught by surprise.

But they responded well. The Sloathe ship came about and fired a devastating round of grapeshot from its dilatory catapult hatches.

The privateer was only saved by the simple fact that the Sloathes assumed their attacker to be of more or less the same construction as themselves. The grapeshot hit the main bulk of the privateer, passing through already half-deflated latex gasbags and effectively causing little additional damage.

And then the privateer slammed into the freighter. Grappling hooks shot from the gondola and embedded themselves in the pickled alien flesh of its side.

The privateer reversed its engines with a shrieking roar of tortured bearings, slowing the Sloathe's momentum towards the Slipstream to a dead crawl.

Oilskin-suited figures, with respirators strapped to their chests and knapsacks on their backs, hauled themselves across the lines and set explosive charges before retiring to a safe distance, shutting their eyes tight, and sticking their fingers in their ears.

The explosions split the Sloathe ship open at a number of strategic points. Its skin slumped flaccid on its bones and several of its internal tubes prolapsed open.

The hatches of the privateer swung open and the pirates swarmed across the gap.

And in the control cabin, Nathan Li Shao pulled a respirator from a storage locker and hauled back the inner butterfly shutters of an airlock. 'Take command of the bridge, Six.'

'Okey-dokey, matey.' A surprising number of extensible manipulatory appendages extended from the black bundle and wrapped themselves around three separate sets of controls.

'We just kill the lot of them?' Kiru fixed his own respirator mask to his face and pulled on a pair of leather gauntlets.

Li Shao nodded as he pulled the butterfly shutters shut behind them. 'Any of the slippery buggers we can find.' He

47

shrugged. 'The main thing, though, is to be on hand to rein the lads in when the fighting's over. We're still heading for the Slipstream, we have less than a couple of hours and I want as much stuff as possible transferred before we hit and it takes us with it. Including prisoners.' He frowned. 'I gave them the standard line about the safety of prisoners, but I don't know how long that's going to last. I just hope I don't have to make an example of anyone this time.'

'What, not like last time?' Kiru said innocently. 'That business with Mad Jack Bumfrey and the dowager duchess of Hokesh?'

'No.' Li Shao pulled his sword and checked the action. Tiny razor-sharp blades extended from the edge and spun on oiled bearings and retracted with a click.

'Or the time before that?' said Kiru. 'The unfortunate incident of Edmond Dagon Teach and the performing Chiangese triplets?'

'No.' Li Shao primed a matching pair of flintlock-action pistols and stuck them back in his belt.

'Or the time before *that*, with Jago "Sheepshagger" Grelks down in the livestock holds with the set of shears, the tub of lard and the rubber waders . . .?'

'You know,' said Li Shao, 'I really think we ought to start associating with a better class of people.' He swiftly totted up the little poisoned throwing-knives slung from his belt. 'Let's do it.'

Li Shao shot the outer hatch. They each took hold of a grappling line, and swung themselves across the gap and into carnage.

———

The hallucinogenic gases and silicate shards of the Ring were seeping through the freighter now, and rasping agony tore at Leetha's throat and lungs as she hauled herself through slick tunnels crammed with brass-bound, jewel-spilling treasure chests, and voluptuous furnishings and suchlike artifacts of surpassing intricacy and subtlety, and old fire-irons, and mangles and interestingly shaped rocks. As ever, in the loading of the freighter for its outer traverse, Sloathe aesthetics had tended to the principle of knowing the value of nothing and taking the lot so as to be on the safe side.

A blue-grey miasma of smoke drifted through this lethal atmosphere: the char of gunpowder and of burning organic and alien meat. The thud of steel against chitinous weapon appendages and the babble and shriek of the wounded and the dying.

The protective inner lids that had shut automatically over Leetha's eyes would have lent the world a blurred and warping aspect even without hallucinogenics in her bloodstream. As it was, they simply made matters worse. Her mind was in chaos, whole layers of memory and association flaking away. She had no idea how she had got here. One moment she had been staring at the Sloathe captain, rooted to the spot as it advanced upon her, the next she had seen it falter with a sudden alarm as the ship lurched – and the next she was here, hauling herself through the jewel-strewn tunnels with one hand and with her lungs on fire.

In her mind, disjointed images flickered and stuttered and pulsed: a brawling mass of Sloathes and ragged human forms. (She had, in fact, wandered through several pockets of the heaviest fighting all unawares, treating them as little more than patches of turbulence in the medium through which she moved, as blades sliced around her and projectiles hit the membrane baulks beside her, missing her in some cases by fractions of an inch. She had been unconscious of them – even of when, for example, the automatic reactions she had developed as a *Seku* had her deftly turning aside the cutlass of a blood-crazed pirate with burning fireworks braided into his beard, and sticking a couple of fingers in his eyes, cutting them on the shattered smoked-glass eyepieces as they punched through. She had also, all unknowing, inscribed a loose and ragged circle through the twisting passages of the ship, and had ended up almost at the point from which she had started.)

In her free hand she still clutched the bulky sheaf of Kimon's notes. She had long forgotten what they were by now, and she had simply forgotten to let them go.

Now she tried to make some sense out of the impulses and images flaring in her head, using the Sun Samurai techniques that allow one to pull a general sense of flow and plan tactics amidst the immediate, mindless cut-and-thrust-and-parry of the specifics:

49

– The Sloathe ship had been boarded.

– The attackers seemed to be winning – but win or lose, in her present condition, there was nothing much that she herself could do about it. It was entirely out of her hands.

– Everything in the universe was all part of the same big glowing thing shaped vaguely like a walrus and contained within itself, so if you looked really close at your fingernail you'd see the universe with you in it and looking at your . . .

'And just what *do* we have here, precisely?'

Hanging in the scintillating air before her, a tall thin man in a shabby black frock-coat and battered stovepipe hat. A black rubber gasmask with two circular smoked glass eyepieces was strapped to his face. His knees were drawn up, as though he were sitting rather prissily on an invisible dining chair and taking genteel tea. His slim pale hands rested on a scuffed and elderly surgeon's bag upon his lap, and one of them loosely gripped a revolver.

'Allow me to introduce myself,' this man said, his voice slightly muffled by the mask, as he brought up the revolver and discharged it. Something tore through the side of Leetha's head, the shockwave of its passing snapping it to one side and concussing her. 'My name,' this man said happily, 'is Mr Pelt. Have you ever felt the urge to breed?'

The Sixth Chapter

In the centre of things, in the centre of the web of cause and effect, a creature squats in a dark and almost dormant orrery chamber and sends its disembodied consciousness out to watch. It likes to watch. It sometimes likes to pretend it is actively participating, interacting directly with the forces it set in motion so very long ago, so many years ago, in the small and self-enclosed System it has made inside its prison. But it can only observe, and to a minuscule degree influence. It can only squat and watch.

There were many like this creature, once. They had the power to warp suns and they made things – and then they all suddenly died before they were ever born, and their artifacts eradicated before they had ever actually been made.

Only this single creature survived the pre-emptive slaughter of its kind – possibly due to a freak space-time anomaly in which it found itself trapped, an osmosizing one-way energy field which masked it from the destroyers of its race. Only it, now, alone in the universe, remembers that its kind had or would or could ever possibly exist.

It is self-referring, and self-regenerating, and it is effectively immortal.

Until now.

Now the jewels within the mechanism of the orrery flicker and burn dimly: they are almost expended, and have been almost expended for thousands of years. The creature is nearing the end of its current life-cycle and can look forward to little more than a millennium of further existence in this particular form – and that an existence of crippled, senile dissolution. The System that it has made, and remade, and made again within its eternal prison, to while away its countless corporeal resurrections, is finally falling apart.

This would, ordinarily, happen during the last stages of a cycle anyway – but the disruptions caused by the sudden and unexpected arrival of the basalt moonlet and its parasite inhabitants have hastened the process – a process which the creature is now unable to halt.

For it is all but immobile now. Oh, it can drag its massive bulk through the purely physical space it occupies, scrabbling across high-density floors with fossil-ancient claws that could rend them if it so desires – but there is nowhere for its massive bulk to go.

Once, it could inseminate its various sub-beings – thousands of them – with its essence, inhabit them, and send them out and move them through the System entire – the mobile and manipulatory components of its self that tended and ministered to its creation and would, when the time came, set in motion the processes of regeneration that would allow it to be born anew.

Once it could send out its sub-beings to slaughter and torture in their millions the various life-forms with which it stocks its creation – the ferrangeous menagerie that it has surreptitiously, but with obsessive precision, ripped piecemeal through the infraspatial gulf, from the very worlds of the eradicators of its race, to seed the sterile medium of its own handiwork with life that is not its own to give or take, and to provide an outlet for its endless venom and its hunger for revenge.

But over the aeons of this particular cycle – by a cumulative series of coincidences that only become an active factor when set against the truly infinite – these sub-beings, every single one, have at some point malfunctioned, or have been killed by the more determined and resourceful of their intended victims, or have simply dropped dead – and the creature's powers are now too feeble to construct more. Only one single sub-being now remains: damaged and stranded and of no use at all.

For millennia now, as its powers have faded, the creature inside has not had a single pair of usable hands with which to grasp the means of its own resurrection.

It can only squat and watch, now, in its orrery room, watching the generations of livestock it once could maim and slaughter on a whim as they live and love and breed –

picking up the subliminal image-resonances that are such a feature of this quasi-space within the System, and twisting them into forms and structures that the creature inside doesn't *want* them to.

The disruption and the mass-killing caused by the eye-blink recent arrival of the Sloathes is an interesting diversion, of course – but it is also hastening the plunge into the final destruction of the creature's creation, and thus its own, ultimate oblivion. The creature cannot anticipate or manipulate it and cannot stop it. Not directly. It can only squat and watch.

But, sometimes, watching is enough.

The process of observation infinitesimally changes the thing observed, influencing it minutely – and when one has had millennia to so observe then these influences accumulate. A single image instilled in some single short-lived hominid craftsman might, out of generations of failed attempts, result in an object with the precisely correct specifications. A single idea instilled in a hominid mind might result, some generations later, in a mind possessed of precisely the correct sense of purpose.

Thus, when it first knew its powers were failing, and that its usual avenues of replenishment were irrevocably shut from it, the creature inside laid other plans.

Given time, and enough permutations, the process might result in an object that needs to *be* somewhere, and someone who wants to take it there . . .

———

Li Shao and Kiru prowled the bowels of the freighter, galvanistic lanterns slung from their shoulders, weapons at the ready, eyes open wide and ears straining for any sounds of nearby combat. Their protective clothing had been battered and ripped in a number of places in the confusion of the initial fighting, but neither had sustained particularly serious damage. A Sloathe claw appendage had grazed Kiru's ribs and an apparently badly aimed throwing axe had laid open Li Shao's upper arm through the padding. He had stitched the wound with a curved bone needle and a length of catgut from the chamois leather poke on his belt and repaired the rip with adhesive tape at the first available opportunity – and made a small mental note to watch his back on the return trip to Sere.

Now they prowled the freighter, through passageways and holds and bivalve chamber-spaces that seemed horribly like the insides of bodily organs, occasionally checking the contents stored within. One hold contained bales of Anean tea – worth a small fortune if they could get it to the industrialized areas of Prometheus, worthless anywhere else. Another contained bauxite strip-mined from the Promethean deserts, which would have had a ready market in the Serean airshipyards, if anybody was actually making airships any more.

The hold they were currently making their way through was filled with corpses, ichor-crusted and fused together in gelatinous lumps.

Nathan Li Shao took in the mass of bodies and frowned behind his respirator mask. 'Why would they want them? They don't *eat* them, do they? They don't eat human flesh?'

'No, they don't eat human flesh,' said Kiru. 'It probably repeats on them or something. Look at this.'

Various items of stray anatomy had come loose and hung in the air around the larger masses. Kiru snagged a severed arm and lost his grip on it momentarily as it demonstrated more inertia than he had anticipated. He took hold of it again more firmly and showed it to Li Shao. 'This is desiccated. Partially mummified. This didn't die recently, not in the last few years.'

Li Shao took the crumbling arm from him and picked at a mass of congealed slime clumped around the forearm. Something shone brightly in the galvanistical lanternlight, which upon closer examination turned out to be a large enamelled scarab secured by golden and now slightly loose metallic bands.

Li Shao evaluated its mass in freefall by tossing it lightly from hand to hand. 'I think this is solid gold,' he said at last. 'It looks ceremonial. I do believe the buggers have been grave robbing.'

His gaze took in the congealed mass of ancient bodies again. 'You know what I'm thinking?' he said.

'What are you thinking?' said Kiru.

'I'm thinking that the fiends have foully desecrated some

54

ancient and undoubtedly sacred resting ground! Some sepulchre inviolate, where the dead should have eternal lain, entombed with jewels and gold and suchlike treasures – the dead who must even now shriek and gibber in the very maw of torment and cry vengeance for this hideous violation!'

'So how are we going to cut the gold and jewels and suchlike treasure off 'em before we hit the Slipstream?' Kiru said. 'We've only got about an hour.'

Li Shao shrugged. 'I'll have a detail string the lot of them behind our own ship, and we can sort them out along the way. It'll give the bastards something to do to pass the time.'

'And in the case of one or two of them,' Kiru said, 'probably something to eat.'

'Takes all sorts. Everybody needs an interest. I think we've got a result, here, Kiru. I think we have a decent ship.'

They left the hold and headed on through the freighter. The worst of the fighting was over now. Occasionally they came across the corpses of Sloathes or the dead bodies of privateer crewmen or the very alive bodies of privateer crewmen loading up on the more valuable-looking of the objects scattered through the passages. Li Shao sent a number of them back to deal with the bodies packed in the hold, and then detailed the rest to locate and free any prisoners being held by the Sloathes. Humanoid response being what it is the whole universe over, he was at length forced to add the immediate rider that the next man, the very *next* man who came back with the rejoinder about people being held by anything else, was going to get a cutlass so far up their backside they'd be able to pick their teeth with the sharp end.*

They came to a large chamber from the walls of which several limp and atrophied tubes depended. Several crewmen were gathered here, nervously examining the contents of a large wooden tub.

---

* 'Tell me, noble grocer, do you have monkey nuts?'
'No, sir, it is just the way that I walk.'
      Incredibly Bad Jokes of the Twentieth Century, No. 4,857
            ed. Professor Bernice Summerfield

Li Shao glanced at the tubes attached to the walls as they twitched and lazily undulated in freefall, remembering past attacks upon other Sloathe vessels. 'This is where the thing was controlled. Those things hook the captain to its nervous system. So where in the various alternative Sheols is the captain?'

He planted a boot against the wall and launched himself across the chamber to accost a native Elysian with frogskin greased with petroleum jelly and a patch over its vestigial third eye. 'Did you find anything else in here? Big bugger, maybe twenty times bigger than any of the others. You couldn't miss it.'

'Broakka, broak-brek,' said the Elysian, shrugging and gesturing towards the tub to convey that this was all they had found. 'Broakka.'

Li Shao looked down into the squirming mass of Sloathe young. 'The captain probably likes the occasional snack. Have someone spray this lot with sump oil and set light to it before we leave. How long do we have now?'

Kiru pulled a hunter's watch from his belt and flipped it open. 'Half an hour.'

'Then I think it's time we thought about disengaging. Put the word out. We take what we've got and we get the Sheol out. I don't particularly want to hang around with a couple of tons of probably highly annoyed Sloathe unaccounted for.' He took in the assembled mercenaries and frowned at a white-furred figure floating casually by one of the sphincter-exits of the chamber with the air of one who was by no means whatsoever ensuring that nobody went through it.

'That Reklonian,' he said thoughtfully. 'That's the chap who hangs around with Pelt, yes?'

'I think so,' said Kiru.

'So where's *Pelt*?'

Her lungs were lacerated. Her breath hitched in her shredded throat. Her left temple pulsed with the sick and searing warmth of powder-burn blisters and somewhere behind her eyes black lights were spinning.

Mr Pelt's face bobbed towards her and one circular smoked-plate glass eye bulged, expanding to fill her field of vision, the remainder of his body dopplering away from it and appended like some hallucinatory humanoid simulcrum of the Most Supreme Captain Trenkor Lep. For the moment Leetha saw the whole world reflected darkly in the lens and then it pulled back and Pelt assumed slightly more human if distorted dimensions.

Mr Pelt pulled open his leather bag and sorted through it. 'The . . . the good captain Li Shao has made it perfectly clear I am . . . I am not to lay a *finger* on you . . .' he said, his voice made hollow by his respirator mask and reverberating back and forth inside Leetha's pixilated head. And she could hear the twisted and leprous thing in his head, chattering and gibbering behind the words he actually spoke: ' . . . and I won't (*but*) . . . I *won't* lay a finger on you (*but*) but (*oh, but oh, but* oh, *but*) . . .'

And beneath it all, like some hard black pearl in the infected guts of an oyster, like the calcine gallstone in a diseased bladder, the very core of his being: the thing that informed his every thought and word and deed.

Something ancient, something old; some almost imperceptible but malignant speck buried deep inside the human brain, every single human brain, waiting for the conditions and the sequence of events necessary for it to flower.

The specifics might alter, minimally, with specific circumstances, but on countless worlds, in countless realities, in every place a human brain occurred, the same quasi-human thing had lived and killed, and would live to kill again.

And here and now Leetha T'Zhan watched Mr Pelt as he found what he was looking for and showed it to her, proffered it as though for her inspection: a lubricated set of stainless steel forceps, glistening and fascinating and polished mirror-bright under their coating of oil.

Mr Pelt slipped them under Leetha's growling semi-sentient body armour and gently peeled it back. They felt warm.

'This won't hurt a bit but (*slit you*) . . .' Mr Pelt said happily, reaching for his side to find a scalpel. 'Won't hurt a (*slit you* eat *you slit you eat you whole*) . . .'

The lead ball took Mr Pelt in the upper right mandible at a point just behind the seal of his respirator mask and below the lobe of his ear. In her chemically accelerated state, Leetha

57

saw it mash the skin and muscle against the bone before it burst through.

The respirator mask burst from Mr Pelt's face with the impact, to trail by a leather strap. His left cheek bulged. A spray of spittle and blood and impacted shards of tooth enamel burst from his mouth to hit her in the face, and then the left side of his head exploded.

Absently, and in the slightly fussy manner of the profoundly traumatized, Leetha rubbed at her cheek with a hand to try to wipe off the blood and bits of bone. She was dimly aware that dark shapes were moving towards her from her left, but then the black lights spinning in her head behind her eyes exploded too.

Kiru found his eyes continuously drawn to the wall of the passageway, or rather a large and particular section of the wall behind a small pile of battered and prolapsing steam trunks and some lumps of rusting iron. The patch seemed slightly damper and more glistening than its surroundings. Some recent and makeshift piece of repair?

Li Shao blew the smoke off his flintlock and rounded on a small collection of crewmen hanging in freefall behind him, their postures suggesting that, under their respirator masks, they were suddenly not a little shamefaced.

'Take this piece of scum back,' he said, gesturing to the decapitated figure of Mr Pelt. 'You're going to be spending the return voyage with him as a small reminder – and someone give that woman a damned mask.'

Kiru pulled a spare respirator from his belt and kicked himself over to the unconscious Anean woman. Her throat was clotted and he stuck a couple of fingers down it to open up a breathing passage before fixing the mask to her face. It was a toss-up between this killing her or saving her, he supposed, but then again she would have died anyway.

Floating by her was a thick sheaf of papers, scrawled in a variety of different-coloured inks, and Kiru absently stuck them in his belt poke for later examination. He listened for a moment to the ragged attempts at breathing, and turned back to Li Shao. 'She's pretty far gone. I think we should have Six go to work on her as soon as possible.'

Li Shao nodded thoughtfully – and then, casually, apparently at random, he stuck out a hand and grabbed hold of the silver-furred Reklonian he had noticed earlier by the throat.

'So what do you know about this unfortunate incident?' he said mildly. Kiru heard a couple of bits of Reklonian cartilage crack.

'Ghaahng,' said the half-suffocated and suddenly very frightened pirate. 'Hagh hogh *ghaahng*.'

'I can't hear you.' Li Shao increased the pressure a little.

There was a general muttering amongst the crewmen with a noticeably sullen edge to it. Kiru glanced about himself at them, noting their posture, and knew that Li Shao was walking something of a tightrope here. Killing Pelt had been fine, they felt – if only for directly disobeying orders – but secondary and more abstract recriminations would be pushing it. Maybe pushing it over the limit.

The problem, Kiru knew, was that Nathan Li Shao loathed those who preyed upon the defenceless with a passion that could temporarily blind him to tactical expediency, plain common sense or immediate survival. Surreptitiously, Kiru put a hand to the butt of his own flintlock, scanning the assembled crewmen for the first hint of an overtly aggressive move.

But again he found his eyes drawn to the suspicious section of wall. It just seemed wrong, somehow; the very fact of its existence and the shape it made in the world was just *wrong*. But then again this was pretty much par for the course with anything to do with the Sloathes. There was nothing for the humanoid mind to relate to or grasp. You found yourself suspecting everything. You found yourself jumping at shadows.

That steam trunk full of empty bottles, for example, resting at an angle by the damp patch, had a strangely glistening and almost *organic* look to it . . .

'Ghoke,' the luckless Reklonian was saying.

'What?' said Li Shao.

'Egh oh ie ghoak!'

'Ah yes. Right you are.' Li Shao released the Reklonian's bruised throat and shoved him away from him to hit the wall choking and gasping through its respirator. 'You were saying?'

'Know nothing,' the Reklonian said hoarsely. 'He say wait there in big room with big barrel in it, so I *wait* there and –'

'Yeah, right,' Li Shao growled, advancing on him murderously. 'Perfectly reasonable. Nothing suspicious about that.' He put a hand back to grasp the hilt of the sword slung across his shoulders. 'So why do I have trouble believing that?'

A number of crewmen were slowly reaching for their weapons.

'Nathan . . .' Kiru said worriedly.

And then all various Sheols broke loose.

A mass of tentacles exploded from the wall, some tipped with clutching scissor-claws, some ending in soft round mouths with jagged fragile teeth, several tipped with silicate barbs which speared a number of startled privateers, who didn't remain startled for long on account of suddenly having nothing to be startled *with*. Several tentacles wound themselves around the Reklonian and dragged him back, squealing, into a gaping maw that had opened up behind him.

'Oh my various gods!' Nathan Li Shao lurched back and wrenched his sword from its sheath, thumbing the copper stud and hacking at a jointed appendage with the buzzing sawtoothed blade – caroming into Kiru who, having been ready for trouble, had been marginally quicker on the uptake, but who had been hampered by taking hold of the unconscious Anean woman in an attempt to drag her to safety.

The tentacles reared and thrashed. The suspiciously glistening section of wall rippled and bulged, various items of apparently innocuous debris liquefying and flowing into the main mass like scattered, semi-sentient and suddenly recombinant drops of quicksilver.

The bulging form detached itself from the wall with a wet and fecund *splop!*, leaving a weeping eaten crater behind. Human eyes, hundreds of them, erupted from its main mass and glowered. The eyelids that blinked across them were like little mouths with human lips.

A set of winglike structures trailing wet tangles of capillaries unfurled from its sides and beat the air, the blast knocking Kiru and Li Shao and the woman tumbling and flailing through the debris, glass shards tearing at their protective clothing and lacerating the skin where it was exposed.

'Excrescent hominids will now cower before my Most Supreme ejaculations!' the thing said, happily.

The Seventh Chapter

And the creature in the centre – in the minute section of its consciousness that could operate upon the order of the momentary – knew a moment of rage. In its millennia of subtly directing the inhabitants of the system it had finally, to a certain degree, come to terms with the basic intransigence of humanoids. Give them a perfectly simple idea, for example, and they'll build a religion out of it. And then that religion will split into factions arguing over the unimportant details, and then one faction will start killing the other faction over some incredibly minor point, and then the other will start killing the first one on account of the killing it did . . . anything, in fact, rather than pull the collective finger out and actually do anything with it.

For millennia the creature inside had compensated and compensated again, adapting its plans to make the best out of the chaotic mess that humanoids manage to make out of anything as a matter of course. And now, finally, when conditions had seemed perfect for success, the massive random factor of the Sloathes had ruined everything.

Admittedly, their bombardment of the Dirigible Cities had provided the impetus to finally send the reptile woman on the Search, but her capture by the Sloathe fleet had been entirely out of the thing inside's control – and it had only been by sheer if fortunate coincidence that the convoy had come under privateer attack.

Still. The situation might have been salvageable. These privateers were based in the free-spinning asteroid they called Sere . . . and for a number of reasons this opened up a large number of extremely interesting possibilities. The thing inside had followed the events taking place in the Sloathe freighter closely, instilling the grain of suspicion that had allowed the pirate captain to rescue the woman in the nick of time . . .

And then it had all fallen to pieces again.

The thing inside watched the monstrous Sloathe as it advanced upon the pirate and the unconscious woman, and knew that it was now, effectively, back to square one.

There was nothing physically present it could manipulate, there was no mind it could influence to any serviceable extent. For a moment the thing inside allowed itself to wallow in its rage; all it wanted, all it really *wanted* was something to throw.

Something to . . .

There might just be something to throw.

If you were looking in the right direction.

Somewhere, someone was screaming. It went on, and on, and apparently without a pause for breath.

Benny hit the wall of the console room, and then the ceiling, and then another wall and then the floor again. It was only after this process had repeated itself a number of times that she realized the TARDIS was literally *tumbling* through the infraspatial vortex of the Implicate.

This had never happened before. Even in the directionless vortex the TARDIS seemed to operate under an internal sense of integrity, some abstract, self-referential centre of gravity. It might be buffeted and tossed by chaoplasmic turbulence like a raft in a storm, but it had always maintained its basic orientation. It never, as it were, tipped over and sank.

Until now.

A double-lurch through dimensions with which she couldn't cope – and she was hitting the ceiling yet again and slowly sliding down it, her elbows skinned, her skin already flowering with extensive bruising.

And somebody was still screaming.

And then Chris Cwej landed on top of her, knocking the wind out of her. Off to one side the slimmer, darker form of Roz Forrester hit, tangled and cursing in the broken-backed remains of a hatstand.

The ceiling juddered under her and Benny heard the familiar oscillating rasp of the central control column – but somehow fractured, tainted with jagged harmonics that sounded like something alive and wounded and shrieking. She tried to make her lungs work, but for the moment they only seemed to want to spasm. Black pinpoints spun somewhere behind her eyes and began to expand . . .

And then Forrester shoved a dithering Cwej out of the way, swung herself on top of her and shoved the heels of her hands into the soft solar plexus under the ribcage, working at the nerve ganglion.

After a while Benny drew a shuddering breath and consciously forced it out; forced herself to breathe in again, forced herself to breathe out.

'You know,' she gasped, 'I usually get a dinner and a date before I get that tactile.'

'Ho sodding ho,' shouted Forrester over the din. 'What the *hell*'s going on?'

'Don't look at me,' Benny rasped back weakly. 'I don't have clue one – but I know a man who probably does. Doctor?' She cast around herself, trying to locate the Time Lord. '*Doctor?*'

'Um . . .' Beside them a worried Cwej was looking upwards – the direction, Benny suddenly realized, from which came the screaming that never ended. 'I wouldn't put money on him knowing anything much.'

<hr/>

The creature inside had made itself ignore the vortex at a wrong angle to reality for a long time now. It was through this, when its powers had been at their greatest, that it had sucked the raw materials and the life-forms that seeded its System – but when its powers began to fade, its quasi-sphere of influence had decreased. Now, all it could extend into was a supremely disappointing collection of swirling debris, randomly displaced from its respective worlds and picked over so many times that, it knew, absolutely nothing of interest remained.

Besides, there was something far more hazardous to consider. This was the medium through which travelled that hated species that had killed the creature inside's kind. In its weakened state they might detect its presence, might locate it, might finally destroy it.

Thus it was with some slight trepidation that the creature inside extended itself. It gave the lumps of rock and the random gas particles and the occasional dead body of some life-form or other the most cursory of examinations. It was, after all, merely looking for something to . . .

There was something new.

A distorted, pulsing, vaguely obloid form, spinning and shrieking and tearing at the fabric of infraspace with ragged pseudopods sprouting from its main quasi-mass. A great rent fouled its side, as though something had, at some recent point, attempted to rip it apart. Within this wound, something sickly phosphorescent pulsed. A little blue growth stuttered weakly on one of its smaller planes, like a beacon.

With a small start, the creature inside recognized one of the half-living conveyances of the hated genocidal race that had killed its kind, and saw that it was wounded, possibly dying.

And inside, all alone, there would be a murderer. Wounded too.

Possibly dying.

Oh, yes . . .

The scream ripped from the Doctor's distended throat without a pause for breath, clashing with the pulsing shriek from the console's central column to lacerate Benny's head with dislocated harmonics and subsonics that were somehow far more horrific than should ever be possible with mere sound. It was a sound that human ears were never meant to hear, no human brain to register. It was a sound that plunged you into a churning pit of alien madness and ate your mental guts.

The Doctor still stood rigid on the inverted console room floor, depending from it, as though paragravity was only something that happened to other people. He gripped the console tightly and he shook and he screamed, oblivious to the chaos around him, lost in some inner and unknowable agony.

Standing groggily on what was ordinarily the ceiling, Benny found that her eyes were more or less level with his. She waved a hand in front of them and they stared straight out of his head, unwavering, unseeing . . . and somewhere inside, behind each dilated pupil, something pulsed like

65

some organically evolved alien equivalent of an LED.

'Oh, damn it . . .' Benny hauled back a hand and slapped the Time Lord across the face as hard as she could.

She then spent a painful couple of seconds clutching at her hand with the other, and trying to work out whether every bone in it had actually been broken or not.

The Doctor simply stopped screaming and shut his mouth. Then he turned his head to regard Benny with his system-reset eyes.

'Oh, she's wounded,' he said, quietly and perfectly calmly. 'I told her it would be like the old days. I told her things would be just like they were, and now she's wounded . . .'

And there was something utterly wrong about his voice, and it was only later that Benny realized exactly what it was. It was as though every word was overlaid upon the din about them, not so much drowning it out as quietly overriding it.

A battered Forrester and a bruised Cwej were on their feet now and crowding round.

'What's going on?' Forrester shouted.

'She's ripped,' the Doctor said, still perfectly and inhumanly calm. 'She was almost pulled apart. She managed to fling herself clear and she's looking for a reality-sequence she can infest, but she –'

His head fell forward. For a moment it was as though the Time Lord had lapsed into dormancy, like a mechanical android with its servocouplings cut. Then he reanimated himself. 'Her screams in my mind. They slice through my mind. She can't remember the routines that stop her remembering the places where she hasn't been, or going where she already is, or building an interface out of living matter and it – are we still heading for Event One, Tegan?' He swung his head around in a sudden bewilderment. His lower lip trembled. 'This is not the Zero Room.'

'What the hell's a Zero Room?' Forrester shouted.

'And what's a Tegan?' shouted a puzzled Cwej.

'After your time, Jamie,' said the Doctor chattily. 'Qantas uniform, incredibly gullible, can't resist pulling a big red knob. You can't miss her.'

'Oh damn!' Benny exclaimed with exasperation. 'Here we go again. He's doing his Musical bloody Companions routine again.'

'Does he do that a lot?' Roz asked.

'Only all the time. He was doing it when I first met him. It either means he's got something incredibly duplicitous and sneaky up his sleeve –'

'Damn. They didn't get her,' said an uncharacteristically short-tempered and vaguely disappointed Doctor. 'I'm still stuck with that irritating blasted perfect-pitch screech . . .'

'Or it means we're suddenly up the transit core without an impeller rod, right?' shouted Cwej.

'I don't know,' Benny shouted. 'I think we're still OK as long as something called the Cloister Bell doesn't start ringing. I gather that means imminent total destruction or something.'

'K9,' said the Doctor, sternly, 'if you don't leave that fibrillatingly evil mechanoid's leg alone this minute, I'm going to give you a core-dump and a reformatting you'll never forget.'

From all around them, suddenly, came a flat and off-key ringing suggestive of a cow-bell writ large, cutting through the ambient din as had the Doctor's voice. *Grong-clonk*, it went. *Grong-clonk-clonk*.

'Y'know, this is probably the point,' Roz shouted, 'where I say what the hell's *that* again, and you give me three guesses.'

———

The spinning form was desperately attempting to open up a hole into some reality, any reality: looking for some way – any way – out.

The thing inside simply reached out with its disembodied consciousness, wrapped itself around a wildly flailing pseudopod and, with the lightest possible force, *pulled* . . .

———

The shrieking from the console suddenly shot up a couple of octaves to a head-splitting squeal – and the TARDIS lurched as though snatched by some monstrous hand, knocking the three humans off their feet again. Benny heard the juddering groan of materialization, palsied and febrile, as though the TARDIS was expending the last of its strength.

Vague and fractured images streamed through her head: (a

67

churning, clashing black iron engine, all cogs and cams and greasy pistons, silhouetted against a sky of fire; a massive eyeball hanging in space, carved from a single perfect crystal, around which spun several, smaller, variegated eyes; a vast flat filigree of silver tracings, along which ornate, artificial insects crawled . . .)

Benny shook her head to clear it. She realized she was still gazing up at the Doctor, who was now casting about himself frenziedly. He flipped himself over and dropped like a half-brick to land on the ceiling by her, and rummaged through an extensive collection of debris that for some reason she had failed to notice before – tossing various scarfs and cricket bats and suchlike items over his shoulder until he finally unearthed his umbrella.

'Is this a dagger I see before me?' he mused.

'No it bloody isn't,' Benny snapped, having finally lost any last semblance of patience she had ever had. 'You can sort of tell the difference because a dagger has more pointy bits and it doesn't keep the *rain* off . . .'

Another shrieking lurch of the kind which Benny, for one, was getting heartily sick. The Doctor suddenly rounded wild-eyed on his companions and waved his umbrella at them fiercely.

'Blast ye for the scurvy knave ye are, mister bosun!' he cried apoplectically. ' 'Twill be a three turn round the scuppers should I hear the dread word o'*mootny* again!'

'What?' shouted a puzzled Forrester.

'What he's basically saying,' said Benny miserably, 'is hello nice transit core and has anybody seen the impeller rod.'

And the TARDIS materialized. After a fashion.

The Eighth Chapter

The Most Supreme Captain Trenkor Lep had spent a particularly uncomfortable hour and a half buried in the hollow it had eaten out in the wall. Like a human being trying his first pickled onion, it had found the taste of preserved Sloathe matter repulsive, and that it tended to repeat – but like a human with a pickled onion, it found that it had suddenly acquired a taste for it. And thus, for an hour and a half, it had tried to remain hidden and immobile while its insides churned with the alien equivalent of wind, and all the while suddenly craving to eat the huge mass of *food* that surrounded it.

Things had not been helped by the fact that several sections of its brain analogue were still in contact with Planet X, and the jabbering voices of Lokar Pan, the Sekor Dom Sloathe and the Most Elevated and Puissant Kraator Xem had almost driven it to distraction.

It was not, therefore, in the most sanguine and temperate of humours.

'Make ready for big inconveniently discorporations!' it roared, ejecting little bits of minced and entirely undigested Reklonian from a couple of sphincter-vents (a thousand little appendages like toothpicks of fleshy stalks sprouting to pick bits of skin and hair out of the teeth around its maw) and mashing aside a couple of other hominids as it shot a tentacle for the larger one in the red leather. 'Is at this moment in time extremely a squish!'

The leather-clad figure hacked frantically at the tentacle with his buzzing cutting-thing, severing it with a spray of slime. The Most Supreme Captain Trenkor Lep felt it no more than a man would feel the bite of a gnat; it was replete with incorporated pickled Sloathe meat and it could build itself plenty more . . .

'Big chompy munching will at this convenience happen upon the head at most precipitously!' The Most Supreme Captain slithered murderously toward the hominid survivors and then something inside it exploded.

—∞—

Nathan Li Shao flung a hand across his eyes as the magnesium light blasted over him. For an instant, even through the protective leather, he could actually see the bones silhouetted in the flesh. There was the wet-silk sound of flesh tearing and the creak and the splintering crack of bones – and a lurching, groaning ululation that seemed to come from every direction at once.

The lights faded. Li Shao lowered his hands and shook his head, blinking to dislodge the swarm of little black-and-purple explosions on his peripheral vision.

Erupting from the feebly flopping remains of the Sloathe captain, like some monstrous and cancerous growth, was a rectangular, boxlike construction – or rather a boxlike construction such as might have organically evolved. It was lumpen and pulsing and juddering as it desperately tried to hold its shape, and crawling with a tracery of vein-like ducts haemorrhaging some bluish pigment. On its roof pulsed something like a blistered luminescent sore.

An opening of sorts, a ragged approximation of a door burst open with a squaptulous *splunch!*

And then a small, crazed figure ran out, actually running on the floor of the passageway even in freefall as though the owner of his own personal gravity.

He was immediately followed by a slightly taller, female figure, who seemed to be attempting to restrain him – and who, it appeared, merely had the use of the gravity available to everyone else and went tumbling. 'Bugger!' She immediately began to retch and choke upon the tainted air.

'Yo-ho-ho and a bottle of rather fine and sparkling Oolonian Chablais!' cried the little man, waving at a momentarily dumbfounded Li Shao what appeared to be that most deadly of all weapons known to man, a razor-sharp umbrella. 'I'm just the man to do the job till something better comes along – so get down, ye heathen scum and *kneel*. Does your mother know you're out?'

And then he fell over.

At this point, the boxlike construction appeared to give up the unequal struggle of existing, and collapsed with a wet *splotch!* into the remains of the Most Supreme Captain Trenkor Lep.

The woman had grabbed hold of Kiru and shook him urgently. She was covered in bruises and bubbles of foamy blood were already bursting from her mouth due to the lacerating effects of the air. 'Help us . . .' she rasped. 'The Doctor. I think he's hurt and Roz and Chris are . . .' She cast around vaguely as the hallucinogenic effects hit. 'There's a dead table!' she said indignantly. 'And it's catslit eyed. When I was little, when I was small the bogiemen and juju lights behind their ragged *eyes* and . . .'

She lapsed into unconsciousness. It had probably been a hard day. Kiru pulled the respirator from the body of the late Mr Pelt and jammed it over her face.

'So what in Sheol was that all about?' Li Shao tapped at his hemp-stuffed respirator box. 'I don't think this is working properly. I think I caught a whiff of the Mister White Man there.'

'I saw it, too, I think,' Kiru said. 'Is the thing dead?'

Nathan Li Shao peered at the prolapsed remains of the Most Supreme Captain Trenkor Lep. It was still moving. As he watched, a lump of it barely attached by a torn string of alien ligament slid towards its main mass. 'I think it's just been inconvenienced. I reckon now would be a good time to emulate the Wise Politician Caught within the House of Ill Repute Suspended by his Nipples with a Bag over his Head and Three Live Lobsters in Little Knitted Berets up an Inconvenient Orifice.'*

'What, hang on like grim bloody death and swear blind our wives'll stick by us?' said Kiru, dubiously.

'I was thinking more along the lines of making our

* Translator's note. This is a direct and almost word-for-word translation from a noted Old Promethean slum-city proverb, save for the term 'Politician', which since that desert world has no formal government save for the despotic Califs of its cities, does not occur in the Promethean tongue. A more direct translation for the term actually used would be an: '*Auspicious-Personage-Whose-*

excuses, hauling up our trousers and having it away on our heels. You.' Li Shao turned to a couple of dazed crewmen who had survived the Sloathe captain's onslaught – the greasy frogskinned Elysian among them – and gestured to the unconscious bodies of the Anean woman and the two new arrivals. 'Give us a hand with getting these back to the ship. We can work out what they were actually doing here later.'

'And if they turn out to be dangerous,' said Kiru, 'we can always throw them out of the hatch.'

Now that the excitement was over, the roaring of the Slipstream from outside could be plainly heard. They were very close now. Li Shao and his men manhandled the three unconscious bodies through the freighter towards the breaches, where the few remaining pirate crew were hauling themselves across the gap.

And behind them the exploded mortal remains of the Most Supreme Captain Trenkor Lep continued to move.

———

Deep under the crust and substrata of Planet X, the Most Elevated and Puissant Kraator Xem was peeved. 'Infamy! Infamy! They've all got it in for me!'

Lokar Pan collapsed out of its transmitter form, through which it had relayed contact to the freighter's captain, and warped itself into something vaguely wasplike – although, in accordance with the mass-to-surface-area ratio, it would have needed two-hundred-foot wings and a small jet propulsion engine if it could ever hope to get off the ground. 'Is gone,' it said. 'Trenkor Lep dead. Boo-hoo and suchlike. Ho hum.' It shot out a pseudopod and idly speared a tempting slimy five-legged quasi-marmoset from an overturned radiogram. Transmitting across the System tended to take it out of one, and it was feeling a little peckish.

The Most Elevated and Puissant Kraator Xem, whose

General-Reputation-for-Extreme-Moral-Rectitude-and-Not-to
mention-Probity-would-be-Severely-Inconvenienced-Should-He
Ever-be-by-Chance-Discovered-in-a-House-of-Ill-Repute-Hanging
by-His-Nipples-with-a-Bag-over-his-Head-and ... etc., etc., etc.' Old Promethean is a remarkably literal-minded, and not to mention self-referential, if not exactly concise language.

visible protuberance had in hir distraction lapsed into an obloid with lots of little baby arms, bounced up and down with a rapid splatting sound and beat the basalt floor with hir little fists. 'Is they *dare*? Take away my things from me! Make them stop now!'

Be calm, the voice of the Sekor Dom Sloathe resonated in their minds. *These aboriginals believe that they have achieved a famous victory, yes? And they will no doubt now return, replete with their ill-gotten gains, to the fetid little bolt-hole from which they came . . .*

'What?' said the Most Elevated and Puissant Kraator Xem, the Ruler of the Universe, suspiciously. 'What you say?'

They going home with your stuff, said the Sekor Dom Sloathe patiently.

'Why you not say that before?' said Kraator Xem. 'Bastards. Don't know where they live. Looked for them before. Lost lots of big ships.'

Ah yes, resonated the Sekor Dom Sloathe. *Their bolt-hole is well protected: a maze of freefloating silicate asteroids through which only the most experienced can safely navigate . . . but none the less, it has been possible to establish a number of admittedly extremely abstruse, but remarkably effective channels of communication. I believe that something might be done . . .*

'What?' said the Most Elevated and Puissant Kraator Xem.

We go get your stuff back, said the Sekor Dom Sloathe.

And somewhere else under the basalt crust of Planet X, in one of its larger repository caverns, the stuffy air stirred amidst the piles of valuables and semi-valuables and outright junk. Gas molecules and motes of dust spun in strange and complex whorls, their atomic structures breaking down, cohering and re-forming into one new and entirely unique long-chain pattern.

There was an injured, juddering, groaning sound that, had any sentience been around to hear it, might have sounded almost alive. And if this nonexistent observer actually existed, then he or she might be put in mind of some exhausted, wounded creature hauling itself with the last of its strength from some raging abstract sea and on to a beach, and collapsing weakly with a sigh of relief.

An oblongatic blue box now stood, at a slight angle
amidst a heap of tarnished and apparently discarded silve
cutlery twenty feet high.

It was slightly ragged around the edges – its blue paint wa
blistered in patches and scraped off the corners and the glas
panes of the little lamp set on its roof were cracked an
spider-web fractured – but its lines were straight and it
structure would appear, assuming our putative observer t
possess a generously rough-and-ready sense of aesthetics
fundamentally intact. Indeed, upon the microscopic level, th
damage was already repairing itself in some complex an
semi-equivalent of clotting and scabbing.

After a while the door of the TARDIS opened and the thin
dark figure of Roslyn Forrester climbed out, lost her footin
and tumbled down the pile of knives and forks and Georgia
silver teaspoons with a cascade of crashes and clatters and
number of vehement and quite unconscionable curses.

The tall blond figure of Chris Cwej – who had taken th
opportunity to change into monkey boots and denims and
scintillating, multicoloured Tyrannosaurus Rex-skin jacket
appeared in the doorway above her. 'You OK, Roz?'

Ms Forrester's reply, alas, has been lost to posterity. Sh
removed a couple of forks from where they had becom
uncomfortably lodged and gazed up at the TARDIS. Th
white band running across it above the door read

pLicMans bOx

in ragged, childish upper and lower-case lettering. 'Take
look at this,' she said to Cwej, who had slithered down th
cutlery with slightly more grace than she had to join her. Sh
pointed up to the letters – and then frowned.

They were slightly less ragged now, and they read:

PoLIS TeFLOn

'I think it's *healing* itself,' she exclaimed. She didn't knov
what disconcerted her more: the fact that the thing ha
almost been destroyed – or this further evidence that i
seemed to live a kind of private life of its own.

Cwej shrugged, apparently unconcerned. 'The Doctor sai
she was pretty much indestructible.'

She, Roz Forrester thought. He's bought into the Docto

lock, stock and single functioning brain cell. It was evident in the way he was looking bright-eyed and cheerfully around himself, as though he were on some holiday outing rather than stranded God knew where and with no hope of rescue.

Just like Roz he had seen the Time Lord go seriously weird, just like Roz he had seen him running from the TARDIS before its materialization was complete and dragging Benny with him – but entirely unlike Roz he seemed to have absolute faith in the Time Lord. So far as Cwej was concerned, and despite all evidence to the contrary, the little bugger was somewhere out there alive and well, and it was only a matter of time before he came storming back to save the day.

Roz took in the surroundings with a sinking heart. They appeared to be in a large cavern: blood-heat warm and damp and smelling of rot – overlaid with the reek of something other and inorganic. It was not exactly a mineral smell, as opposed to animal or vegetable: there was something intangibly alive about it. She was put in mind of a case, years before, involving a Ruul from the Proximan chain rafts – a silicate-based life-form living in liquid ammonia, and who had boiled to death in what Roz's metabolism thought of as room temperature. The smell was something like that.

The walls of the cavern pulsed with phosphorescence, limning the piles of miscellaneous objects. Roz saw, in particular, in this order:

a horsehair-stuffed red leather sofa piled with porcelain dolls and glove puppets and marionettes. The eyes of the dolls had been poked out and replaced with fossil finger bones;

a heap of books soaked with some sort of viscous slime and degenerating into sticky papier-mâché. Visible titles included: *Tristram Shandy*, *Titus Andronicus Restored*,* *Paradise Mislaid* and *Fly Fishing* by J. R. Hartley;

* Literary note. In 2001, polyfractal text-enhancement convincingly demonstrated that Shakespeare's *The Most Lamentable Tragedy of Titus Andronicus* as printed in the 1623 Folio was in fact incomplete, and was originally intended to be played as farce with a cunning series of sight-gags and an injection of unfortunate and utterly gratuitous smut – including an entirely distasteful set-piece involving Lavinia, Sempronius, a tooled leather psalter and a mixed fruit salad. The restored *Titus Andronicus* was later, in 2004, holographically filmed as *Carry On Amputating*.

a large pile of Bakelite telephones and stuffed animals including a ring-tailed lemur, a slightly limp water moccasin and a puma with an expression of extreme umbrage.

The cumulative effect was extremely disquieting. This was not like some of the weirder areas she had recently encountered in the TARDIS – which, she was dimly aware, had been the result of the human mind and senses trying to make some sense out of a fundamentally inhuman environment because although the TARDIS was inhuman it was, she thought, fundamentally benign.

Here, the objects were real. They might or might not have originated on Earth, they might or might not have been actually *made* by humans, but they were as fundamentally human as a napped flint axe or the roof of the Sistine Chapel. It was the arrangement of them that was at fault.

Even dumped in rough-and-ready piles like this, they had been dumped by things as far removed and unknowable to man as a man is to a microbe on a slide – and the canisters were coming. Surrounded by these commonplace and human things, Roz Forrester felt an alienation far worse than she had ever before felt in her life.

Chris Cwej, on the other hand, was rooting through the stuff as happy as a kid in a junkyard. 'Hey, is this neat or is this neat? It's really weird.'

'Yeah,' Forrester said miserably. 'Right.' She looked up at the TARDIS again and at the legend which now read:

POLICE TELEFONE

There was probably enough food in there to last them for the rest of their lives. The best plan would probably be to go back inside, triple-lock the door and spend the rest of their lives eating. She turned to Cwej to say as much – and found that he was now almost a hundred metres away and scrambling over the junkyard dunes. With a sigh, she checked the charge on her flenser-gun again and set off after him.

'What the hell do you think you're doing?' she puffed when she had finally caught him up by a small mountain of polished chicken bones.

'The Doctor and Benny are out there somewhere,' Cwej said firmly. 'They might be in *peril*. It's our honour-bound duty to find them and save them.'

'Yeah,' said Forrester. 'Right.'

They came to the cavern wall and followed it around until they came to an opening of sorts, choked with solid slime. Roz decided that her justly famous non-expertise with a power-weapon would probably not be a factor at this sort of range, so she and Cwej broke out their flensers and peeled the wall off layer by layer. Sometime later there was a hole wide enough to crawl through. Roz went first, cautiously, gun at the ready.

And then she saw what lay beyond it.

———∞———

And in its flickering, churning orrery room, the thing inside knew a sudden sense of doubt. It had not anticipated that the space-time conveyance would use its brief respite of actuality in the freighter to reorient itself and fling itself to some more tenable environment in which to heal. The thing inside had also not anticipated that the creature calling itself the Time Lord would be travelling with pets. This introduced whole new complications to an already overcomplicated probability matrix.

Never mind. The basic purposes had been achieved. The pawns were now in place. The thing inside crushed its momentary uncertainty.

It was ready to begin.

Canto Second:
A Question of Finance

PATRON: n.s. One who countenances, supports or protects. Commonly a wretch who supports with insolence, and is paid with flattery.

Samuel Johnson (1709–1784)
Dictionary

The Golden Rule is that those who have the gold, make the rules.

Anon. And not some alien who never existed in the first place and even if he did I never met him.

(As quoted by Sentient Citizen FLORANCE in *My Life as a Self-Referential Bioware Operating System Who Got Wise*)

The Ninth Chapter

It was later and the pirate ship was under weigh, winding through the three-dimensional maze of the Ring on the couple of spluttering diesel engines that had survived its recent high-speed manoeuvres – and the strain of pulling itself away from the periphery of the Outer Slipstream, which had flung the deflated remains of the Sloathe ship away bare minutes after it had been released.

Lashed to its superstructure under tarpaulins were the fruits of the pirate haul, including an extremely large number of mummified corpses and their ceremonial gold and jewels and suchlike treasure. Amongst these crawled the oilskinned crewmen, cutting free what they could and jettisoning whatever remained over the side.

Nathan Li Shao, meanwhile, had been making an inventory of the other booty. Now, as he hauled himself up to the bridge, he passed the living-quarters he himself shared with Ciru and Six – little more than a pair of packing cases nailed together as a place to put their bedrolls – in which he had established a sick-bay of sorts.

The practicalities of combat meant that the pirate crewmen themselves had only suffered minor injuries or major death, and the majority of the Promethean and Anean prisoners liberated from the Sloathes had been found safe within the airtight polyps of their cells. They were now helping to sort the gold and jewels and suchlike treasures from the corpses. The quarters were only occupied by the Anean woman and the two strangers who had appeared so mysteriously on the Sloathe ship. When Li Shao stuck his head through the hatchway, he saw that the odd little man in the baggy and mismatched clothes was still locked rigid, his eyes closed, a faint smile on his face and his hands clutching his umbrella to his chest. Only the almost imperceptible rise and fall of his chest suggested

81

that he was alive. The strange woman appeared to be sleepin
naturally now, occasionally stirring and murmuring.

Six was still at work on the Anean woman: floating over he
with an appendage stuck down her throat – working wit
microscopic precision, Li Shao knew, to remove the gla
fragments and repair the thousands of small injuries to h
lungs. Li Shao had gone through the same procedure once aft
accidentally losing his respirator mask, he remembered, ar
he wished he could forget about it. The woman's semi-sentie
armour was gathered around her waist and muttering sullen
in a way that managed to suggest that it just happened to b
there, and wasn't attempting to get as far away from th
polymorph as possible in any way, shape or form.

'How's it going, Six?' he asked.

An eye-stalk surfaced from the rags and tracked round
regard him. 'Is okey-dokey, think we, pretty much. Funn
woman, little damage much. This woman big damage, tak
bigger lot of time . . .' The polymorph paused, thoughtfull
its work on the Anean woman continuing all the whil
'Funny man really strange though. No damage. No thing
inside lungs – and lungs all wrong. Filters and stuff. Nev
seen wrong lungs like before, say we. Sound like he have tw
hearts go boom-boom also, think we.'

Li Shao gazed at the immobile man again. 'Has he mad
any kind of move at all?'

The polymorph waggled their eye-stalks dismissively. 'Mov
nothing. Say nothing. Just float there like a boring thing.'

'All right. Let me know the minute he does.' Li Sha
hauled himself out and continued on his way to the bridge.

This was one of the easier sections of the traverse: almost
hundred leagues with nothing much in the way until they b
the dense asteroid cluster that surrounded Cere. Kiru had tie
the helm and was examining a thick and mismatched sheaf
papers he had picked up from somewhere.

He looked up when Li Shao entered. 'Anything particularl
exciting?'

Li Shao pulled his inventory from his belt poke an
skimmed through it. 'Apart from the stuff on the bodies,' h
said, 'we've got about four hundred and fifty of what yc
might call *objets d'art*. Anything from a Hokeschi nine-strin
guitar to a set of nesting tables and a stuffed toy bear on

82

stick. There was a lot of food, too – the lads found a whole hold full of rotten oranges – and some of it was salvageable: pickled vegetables, tinned fruit and some sides of salted meat that should be all right when we peel the slime off. Forty blocks of Anean zombie-hemp resin –'

'Any good?'

'Pretty colours.'

'We'll be able to shift the food and the hashish on Sere at least,' Kiru mused. 'The market for consumables and potables is going through the roof. Enough to cover expenses?'

'And pay off the crew,' Li Shao said. 'Nowhere near enough for a new ship. We're going to have to put together some sort of deal.'

'Solan again?'

'I reckon. His credit's good – whatever else about him stinks.' Li Shao glanced at the papers in Kiru's hand. 'What's that you're reading?'

'Something I picked up on the freighter.' Kiru showed him a sheet of yellowed vellum: a crude representation of the System elaborated with a large number of entirely unnecessary curlicues. In the centre of each of the circles representing the Wanderers, in different coloured inks, was an eye. 'They look like research notes based on one of the Anean sub-sects relating to what they call the Eyes of the Schirron.'

Li Shao nodded. Throughout the many and various religions of the System a recurring theme, for some reason or other, concerned a set of mythical entities known collectively as the 'Eyes'. These Eyes were variously defined, depending upon to whom you talked, as anything from the four actual eyeballs Kloi-Kloi-Seki's young ripped from their father to make the Wanderers themselves, to the eyes of the creator-god who watched over every world from sparrow-fart to sunset, to the physical embodiments of the four elements of Earth, Air, Fire and Water, to metaphors for any number of variations on the Four States of Being* – and were probably

---

* The Elysian Evangelical Pontoon-cult of the Frantically Wobbling Dipsomaniac, for example, held that the four states of being were: (1) Sober as a Judge, (2) Happy as a Sand Boy, (3) You're my Best Bleedin' Mate You Are, and professed to a guilty and extremely uneasy total blank concerning (4).

the result of some original religion, long lost to the mists of history, from which all of the others had evolved.

The various Eyes were inextricably linked with the various prophesies concerning the End of the System, and as with most religions they tended to share some basic common factors while flatly contradicting each other in everything else. Simply, in the Last Days, the Eyes would come together in a mythical place where there were No Shadows (certain and slightly earthier sects held that they would be stuck where the Sun didn't shine) and either destroy the System utterly, or save it. Seas of fire were in evidence. You couldn't move for the rivers of blood.

'So what?' Li Shao said. 'Another specious cosmology, like we're all living inside a big hollow ball or we're falling from eternal ice and into the Sun. Big deal. It's not as if we could make any money peddling it – I mean, fiendish piratical rogues who'd sell our grannies for the price of a beer and a hamster in a bap we may be, but there are certain limits.'

'It's vaguely interesting, all the same,' Kiru said. 'Whoever wrote this was convinced that these items are actual artifacts, and there's some slightly obfuscated but remarkably specific directions for finding them –'

'What sort of artifacts?' Li Shao said.

'Diamonds as big as your head, apparently, with lights of a Most Attractive and Coruscating nature inside them.'

'Now that,' said Nathan Li Shao, thoughtfully, 'puts rather a different complexion upon things. Directions, you say?'

'Directions. They're scattered through the System, it seems, but our unknown writer's narrowed down the area of search. On Prometheus, for example, he mentions something called the Valley of the Scorpions of Glass – ring any bells, Nathan?'

'Yes,' said Nathan Li Shao, quietly. 'It rings some bells.'

Quite which bells in particular we may never in fact learn, because through the hatch behind them, from the direction of the makeshift medical bay, there came a loud and piercing shriek.

———

There was something sliding through her *lungs*, slipping through them and probing at them with a thousand little cilia fingers. Leetha choked and the slippery things whipped themselves from her and into the black and ragged mass hanging in the air over her face. Automatic reflex action had her punching a couple of fingers into it – and failing to connect. The black thing darted away from her and, for an instant, appeared to shimmer and –

And then looming over her was something that might once have been human. It was dressed in a suit of skin, skin flayed from human faces, and stitched so that their eyeholes gaped and their mouths hung open in soundless screams, stained alternately crimson and black with fresh and ancient, crusted blood. His teeth were filed to points and had shreds of meat in them. Coarse black hair sprouted from his cheeks in pus-encrusted plaits and fireworks burned in it. His catslit, feral eyes pulsed with light, one yellow, one red, and his sore-split lips leered, and he slashed at her with a jagged cutlass-blade . . .

When Leetha was a child and training as a *Seku*, her cadre would occasionally frighten each other at night, in the dormitory-chambers, with the tales that filtered into the Dirigible Cities of the pirates plying the traverses of the System, and their atrocities. As such surreptitious late-night conversations tend to go, they had comprised one part out-and-out horror, one part elaboration, one part horrified fascination and one part vaguely suspicious speculation . . . but the tales of one man in particular had held an absolute terror for Leetha. So visceral and foul had they been, so lacking in common humanity, that she had lain awake for nights locked rigid, knowing that the moment, the precise *moment* she relaxed, he would burst from his place of concealment and fall upon her. And he would leave her alive, for a while.

The thing before her was exactly and precisely how she had imagined him. That was when she screamed.

She wrenched a blade from her living armour (which squeaked in protest) and hurled it at the apparition. It passed right through it and the thing seemed to collapse, folding in upon itself until all that remained was a bundle of rags, cowering against the wall and regarding her warily with three eyes on stalks.

Dimly, Leetha was aware that there were other people in the cabin: a strangely dressed little man, and a taller, younger

85

woman in a khaki shirt and pair of shorts. The woman, it seemed, had been awoken by Leetha's scream.

'What's going on?' she said, rubbing at her lips with the back of a hand. 'Ugh,' she continued to nobody in particular. 'My mouth tastes like something small, dead and furry and I don't mean my –'

'Is not going on nothing, we!' the black bundle squeaked in strangely polyphonic tones. 'Is bleeding thanks get we? Ho bleeding ho. Damn reptile-woman nearly frightened the life out of we.'

'Oh yes?' Leetha pulled another blade from her belt and advanced upon the thing with discorporational intent, her voice roughened, sibilants extending in a reptile hiss. 'You want to try it, yesss . . . ?'

'Ah, I see you're awake at last,' a deep and cheerful voice said, and through the hatch came a big man in blood-red leather jacket and trews and with a large sword slung across his back. There was a silver band around his head and a personable and vaguely humorous smile on his face. He flicked his mismatched eyes to the still-rigid little man. 'Some of you, anyway.'

'Damn reptile woman hit we,' said the black bundle of rags sullenly. 'Bleeding mad reptile woman.'

'Well, I'm not exactly at my best in the mornings myself.' The big man turned his smile on Leetha, who had been caught slightly flat-footed by his arrival and deflated somewhat, and now pegged him as somebody to watch extremely carefully. There was something about his manner that would have an incautious Anean mugwop dropping out of the banyans and scrambling up the evolutionary tree so it could make some money and give it to him straight away.

'Don't mind Six,' he said, indicating the black bundle. 'They have a sort of automatic sting-reflex if they're startled. Whatever you're most frightened of, the worst thing in the world, that's what they look like.'

'Excuse me.' The human woman, who had been worriedly checking over the unconscious man, turned back to the new arrival with the sort of bright and utterly sincere smile commonly worn by those dealing with children, mental defectives and large men with prominent weapons. 'Silly question, I know, you probably get asked it all the time – but

86

where exactly are we?'

The big man shrugged. 'You're safish.'

'Go-od.' The woman nodded intelligently. 'So where, precisely, are we safish?'

'You're on what might be called a privateer vessel,' the big man said, and grinned. 'Though we tend to think of ourselves more as freelance entrepreneurs filling an unofficial niche in the commodities market. We're currently headed for Sere. Nathan Li Shao' – he sketched an elaborate little approximation of a bow in freefall – 'at your service.'

———

'Problems?' said Kiru when Li Shao and Six returned to the bridge.

'Not really. I just had to lock them in, that's all.' Li Shao absently fingered a bruise and a couple of scratches on his face. 'Everything was going fine till I mentioned my name. Can't think what was wrong with mentioning my name.'

———

'He'll be back,' the saurian woman said darkly. 'He's locked us in and he knows where we are. Oh *yes*, he'll be back . . .'

At least, Benny thought, whatever had happened to the Doctor, the strange process by which the words of those around them were translated into human terms was still operating.

This was something of a mixed blessing, of course: the saurian woman – Leetha? – seemed extremely distressed, and this boded ill for such words to be of much actual comfort.

'So who is this guy?' she asked.

'You don't *know*?' Leetha stared at her incredulously. 'Li *Shao*. The Barbarous Buggering Butchering Buccaneer of a Billion Bloody Battles!'

'Right,' said Benny uneasily.

'The Sky Wolf! The Child Slayer! Wet with the blood and entrails of a thousand innocents!'

'I think I've got the picture,' said Benny.

'It was Li Shao who boarded the *Dauntless* and tied the captain to the bowsprit with his innards and cut his *name* into him!'

'Cut his name into him, right,' said Benny.

'It was Li Shao who stormed the stilt-walking Citadel of Hokesh, and personally subjected every man, woman and child therein to the most obscene improprieties and usages of a sexual nature!'

'Usages, yeah,' said Benny, who had a horrible idea of where this was heading.

'My people have a song about that,' said Leetha.

'Look, it really isn't necessary . . .' Benny began, but it was too late. The saurian woman had adopted a stance which Benny would come to know and loathe as the Way of the Pontificating Lemur – one finger in the ear, one hand free for complementary gestures of an expressive nature, and the only correct posture for a Sun Samurai relating oral history such as is passed down the ages. A vibrato and slightly nasal preparatory whine came from her, and Benny started looking around for somewhere to hide.

But it was to no avail.

And it is at this point, sadly, that we run into an insurmountable problem in the translation of these chronicles – in that the sublime majesty of Leetha's song, its lyrics surpassing even such renowned nineteenth-century wordsmiths as Mr William McGonnagall or Mrs Amanda McKetterick Ros, is literally impossible to convey in the English tongue. Indeed, such was the enormity of their task that our highly trained team of xeno-semanticists were barely able to complete one stanza, to whit:

> The good people of Hokesh
> Were having fun and frolics,
> When a fiendish horde of pirates came
> And cut off their communications . . .

. . . when one suffered a *petit mal* seizure depriving him of the use of his right hand, one flung himself under a No. 57 omnibus, and one was finally discovered some months later, living as a fur-trapper in Goose Crag, Colorado, and firing with a 12-gauge shotgun upon anyone who came within a fifty-yard radius with a scrap of paper.

Suffice it to say that, as Leetha detailed the virtuous lives of the people of Hokesh, its principal exports, its places of great civic beauty and interest and the havoc subsequently

88

caused to them by Li Shao and his men – suffice it to say that one Bernice Summerfield found herself suddenly force-evolving psychomanipulative powers almost to the point where a large claw-hammer would crystallize out of thin air by wishful thinking alone.

It was therefore probably fortunate for the fabric of the universe, and certainly fortunate for Leetha that the still body of the Doctor suddenly gave a massive shudder and opened its eyes.

'Well, I certainly don't want to go through that again,' he said briskly.

'Doctor!' Benny swung herself round to face him, mis-judged the momentum and tumbled in the air.

The Time Lord casually stuck out a hand to steady her. He was looking around with bright-eyed and cheerful interest, as though his recent collapse had simply never happened. 'Hello, Benny. Why do we appear to be in an overgrown tea-chest?'

'Uh.' Benny was momentarily nonplussed by the abrupt transition. 'I, uh, think we've been captured by space pirates and put in it. Here to await advances of a foul and unnatural nature and stuff. I'm rather looking forward to it, myself. Listen, Doctor,' she continued urgently, 'we've lost the TARDIS and Chris and Roz. I think they might be dead, and I really think we –'

'Oh, the old girl's tougher than that,' the Doctor said reassuringly, absently patting her hand. 'And if the TARDIS was destroyed I'd know about it. Don't worry about Chris-topher either – he's just the sort of chap that the gods, or the nearest local equivalent thereof, like to smile upon. Trust me.'

He turned to regard Leetha – who had by now stopped singing and had distrustfully backed off to the boxwood wall – with politely raised eyebrows. 'And the young lady is . . . ?'

'Leetha,' Leetha said suspiciously. 'Leetha T'Zhan.'

'I like the symbiote. You're a saurian? Or what do you prefer to call yourself these days – whatever these days actually are? I seem to be a little disadvantaged, temporally speaking, at the moment.'

'I'm a Sun Samurai,' said an increasingly bemused Leetha. 'I'm from Aneas.'

89

'Hmm,' the Doctor said thoughtfully. 'I don't recall that particular planet or sect. Possibly there are more holes in my mind than I thought.' He raised a hand and made a strange, tentative gesture in the air – probing it in a direction in which Benny, who was watching, found her eyes watering trying to look.

'Something odd about these dimensions,' he mused. 'Not so much unreal, exactly, as . . .' He shook his head and turned back to Benny. 'Space pirates, you say?'

'Something like that,' Benny said. 'I haven't got it quite straight in my –'

'I can tell you about them,' said Leetha.

'Really?' The Doctor beamed at her.

'Yes.'

'Um,' said Benny. 'You really don't want to . . .'

'Why don't you tell me all about it,' smiled the Doctor.

Leetha stuck her finger in her ear and took a deep breath.

'Oh no,' said Benny, miserably.

And the pirate ship chugged on toward Sere.

The Tenth Chapter

'. . . ohdamnwereallgoingtodieohSHITohbugger . . .' a voice was saying beneath the basalt crust of Planet X. ' . . .ohsod-ohbugger*WAAAAAAAH!*buggerchristweregoingto*AARGH!*-godohgodoh*JESUS!* . . .'

'Look, I'm really sorry about this,' Cwej said to the thing (currently in the form of a hairless betentacled ten-foot-long mouse on caterpillar treads) who was dragging them through the tunnels. 'She just has this problem with sentient beings who aren't of the, um, carbon-based bipedal persuasion. She doesn't really mean anything by –'

'Silence!' squeaked the thing.

'Suit yourself,' said Cwej.

Roz continued her half-whimpering trauma-monologue, only punctuated by her exclamations when another of these aliens went past. She had been like this ever since they had burst out of the junk-filled cavern to find themselves in a main thoroughfare of sorts, packed with hundreds of these creatures going slimily about their business. Roz had opened fire without a second's thought, scoring a direct hit on the tunnel wall – and Cwej had been forced to take the gun away from her before she could do more fatal damage. They didn't know a thing about these creatures, and liquefying their flesh with a flenser-field and blasting it off whatever they used for bones didn't exactly seem the best way of opening friendly relations.

He was starting, however, to suspect that he had made a mistake.

The rodentular thing dragged them around a curve in the passage and they suddenly found themselves confronted by a pulsing slimy blockage with eyes, which dilated like a sphincter-valve and the thing threw them through. Cwej remembered his Guild training, hit the floor rolling on to his feet and cast about himself cautiously. He got the impression of a largish chamber, packed with vaguely humanoid figures. Then the opening irised shut behind him, leaving him and Roz in darkness.

The first thing he noticed was the smell of large numbers of creatures confined: their food gone rotten and their body odour gone sour, their wastes and their various illnesses. The reek threatened to shut down his respiratory system – but at the same time, in some indefinable sense, it was slightly comforting. Anything living in here might be different from him, but not upon the same order of difference as the things outside.

The second thing he noticed was the sound. The creatures in here had been almost silent on their entrance – and now they began to murmur amongst themselves. There were a lot of them.

The sound of things moving in the dark. Something warm and dry and scaly brushed against him. 'Uh, Roz,' he said. 'I don't really know what to do, here . . .'

But Roz Forrester was screaming again.

———

Let the eye pull back like some insubstantial camera, through the tunnels and substrata of Planet X and through the crust. See, here, on the surface, the tethered hunks of Sloathe destroyer vessels, protected from the shrieking winds by membranous windbreaks. The destroyers are unfurling their launching sails.

See how a number of Sloathes in protective carapaces are crawling over the windbreaks. They make a few, small, strategic cuts *here* and *there*, and the breaks split wide open.

The wind hits the sails, the mooring lines are loosed, and the destroyers lumber into the air.

Now pull back further. Here we see a number of fighter vessels sailing dispiritedly for the planet hanging like a sullen and cancerous blister in the wound it has made in the energy field that encapsulates the System entire. These are the vanguard of a freighter escort, split from their charge and hurled thousands of leagues from it by the Great Outer Slipstream.

Farther back still, the Slipstream itself, collapsing into chaotic turbulence, its force dissipated. Several items have been ejected from it: the wrecks of incendiary-incinerated fighters, miscellaneous items of cargo and the bodies of Sloathes ... and finally the ruptured wreckage of the freighter itself.

It hangs in the air, pickled skin flaccid on its bones, without power; without, apparently, life.

———∞———

In the bowels of the freighter, the thing that had once been the Most Supreme Captain Trenkor Lep stirred.

The Eleventh Chapter

The asteroid of Sere – a massive and irregular lump of impure quartz some twenty miles along its greatest dimension, clustered with dockland and shipyard, twisting inorganic forests of pipes and pylons to which are tethered a thousand craft in varying stages of completion and dereliction and abandoned repair. Ancient transperihelic triplanes, patched and repatched with tissue paper and varnished with cellulose, jostle armoured eight-engined dreadnought bombers; sungliders with their massive tinfoil wings in tatters tangle inextricably with clockwork gyrocopters; deflated airships drape themselves around the peeling superstructural skeletons of ironclad freighters, depending outward from the pitted glassy asteroidal surface under the torque of Sere's spin, so that if it were possible to stand *on* the surface, the whole world would be upside down.

And in the warrens beneath the surface, inward-facing floors swarm with the human and humanoid dregs of the System, milling through taprooms and ordinaries and shebeens, taking their ease in opium dens or gambling hells or houses of ill-repute. Once Sere was a major trading centre of the System, a crossover point for the inner and outer traverses. Now it has become nothing more than a refugee camp writ large, servicing only those privateers brave or foolhardy enough to venture into Sloathe-occupied airspaces.

Once you could buy anything here.

———∞———

In a side-tunnel off the Street of the Intermittently Agreeable Anacon a hansom drawn by a team of miniature steam engines juddered to a halt. The jarvey stuck his head through the flap of the cab. 'Big Happy Snake. Forty thousand marks.'

Li Shao handed up a greasy roll of banknotes overstamped with figures twenty times their face value, the result of selling his ship for scrap and all of the inflated Serean scrip he actually owned. He had paid off his crewmen and rescued labour in foodstuffs, and had set Kiru to guard over the rest: if a deal with Solan fell through, this would be all they had to live on.

He climbed out of the cab, shouldering a bulky pigskin bag. He had shaved in the last two days and wore a slightly shiny, grey woollen suit from which the more dubious stains had been scraped.

Six floated out of the cab behind him. Polymorphs floated everywhere, possibly due to flotation sacs under their rags, though there was some dispute about this since those in a position to tell for sure were, without exception, curled up whimpering in the corner of some bedlam somewhere, with their eyes as big as saucers.

The jarvey released a series of clutches by way of pulleys and string, and the cab chugged off. Li Shao and Six headed up the tunnel.

Humans, humanoids and other sentient beings in various stages of malnutrition, salubrity and intoxication milled through the tunnel, clustering around food stalls trading anything from raw grain dough, to Anean *Kimu*, to waste products of some creatures to other creatures who could metabolically assimilate it. Children darted to and from the doorways set into the tunnel sides on indefinable errands, flushed with energy and cheap gin, and street whores of every available species and gender plied their trade. Nobody except for the beggars seemed particularly starved – but Li Shao noticed that, in the months he had been gone from Sere, the stalls selling anything other than food had disappeared. The situation had devolved to the point where nobody could afford more than their basic needs.

'Hey, sailor boys!' an Anean woman with golden scales, and a costume that wouldn't be worth much even if the gemstones that comprised it were real, called as they passed a stall selling boiled maize. 'Jou wan da goot time dirty stuff an ting?'

Li Shao shrugged and waggled a hand noncommittally. 'How much?'

'Seventy million, all same.' She turned to the stallholder and muttered something in Serean tunnel-argot to the effect that sailor-boys back from a voyage had ready cash falling out of every available orifice and knew the value of nothing.

'*Tleki lamo baya,*' Li Shao told her. '*Peh no sako de le trasla, he?*'*

The girl shrugged and returned to her conversation with the stallholder. Li Shao and Six wandered on, detoured around a green-furred Reklonian simian cranking a hurdy-gurdy while a scrawny two-foot-tall Anean marmoset capered, took a sharp left and slid through a doorway partially concealed by a *kimu* stand.

Inside, a small but tasteful foyer in gilt and velvet plush. Flanking a large inner hatch, two figures in black and pristine tuxedos, one a snow-white Reklonian, one a jet-black human. Another human, female and ice-cold-elegant and bouffanted, sat behind an ornately carved jade table.

'We're here to see Solan,' Li Shao told her.

The hostess looked him up and down with a faint sense of scorn. 'Do you have an appointment?'

'He knows we're coming.'

She wasn't necessarily going to believe this. 'And shall I give your names?'

'He'll know us if you describe us,' said Li Shao.

The hostess cranked the handle on a brass and Bakelite telephone. 'Camo? Danielle. Two, uh, gentlemen to see Mr Solan. Rubri Polymorph and a human. Built like a strawbrick outhouse and dressed like a bookie's runner. Silver band around his head and . . .'

She listened, nodded, and replacing the receiver on its cradle she turned back to Arcane. 'That seems to be in order.' She motioned towards the Reklonian bouncer. 'Mischa will take you up.'

---

* 'Apologies, mystic jewel of the Disorient, but I have neither the inclination nor the four and a half days spare at this present point in time.'

Benny stacked the pewter pint pots and toby jugs and lead crystal decanters on to a tray and carried it off through the salon, winding through the various species of females and males and the graduations of hermaphrodism as they danced or chatted or fumbled with their various clientele. Intermingled smokes and perfumes and pheromones wound through the room and gave her a vague and peripheral sense of being sexily stoned.

In the corner, under tatty velvet drapes that had long-since seen better days, the Doctor had his sleeves rolled back and was cranking a barrelhouse harmonium. He seemed entirely at home, fitted into the space around him as though he had lived there all his life. Indeed, Mama Roca in her red velvet and ruff, maternally surveying her domain from her chaise longue and adding to the psychochemical content of the air via her hookah, now seemed to be under the impression that she had known him for years – though if pressed, she would be hard put to recall precisely when and in what circumstances she had actually met him.

'Do you know,' he said to Benny as she passed with her tray, 'this reminds me of a little place I used to run in the Yukon some time around 1849, Gregorically speaking. I'd forgotten about that. I think the holes in my head might be filling up again.' He grinned at her with a kind of totally innocent mischievousness. 'Are you enjoying the Serean sights? What do you think?'

Benny glanced across the salon to where a smaller woman of the same general frogskinned breed as Mama Roca was leading a couple of naked men (one human and brown-skinned, one humanoid and black-furred) on leashes into one of the back rooms. Benny already knew what that particular back room contained, having gone over the pig-iron manacles and the inflatable India-rubber ocelot an hour before with a feather duster. She turned her attention to an alcove in which was taking place a quite remarkably improper (and not to say physically improbable) and impromptu amateur display.

'Well, I don't think I'll ever look at a coconut, a rubber glove and a tube of water-based lubricant in the same light ever again,' she said. 'Couldn't you have found us somewhere with a little bit more class?'

The Doctor shrugged, unconcerned. 'Class isn't everything. There are worse places to be.'

When the pirate ship had docked on Sere, Captain Li Shao had turned Benny, Leetha and the Doctor off without so much as a penny loaf, on account of how they had merely been dead weight and were getting off lightly since he hadn't charged them for the journey. Usages of an obscene and sexual nature had failed to materialize at any point.

'Just you wait,' Leetha had said. 'He's biding his time, that's all.' Benny got the impression that the saurian woman was vaguely disappointed.

Benny had stood on the inverted wharfyard platform and looked down gloomily at the ships hanging from their hawsers. Only one in ten of them was showing any sign of activity, and each of these was in an extreme state of dilapidation. Somewhere out there, in the variegated lights zipping past under asteroid's torque, was whatever remained of the TARDIS and there was no way of getting to it. Nobody was going anywhere. They were stranded.

'So what do we do now?' she asked the Doctor.

The Time Lord shrugged and laid his umbrella jauntily over his shoulder. From somewhere he had found a large red spotted handkerchief and tied it in a bundle to the ferule. Benny had no idea what was in the bundle.

'Now we make the best of things,' he said, following the last stragglers on the ladder to the hatch set into the surface of the asteroid. 'Don't worry about it. Something's bound to turn up.'

'If you start whistling a happy tune I'm going to throw,' said Benny.

'Something' had turned out to be a hinterland establishment going under the entirely unlikely name of 'Mama Roca's Nookie Bang Bang Emporium for the Strenuous and Reasonably Priced Knocking of All Same Matey' – a name to which, when the Doctor had translated it for her, word-for-word from what looked like a luminescent scribble by a paraplegic who had temporarily lost the use of his little suction cup on a pole, Benny's immediate reaction had been: 'Oh my dear Lord, somebody's taking the *piss* and I hope it's you.'

Obviously once a prosperous house of ill-repute offering sybaritic and luxuriant delights that would make your toes curl, it had lately fallen upon hard times. The salon was presided over by an enormously fat and apparently good-natured amphibian woman with slick and froglike skin, who had simply taken a long drag from an ornate, sweet-smelling hookah, idly caught a fly with her tongue and said: 'Room and board if you make yourself useful. Brek. Anything else, you make your own arrangements so long as you keep me happy. You'll know it if I'm not. Glop.'

Benny had looked at the prospective areas of usefulness currently on offer, and had plumped for a career in the glassware cleansing and lateral catering surface maintenance industries like a shot. It was only some days later, when she had some idea of the Serean situation insomuch as it pertained to finding even the most menial of employment, that she would recollect how the Doctor had stood unobtrusively close by, his eyes never leaving those of the frogskinned woman.

'You know, there's something slightly odd about this place,' she now said thoughtfully. 'I don't mean just here, I mean this whole so-called "System". I mean, OK, there's a fair number of humans – but there's a whole bunch of aliens. Silurians, Sasquatches, Draconians and Siva knows what else. I mean, they're calling themselves "Aneans" and "Elysians" or whatever, but that's what they are. I think I even saw a *Solarian* in here a while back, plus a number of things I couldn't even begin to identify.' She frowned. 'Why aren't we hip-deep in various sorts of oxygenation fluid, I ask myself? Half of the people here must instinctively hate the other half's respective digestive-tract analogues.'

'I wouldn't be so sure,' the Doctor said, cranking on the handle and running a complex glissando up and down the harmonium's keyboard. 'I still have a reasonably good receptivity to morphic resonances, and I suspect that those people you're calling "human" are in fact rather less human than you think they are, genotypically speaking – and those you're calling aliens are far more human than they look. They're all hybrids. This whole society seems to be massively hybridized.'

A human being born even a quarter of a century before, or a quarter of a century after, might have flatly and even hysterically refused to believe this, would probably have been disgusted by it and would certainly have been more than a little taken aback. It would have been, basically, the general cultural equivalent of a twentieth-century human being asked, quite cordially, whether he or she would care to participate in an act of sexual congress involving three live chickens and a large Alsatian dog.

Benny, on the other hand, was fortunate in that the people of her own time had by and large developed a happy and relaxed and generally unobtrusive ambisexuality. She had read of such human aberrations as homo- and lesbophobia in the course of her historical studies, but like the vast majority of her contemporaries she had never been able to understand how the people in history could have made such a big deal of such things. It was as mystifying to her as accounts of race-hatred between the already almost entirely homogenized human sub-groups.

Additionally, she had been born into a time when a large number of broadly similar life-forms had banded together to fight the far more immediate and inimical threat of the Daleks, and before this alliance had degenerated into the inevitable internal squabbling and conflict. Her various travels with the Doctor had occasionally pitched her into such conflict at the sharp end, of course – but while being able to recognize the factors that produced it intellectually, she remained puzzled by it rather than anything else. She might loathe and despise the Daleks or the Cybermen or an individual of any other race for specific reasons, but she did not have the emotional tool-kit for mindless bigotry and she was therefore the last person to baulk at the concept of a bit of interspecieal how's-your-father.

'Is that possible?' she asked with genuine interest.

'Not impossible, just highly unlikely.' The Doctor finished his piece on the harmonium with a flourish and launched into a sort of hybrid Bangra/twelve-bar-blues. 'Even in your own time, one in ten thousand Solarians, let us say, was biologically capable of interbreeding with maybe one in a thousand humans – the odds against that actually happening were astronomical of course, and interspecies breeding doesn't happen to any great extent for some tens of thousands of years up your particular time-line.' He glanced around the salon. 'Here, I think, the process has been accelerated in

100

some way. I think these people are the descendants of a relatively small gene-pool who just happen to be viable with each other . . .' He frowned. 'Either "just happened to be", or were actively selected. There's something else I've been meaning to tell you. Something I've noticed about these people. They seem to be –'

'Hey, you!' Mama Roca called to Benny from her chaise longue. 'I'm feeding you to stand there and talk?'

'I think I'd better go,' Benny told the Doctor. 'You can tell me about it later, yeah?'

———✦———

Mischa took Li Shao and Six up through the casino. Although by no means packed to capacity, the roulette wheels and the baccarat tables and the steam-driven one-armed bandits were well attended – the distinctions between rich and poor still obtained on Sere, though now scaled down a number of levels to the point of microcosm. The jewellery might be slightly tarnished here, the clothing a little frayed around the edges, and the money changing hands inflated to astronomical and all but worthless sums, but there were, one felt, simple standards that had to be maintained. One must be seen to keep one's end up.

The sumptuous casino-chamber under its twinkling electrical chandeliers was merely the most public face of Solan's operation. Elsewhere, Li Shao knew, other tastes were catered for. There were dark and smoky back rooms where vast sums changed hands over knucklebones or Three Chimneys. There was a perfect, if slightly compact, representation of a Promethean arena, complete with especially imported desert lions and the facility for the clientele to make vaguely entertaining use of their thumbs. There was a rather larger warren of tunnels filled with mechanical deathtraps of a most indecorous nature, into which subjects would be regularly introduced and bets taken upon how long they would last.

Or one could bet upon which would be the first to die of a pair of identical twins injected with strychnine.

Or one could bet upon whether a child would in fact complete a particularly ambitious tower of wooden blocks.

Or one could bet upon the precise gestation time of an Anean *gleki* larva – which microscopic parasite burrows into

the host and promptly expands to fifteen thousand times its
original size.

Or, for a fee, one could be the subject oneself of such
wagers. Solan's gaming house catered for every taste.

The Reklonian led Li Shao and Six to a highly polished
elevator cage, which rose smoothly and silently into the
ceiling. The elevator was a new addition; they had not seen it
before. Six ran an absent manipulatory appendage over the
shine.

'Classy,' they said.

'It's a departure from Solan's usual style,' said Li Shao.
'Last I heard he was investigating the recreational possibilities offered by small furry animals and galvanistical
power tools. Makes no odds. Everything he touches turns
slimy after a while.'

The elevator deposited them in a stark and white-
tiled antechamber, lit by fluorescent tubes that buzzed
megrimously and smelt of ozone. The chamber was empty
save for a thin Anean woman in a spotless smock and rubber
gloves, and a tank of clear fluid on a steel table. The woman's
scaly skin seemed clean to the point of sterility, desiccated
and cracked, as though depleted of its subcutaneous oils by
overscrubbing with some particularly astringent detergent.

She glanced at Li Shao's pigskin bag. 'Anything
dissolvable?'

'One or two documents. The ink, maybe.'

'Take them out.'

Li Shao pulled out a thick sheaf of inventories and
receipts. The bag still bulked heavily. The Anean woman
took it from him and, without preamble, dropped it into the
tank. The liquid seethed. She pulled it out, its outer surface
crumbling slightly, its clasps now untarnished and mirror
bright. She handed it back to Li Shao, and then sprayed both
him and Six with a sick-smelling fluid from a handpump.

'What the hell was *that*?' a dripping Li Shao said.

'Antiseptic.' The woman gestured toward an airlock hatch.
'Who knows what dirty little germs you might be carrying.'

This chamber was also walled with tile and lit by neon. Lead
pipes crawled around the walls, looking for a way out, failing

to find one and settling in the end to be connected to a collection of wash basins and baths and wallowing troughs. Rubber hoses snaked and tangled on the floor. The air was blood-hot and moist and stank of sweat and vaguely diseased flatulence and Epsom salts.

'My dear Li Shao!' something pale and bloated said from a bank of steam. It was a blubbery voice. It sounded like a Reklonian ice-whale being flensed. 'I gather that your recent, ah, exploits have been something of a success.'

Li Shao shrugged. 'Some you lose and some you win.'

'But the man with the money loses never.' The voice chuckled gloatily. 'Sit down, sit down. Can I tempt your colleague and your good self with a little something in a camphor and sodium preparation? Marvellous for piles, I'm assured. The late Rear Admiral Crighton used to swear by them, as I recall. Though you'd know better than I about that.'

The pale mass waddled heavily close and resolved itself into an enormously fat and naked human male. Arcane had heard it rumoured, once, that Solan was in fact a woman or some form of androgyne. He was always, however, referred to in the masculine, and the expanse and the pendulous rolls of his flesh made hard corroboration unlikely unless one had a handy haulage crane about one's person and, as it were, the stomach. Be that as it may, and leaving the matter of gender aside, Solan was probably the single most powerful individual in Sere, with fingers in more pies than a paraplegic butcher, and you talked to Solan if you wanted things done. Things he didn't want done, didn't happen.

'I came to talk business, Solan,' he said.

'But of *course*, my dear captain.' Solan waddled closer, trailing a number of tubes. 'Of course you want to talk business. Talking business is what I do best.'

Li Shao proffered the manifests. Solan took them with raw-sausage fingers and flipped idly through them. 'When you contacted my people,' he said, 'I believe you mentioned samples.'

Li Shao snapped open the case and pulled out an item as big as his head, solid gold inset with jetstone and blue enamel: a burial mask. Its patina of ingrained dust and Sloathe ichor had been removed by the solvents in the tank

103

outside and it shone like a little stylized sun, since that was what it had been fashioned to resemble. The little face in the middle shone with a perfectly fatuous imbecility.

Solan raised an eyebrow. 'Interesting. Quite worthless, of course, under the present conditions, here within Sere.'

'That's the point,' Li Shao said. 'There's no market here – but there's still a market of sorts on the Wanderers. I propose to reopen trade links, and for that I need a ship.'

'Which,' Solan said, 'is of course going to end up as several items of charred and orbiting debris the first Sloathe blockade you meet.'

Li Shao shrugged. 'Possibly. But think on this. The war with the Sloathes hasn't all been one way. People on the Wanderers have organized resistance, and there are still a few members of the old Fleet around – I used to be one of 'em myself. It's just possible that the balance could tip the other way . . .'

'Possible, but hardly probable,' said Solan.

'Be that as it may, it comes down to only two possibilities. Either the Sloathes are going to win right down the line and we're all going to die, in which case there's nothing we can do about it anyway – or the situation's going to stabilize and any trade links we can forge at this point will be invaluable. Think of it as a long-term investment.'

Solan was silent for a moment. Then he regarded Li Shao steadily with his cold, dead, piggy little eyes. 'Do you know what I think, Captain? Do you know what I *know* is going to happen?'

'What's going to happen?' Li Shao said.

'The Sloathes are going to win, as you say, down the line. In a matter of years, and possibly months, we within Sere will be the last surviving of the indigenous species of the System, and we will fight each other over the last scrap of food, and then the food will run out, and then we will fight each other to the last bone . . . which *I* will split open, and from which *I* – make no mistake about *that* – will suck the marrow. And then of course I myself shall starve, after eking out my own extremities as much as is physically possible.

'This is what I *know* will happen, Captain.'

'But of course . . .' Solan smiled without a shred of humour, 'there is always that one chance in a thousand, or in a million, and one must cover every eventuality. Buy your

104

ship, Captain. Use my name. You'll know, believe me, when the time comes for you to repay.' He gestured vaguely, like a massive baby blatting, dismissing Li Shao from further consideration. 'Mind you don't trip over the tubes on your way out.'

<hr />

After Li Shao and his polymorphic companion had gone, Solan lay back upon his especially customized surgical table and pensively infused a cobalt and juniper preparation. At length, he pressed a galvanistic button and a bell rang outside. The Anean nurse entered.

'Call down to the foyer,' Solan told her. 'Have the good Captain Li Shao followed. Our Mr Glome, perhaps.' He thought for a moment. 'Also, he'll be recruiting for the next few weeks. Have some of our people sent to him. Perhaps it's my distrusting nature, but I got the distinct impression that there was something he wasn't telling me.'

The Twelfth Chapter

After three days (or, at least, given the dayless quality of life in Sere, an endless parade of beer glasses, dishwater and tabletops, interspersed with three periods of fitful sleep) Benny found that she was rather enjoying the atmosphere of the house of ill-repute – and she wanted nothing better than to get the hell away from it as soon as humanly possible.

She enjoyed it because, for one thing, these people as a whole seemed to be relatively free of the artificially imposed and gender-based oppressions that proliferated in other, less enlightened and less homogenized societies: the people here seemed to be evenly split between the various sexes and sexualities, and it was as common to see two beefy males, say, heading for a back room together as it was to see a heterosexual couple, or two females, or a big strapping woman with a frail and doll-like male and him in charge of matters, or some incredibly complex variations on the theme of the multiple and with some confusion as to who was actually paying whom and for what – an almost academic distinction by now since, Benny gathered, money as such in Sere was now next to worthless. Payment for services, as it were, rendered was now taken almost entirely in food and other consumables, from which Mama Roca took her cut to feed herself and those actually in her employ, and which she held for those who had more than their day-to-day needs in a way more or less analogous to a bank.

Perhaps as a result of this – and the exchanging of actual food and drink is a subtly different transaction from the exchanging of abstract cash – the distinctions between employees and clients were fast eroding and there seemed to be a singular lack of coercion involved with their respective activities. And the tragedy of coercive power imbalances,

whether sexual, racial, specieal or financial, is not so much
that they are 'wrong' or 'evil', but simply that one faction
gets to have all the fun.

Here the distinctions were breaking down and there was
more fun for everyone than you could shake a dubious
implement at: hey, the process went, the outside world's
collapsing and we're completely isolated from it anyway; the
food's running out and the social matrix is falling apart
spectacularly and we're all going to die. So let's have one last
party before we die. Bring a bottle. And anything you feel
like doing with it is up to you and anyone else concerned.
And if you can find someone willing to pay *you* for doing it
then hoo bleeding ray.

The only unbreakable rule seemed to be that of simple
mutual consent – a rule which Mama Roca had established,
and enforced by the presence of bodyguards, even in the time
when the house of ill-repute had been a purely financial
concern – upon the simple basis that it wouldn't be any fun
otherwise. Nobody here was giving of themselves any more
than they were willing and prepared to give – and if all
Benny Summerfield wanted to give were her services waiting
tables in return for minimum board and a place to sleep,
nobody was going to force her to dance on them or do mucky
things under them. The practical upshot of all this was that,
basically, in the short term, Benny got to eat and got to watch
a hugely entertaining, sexy, round-the-clock floorshow that
would have made the inhabitants of Sodom and Gomorrah
feel the need for a quick lie-down, while remaining almost
entirely free of moral qualms.

But she knew that it was never going to last – and that was
what worried her. Benny had seen the phenomenon at close
hand before, once on an excursion with the Doctor to an
inflation-hit Berlin between the twentieth century war-phases
one and two, once in the twenty-second-century Puerto
Luminan colonies immediately prior to Earth Force annexation, and in any number of other basically self-contained
environments teetering on the lip of the catastrophe curve –
and she knew that it was a common pattern.

This was currently that magic point in the cycle before
the party broke apart spectacularly into mass violence. The
social mechanisms that inhibited Sereans *en masse* from the

more extreme forms of enjoying themselves were gone – and next, catastrophically, would go the last vestigial mechanisms that restrained them from wholesale assault and murder. For pleasure and hatred, and revenge, and for the hell of it and then, when the food at last ran out, for bare survival.

The escalating tensions were reflected in the fact that Mama Roca had, apparently, been forced to adopt increasing numbers of bodyguards of late, ostensibly to enforce the rule of consent and to guard the stocks of food. The majority of these guards were drawn from patrons of the establishment itself, by the simple process of being offered the work if Mama Roca liked them when their credit ran out – and more than once Benny had overheard remarks to the effect that they regarded the place as being their home. Looking about the salon, Benny believed she was watching the nascent cohering of a tribe, who would band together when the real troubles came – and wondered how many similar tribal groupings were forming throughout Sere. The people here seemed relatively benign, if naturally a little overstimulated given their particular focal point – but what would they be like a year from now when the cannibal tribes were the norm?

Thus far the process still operated upon the subconscious level. It was business more or less as usual and the place still welcomed passing trade – it was just that more and more of it seemed to be suddenly moving in here on a permanent basis. Benny gathered that immediately prior to the Doctor's arrival and her own there had been a new influx of paying clients: paid-off crewmen, she was vaguely aware, from Li Shao's ship. They had food to bring in and they were tolerated, and some might eventually join the main body of the tribe – but not many. Several had been summarily ejected for breaking Mama Roca's Rule and none had been asked to stay on once their food-credit was expended.

A remaining group of them were currently in an inevitable alcove with a number of women – a small number, since the vast majority of those here wanted nothing to do with them. One of the men leered up at Benny as she dumped a trayful of drinks on the table before them (Mama Roca converted one item of credit for another, and was scrupulously honest about it after she had taken her cut, and the crewmen had converted almost all their food into drink). 'You look like a likely lass, yes. Why don' you come and have a bite on my big sausage?'

'Yes? Well, why don't you go and stick your sausage sideways,' said Benny sweetly, reflecting that given the guy's general standard of material, even this level of witty repartee was in danger of going over his head. This was probably someone who could use the word 'feisty' in cold blood.

She was right. The man, a piebald human with an old, puckered scar running down his face and through the empty socket of his left eye, muttered something about receiving a deal of gratification from the person of a girl with spirit and grabbed her left breast, hard enough, she later discovered, to leave bruises.

Had Benny not to a degree become acclimatized to life in Mama Roca's house she would have seen this coming a mile off and avoided it in the first place. As it was, she was startled and shocked by this breaking of the unbreakable Rule – so she automatically straight-armed the man in the face and broke his nose. And then he was out of his seat and coming for her, so she ducked under the blow and applied an interesting TerraFed military technique – learnt in the time when she had been drafted into the Dalek Wars – to laterally dislocate his arm.

And then of course a couple of his companions, an Elysian and an Anean, were out of their seats and pulling their knives, spilling a couple of alarmed and frightened women, who had not quite had time to react, off their laps, and –

Two slim and razor-sharp and dull-sheened blades went through their throats. They fell back with a couple of aspirating gurgles.

'Need any more help, Benny?' said the voice of Leetha T'Zhan behind her. Leetha had been hired by Mama Roca on sight as a bodyguard, and without the need of any persuasion from the Doctor whatsoever. 'I think I'd like to be some more help.'

The man Benny had inconvenienced was sitting on the floor and clutching at his arm and moaning. Blood ran from his broken nose. Benny risked a glance behind her and saw that Leetha was standing very, very still and simply looking in the general direction of the remaining pirate crewmen. It would probably be better, she thought, if *nobody* made any sudden moves at this point, not even her.

'I don't think that's going to be necessary, Leetha,' she said very softly.

She became aware of a larger, lumbering presence behind her. Mama Roca had left her chaise longue – something Benny had never seen her do, not even once, in all the quasi-days she had been here.

'I think you'd better find other business, girls,' Mama Roca said to the women in the alcove, who were already leaving it – one merely remaining to carefully spit on the bodies killed by Leetha's blades, another aiming a sharp kick at the wounded man's elbow in passing that caused him to shriek and pass out. Then Mama Roca turned her attention to the remaining, living and now slightly alarmed occupants of the alcove, three of them in all.

'I think you've overstayed your welcome, lads,' she said lightly. 'Take your friend away. Leave the bodies. Rek. I have a cold room and I'll ... keep them safe to be collected by their next of kin.'

This last caused Benny to turn sharply and look at Mama Roca's eyes. And Mama Roca's eyes told Benny that she, Mama Roca, knew, precisely, the way things were going.

'This is *not* going to be a good place to be, soon,' said Benny. 'We have to get out of here or we're going to end up asking for a slice off the leg or the breast and really meaning it. Donner kebab, anyone, know what I mean?'

'I regard that remark as being in the worst possible taste,' said the Doctor sternly. 'Take it from one who knows.'

They were in a communal chamber set apart for employees to sleep, sharing their daily meal of cabbage and onion potage and murmuring quietly so as to avoid waking the sleepers. Benny had been slightly piqued to learn that the Time Lord's harmonium playing was worth more to Mama Roca than her own skivvying: yesterday he had been given an extra handful of carrots and today he had been given a couple of leathery strips of curried pemmican. Benny was no gourmet, but she had a nasty suspicion that an elderly donkey was involved somewhere in its ancestry.

'I just hope Leetha can find something,' Benny said between chewing. 'Anything.'

Despite the unfortunate tendency to fixate, Benny had come to like Leetha T'Zhan on the journey to Sere. When she wasn't muttering darkly about impending foul and sexual usages and the like she was just the sort of dangerous and capable person you wanted at your back in a crisis.

Leetha was also determined to get away from the asteroid – for reasons the nature of which, though the Doctor had tried repeatedly to draw her out, she seemed strangely uncommunicative. As a bodyguard – and thus worth more to Mama Roca than both the Doctor and Benny combined – she enjoyed a number of advantages including a tacitly agreed amount of time free for something other than sleep, most of which she spent wandering the wharfs looking for any ship that might be hiring crew.

'I think she'll find something. In fact, I have the feeling that it would be almost impossible for her not to.' The Doctor chewed pensively on his strip of meat. 'It's something to do with the very nature of the System. You'll remember that I told you there was something odd about these people?'

'I remember,' Benny said. 'I've been thinking about it.' She spat out a particularly intransigent bit of gristle and continued, waggling her hands for emphasis like a puppet on a string. 'They're like people in a particularly formulaic movie, going through their routines even when there's nobody else around. They act like somebody, or something, is watching them all the time. They're like actors who are always *on*.'

The Doctor nodded. 'Something like that. It's a little like pre-fifteenth-century Güttenberg before old Martin Luther put the worms among the diet, where every act was based upon the quite erroneous but fundamental certainty that one was being watched by an omnipresent God – but it's more like a time I recall in Mesopotamia when people actually *were* being watched over by "gods" and they didn't consciously know it. Messy business, that. Took almost a century to sort it out, and you still ended up with the King James's version of Genesis.'

'Do you think something's actually controlling these people?' Benny said.

'Influencing rather than controlling.' The Doctor's face clouded briefly. 'But that just makes it all the more insidious,

111

all the more loathsome. All the more sly. I can't stand things like that.'

'Oh yes,' said Benny. 'Can't have someone mucking around behind the scenes like that. Manipulating people and manoeuvring them into the right place at the right time. Next thing we know, we'll have a pyrotic in a big skin balloon full of methane, just when it needs to be exploded or something. Can't have something like that, right?'

'I'm going to pretend I didn't hear that,' said the Doctor.

'The thing that worries me,' Benny said, 'is that I can feel myself starting to think the same way. Becoming one-dimensional. Playing the part that was slotted for me.' She looked at the Time Lord, suddenly, sharply. 'How much of that are you doing? Suppressing this and emphasizing that and greasing along the other? Making us fit in where we don't really belong?'

It was at that point that Leetha T'Zhan entered the chamber and picked her way through the sleeping forms, the silver corslet under her leather tunic gleaming dully and her eyes glinting yellowly in the flickering nightlights. Benny noted how she moved: lithe and silent and never putting a foot wrong, like a cat.

She crouched down beside them and pulled a scrap of thin paper from her tunic. 'I've found a ship,' she said.

The Thirteenth Chapter

In a chamber inside Planet X, Roz Forrester picked up a vaguely human form and peeled off its lumpen coating of solidified Sloathe ichor to reveal a slightly tarnished two-foot-tall silver figurine, reminiscent of the Winged Victory of Samathrace. She tossed the lumps of ichor aside, to be fallen upon by a number of squirming little three-eyed ratlike things, and set the figurine down at the end of a line containing various approximate human forms ranging from a tiny porcelain doll, to a tailor's mannequin with a flying helmet, to a classical marble statue fully ten feet tall of a man with a discus. Then she turned to the Sloathe in the form of a novcar-sized, soft-shelled tortoise on a pogo stick. 'Yes?'

The Sloathe bounced up and down on its single limb thoughtfully. 'Is good,' it said at last. 'Next one.'

Roz wandered over to a pile of miscellaneous items and perused it for something else even vaguely human. Around her, throughout the cavern, similar scenes were taking place as the captive workforce sorted and arranged Sloathe acquisitions into whatever order each particular Sloathe had decided upon this time. Last time it had been big square things, the time before that it had been things beginning with the letter 'S', and the time before that it had been things you emotionally associated with the colour blue – it wasn't actually this, of course; you had to find some sort of system more or less equivalent in human terms to whatever was going on in what passed for the Sloathe's mind at the time, and you had to work it out by a laborious and painstaking process of trial-and-error.

There were maybe a hundred other prisoners currently in the cavern, taken on Sloathe incursions into what Roz still assumed to be a planetary solar System, and she had gathered

113

there were thousands more scattered throughout Planet X.

So far as days as such could be reckoned, Roz judged that she had been here slightly more than a week, but time as such was almost impossible to keep track of. The Sloathes had a dim idea that their prisoners needed regular sleep and food – but in practice this resulted in the prisoners being herded *en masse* into darkened chambers for what might be five minutes, or six hours, or twenty-four hours. It had been into such a chamber that she and Cwej had been deposited upon their arrival and capture, and after she had finally gotten herself under control enough to stop shrieking every time something moved in the dark and actually talk to her fellow prisoners, she had heard tell of a 'sleep' period, some years before, that had lasted for the equivalent of fifteen weeks. Without food or water. None of those she had spoken with had been there at the time, having been taken prisoner some time later – and some of them were extremely vehement upon this point.

That first 'night' had lasted, so far as Roz could reckon, a mere seven hours, during which she had formed the impression that her fellow captives were human. She had been slightly taken aback to emerge, blinking, into the now-dazzling faint subterranean phosphorescence, to discover the sheer number of different species with which she had been incarcerated.

She had also been mortified to discover that a couple with whom she and Cwej had struck up a nascent friendship, and whose friendly voices in the dark had done more to bring her out of her debilitating terror than anything else, were in fact a human and a hairy, ursine alien hominid – and they seemed to be totally unashamed of the fact. Roz had tried to conceal her disgust, merely making a mental note to avoid them if at all possible and be polite when it was not – and she was only just starting to suspect that they were now doing the same to her.

This annoyed her and, in some unaccountable way, it hurt. It wasn't after all as if *she* were to blame for their perversion, it wasn't like she was a speciesist or anything, but there were some things that were just so . . .

'Hurry up there, pretend-move monkey thing,' called the Sloathe on a stick imperiously. 'Is want aesthetically type pleasing thing here right *now*.'

114

Roz Forrester shrugged, and hauled a slightly bent lampstand with a pelmet out of the pile. It stood more or less upright, so the Sloathe probably wouldn't notice the difference.

———∞———

Later there was a food break. The Sloathes accomplished this by gathering the prisoners together in a relatively junk-free area of floorspace by the wall, tossing in a collection of approximate foodstuffs and letting the prisoners get on with it. The prisoners had organized a rota of sorts, and today it was slightly squashy raw turnip and extremely rotten bacon slices cooked over a scavenged fire. Chronic malnutrition was beginning to take its effect: Roz hunkered down by the wall and bolted the food without a second thought.

Around her people of various species and races were either eating or conserving their energy, but there were a few of them who were slightly more active. A group of maybe ten were weakly performing exercises with a makeshift and inexpertly carpentered vaulting horse, to the exhortations of a thin, grey-skinned man with a hairy string pullover and a forage cap and a swagger cane tucked under his arm. Several other figures wandered around the Sloathe-guarded perimeter, flapping their ragged trousers suspiciously.

Vaguely interested, Roz wandered over to one of them: a reptile-skinned and saurian man – an Anean, she gathered – with several long-healed stitchmark scars across his chest and his hands thrust deep into his trouser pockets.

'Um, what exactly are you doing?' she said.

'*Shhh!*' The Anean cast around at the nearby Sloathe guards, mugging furiously, and then deflated somewhat. 'Doesn't matter. The frightful buggers never notice anything anyway, so long as you don't try to go past them.' He turned back to Roz confidentially. 'Escape committee,' he hissed. 'There's something very interesting in my trousers.'

'I'm sure there is,' said Roz.

'There's these little sack and drawstring arrangements,' the man said patiently. 'Took us ages to make them. Y'see, what happens is, Smudger and Nudger dig the tunnel and they pass the stuff they dig out to Dodger, Todger, Shiner, Tonker and me and we dispose of it.' He flicked his head towards the

115

vaulting horse, coincidentally at the point at which one of th
people vaulting over it caught his foot and fell flat on hi
face. 'Meanwhile, we've got Cholmondly and Beauchamp i
there, stitching Sloathe suits together. So when the tunne
hits the open air, we take the vaulting horse down it, and tro
across the surface using it as a break against the two
hundred-mile-an-hour winds until we find a ship – and the
it's into the Sloathe suits, bluff our way on to the bridge an
we're away.'

Roz nodded slowly and looked down at the ground. Larg
quantities of excavational debris were conspicuously failin
to be deposited there. 'If you don't mind me saying so,' sh
said, 'you don't actually seem to have all that *much* dow
your trousers. How far exactly has this tunnel gone?'

The saurian man was crestfallen. 'Not that far, really. Ba
hands on living rock you see. We used to have a teaspoo
once but it broke. Still,' – he brightened up slightly – 'neve
say die, eh? You have to do something or you'd go mac
Ah-ha, ah-ha-ha-ha.'

'Excuse me,' said Roz. 'There's someone I really have t
go and talk to.'

Chris Cwej was sitting by the fire and chatting to Laseer
and Holf, the human and the bearlike humanoid of thei
recent acquaintance, as they ate. Roz tried not to notice th
fact that the pair of them suddenly had to be somewhere els
the moment they saw her heading for Cwej, and sat dow
next to him.

'We have *got* to get out of here,' she said. 'While we stil
have some of our strength. Three more days of this and we'l
be as bad as them.' She glanced speculatively to the ring o
Sloathe guards, none of whom seemed to be paying th
slightest attention to the people they were supposed to b
guarding. 'We can get past that lot, out into the tunnels . . .'

'People have tried before, apparently,' Cwej said. 'Laseer
told me. Some of them came back alive, some of them cam
back in bits. Some of them came back . . . changed. I thin
we were lucky that the first Sloathe we met wasn't in a moo
to play with us. Nobody made it to the surface.'

'And the surface wouldn't do us any good anyway,' sai
Roz. 'I wasn't thinking about the surface. I was thinkin
about the TARDIS.'

116

The Fourteenth Chapter

In the spinning asteroid of Sere, in his white-tile chamber smelling of corruption only partially masked by antiseptic, Solan turned his massive head towards the hunched figure in the black cloak and cowl.

'I'll hear your report now, if you would be so kind,' he said.

The figure nodded slowly. 'I felt them. I put my fingers in their *minds*, little sliding fingers and they felt I feel it and . . .'

'In your own time,' said Solan, patiently.

The figure put its splayed and bone-white fingers into the cowl, presumably pressing them against the face within. ' . . . They are concealing something. They told you the truth, so far as it went, but they . . . have another agenda, yes? They think that they are . . .'

At this point Solan was distracted. In a marble washstand in the corner was a soggy pasteboard box, and from within this came the scrabbling of little claws, a squealing.

'Excuse me one moment.' Solan hauled himself from his surgical chair and lumbered to the box. He pulled off the lid and something inside chittered and squealed at him. He nodded thoughtfully.

'I understand,' he said quietly to the thing within. 'Left a bit, forward a bit, left a bit again.' Then he turned back to the figure in the cowl and smiled politely. 'My apologies for these continual interruptions. Pray, Mr Glome, continue.'

———

In the back room of the Notional Dragon, Nathan Li Shao said: 'You know what's bothering me? That little bugger in the black wasn't out there today. It's possible Solan's

117

making other plans. I keep waiting for the other shoe t drop.'

'Just so long as he gives us three more days,' said Kir 'We're nearly there. Three more days and we'll have a fu complement.'

'Maybe.' Li Shao scowled. 'If we can find anyone else th damn thing likes.'

Hiring a crew had presented problems. In the old day before the blockades, you simply block-printed up a handf of fliers and waited for the mad rush. Li Shao had expecte things to be even more hectic now – but it seemed that th population of Sere had developed something of a sieg mentality in his absence. They were digging into bolt-hol and pulling the rocks over their heads and they didn't seem t have the stomach for adventurous exploits of utter peril an danger any more. In the days they had been hiring there ha been less than fifty applicants, and it was some time before L Shao realized that this was something of a blessing i disguise: anyone who still had a spark of fire in their guts wa probably the best anyway, and the applicants had hardly to b winnowed down by selection.

The major problem was the ship itself.

They had found it amongst the rusting hulks of a run-dow broker's dock, and for Nathan Li Shao it had been love at fir sight – albeit the edgy, worried kind of love in which yo know you're going to regret this and you're going to hat yourself in the morning, but you're going to do it anyway. had hung, almost inconspicuous in its unadorned elegance between a salvaged Fleet destroyer and a reconditione long-haul freighter – and indeed the little Reklonian broke had almost led them right past it on the viewing gantry, an appeared to have been unaware of its very existence until hi attention had been drawn to it.

'Was found drifting,' he had said when prevailed upon t check the documentation. 'Years back. Nobody inside. Noth ing inside it.' And then he had shrugged and simply seeme to forget about it. He had to be forcefully reminded a numbe of times that he was actually selling it.

Inside, it was even more worrying. The engines wer sealed off, encapsulated in big streamlined lumps of som bonelike substance – and Li Shao had the horrible feelin

hat they were atomic, of the sort that had powered the
vessels of Fleet suicide squadrons (the 'Black Pigs') during
the early years of the war with the Sloathes. The last thing he
felt like was coming down with the radium pox. Six,
however, had detected none of the killing emissions that
characterized these dirty-cobalt reaction engines.

Its interior spaces had been disquietening, too. The very
shape they made in the world seemed to affect the mind upon
some subliminal level. Li Shao had been put in mind of the
process by which, upon first impressions, one can instantly
like or loathe an acquaintance. The problem was, of course,
he knew perfectly well how incorrect these first impressions
usually are.

The reactions of its prospective crew to this had varied.
Some, just over thirty in all, had liked it and made themselves instantly at home, others had remained relatively
indifferent – and some had thrown something like a hysterical fit upon stepping through the hatch. It was like the ship
was doing Li Shao's selecting for him. It was like she was
alive. It was this sense of coming under outside pressure that
was gnawing at Li Shao's gut – but he was committed. He
had used Solan's name to buy the thing, and you don't back
out of a deal with Solan. Besides, she was the best ship they
had been able to find and whether it was due to outside
influence or not he still had a good feeling about her. Mostly.
Most of the time.

And then there was that matter about the damned
name . . .

It had just been there, the first time he saw her. In his head.
And when he had broached the subject of naming the ship to
Kiru and Six, they had instantly suggested the precise same
name simultaneously.

'We won't get many now,' Kiru said. 'Word's getting
around. It's like we were hiring for a corpse boat or
something. I say we go now, before the people we've already
got eat our foodstock out from under us.'

Li Shao shrugged. 'That's not going to happen for a
while – and we're still seriously undermanned. We can
afford to wait. Nobody's exactly holding a pistol to our heads
at this point.'

Benny looked up at the Chinese dragons painted across the tunnel wall over the inset door, mentally comparing them with the other such signs she had seen in Sere: Japanese ideograms, Maori sky gods, Hindi temple-carvings, Ice Warrior cohort-sigils . . . she was struck by the fact that these elements and images, like the people here, seemed to be almost entirely dislocated and discontinuous: as though they had been simply cut and pasted-on from a variety of sources rather than evolved from any natural and coherent culture.

'Is this the place?' she said.

Leetha took a greasy handbill from her jerkin, potato-printed in what Benny gathered was the single actual printed language of the system, and from which Benny had been able to make neither head nor tail. '*Free trader* Schirron Dream', she recited. '*Now signing for Maiden Voyage. Sere Dock to Sere Dock, indefinite. Ships rations and one share one tenth profits. Apply Notional Dragon tap.*' She put the flier away. 'It's the place.'

The Doctor frowned. 'You know, there's something about that name,' he mused. 'Something I remember from the past. Or possibly the retrogressive future, of course. It's –'

Leetha looked at him sharply, almost suspiciously. 'Yes?'

'Nothing.' The Doctor shook his head. 'It's gone. Sorry.'

He beamed at Leetha – and Benny found herself suddenly wondering exactly how much the Time Lord was putting the Anean woman on. Admittedly the Doctor was still acting a little erratically – but there was altogether too much of the wide-eyed *who-me?* innocence of which she had learned to her cost to be very, very wary.

Leetha, for her part, simply dismissed him from further consideration. She barely tolerated the cracked little fool and his babblings because Benny seemed to dote on him – and because Benny was going to be useful. The loss of Kimon had been bad enough – but the loss of his notes had been a disaster. (And somewhere in the back of her mind, a little self-disgusted voice was telling her, over and over again, that she should be ashamed of these priorities. She stilled it by pointing out, over and over again, that if she gave in to grief and fell apart now, the lives of Kimon and all those countless others in Rakath would have been spent in vain. Time to count the dead and grieve later.) The loss of Kimon's notes

120

meant that all Leetha had to go on, if she were to complete
the Search and give her people's deaths some meaning,
was her copy of the Book – of which one of the least
impenetrable passages was the *'Sheweth Now unto the Gods
of Worlds and Sundry Browsers with Insolent and Nefarious
intent that this Tome, ex libris, cometh to the Possession by
unlawful Means of . . .'* legend at the front, and which she had
just about penetrated to the point where she was seriously
considering writing her name under it.

In their days of incarceration together in the pirate ship,
Leetha had learnt that Benny was a xeno-archaeologist,
and while not being entirely sure as to what a 'xeno-
archaeologist' actually was, she gathered that it involved the
finding of ancient artifacts and relics from the slimmest of
remaining clues. This was going to be very useful indeed.

Fortunately, Benny and her idiot travelling companion had
been as desperate to get away from Sere as Leetha, and
Leetha had been more than happy to assist them. Time to
broach the subject of the Search to Benny later – the
important thing now was that there was a vessel leaving this
self-enclosed hellhole and she had a chance to attempt it.
Even the name was a good omen . . .

And of course, she thought with a barely suppressed
shudder, there was another reason for leaving. Li Shao was
still in Sere, and Leetha T'Zhan for one wouldn't breathe
easy until she was a couple of thousand leagues away from
him. She had tried repeatedly, on the pirate ship, to impress
the very loathsomeness of this man upon Benny, but for
some unaccountable reason the human woman had seemed
uninterested. It was as though she simply didn't understand
the danger they had all been in, the absolute evil of the man
that evidenced itself in his every deed.

Even the first stories of him epitomized his nature: how he
had as a youth lied his way into the System's Fleet (then
existing) and had risen, through a simple policy of crawling
sycophancy to his superiors and downright brutality to
his inferiors, to the rank of first lieutenant of the *Wayfarer*, a
rocket-powered pocket gunboat of the sort used to escort
supply convoys through Sloathe-occupied airspaces. It had
been on one such tour of duty, some eight years before and
escorting a refugee ship as it rose from Elysium for its

121

traverse towards the inner Wanderers, that they had encountered a raiding party of three Sloathe destroyers.

At this time, the Sloathes had little experience of th System. With the *Wayfarer* outnumbered three to one th situation was difficult and dangerous, but not entirely hop less – and it was at this point that Li Shao showed his tru mettle. He shot his captain in the back with a flintlock, too control of the bridge and made a run for it.

Even then, the gallant Li Shao's reserves of treachery ha not been sucked dry. Whether by design or by sheer incom petence he had brought the ship down on the Elysia bouncing moon of Rubri, there to sell the entirety of h remaining crew into the fearful bondage of its degenoma cers and their hideous experiments, in return for safe passa to the Ring and his subsequently notorious piratical career.

The time Leetha had spent on board his ship had been o long, slow torture of dreadful anticipation, and the fact th he had apparently released them showed just how sly an devious this man actually was. He was like a mouse toyin with a cat,* and Leetha knew the moment, the very *momer* she lowered her guard, the very moment she began to fe safe, she would hear that chilling, if deceptively friendl voice behind her and . . .

'So we going to stand out here all day or what?' sai Benny.

The Doctor, who had been absently balancing h umbrella, still with its red and white spotted bundle, on h nose, let it drop, swung it jauntily over his shoulder, bowe to Leetha and Benny and gestured with elaborate courtes 'Shall we, children?'

'Children?' said Leetha suspiciously.

'I'll tell you about it later,' said Benny. 'It's a littl complicated.'

'No it isn't,' said the Doctor.

'You want to bet?' said Benny.

---

* By a small quirk of System force-evolution, mice were two-foo long feral predators with razor-sharp claws and a bite that shut yo renal system down in shock. Cats, on the other hand, were timi neurotic sacks of suet with chronically weak hearts and a predile tion for quiet and darkened rooms.

They went inside. A number of people in the opium-
moky interior turned on them that impassive but slightly
vary examination that typifies the regulars of any establish-
nent – with an edge to it that told Benny, for one, that the
ame unconscious tribal processes she had noticed in Mama
Loca's were operating here. A surly, scrawny blue Rek-
onian, with intertwining Anean taipans shaved into the fur
f its biceps and forearms, grunted and indicated a shadowy
oorway towards the back of the room. 'Through there.'

They picked their way through the rush mats and
itricately carved couches whereon sundry supine figures
ere informally investigating the recreational possibilities of
arious alkaloid derivatives and endorphin analogues, and
ent through the door.

Nathan Li Shao and Kiru looked up from where they were
laying desultory hands of Three Chimneys to pass the time.

' 'Evening.' Li Shao pushed his little semi-circular trans-
icent green-stained cellulose ritual Promethean nomad card-
laying hat up his forehead. 'Don't I know you from
omewhere?'

———————

nd then everybody started talking at once:

'Kill you,' Leetha snarled, reaching for her armour. 'Make
ou dead and kill you now!'

'Pardon?' said Li Shao.

'Settle down, Leetha, please,' said the Doctor hurriedly.
'ake that off her and calm her down, would you, Benny?
hank you. Now. I gather that you are hiring crew for a
oyage, is that correct?'

'That's right,' said Li Shao. 'Is she all right?'

'Let me go!' shouted Leetha.

'That's an interesting hold,' said Kiru. 'I've never seen a
ody hold quite like that before.'

'Good, isn't it?' said Benny. 'I learnt it in the Service.
oesn't take a lot of brute strength and it's almost impossible
• get out of –'

'Ow!' Leetha exclaimed.

'– and it hurts quite a bit if you try.'

'Thank you, Benny.' The Doctor turned to Li Shao again.
believe I can be of some help with your endeavours. I have

a certain amount of experience with exploits of a hazardou
and perilous nature.'

'Such as?' said Li Shao.

'In my time,' the Doctor said, 'I have come up again
Daleks, Draconians and acid slugs down a coal-mine. Cybe
men have been known to break out the gold dust at the me
mention of my name. Time and again I have bested tl
Master in a battle of wits – which I fancy says not
little for my cognitive abilities, sartorial tastes and a
round general spunkiness.' He took a deep breath. 'Hootl
Solarians, Greki, Sea Devils, Yeti, Silurians, Nazis, corpora
arcologies, bogiemen, vampires, bodysnatchers and Bo
woppets from Altair XIV have variously known what
means to be my enemy or my friend. I am the Doctor. Tl
Doctor is me. Who do you think it was,' he said with a litt
smile and his fingers crossed behind his back, 'who gave tl
Clangers their big break?'

'I've never heard of any of them,' said Li Shao. 'What is
that you do, exactly?'

'Oh, I generally muddle along,' said the Doctor.

'Muddling along,' said Li Shao, 'is not exactly a skill (
the top of our list. Can you cook?'

'I've been known to,' said the Doctor.

'You're in.' Li Shao turned to the two women. 'We cou
do with a master at arms if you're interested. You look li
you could be handy in a scrap.'

'I would rather slit my wrists with a leatherman's awl th
work for such as you,' Leetha spat.

'I wasn't talking to you,' said Li Shao.

'I suppose so,' Benny said while Leetha splutter
apoplectically. 'I'd want Leetha along, too, to back me up.'

'If you think I'm going to spend so much as a minute
the same ship as *him* . . .' Leetha said.

'Sorry.' Li Shao rubbed at the side of his head thougl
fully. 'I'm not as fond of impact trauma and seconda
haemorrhaging as I used to be.'

'I can keep her under control,' said Benny. 'Listen, fro
what I hear, we're going into peril and danger such as v
might never live to tell the tale of and stuff. You're going
need dangerous people like Leetha for stuff like that.'

'She has a point, Nathan,' said Kiru.

Li Shao nodded slowly. 'All right. If you can control her.'

'Listen, Leetha,' Benny hissed in the Anean woman's ear. 'Don't be more of a fool than you have to be. This is the last ship *out*, understand? No more chances. Just don't blow it for all of us, OK?'

Leetha subsided somewhat and ceased struggling against Benny's grip. 'He better not come near me,' she muttered sullenly. 'Cut him up and gut him if he comes near me.'

Nathan Li Shao shrugged. 'Remind me to avoid any wild horses travelling in your general direction.' He found a scrap of paper in his leather jacket and scratched a brief note on it with a dip pen. 'Take this with you to the third quadrant wharf. We're in berth seventeen. Give it to Six and . . .'

'My dear Captain Li Shao,' said Solan, stepping through the door of the backroom, followed by a pair of burly humanoids.

He was strapped into a straining corset and elasticated support stockings, and wore what on a slightly more diminutive form would have been a voluminous smoking jacket, but which upon him was as tight as a sausage-skin. A huge blunderbuss was clutched in his hands.

'I must confess to delight,' he said, 'if not exactly surprise, at finding you still here. I believe you've met my associate, Mr Glome?' He gestured negligently to the small figure in the black cowl who had entered cringingly behind himself and his men.

'I've seen him around,' Li Shao said. 'Can't say I know him.'

Solan chuckled wetly. 'Ah, but Mr Glome knows you, Captain. Mr Glome tells me that you have been, shall we say, slightly economical with the truth with me? You have made plans within which you have not seen fit to include me. I am disappointed in you, Captain.' He raised the blunderbuss until it was pointing directly at Li Shao's head. 'Very disappointed indeed.'

The Fifteenth Chapter

The Sloathe destroyers wormed their way through the mazy crystal debris cloaking Sere. In the bridge of the final one – for it was, after all, no fool – slumped the Sekor Dom Sloathe: steering this particular vessel directly, and indirectly controlling the rest by remote control transmitter-analogues warped from several outer sections of its main mass.

The Sekor Dom Sloathe still presented a vaguely brain-like aspect to the world: form is dictated by the demands of function, and it had learnt that if it twisted hirself into the form of a brain it was highly intelligent, while if it assumed the form of, for example, an avocado with a hat on it was, basically, incredibly dumb.

Currently a pair of sallow-skinned System-aboriginal slaves were scrubbing at the Sekor Dom Sloathe's bulk with brooms dipped in buckets of soapy water. In addition, the bridge contained hir foodstock of Sloathe young in a tub and a globular tank of lead crystal.

Within this, a young Sloathe that had yet to reach the size of maturity and awareness, clamped into a tortuous trans-mission-shape transmitting on a number of very specific frequencies.

Now the Sekor Dom Sloathe exuded a pseudopod and pushed it through a hatch in the tank. The tentacle grew several bony claws upon its tip, and affixed itself to the flesh of the thing with a *clunch*.

———

In the back room of the Dragon tap, the majority of Nathan Li Shao's attention was fixed, not unnaturally, upon the bell of Solan's blunderbuss. He was peripherally aware, how-ever, that one of Solan's men – Mischa, the white-furred

Reklonian he had encountered days before at the gaming house – was carrying a large wooden box. From this there now came a squealing, the frantic skutter of claws.

'Excuse me one moment,' Solan said. The blunderbuss was suddenly removed from Li Shao's face – which was not that much of a relief, since the other of Solan's men, an ebony-black human, was standing by the door and covering the room with a clockwork-operated machine-gun capable of expending lead pellets at a rate of almost thirty a minute.

Solan lumbered over to the Reklonian and opened the box. 'Nearly there,' he said. 'Starboard and then dead ahead for one half league.' He turned back to Li Shao, cradling his gun in the crook of one arm. 'My apologies, Captain.'

'What are you playing at, Solan?' Li Shao said angrily.

Solan chuckled. 'No games, Captain.' With his free hand he gestured vaguely to the cowled figure. 'I believe this might be the ideal time for our Mr Glome to present his credentials, as it were.'

The bony, palsied hands of Mr Glome went up to the cowl and pulled it back. The flesh, such as there was, upon Mr Glome's face was dead and dry, puckering around the cranium where it met a smooth glass dome within which, pulsing in its cephalic fluid, was his living brain. A tracery of verdigrised copper wires entwined itself around it.

The eyes of Mr Glome were sewn shut with catgut – although, Li Shao knew with a lurch of clammy and unmanning terror, this would not inconvenience him in the slightest. Mr Glome was a degenomancer – one of that strange and horrible race of the Elysian satellite, Rubri, who systematically killed themselves while keeping their brains alive, and derived foul unnatural powers and perceptions from the specific energies released by the chemically controlled decomposition of their mechanically assisted corporeal bodies.

Li Shao knew the degenomancers. They had opened him up and done things to him – and once you had been touched by them there was a little piece of you that was for ever in their power. His stomach crawled. He tried to force muscles suddenly slack as cotton into motion, and failed.

'In my mind . . .' said Mr Glome, breath rattling through lungs clotted with scab-tissue and desiccated pus. 'In my mind, I think, I saw it in my *mind* and . . .' He put a hand into his robes at sternum level and there was the ratcheting sound of a little clockwork mechanism being wound. 'Into my mind it went and . . .'

'Quite,' said Solan. 'The upshot is that I know your every thought and every plan. I know that this trading voyage of yours is merely the cover for an attempt to find the Eyes of the Schirron . . .'

Li Shao was aware of a little gasp, and then an angry muttering and a hissing from the Anean woman.

'Now,' Solan said, silkily, 'I am of course aware of the legends, and there might or might not be some truth in them – but frankly, my dear captain, I could not care one jot. What hurts me and, I must confess, angers me is that you did not see fit to make me aware of these plans. That shows a singular lack of faith, and not to say professional courtesy, and I don't like it.' Solan raised the barrel of the blunderbuss until it was again levelled squarely at Li Shao. 'I think it's time we relieved you of your responsibilities –'

'Excuse me,' a voice said politely.

The little man in the pristine linen suit who had called himself the Doctor had faded into the background during this exchange – had not become invisible as such, Li Shao was dimly aware, just unnoticeable: some unimportant part of the scenery.

Now he bustled forward, all energy and business, and it was as though everything and everyone in the room had become mere background to him.

'If you don't mind,' he said, brushing neatly past Mr Glome the degenomancer and casually reaching out a hand to push a slightly nonplussed Solan's blunderbuss out of the way. 'Thank you. Ghastly things. Never could stand them. Now.' He glanced around the little room full of astonished and incredibly dangerous people with a brisk little smile. 'If you will attend to me carefully, you will note that I have absolutely nothing whatsoever up my sleeves . . .'

Somebody was nudging Nathan Li Shao repeatedly in the ribs. He risked a brief glance round to see the dark-haired woman, who a couple of seconds before had been involved in a tense *sotto voce* conversation with the Anean woman.

'I've been here before,' she said quietly to him out of the

orner of her mouth, 'so take it from someone who knows. Any minute now all hell's going to break loose, and I think it might be a really good idea if we all got ready to run . . .'

I don't believe it!' Leetha gasped as they pelted through the twisting tunnels of Sere. 'How he started singing that song, with appropriate gestures, about an elephant* and then he just turned and looked at the degenomancer, who lurched back with an ululating scream of terror, clutching at his sewn-up eyes, and then collapsed whimpering most piteously about how big putrescent slug-things with napkins knotted round their necks were bursting out of his face and eating his nose with knives and forks of the finest Sheffield steel.' The clockwork machine-gun previously in the possession of the Reklonian slapped against her side on its strap as she ran.

'Frightened the life out of me,' Benny panted. Up ahead he saw the big running form of Li Shao and the more diminutive of his friend Kiru, and slightly ahead of them she saw the Doctor sidestepping an Elysian beggar, dropping something into its bowl, tipping his hat as he passed and taking a corner with a little hop-and-skid to lose a little of his momentum. Sometimes, she thought, the Time Lord was like something out of a particularly manic Chuck Jones cartoon.

In the interests of completeness, it is perhaps apposite at this point to interpolate Benny's later recollection of the Time Lord's song, with appropriate gestures – for it would, subsequently, become the basis on countless worlds and in countless times for the cautionary proverb: 'If a strange dark woman, after the tenth drink, suddenly begins to sing:

> What is this that I hear? (*put your hand to your ear*)
> Upstairs in the attic? (*point up*)
> It is an elephant (*make like a trunk*)
> Riding around on a bicycle. (*stomp about stupidly*)
> It is an elephant, (*ditto last line but one*)
> So *chic* and elegant, (*flounce!*)
> With one trunk here and one tail there. (*thing with the trunk
> again and then bump and grind*)

do not under any circumstances approach her for she shall immediately fall over and be violently and spectacularly ill on you.'

For some reason the thought was strangely chilling, and she couldn't quite work out why.

'And then he turned back to the fat man,' Leetha gasped 'and did all those jokes about the oven-ready mallards and the custard while pulling delicately monogrammed handker chiefs out of his pocket! And then the fat man tried to shoc him, and the flapping white doves and streamers and clock work teeth came out of his sleeves, and he just pushed th gun out of the way and all the tin-tacks went up into th ceiling!'

'You were of no small assistance yourself, you know,' sai the Doctor, popping up beside them as if from nowhere an apparently not out of breath at all.

Very like an old-time cartoon character, sometime thought Benny. Like that little Tex Avery dog – Droopy, o whatever – when the bad guy slams and bolts the door o him, and loads it with chains, and piles anvils against it, an hops in his car, and then a plane, and then a rocket ship t Mars or somewhere, and when at last he falls to his knee gasping with relief, he hears this little voice behind hir and . . .

'You mean with the Reklonian?' Leetha said. 'Guns ar only useful if you're fast enough to use them – and I'r faster. You should have let me kill him. You should have le me kill them all!'

'I do not,' said the Doctor primly, 'believe in unnecessar killing.'

No you don't, Benny thought as she ran. You don't ki people. You might just leave the bad guys alive and forge about them, stranded on that martian desert to die of anoxi or starvation, but you don't believe in actually killin anything. Unless you can't get out of doing it. When yo can't get someone else to do it for you.

Unbidden, another cartoon image came back to he There's a dog who guards the fold and there's a wolf wh wants to eat them. The wolf is very wily, and constructs hi intricate plans, and orders rocket-powered scooters an dynamite from the Acme corporation, while the dog ju strolls through it all, apparently all unawares, and wreck those plans, or sticks a sudden crowbar into the machinery, c casually hands the fizzing stick of dynamite *back*. (Benn had once written, in a long-forgotten and mercifully unpublished dissertation upon the history of cinema, that one of the major underlying points of this scenario was the internal tension between the fact that the supposedly animal and mindless wolf was in fact the culturally and technologically literate, tool-using product of a coherent and constructive social order – while the apparently good and civilized and above all insouciant dog was really the primitive, even elemental, agent of chaos: the fall of the prat, the punchline to the gag, that butterfly-beat moment where things fall catastrophically apart.)

And it makes no ultimate difference to the sheep of course, who are destined for slaughterhouse anyway. But not today. The fact that no sheep died today is the sole justification for any moral superiority that the dog who guards them has, and an entirely specious one at that. Nobody dies in cartoons anyway, when the rostrum camera's on them – but notice how there don't seem to be many *lambs* about? The positions switch again: the wolf as noble anarchist who merely tries to take what he must to survive, the dog the lackey of a larger order which by its very nature kills, and kills, and kills again on an industrial basis . . .*

And at the end, of course, the whistle goes, the shifts change and both the dog and the wolf pick up their lunch pails, clock off and go home.

Levels, Benny thought uneasily as she ran through the twisting tunnels. Strata of truth and consequence, of culpability and blame. Just what levels are you in fact operating *on*, Doctor?

And why am I suddenly starting to think like this again? Is

---

* Benny's thesis had continued in this vein at some length, had contained the words 'Apollonian' and 'Dionysian' some three hundred and twenty-five times, and had eventually concluded that the world was just one total hellhole that ended in misery and death whichever way you looked at it, that your mum and dad they messed you up whether they were in fact dead or not, and that she was glad she didn't have a boyfriend or a girlfriend, because they were all entirely and without exception stupid, and seemed almost wilfully uninterested in the inherent, self-evident and entirely serious truth of their so-called jokes, even when she tried repeatedly to make them aware of it. Benny was fifteen at the time.

131

a certain little bit of *your* mind currently too busy concentrating on other . . .

Ahead of them, Li Shao and Kiru had stopped before a number of red-painted wood and glass cabinets bolted to the tunnel wall. Within them were telephone apparatuses, and Li Shao pulled the receiver from one and cranked the handle.

'We have to give Six some time for the engines to warm up,' he called as Leetha, the Doctor and Benny went by. 'We left Solan out cold, but who knows how long that's going to last? Go on ahead. We'll catch you up.'

'He's letting us go ahead into a trap,' Leetha muttered darkly as they pressed on through the tunnels. 'I know he is. That's just the sort of thing he'd think of.'

'You know,' said the Doctor mildly, still apparently not out of breath, 'I really think you're being a little hard on the man. Admittedly, we've only known him briefly, but he's treated us with nothing but courtesy. And you must admit that he and his friend were also of some help with the obese gentleman in the rather fetching latex – Solan, was it? – and his men.'

'Then you know *nothing*,' Leetha spat. 'When I think of someone like Li Shao defiling the Search for the Eyes with his foul attentions, I –'

'Ah yes,' said the Doctor. 'I believe that this Solan mentioned something about that. Would you care to elaborate?'

Leetha almost lost her footing trying to stare at him aghast while running. 'You mean that you have *never* heard of the Eyes? The Eyes of the Schirron?'

'Well, I haven't been well.' The Doctor frowned. 'I believe the name "Schirron" is vaguely familiar – I think I may have mentioned that before, but – no. I'm afraid you have me at a loss.'

'The Eyes of the Schirron are the very souls of the Wanderers! When the very System seems to die and the Sun burns black they must be disposed!'

'What?' panted Benny. 'Like destroyed or something?'

'I think she means "disposed" in the sense of being put in their correct place,' said the Doctor.

'With rituals of much complexity and solemnity,' said Leetha.

'Now why,' Benny said, 'does that not surprise me?'

They had passed through the hinterland zones by now; public tunnels had given way to the wide and absolutely deserted commercial areas of a trading centre and crossover point where nobody was now going anywhere. Once or twice they passed the dead and rusting iron and perished rubber remains of derelict haulage mechanisms and conveyor belts, left to rot where they stood.

And then they came to the cavernous chamber of the wharf. The hatches set into its floor were dark, save for one, from which came a diffuse and bluish luminescence.

The air here crackled with static and smelt of ozone. Benny felt her cropped hair prickling in her scalp.

'Could it be?' The Doctor sniffed the air, and smiled beatifically. 'Is it really?'

'Is it really what?' said Benny uneasily.

The Doctor merely twirled his umbrella and marched towards the glowing hatchway. Benny and Leetha, independently but simultaneously, shrugged and followed him.

Rope ladders and communications cables depended to the docking platforms. And below that, against a multicoloured inverted sky that blurred past, tethered by hawsers, was the ship. The good ship *Schirron Dream*.

Benny heard Leetha gasp.

It was the brilliant matt-white of porcelain fresh from the kiln, all inlaid with interlocking and vaguely runic symbols of purest gold. Three winglike structures swept, gull-like, back from its main body to razor-sharp points. It was sleek and fast and it looked like a love-song addressed to the Cosmos, or at least addressed to the microcosmos of the System – Benny was reminded of how the TARDIS and the Doctor, no matter how apparently incongruous upon the surface, somehow just happened to fit wherever they happened to be.

The very shape the thing made in the world declared that, quintessentially, the ship was there to be used. Just looking at it made you want to get in it and see how fast it could go.

The engines were alive and idling. A shimmering blue light throbbed in their propulsion vents.

'I knew it!' the Doctor exclaimed triumphantly, pointing dramatically at the engines with his umbrella. 'Orgones!'

133

'Oh, bloody hell . . .' said Benny.

The sound of trotting feet behind them. Li Shao and Kiru came out of the gloom. Li Shao opened a storage locker by the hatch and passed out a number of respirator masks. 'Made it all right, then?'

'I'm not so sure,' Benny said. She turned to the Doctor. 'You're having me on again, aren't you? Tell me you're having me on again.'

The Doctor merely beamed at her.

'What's an orgone?' said Leetha.

Benny sighed. 'You don't want to know. Let's just say I really hope we don't have anything wrong with our sex drive.'

———

Some three minutes later, detonation-bolts detonated, severing the hawsers and communication lines, and momentum flung the ship from Sere. Some two minutes after that, several muscular men, in the ragged uniforms of what had once been the Serean militia, burst into the wharfside loading bay. Below them, through the hatch, they saw the hanging hulks of decommissioned ships and dangling cables. In the whirling sky of the Ring beyond they occasionally caught a glimpse of a brighter, bluish streak that might or might not have been an exhaust trail.

The ex-militiamen retraced their steps until they came to a telephone booth, where their leader called the man who had once paid them off by the week, and now employed them on a more formal basis.

The Sixteenth Chapter

The Sloathe bulked squebulously over the supine forms of Forrester and Cwej and pulsed, constantly forming and re-forming: now a double-headed stoat with a slick oyster skin, now a toad with human heads growing from his tongue like boils, now a monstrous glistening kidney, trailing its tubes and supported by elongated insectoid legs.

'Is tried to get away from us,' it said. 'Is must you know that this not good thing.'

We'd have made it, too, you squishy polymetamorphic bastard, thought Roz sourly. We were just unlucky.

It was the food time of the fifth 'day' of their captivity that they had made their break. With the aid of the Escape Committee they had organized a mock-riot and, as the ring of Sloathe guards had moved in to break it up, they passed by an apparently discarded vaulting horse, from which Forrester and Cwej had subsequently emerged to make their attempted escape.

They had made their way out of the repository cavern and crept through the tunnels of Planet X, hiding behind discarded junk, avoiding the worst concentrations of the Sloathes (who seemed to pulse through the basalt moon like bulbous platelets through a pulmonary system) and trying to locate the chamber in which they had left the TARDIS. They had no real hope of being able to actually operate the thing, but there were vast stockpiles of equipment and weaponry in there – and if the prisoners of the Sloathes could be freed and armed, Roz had dreams of subsequently wandering the squabmous corridors *en masse* with a bunch of atom-pack-powered ion-skreemers with flame-thrower attachments gaffer-taped to the barrels.

It had been while they were hiding out, in a tunnel behind

a couple of overturned display cases of interesting Euryapsidic fossils, that disaster struck, in the form of simultaneous and catastrophic bouts of sickness and diarrhoea, which, had they not been too busy projectile-ejecting from both directions, they might have put down to the rancid chicken skins and spoiled cabbage with which they had repleted themselves to give them much-needed strength for their escape. The food available to Planet X's prisoners was a continual game of Proximan Mah Jong and they had merely had the bad luck to pick the exploding domino.

It had also done little for sartorial standards already slightly lowered by days of sorting through slimy debris and communal sleeping and no way of washing. Roz Forrester, for one, was seriously beginning to fear for the safety of her underwear.

In any event, the interesting noises issuing from behind the display cases had attracted a number of Sloathes, and Forrester and Cwej had been hauled to a chamber in which squatted a Sloathe markedly larger than the rest. Its name, apparently, was An Tleki, and she gathered that it was the administrator for all things prisoner.

'Is to be just not good thing enough,' said An Tleki. 'Is have enough upon the plate-type thing without pretend-move buggers getting out all the bleeding time. Is pain in the bleeding fundament is what it is. Yes.'

Forrester turned to Cwej's pale and befouled face. 'You know, Chris, I'd kill for a hip-bath and a loofah.'

Chris Cwej tried to grin back. 'I think you should be thinking more on the lines of an industrial jet-blaster and a suction sluice.'

'What?' A large eye on a pseudopod shot for them and peered at them intently. Then its outer membrane formed a soft and perfectly clear pair of lips. 'What thing say?'

'We said we're very, very sorry and we'll never do it again,' Roz told it. 'You wouldn't believe how sorry we are and how we'll never do it again.'

'Don't believe you,' said the Sloathe, rather huffily, Roz thought. 'Never mind, though . . .'

A little slit opened up in the main mass of An Tleki, and a new and entirely horrifying appendage burst from it: a ribbed and needle-like appendage with a channel running through it, membrane sacs clustered around it. A trickle of clear fluid drooled from the needle.

'Got a way to make sure you never go away,' said An Tleki. 'Not never again.'

The Seventeenth Chapter

The bridge of the *Schirron Dream* was obloidal and walled with a substance similar to that which encased the engines: extruded panels that felt like the surface of a fingernail or some animal's hoof, inlaid with whorls of pink and pale blue like mother-of-pearl.

The controls seemed to be designed for something vaguely humanoid, and after a few hours' trial and error Li Shao thought he had the hang of the important ones: so long as you knew how to start and stop and steer the thing there was no problem. In the days since they had bought the ship they had bolted seats scavenged from a junkyard on to projections apparently designed for sitting on, but could only actually be sat on if you had a third leg or a muscular and prehensile tail. The only other important modification was the installation of radar and sonar readouts – since Li Shao didn't trust his expertise with the clusters of what were presumably instruments and viewing screens, but looked disquietingly like inset, globular, blank and milky eyes – and radio and intercom rigs since the ship did not appear to have any internal or external communications systems at all.

Now Li Shao sat strapped in at the communications console, the throbbing of the engines working at the muscles along his spine, idly cranking through radio channels and trying to think. His hands itched to be at the helm, taking them through the tortuous path that led out of the Ring, but Kiru was perfectly capable of doing that while Six sang out vectors from the radar – and as captain it was his duty to delegate, to form policy and give the correct orders, without cluttering his mind with the specifics of actually carrying them out. Perhaps because this was a real ship, with a real crew, as opposed to what was basically a floating patchwork

ransport full of cutthroats, he felt he owed it that duty. He
adn't felt this way since the Fleet, all those years ago . . .

Solan had rushed their departure, and the *Schirron Dream*
vas pitifully undermanned. On the plus side, that meant an
xtended period before restocking of supplies – he estimated
hat the ship and crew could sustain itself for six solar
nonths or more – but that would be academic if they ran into
rouble. There were barely enough people to man the newly
nstalled weapons systems, let alone fight off any attackers if
hey boarded.

And then there was this business about the Eyes. It had all
eemed like a good idea at the time. Bit of high adventure, bit
f excitement, trade with every Wanderer we go to – but
vhat, precisely, when it came right down to it, was the point?
ix months, a year, two years from now, the System would
e completely crushed by the Sloathes. Nobody was going to
e *left* to talk for years to come about these heroic exploits in
earch of a bunch of mystic jewels with lights inside them
hat might be the crux of the religions of worlds, but which
ne Nathan Li Shao could not personally give a fart and a
alf about.

So just why, said a sneaky little voice inside him, are you
oing it? If you want panoplied action and bags of adventure
nd a gloriously stupid death, then why don't you simply
aunch a last desperate attack against the Sloathes?

Three reasons, he thought. One, it won't do any good; two,
: would be to betray thirty-five odd people who signed on in
ood faith for a trading voyage; and three, it's precisely what
ve're doing anyway.

And then it was there, quietly, in his head. All of it.

It wasn't about the Eyes and it had never been about trade.
here was no trade left in a System blockaded by the
loathes, and any lone ship that tried to run the blockades
vas going to be taken apart spectacularly – but it was going
o take out as many of the bastards as it could in the process.

This was a suicide mission, plain and simple, with the
yes of the Schirron merely a convenient hook to hang the
oose on. Li Shao, Six and Kiru had known it when they
onceived it, the crew had known when they had signed on
or it, and they were all of them going to die.

Nathan Li Shao suddenly felt happier than he had in years.

He wanted to burst out laughing, and he might have given in
to the urge, save that it was at this point that the transmission
bands from Sere began to squeal, and a voice spoke over
them, and the incipient laughter died in his throat.

'My dear captain,' said the voice of Solan. 'You didn'
think you could run out on me quite *that* easily, did you?'

Nathan Li Shao broke a thumbnail hitting the reply switch.

'Oh yes?' he said, perfectly calmly. 'What are you going to
do? Send out a couple of rowboats after us?'

'Hardly,' said the voice of Solan, happily. 'You see, for
some time now, much as it pains me to admit it, I have been
what you might call something of a double agent. The
Sloathes, you see, have offered me some degree of advantage
should I assist in their general assimilation of the System
and of Sere in particular . . .'

'What?' Li Shao snarled.

Then he remembered to depress the reply switch.

'What?' Li Shao snarled.

'. . . time now,' the voice of Solan said, having not paused
for a reply, 'I have been in communication with certain, shal
we say, pacification forces even now *en route* to our littl
asteroid. Indeed, I understand that your course should lea
you to intercept the first wavefront around about now –'

Li Shao snapped off the switch cutting Solan off. He stared
at the speaker for a moment, disparate eyes suddenly blank
with a murderous fury simply too big to get out of them.

'Bastard,' he said quietly.

Then he turned to Kiru and Six and snapped: 'Action
stations! New deployment!'

The smaller man and the polymorph had remained intent
upon their work, ignoring the exchange at the radio station
Now it was as though they were galvanized. A couple of
Six's eye appendages snapped round towards Li Shao and
Kiru slapped controls to slow the ship into a safe holding
pattern. The ship lurched.

'Problems?' he said.

'We've got problems,' Li Shao said, sliding into the contro
seat and buckling the straps as Kiru vacated it, losing not so
much as a second between them. 'Sloathes ahead. A lot of
them. Coming through the maze. Any sign of them, Six?'

Neither Six nor Kiru wasted time with expostulations

'Nothing yet,' Six said simply. 'Big lumps, little lumps and particles, see we. Random movement see we and . . . something there now. Something there. Is right. Is *lots*!'

'Excuse me,' said a quiet voice by Li Shao's ear.

'Deployment?' Li Shao said.

'Is single file,' said Six. 'Look like big, big gunship in front. Convoy stretching back through maze gods know how far.'

'Excuse me,' the quiet voice said again. 'It's nothing really, but I couldn't help noticing . . .'

Li Shao shook off the annoying presence. 'Alternative routes?'

'None. No way out. They coming for us. Coming fast!'

'Oh, bugger,' said Li Shao.

'I just wondered what would happen if I did *this*,' said the Doctor.

The engine-vents of the *Schirron Dream* pulsed and stuttered – and then blazed with a searing, blue-tinged light, bright as burning magnesium.

The ship shot forward as though fired by a gun, shattering and scattering crystal asteroids and several unfortunate Sloathe ships with its shockwave and a sound like several million little glass bells simultaneously exploding. Had any vessel, Sloathe or otherwise, been capable of following in its wake, it would have reported that the *Schirron Dream* burst through some fourteen hundred miles of the Ring in a matter of minutes. Away from Sere and Solan and the ships he was calling to him.

Out, finally, into the System.

'Oh, bloody-humpbacked Cruag, hairy-nostrilled Seth and the inordinately fecund Bel Shebedebededeth!' Nathan Li Shao exclaimed as the bridge juddered around him and blinding lights stuttered and strobed on the globular screens. 'What the various hells is happening?'

'Well,' the Doctor said, standing calmly by him on the deck and seemingly oblivious to the lack of relative gravity and the acceleration. 'I just happened to notice that you

141

weren't using the engines to their full capacity. You just press this projection here and . . .'

'Make it stop,' Li Shao growled murderously. 'Make it stop *now*.'

The Doctor shrugged. 'Suit yourself.' He passed a hand over the console and a section of it glowed briefly.

The deceleration flung Li Shao so hard against his straps that he almost passed out. When his head stopped swimming, he turned it to glower at the little man.

'You know about these controls?' he said.

'Not as such.' The Doctor waggled a hand noncommittally. 'But I have a little experience with some of the more abstruse aspects of alien design, and there are some general configurational principles. This here, for instance, seems to be the central control for a crude form of simulated gravity . . .' He passed a hand over another small and almost unnoticeable projection on the console.

From the hatch to the aft of the bridge came a sound that could only be described as every single unsupported object in a ship hitting what was suddenly the floor.

'Whoops,' said the Doctor.

In the cartilaginous cabin that they had been assigned upon arrival, Leetha was doctoring Benny's split eyebrow when the Doctor entered. 'Let me guess,' Benny said. 'That was your fault. I'll just bet it was your fault.'

'As much as anything is anybody's fault, I suppose,' said the Doctor. 'I blame society, myself.'

He sat on the bunk assigned to Leetha and rubbed his hands with a genial smile. 'Well, I'm sure you'll be glad to hear that we're on our way at last – and that, due to a little practical advice I was able to give our captain, we're talking in terms of days and weeks rather than months. First stop is Prometheus. That's where he was born, apparently.'

'And that's a planet, right?' said Benny.

'Well, I must admit that was my first thought. It's probably easier if I show you. Come and have a look.'

He left the cabin with Benny and Leetha trailing behind and led them through a couple of curved and vaguely organic corridors to a larger, communal cabin, which had been fitted with scavenged, mismatched fixtures to serve as a refectory of sorts. The only problem was that, under the artificial gravity, all the tables and benches were now bolted to the ceiling.

In the wall was a large, circular panel.

'It's a viewing port,' the Doctor said. He passed a hand over a projection in the wall beside it and it hazed to life, displaying a view now unobstructed by the crystalline chaos of the Ring.

Benny gazed out upon the distant, massive forms.

At the clockwork.

'Oh, hell . . .' she said.

'What's the problem?' said Leetha. 'Are you all right? It's only the System.'

'Don't mind me,' Benny said. 'I should have got with the programme long before now. It was just that I was probably expecting more of the same old balls.'

And the creature inside allowed itself a quiet quasi-moment of smug self-congratulation, in its orrery room. Several crucial junctures had been passed, its forces were in motion. It could see the future unfold before it, now, the process of cause and domino-effect operating right down the line and running like clockwork. Events had taken on a shape of their own and there was not a single random factor with the force to disrupt that shape.

There could only be one end, now. Life and revenge for the creature inside. Death for everything else.

There was no possibility of failure. None.

None at all.

The dead remains of the freighter that had once been conned by the Most Supreme Captain Trenkor Lep had been drifting towards Planet X for weeks now.

Now, finally, it entered its gravitational field. It began to fall.

Now it entered its microecological atmosphere. It began to burn.

The winds of Planet X whipped it. It hit the surface of

Planet X in an elliptical trajectory trailing black and greasy smoke, a lacerated, burning lump of Sloathe meat, impacting to spread its mass across a radius of a quarter of a mile.

Damp little fires smouldered for a while and went out.

The remains of the freighter began to coagulate.

They twitched.

Canto Third:
After the Rains

Jack and Gye
Went out in the rye,
And they found a little boy with one black eye.
Come, says Jack, let's knock him on the head.
No, says Gye, let's buy him some bread;
You buy one loaf and I'll buy two,
And we'll bring him up as other folk do.

Trad. Nursery Rhyme

'Tell me lovely fishmonger, do you have prawn balls?'
'No, sir, that is just the effect of the cold.'
Incredibly Bad Jokes of the Twentieth Century No. 15,478
ed. Professor Bernice Summerfield

The Eighteenth Chapter

Some small degree of time passed. In the water, bodies of the Wanderers rose and fell, tides swelled and yawed under unfamiliar and cumulatively destructive stresses, volcanoes burst from the earth and exploded and in the centre of the System the Sun pulsed, bathing the Wanderers in the light of day and the black light of night. People were born and rather more people attritionally died. Sloathe forces continued their consolidation of the outer Wanderers and their harassment of the inner.

Across the System, regular as clockwork, the steady stream of incident and event continued its inexorable march from the *now* to the *then*. Some of these incidents, strung sequentially like dead and glittery flies through the web of causality, would later, in particular, prove extremely and even supremely important. Others not. That's the way it goes with events.

———

In a black and stagnant watercourse in the jungles of Anea, a particular swampwater bloater almost dead from starvation because its dorsals and eyeballs were deformed to the point where it was evolutionarily unable to compete, burst the viscous surface in a last desperate attempt to escape a needle eel, found itself flopping weakly on a mudbank – and found that it could breathe. With whatever a swampwater bloater in fact uses for trepidation it took its first, tentative steps upon comparatively dry land.

———

Later:

In the tunnels of Sere, now, there was nothing but the living bodies of the Sloathes and the rotting bodies of the

147

dead. Even before things had begun to fall apart, the defences of the asteroid had been casual at best, relying more upon the crystalline maze that surrounded it than upon observational posts and gun emplacements. The Sloathe destroyers had simply bombed the surface with incendiaries to discourage anyone still actually on it, blocked off every exit point they could find and then swarmed through the asteroid killing anyone and anything they found.

Those who survived long enough noticed that there was something odd about their actions. Sloathes were known the whole system over for bickering amongst themselves like a troupe of baboons over a windscreen wiper – and it was this innate disorganization that had, in the earlier years of the System's occupation, more than once allowed indigenous forces to snatch desperate victory from the mouth-approximations of abject defeat.

These Sloathes were different. They moved like well-drilled troops, like bodies controlled by a single head.

Some Sereans survived. They had already been building their own little microsocietal bolt-holes against the coming famine, and some of these (the establishment of Mama Roca, for example) were able to seal these bolt-holes off. They cowered in them, now, waiting for the rescue that they knew would never come.

Some survived by other means.

In the central chamber of a destroyer tethered to the quartz asteroid with ropes of tendon, Solan hung from a hook with grey shapes jostling around him; he was looking upon the massive brain-thing of the Sekor Dom Sloathe. The bruising inflicted upon him by Li Shao had faded slightly, but a ragged scrap of bandage bound together a fractured skull and his left arm hung limp from a broken humerus – injuries sustained in the Sloathe annexation, when a step-ladder in his private tunnels had fallen out from under him, as he tried to make his escape.

You can get out of this, he said to himself, his mind hunting, as it had hunted all his life, for every last available option. You can get out of this alive. You can cut some sort of *deal* . . .

'Hey, listen,' he said. 'I can get you big pretty things. Pretty things for you! I show you!'

The massive brain thing juddered slightly, regarding him with squidlike eyes. A mouth formed and opened stickily.

'I think, perhaps, that your direct contact with my species has been limited to those marginally less cognitive than I. Would I be correct in assuming that?'

'Um . . .' Solan knew when he was on a hiding to nowhere. He changed tack a little. 'I did expect a little gratitude,' he said. 'It was, after all, I who made your victory possible.'

The Sekor Dom Sloathe appeared to consider this. Then: 'You have my gratitude. That is why you are still alive. I estimate that my gratitude will last, oh, another three and three-quarters of your minutes.'

The Sekor Dom Sloathe paused for a moment. A lumpen, organic approximation of a pocket-watch on a stalk burst from it, dangled over one of its eyes for a moment and then whipped back into its mass. 'Three and one half minutes, now. Now. What, precisely, are these "pretty things" to which you refer?'

In the pocket of his shredded rubber robe Solan felt the pressure of a sheaf of papers, painstakingly copied by the degenomancer, Mr Glome, from the images he had pulled out of Nathan Li Shao's head. The notations on them were coloured by Li Shao's disinterest, illegible in certain places, but legible enough – and for a certain, fundamental reason, he knew the true importance of what they described.

He thought of his own private treasure stores, next to worthless in inflation-struck Sere and utterly worthless now.

Worthless save for one particular thing.

'Let me live and I can give you the Eyes of the Schirron,' he said.

~~~

Later:

On a becalmed, partially destroyed and all but deserted raft city on the water world of Elysium (the single Wanderer, incidentally, that for various reasons could claim to be globular with any degree of verisimilitude), on a ship's desk crammed with yellowing nautical charts, in a cabin directly under the starsail, a small, mottled blown glass globe which had been teetering on the edge of the desk for more than half a solar year, finally toppled to hit the bare timbers of the deck. It didn't break.

Simultaneously:

'Bugger off and leave me alone.' Roslyn Forrester feebly blatted away the hand that had gripped her and curled into a foetal ball, trying to press herself into the greasy rock wall of the sleeping chamber. The desiccated, enervated feeling was just about bearable if she clutched her stomach and didn't move.

The hand shook her again. She uncurled herself and made to launch herself at the presence with a snarl.

It was Cwej, grey-faced and red-eyed, jerking a little.

'We have to *go*,' he said urgently.

Roz staggered to her feet. The dark forms of the other prisoners were already stumbling to the mouth of the chamber. Roz dry-heaved and shook and pressed her hands to her stomach and then lurched after them, praying that she would get a Sloathe who understood what she needed, and felt like giving it to her.

When the slave administrator, An Tleki, had plunged its needle appendage into her neck and pumped its fluid into her, she had experienced a whole-body kick remarkably similar to the effects of Earth-produced heroin (which she had experienced by electroencephalic stimulation as a part of her Adjudicator training, and which, in the thirtieth century, was coming back in fashion as a more wholesome and natural alternative to micro-customized synthetics and electroceph-stim) but jacked up, as it were, to the nth degree and with a strangely crawling edge to it – before almost instantly crashing down to the nausea and crawling need. After she and Cwej had been dragged back to their fellow prisoners, she had learnt that the Sloathes generated this substance by way of little vestigial chemical-cracking venom glands inside them, and used it to deal with troublesome prisoners if they didn't feel like simply killing them.

Well, fair enough, Roz had thought, I can cold-turkey it out and so can Cwej. No problem. We can do that.

It was only later that she learnt that the euphoric and addictive effects were merely a by-product of the suspension fluid.

150

Suspended in it were millions of mutated Sloathe miscrospores, even more voracious than their progenitors. First they would feed amongst themselves until only one microscopic spore remained, which would then simply latch on to the wall of a convenient blood vessel and wait for more of its smaller brethren to go past.

And then, unless it was periodically fed, it would attempt to feed on anything. A little organism munching through your body, ejecting undigested biological matter behind it, eating, and eating, and eating, and eating . . .

And, of course, every time it was fed by another injection of microspores, it would get bigger.

And bigger.

Roz Forrester and Christopher Cwej stumbled out into the tunnels of Planet X. The first thing Roz noticed was that the tunnels seemed to be full of prisoners, more than she had ever seen before. The second thing she noticed was that they were all being herded in the same direction. The third thing she noticed was that this direction was away from the repository caverns and upwards.

'What are they doing to us now?' she said to Cwej.

He shrugged, dull-eyed and exhausted, the puppylike bounce and energy of him almost completely gone – and if Cwej was that bad, Roz thought, what the hell must she look like? It wasn't as though one Roslyn Forrester, Adjudicator of this parish, had been an odds-on favourite in the bouncy enthusiasm stakes in the first place.

'I don't know,' he said, vaguely. 'There were rumours, though, coming back when I woke up. Somebody said that the Sloathes are suddenly taking every prisoner somewhere else. Somewhere off the planet.'

———

Later:

Under the packed snow and permafrost of Reklon, an ice-worm burrowed out into a cavern, although it had no way of knowing this. From its point of view, the world just suddenly went away, and then suddenly came back on only one side.

Despite the name, ice-worms were a kind of heat-seeking hot-blooded snake, with thick directionally aligned white fur and rows of vestigial limbs adapted in the form of little ice-cutters and shovels vibrating at some fifteen hundred cycles per second. Many a Reklonian had come to know and dread the ascending whine that meant that any second now a buzzing streak of fur would come shooting at you from the ice, wrap itself around you and attempt to snuggle up – a process which, given that an ice-worm was effectively a flexible boring saw capable of cutting through five feet of supercooled ice in less than a second, proved invariably fatal.

The ice-worm was blind, but it had heat-sense and knew there was something *warm* ahead of it. It had pressure-sense, and it whined forward until it encountered something *hard*.

It had time-sense, and it realized that it was suddenly getting very, very *old*.

Very, very quickly.

The Nineteenth Chapter

'No, Yani! You pull the housing back, feed the belt through
like this, engage the locking catch and then you twist this.'
Benny fed the belt of impact-detonated mortar shells into the
ejection gun and pushed the housing back into place. The
weapon reminded her of a miniature version of the ejectors
used to deposit canisters full of exo-enhanced TerraFed
stormtroopers during the Dead Geek Wars – a particularly
insane and vicious period of Earth history, under the New
Old New Old Good Old New Old Little Old Islam-Christian
Fundamentalist Republican Right Party premier 'Resurrection Bob' McGobglurk, and his lovely wife Yoko, when the
combined might of the Terran empire had, simply, attempted
to stomp every other sentient life-form in the galaxy into
their respective grounds. It was just another example of
the mismatched and dislocated technology of the System:
objects and concepts ripped wholesale from wherever they
once were, and just suddenly there.

The tubes of the ejector protruded from the ship through
rubber-gasketed holes drilled into a glass bubble. Through
it, Benny could see the distant brassy forms of cogs and
flywheels and rockers, hanging in the air, seemingly unrelated to each other. The Doctor had told her that these
were mere projections of a multidimensional structure into
dimensions with which the human mind could cope. Benny
found she could cope with them if she didn't actually look
at them.

Beside her, Yani took hold of the ejector and pulled, fed,
engaged, twisted and replaced. 'Good?'

Benny looked down at the cheerful evil little pale grinning
face of the Anean pigmy and nodded. 'It's good.'

'Can I fire it now?' Yani pantomimed two hands gripping

153

the firing mechanism and juddered them. 'Bang! Bang-bang! Kablam-a-blam-a-bang-bang!'

'Only when the captain orders action stations. Only when you can't avoid it. Promise?'

Yani shrugged and made a disproportionately large moue of disappointment with her disproportionately large and whorl-tattooed platelet-implanted lower lip. 'Promise.'

Benny left her and continued through the ship, checking up on the other weapons stations. Upon boarding the *Schirron Dream* her position as master-at-arms had been merely probationary, but over the past few days her familiarity with a wide number of technologies had consolidated it – and her expertise in the group-psychology of supervision had made her invaluable in dealing with the various problems of what were, effectively, more than thirty strangers suddenly shut in together. It was one of those problems with which she was now going to deal.

The *Schirron Dream* would operate upon a two-shift system until she hit the Anean orbit, and Benny found Leetha in their shared cabin, pacing the deck with the sort of wound-up frenetic energy that was surely, at some point, going to snap.

'What do you want?' the Sun Samurai said irritably.

'Just thought I'd have a chat,' Benny said brightly. 'Well, actually, you seem to be having a few problems and I thought you might want to talk about them. Hints, basically, have been made.'

'What in the name of Gog Bel-Shabababelbeth would I have problems about?' Leetha turned to peer at Benny suspiciously. 'What sort of hints?'

Benny shrugged and waggled a hand noncommittally. 'Oh, you know, just the usual stuff. Stuff like the captain saying, "That damned woman's going round with a face like a jackal licking piss off a scorpion, Benny, and people are getting annoyed. Sort it out, would you?" Stuff like that, y'know?'

'Hah!' Leetha flopped down on her bunk. 'Our "captain". Li Shao the despoiler and ravisher. Li Shao the traitor. Have I told you about his foul and loathsome treachery?'

Benny sighed and sat down on her own bunk. 'Probably.'

154

Kiru sat in a galley-cabin, now rearranged for the ship's internal gravity, nursing a small beer and idly glancing around himself at the others gathered there: eight of them in all, eating and drinking and generally relaxing before turning in to sleep. Over the last few days Kiru had got to know almost all of them, and they gave him a good feeling.

It wasn't quite like the old days in the Fleet which he had joined after leaving the floating cities of Elysium – the *Schirron Dream* had no truck with some of the harsher aspects of Fleet discipline, for a start – but there was a similar sense of camaraderie, of people united towards one common aim. Except for that bloody Anean woman, he recalled, pleased to note that she wasn't here even though she was off-shift. Just what, exactly, was her problem?

Kiru shrugged to himself and pulled out the sheaf of notes he had retrieved from the Sloathe freighter. A lot of them were written in a private cypher, which he had almost completely cracked by now. He studied the passages relating to Prometheus again:

> ... it was in this time, I believe, that the Stone was secreted in a Vault within the Valley of the Scorpions of Glass, that it might remain inviolate until the Sun burns cold. And the Vault was barred with Cantraps of a most Strange and Horrifying Nature, said to drive a man Mad, wherewith he pull his own eyes out and eat them ...

'What do *you* think, Kiru?' said a quiet voice behind him. 'What do you think of the Eyes?'

Kiru started, and turned to the diminutive figure of the Doctor as he stood, holding a steaming cup of the tarry-smelling tea to which he was partial. He forcibly reminded himself that the little man had of course been present in the Dragon tap when Solan had mentioned the Eyes. That was the only possible explanation, of course, and the Doctor hadn't been reading his mind like a degenomancer at all.

'May I?' The Doctor sat across the table from Kiru and regarded him with polite enquiry. He was in his shirt-sleeves and an apron and he wore a starched, white chef's hat at a jaunty angle, perched on top of his other hat which he had for some reason neglected to remove. A gnawing little part of

Kiru found itself wondering about this man, if that was what he in fact was. First there had been all that business on the asteroid, and then the bridge of the *Schirron Dream* . . . and then he had simply settled into his position as cook, doling out speedily but perfectly prepared meals made from ingredients Kiru could not recall ever actually being on the supply manifest. Kiru had the uneasy feeling that if he ordered, say, Reklonian ice-worm sandwiches with particularly retiring Anean swamp chameleon-truffles and a side order of Promethean myrrh, the Doctor would apologize, profusely, that they were off because he'd suddenly run out of bread.

There seemed to be a recurring pattern, here. The Doctor would simply fade, unobtrusively, into the background so that nobody gave him a first, let alone a second thought, until he suddenly wanted some question answered or something done and then he . . .

What was it he had been thinking about? Oh, yes. The Eyes.

'I don't know,' Kiru said. 'I really don't. I mean, Nathan, he doesn't believe a word of it and he's using it as an excuse for this fool's errand – this last doomed battle against the Sloathes. So far as he's concerned, I think it could have been anything from a stolen carved jade penguin to a missing man in a hat. I think anything would have done. As for myself . . .'

'Yes?' The Doctor sipped his tea.

Kiru shrugged. 'I don't believe in them. I think that even if they exist, they're probably just some prehistoric burial totems with the hideous curse that everyone dies within seventy years of touching them, know what I mean? But . . .'

'But?' The Doctor sipped his tea again.

'But then again, what if I'm wrong? What if by some million-to-one chance these things have some power that could destroy the Sloathes for ever? We're all going to die anyway, so what have we got to lose by trying?'

'A commendable attitude,' said the Doctor. 'If everybody gave up because things were hopeless, the whole vast panoply of galactic history would be reduced to an exponentially expanding mass of fissioning protozoa.'

He looked thoughtful for a moment. 'Then again, it'd save

156

a lot of shrieking misery and death, you'd get a net gain in biomass and nobody would find themselves at a loose end on Saturday nights.' He shrugged, and changed the subject. 'Tell me,' he said. 'I have it on good authority that our good captain is at some point going to murder us all in our beds. Is this in fact going to occur at any point? Will I have time to go and get my box Brownie?'

'What?' said Kiru, who had understood possibly a third of this. 'What are you talking about?'

'Many, and varied, and not to mention extremely protracted have been the tales of the fiendish Captain Li Shao, is the point to which I am referring,' said the Doctor, handing Kiru another ice-cold and brimming small beer which seemed to have simply appeared out of thin air.

'Ah yes,' Kiru said. He downed half of the beer. 'The "Fiendish Captain Li Shao". Let me tell you about the fiendish Captain Li Shao . . .'

<hr>

'. . . and they were still hanging out,' said Leetha, 'and so he made them clean up all the mess behind them afterwards! And then he took a great big butcher's hook and —'

'Right,' said Benny. 'Mouse-powered electrostatic egg whisk. Chamois-leather glove-puppet. Great big butcher's hook. Must have made their eyes water.'

'Oh no,' said Leetha darkly. 'Because he'd already personally and with much demonic sniggering and gloating . . .'

'I should have known,' Benny muttered to herself. 'Silly me for walking into that one.'

'If a monster like Li Shao gets his hands on the Eyes it would mean the end of us all!' the Sun Samurai cried. 'We must get away from him. We must conceal the Eyes of the Schirron from his filthy and unconscionably bestial clutches!'

Benny sighed. 'OK. The moment we land, we're over the horizon.'

'Horizon?' said Leetha.

'Sorry,' said Benny. 'I was forgetting. Let me see that book of yours again.'

Leetha handed over her soft-bound copy of the Book and Benny opened it at one of the pages she had marked with a scrap of paper (Benny was personally one of those who regarded the message more important than the medium, and would as happily read old chip papers as the finest illuminated chap-book. Leetha, however, had started growling menacingly the first time she made to turn a corner over, so she hadn't). The relevant passage read:

XIV: (ii)   And when the chosen does at last negotiate the Dread Portals of the Valley of the Scorpions of Glass, then shall She walk in Darkness for a Month of Days with neither Food nor Water. And the Jackals shall strip the Flesh from Her Bones and make to gnaw upon Her soft Members with many small noises of appreciation, and gusto, together with certain gaseous eructations of an indigestive and flatulent nature.

XIV: (iii) And then the Chosen shall walk through a Cleansing Wind, that shall scour Her Bones as though with a Scourge of Flails comprising knotted strings of neither more nor less than two and one-third Fingers in length.

XIV: (iv)   And then the Chosen shall walk through the Mouth of the Sand Snake, and shall pass through the Gullet of the Snake to a most wonderful Oasis where there is always Rain. But she shall turn Her Back upon this Oasis, for it is an Evil Place, and in that Act of Turning shall She discern the True Nature of the Treasure Within.

XIV: (v)   Thus spake Jastracoasto the Nabob, whereupon those assembled did make such Great Excoriations as, 'Give over!' and, 'Pull the other one, Fuzzy, for it does have Bells attached withal!' And Jastracoasto did then wax with Wrath unparallel'd, and did Smite them Mightily, shouting . . .

Well, I hope that's allegorical,' Benny said, 'because I for one don't particularly like the bit about the jackals.' She thought for a moment, then shrugged. 'Could mean anything

158

from a spiritual rite of passage to a set of literal directions corrupted through a couple of thousand years of reinterpretation. Possibly it's describing ablation. You know what ablation is?'

'What's ablation?' said Leetha.

'Something non-desert-dwellers experience in the desert.' Benny gestured vaguely to take in the entire world. 'In any environment there's all these little packets of information that you never notice because they're so familiar. They're just part of the world. I mean, you grew up in the jungle –'

'A city,' Leetha said. 'Rakath.'

'OK. You grew up in a jungle city. The point is, everywhere your eyes rest, they rest on a plant, or an insect or a bit of brickwork, or an item of clothing . . . God knows what else. It's around you all the time and you never notice it.

'In the desert there's nothing – at least, nothing that a mind unused to dealing with such a rarefied environment can recognize. There's nothing to see, nothing to hear and nothing for the mind to think about, so it lapses into fugue. The result is a sort of waking dreamstate: levels of cognition and association peeling off to expose the core, and that's ablation.'

'What?' Leetha said.

'The desert makes your mind stop and you see strange things,' said Benny patiently.

She became thoughtful for a moment. 'It's actually remarkably similar to the displacement trauma you find in urban warfare,' she said after a while. 'Not just because of the horror and the suffering and so forth, but through the simple ablation of environmental information – familiar buildings into piles of rubble, people you care about into sides of meat. It changes people. It dehumanizes them and simplifies their thinking. They do things automatically, think their simple thoughts automatically – for the simple reason that if they'd let themselves think or feel with any degree of complexity again, or tried to establish simple human contact ever again, the screams would be too big to get out of their mouths and they think it would kill them.' She frowned. 'It breeds fanatics, that terror. Compulsives. Any actual purpose will do so long as they can perceive it as paramount – absolutely overriding anything else.'

Leetha, suddenly, became aware that Benny was now

looking at her with a kind of sadness. 'I don't know what you're talking about,' she said angrily.

'No,' Benny said sadly. 'You probably don't.'

———∞———

Thus the good ship *Schirron Dream*, through the insubstantial clockwork, *en route* to the desert Wanderer of Prometheus and, subsequently, the destruction of worlds.

The Twentieth Chapter

On the surface of Planet X, a circular hatch opened with a rusty squeak and Pon Fuki Gek slithered out, gripping several iron rings sunk strategically into the planetoid's crust with hooked appendages, extending a streamlined carapace of hard, smooth platelets over itself against the abrasive wind. Pon Fuki Gek glanced, briefly, about itself with heavily protected eyes, then shot an extruded grappling line (a little sac of combustive gases in its clawed head carrying it some three-quarters of a mile) and began to haul itself across the surface.

Seismographs in the observation room of the Most Elevated and Puissant Kraator Xem (or, properly, a row of little Sloathes twisted into shapes approximating the function of seismographs) had detected a particularly heavy impact on the surface some time before, largely unnoticed during the general mobilization of the Sloathe fleet and the attendant relocation of Planet X's prisoners. Now the Most Elevated and Puissant Kraator Xem had had time to recollect it. In this particular section of the planet, it was Pon Fuki Gek's job to investigate such impacts, and to salvage what was salvageable.

Pon Fuki Gek dragged hirself across the surface, sucking hir slippery tendon line back into it, little rollers under it rolling across the ash and slag. Twice it repeated the process of firing hir grappling line and hauling it in.

As it approached the centre of the impact site, Pan Fuki Gek could not believe hir eye-analogues. Various items had hit the basalt moonlet before, and indeed hit it on a constant and regular basis, but these were commonly little more than extremely boring rocks, or lumps of rapidly melting ice, or the occasional crushed and decayed body of some aboriginal lost in the airspaces of the System. Occasionally there was something that the Sloathes thought of as a *nice* thing, or a *pretty* thing, but only very rarely, and hardly any of such nice and pretty things survived the fall.

Here, however, there were riches such as might be imagined in the dreams of Sloathe avarice. Artifacts and *objets d'art* lay everywhere or were scattered by the wind. In rapid succession, Pon Fuki Gek passed: a ruptured packing case spilling variegated globes of volcanic glass, some of which had survived intact and inside which, suspended in water, flecks of some glittering white substance swirled; a collection of battered and twisted brass instruments including a tangle that had once been three trombones, and a dented euphonium; a large and wide-scattered pile of interesting driftwood; a stuffed bloater affixed to a polished rosewood plaque; a large brass flywheel, fully ten feet across, from some long-disassembled internal combustion engine; a crushed gilt picture-frame twenty feet on a side, its actual canvas indiscernible since it was obscured by the five-ton galvanistical rotary lathe that had crushed it . . .

Pon Fuki Gek was so engrossed by the nice things and the pretty things around it that it entirely failed to notice as it trundled up a large and bulbous and suspiciously squishy hillock of ash. It was still inspecting an interesting collection of granite tombstones when the ash opened up and swallowed Pon Fuki Gek with a gulp.

There was the muffled sound of crunching mastication under the ash. Acidic vapour shot from buried vents. Then a massive and amorphous lump exuded itself from under the concealing crust, hundreds of small tentacles around its outer edge dragging its bulk in the direction from which the luckless Pon Fuki Gek had come.

And at length, it came to the hatchway. It spun the circular protruding handle, opened it up and then poured itself down it.

———✺———

The Sloathe ships were approaching the orbit of Reklon: hundreds of them, ranging from little nippy gunboats little larger than an actual live Sloathe of slightly larger than average size, to the massive dreadnoughts fully four hundred yards across.

In a polyp-chamber in the bowels of one of the smaller

freighters, close to the rear of the convoy, Roz Forrester gave a Sloathe in the form of a large and humpty-backed, three-eyed perambulatory porpoise on crab legs a final wipe with her chamois leather. 'OK?'

The Sloathe extended an ocular stalk and regarded its newly beeswax-and-lavender-sheened skin. 'Okey-dokey.'

'Give me my stuff, then,' said Roz. 'I need my stuff.'

'Hm.' The Sloathe regarded her. 'I don't think you want it.'

'Yes I bloody do,' said Roz.

The Sloathe appeared to be debating with itself. 'Okey-dokey,' it said at last. It extended a needle-appendage.

For a moment it hesitated, and for a horrible moment Roz thought it was going to put it away again. Then it whipped for her, fast as a cobra-strike and bit into her neck, just above the collarbone, where there were already an even half-dozen other half-healed punctures. Roz felt something splurting into her, and the warm relaxation that had lately come to take the place of an actual high. She was Red-Queen-racing now, she thought, busting her guts to stay at the exact same point where she started. She wasn't even getting the pop any more.

It would keep the little gestating thing inside her happy for a while, though. Was it big enough to feel, now, if you pressed your finger to a particular vein? Was it big enough to clog yet, like some ambulatory microtentacular blood clot? For days now she had reacted to every vascular twinge with the same vague and crawling horror as one would ordinarily experience looking in the mirror to suddenly find a new and crusty-looking mole.

She made her way through the slimy tunnels worming through the ship, avoiding the clusters of Sloathes wherever possible, heading for the areas where the System aboriginals were kept. As one who had been marked by the Sloathes, with the right smell on her, her position was something like that of a trusty in a prison block – and she and others like her had more or less the run of the ship, serving as degraded slaves in return for the alien substance that kept them alive. There was, after all, nowhere else for them to go.

The Sloathes never seemed to tire of being washed and groomed – though they had some difficulty in differentiating between various toiletry and cleaning products, so it was well to be wary if you didn't want to find yourself plunging your

hand into a bucket of caustic soda. They liked to keep a
number of slaves on manipulatory appendage, as it were,
should they ever feel the sudden need for a good scrub.

As much as possible, though, whenever she wasn't forced
to go out and score, Roz preferred to stay in the prisoner-
occupied holds and be with people of her own kind. She
wasn't quite sure when she finally had started to define this
collection of disparate captive hominid creatures as 'people
of her own kind', but it was probably a question of degree, of
utter inimicability versus relative empathy, the possibility
of basic emotional connection. She no longer found the
attempts of the prisoners to improvise catering or sanitary
facilities amongst themselves with what little they had, or
even the pathetic antics of the 'escape committee', laughable.
Now she saw them for what they were: a doomed but utterly
courageous attempt to retain a social cohesiveness, even in
the face of the destruction of their worlds and certain death, a
cohesiveness that on some indefinable level the Sloathes
never had and never would possess.

Bloody hell, thought Roz sourly, stroky nurture sicky-poo
or what? You'll be organizing a sodding group hug, next.

Thus Roz Forrester as she hauled herself through the ship.
Presently, she came to a place where the tube she was hauling
herself through bulged globularly, one side of its membrane
protruding through the leathery skin of the hull and perfectly
clear. This was presumably the hollowed remains of a
massive Sloathe eye-analogue, now serving the function of a
viewing port. Roz had passed through such chambers before,
but had merely seen the swirling flares of the energy field
that, she gathered, encapsulated the System.

Now she pressed her face to the slightly springy membrane
and peered through, hoping to catch some sight of their
eventual destination.

Chris Cwej, on his way back to the prison-holds from
giving a Sloathe a particularly frothy bubble-bath, found her
still staring, aghast, through the membranous porthole.

'Are you OK, Roz?' he said, laying a concerned hand on
her shoulder.

Roz shook him off. 'Can you see it?' she said in a small,
tight voice.

Cwej peered through the viewing port. 'Oh, yeah. That's

Reklon, apparently. I've seen it before, a day or two ago. I didn't tell you about it because I didn't want to upset you.'

'Well, thanks a lot.' Roz turned away from the awful spectacle and looked at him. As had she, Cwej had taken the advantage of regular access to sundry cleaning products to clean off the filth of their captivity on Planet X, but he still looked a mess: ashen-faced with bloodshot, red-rimmed eyes, hunched and twitching in his stained and battered tyrannosaur-skin jacket.

'How did you know I was here, anyway?' she said.

Chris Cwej shrugged, and the ghost of a grin twitched the sides of his mouth. 'Well, to tell you the truth, you could hear your distinctive mating cry of "Jesus sodding *Christ*!" halfway across the ship.'

———

The ice-Wanderer of Reklon comprised three separate irregular masses of core-rock caked together by permafrost and packed snow. Its pristine whiteness was disfigured by clumps of pine forest strewn along its central mass, and by an irregular collection of peaks upon one of its outer – several of which were, intermittently, volcanically active, belching smoke and ash or glowing like hot coals. A particularly interesting feature of this outer mass was what was known, by the native Reklonians, as the Headlights: a standing electromagnetic field producing a shimmering corona that extended into the visible spectrum from the ultraviolet.

It was pure coincidence that as one approached the Reklonian orbit, from a certain angle, it looked exactly like a huge, plump and fatuously jolly snowman, with a pipe. With a mauve hat on.

———

The Sloathe ships swung down into the Reklonian skies, skimming over the snowfields in single but jostling file like a crocodile of unruly, corpulent and snot-covered toddlers.

Reklon was now fully under Sloathe occupation, its settlements in blasted ruins, the vast majority of its original inhabitants slaughtered save for those who had been taken prisoner or those who had managed to escape to the inner Wanderers of the System. There were, however, a small minority of survivors. There were things that lived under the snows and were not detected. There were things, horrible things, that had concealed themselves by way of most foul and unholy magicks. There were the vestigial Reklonian brigand-tribes that roamed the ice-wastes, relentlessly pursuing a war of resistance against the occupying forces.

As the Sloathe ships passed over a certain snowbank, wolf's-fur-wrapped figures pulled back camouflaging tarpaulins piled with snow to reveal mortar racks and squat gunpowder rockets with stars and whooshes and explosions painted garishly and ineptly on them. They lit the blue twists of touchpaper, retired to a safe distance and shouted 'Hurrah!'

The rocket fusillade took out the final three ships of the rearguard, blowing them apart in the air like hydrogen-filled balloons touched by the burning tip of a cigarillo. Slightly forward of them, a moderately sized transporter, crippled by a nearby airburst, dropped out of the sky and plunged towards the snowswept plain.

Outside Roz heard muffled shouts and screams and rifle-fire, the chaos of pitched battle, though as she listened it seemed now to be diminishing in intensity: the screams of the desperate and dying supplanting the battle-screams of those who were actually killing. She hauled at the collapsed tangle of bonelike support struts that had caved in, crushing a number of prisoners, shutting off the exit of the hold in which she had been sleeping when the ship was hit. There was a large and warmly pulsing tender area down one side of her head, and she had no idea how long she had been unconscious before surfacing into the world to find that it had fallen in on her and she was trapped.

'Come on,' she snarled with desperate frustration. 'Come on . . .'

A slightly rank presence behind her. A hairy hand grabbed the strut. 'Let me help.'

It was Holf, the Reklonian she and Cwej had known on Planet X. One eye was swollen shut and his left arm hung dislocated and limp. Muscles bunching and shaking under the fur of his good arm, he wrenched at the fallen support with an inhuman strength. It creaked ominously for a moment, then came away. Holf shoved it to one side. He turned to regard her with his small bright functioning eye and gestured back towards the other shocked and wounded survivors in the hold, maybe twenty in all. 'Let's get them out of here, yes?'

Roz looked back at him. 'Thank you,' she said. It was all she could think of to say.

With the big Reklonian's help it was easier to clear the blockage, although Roz noticed that as he worked Holf kept his eyes fixed solidly on his hands and whatever was in them, flatly refusing to take in anything else. Laseem had been one of those crushed under the struts.

They hauled the tubeway open and a blast of chill air hit them. Deciding that the wounded would be as safe here as anywhere else for the moment, Roz and Holf made their way cautiously out into the partially collapsed tubing.

Bodies were strewn through it, Sloathe and humanoid, all bearing similar gunshot and puncture wounds.

'What the hell?' said Roz, puzzled and not a little alarmed.

They rounded a corner and came across their first living thing: a scrawny Reklonian in silver wolf's-fur robes, hung with kitbags and bandoliers of ammunition and knives, a clockwork machine-gun slung across his back; he was going through the clothing of a dead Anean. The Anean was now dusted with a bloom of frost, save for where thin strings of steam still rose from a number of knife wounds.

'Hey!' shouted Roz, furiously. 'What the hell d'you think you're doing?' She reached for her gun, preparing to bring it up in the procedurally correct two-handed manner – and was deeply shocked and startled when her fingers closed on thin air. It was only later, recalling it, that she realized she had momentarily slipped back into a street-cop mindset. Street-cop suddenly coming up against a looter in a riot.

The Reklonian spun on them with a snarl. She saw that he was wearing a little beret. 'We are glorious Reklonian liberation resistance movement,' he growled. 'And you are filthy collaborators.'

Then, with a simple casualness that gave them no chance to react, he simply raised his machine-gun and emptied the clip into Holf. At the time, Roz was merely aware of something falling with a thump on her periphery and spraying her with something warm and she didn't really feel much about it either way. It was only later, when there had been time to assimilate things, that in the privacy of her head she would relive the instant again. And again. And again. And again.

'Thus die all foul traitors,' the Reklonian guerrilla said calmly. Then he looked at Roz, and something in his eyes made her start to back slowly away.

'Thought we'd used up all the women,' he said happily, appraising her as he advanced. 'Little bit stringy but a little bit tough, I think. Might last longer.'

Her heels hit something that she could not, at this point, connect with Holf and she pitched backwards to hit the springy wall of the tube and slump down it. She looked up at the Reklonian with the gun, and at the second fur-clad figure who had appeared behind him, with another gun.

'Longer'n you,' she said as the butt of this second gun piledrived into the base of the guerrilla's skull.

———

Chris Cwej was wearing slightly bloodstained furs remarkably similar to those of the Reklonian guerrilla, and was similarly bedecked with scavenged weapons. He looked down at the guerrilla, and kicked him in the ear for good measure. There was a large bruise on his left jawline and a half-clotted gash across the back of his right hand. He looked at Roz with eyes wide and slightly dazed from recent trauma.

'I should kill him,' he said, perfectly calm – but with that calm that comes from profound emotional shock, where hatred or loathing or terror overload and simply fail to operate any more. 'But I'm not like him.' It was like a child being absolutely firm on this point. 'So I won't.'

He bent down and methodically began to strip the furs and weapons from the supine Reklonian, passing them to Roz. 'We're going to need them.'

'What happened?' Roz didn't want to say it, but she wanted to know what had happened.

'When we hit everything went crazy,' he told her. 'People and Sloathes just streaming out of the ship, trying to get out –

168

nd the Resistance people just cut down the lot of them. People
nd Sloathes alike. They didn't care.'

'Hey, listen,' said Roz, pulling on her new furs. 'Chummy
ere was talking about using up the women. What did he –?'

'I don't want to talk about it,' said Cwej.

'But he said –'

'I don't want to *talk* about it.' Cwej rounded on her with
sts clenched so tight that they shook.

'Oh, Jesus,' Roz said, quietly. 'We're just like the
loathes, aren't we? Only worse. We know what we're doing
nd what it means.' She was referring to the Reklonian
uerrillas and it didn't occur to her, then, that she was now
utomatically lumping together all the disparate aboriginal
habitants of the System, broadly, as people like herself in
er mind.

'I was held up in a crush,' Cwej said shortly. 'I had time to
ork out that something was wrong. I managed to pick up
me stuff from a guerrilla killed in the fighting and then I
ame looking for you.'

Roz got the distinct impression that he was glossing over a
umber of incredibly horrible facts at this point, but she
oked into his eyes and decided not to push it. 'So what do
e do now?' she said.

'We have to get away from here,' he said. 'They'll kill us if
ey find us.'

Roz checked over the clockwork gun and, after a certain
mount of trial and error, worked out how to load it. They
ade their cautious way through the body-strewn wreckage
f the ship. Occasionally, somewhere distant, she heard
aguely brutish voices raised in laughter and cheering.

Somewhere towards the outer skin, she caught a sudden,
rching movement amongst a pile of dead prisoners. She
auled back the half-frozen body of an Elysian, who had
een shot through the mouth with a musket ball, to find a
edium-sized Sloathe, lapsed into a trembling obloid and
ashed in several places to show the amorphous and complex
mi-solid structures within. Its exposed insides were filmed
ith glittery frost.

Roz caught the faint smell of lavender and beeswax. She
umped at the weakly twitching obloid, trying to bring it
ack into some semblance of life.

169

Eventually, an eye of sorts formed itself out of the mess in one of the gashes. It regarded her fearfully.

'Can you move?' she said to it. 'If you can come with us, we can help you live.'

'What are you doing?' a puzzled Cwej said. 'Leave it.'

'We can't,' Roz said. 'The Sloathes make the stuff we need to have to stay alive. How long are we going to live without it?'

The Twenty-First Chapter

From orbit Prometheus resembles a vast rock bowl, its dust-strewn concave face directed permanently to the Sun, of which it is the nearest Wanderer, its rim comprising lofty and impassable crags.

Across the deserts, the Promethean nomads range and conduct their sporadic but constant intertribal wars – and above them, intermittently, stalk the petroleum-powered slum stilt-cities – each following some complex pattern of its own, its internally combustive pistons churning, its hydrocarbon smokes belching, alternately wheeling and jostling with the others in an erratic and unending interactive dance.

The progress of the cities might be random, *is* apparently entirely random save that, at the correct time, all the cities come to rest on the tors at the centre of the Wanderer where, for this instant, the tribes have gathered in uneasy truce.

This is the Raintime, which occurs at an interval of eighteen solar months. The aquifers of Prometheus contain osmotic valves, which lock the water away until it can be pumped, *en masse*, under pressure, into the atmosphere to precipitate in a matter of hours.

The Raintime comes once every eighteen solar months, and when it comes it changes the world. Flashfloods burst the sides of gullies and stream across the dustbowl, swelling bone-dry oases to the size of lakes, which flow together, and still the waters rise, until fully half the habitable Wanderer is inundated to the height of a man. The fauna of the desert breaks, desperate, for the high ground towards the rim: jackrabbit and coyote and jackal, badger and bullsnake and kangaroo, packrat and gila and bobcat . . . their vicious private ecologies of predator and prey forgotten in the rush to escape the deluge. Vulture and thrasher and rubber-shrike respectively soar and flutter and bounce over these sudden new lakes in bewilderment, before lighting upon any perch they can find and sticking their heads under their wings to wait it out. And then the floods subside in a matter of hours and, briefly, the desert flowers. New-bloated cacti jettison pollen into the clean air, and their too-long-dormant floral cousins, too long trapped under heatcracked, blistered earth, push forth and ephemerally burn. Dandelions and the delicate, crisp white evening primrose, purple verbena, mariposa. Fragile jewels with lights inside them, sprouting from the dust.*

───▰▰▰───

As you progressed towards the mountains, the already wilting desert flowers gave out to brittle perennial scrubland and to zones where nothing would ever grow again. Not now. These were the battlegrounds of the nomad tribes, wrecked by centuries of warfare and, latterly, by incursive Sloathe attack. The ground was black with ash still sludgy from the rains, solidifying to a brittle and crunchy crust, here and there still smouldering slightly from what had once been blazing petrochemical fires.

The remains of makeshift fortifications, moats and trenches and craters devolved into each other like the whorls of a vast and grubby thumbprint; spent shell casings and germ-bomb canisters and subterranean mole-torpedo shrapnel covered the ground; the remains of brewed-up tanks and the shattered crystal frapranistan mesoreplivators of fiendish patent Death Ray machines protruded from it at sad angles; clockwork time-mine detonators ticked and ratcheted and atom bombs in suitcases hummed and bleeped menacingly under it. The air smelt of cordite, and pepper gas, and chlorine.

Somewhere one of the ravens, who wheeled constantly over the battlegrounds, lighted upon a particularly sensitive landmine and went: *Raaak*-**KABLAM!**

The sound startled Benny's pony; it snorted, and then broke into a fit of asthmatic coughing. Ahead of her, Leetha

* And coruscating.

reined in her own plodding and bronchially wheezing mount, and waited for her to catch up.

The *Schirron Dream* had landed on the Promethean central tor directly after the rains. This was a time of festival, apparently, and in the shadow of the stilt-cities with their watchful anti-aircraft guns trained on the skies in case of Sloathe attack, the hill had been decked with the horsehair and behemoth-skin huts of nomad encampments, bustling with commercial trade and the complex rituals by which the K'ans traded husbands and wives.

Li Shao had decided to stay here for a couple of days to trade the Promethean burial artifacts he had liberated from the Sloathe freighter, and Bernice Summerfield for one had been looking forward to a few days of rest and relaxation.

Leetha, however, had other ideas, and had eventually prevailed upon Benny to join her. The Doctor had elected to stay with the ship, merely asking Benny to try and keep the Sun Samurai out of trouble if that were possible.

Benny and Leetha had wandered through the encampments asking after the Valley of the Scorpions of Glass, eventually being directed to the tent of the *Shi Noor*, where they had learnt, from a wizened and stumpy-legged old man in a yashmak, that it was a place that was not to be talked of, best to be forgotten about and definitely not in the N'han Crags of the rim, over there. They had pooled their shore-leave money (strips of woven silk that were valid for the duration of the Raintime festivities) for a couple of elderly pack ponies, politely refused the offer of having them converted into pony kebabs at no extra charge, loaded up with as much food and water as they thought the ponies could stand without falling over and expiring, which wasn't much, and set out.

Now Benny gazed around herself at the blasted battle-grounds inclining to the foothills. Soon they would be packed with nomads thundering over the steppe and stuff and going at it hammer and tongs – but for now they were silent. A soft, hot wind blew over the ash and it smelt of swimming pools and fireworks. She settled her tinted desert goggles over her eyes again and pulled her grubby bandana up over her nose and mouth.

They seemed to be relatively safe here, so long as they

stuck to well-worn tracks – but Benny was feeling a sense of foreboding that seemed somehow unconnected with this desolate place: a pressure, a tension, almost unnoticeable at first, but which had been building up inside her for a while now. A faint ringing in the ears, like tinnitus, as though a strange music was playing at a pitch too high for the human ear. A vague enervation that made her body want to twitch rhythmically.

She mentioned it to Leetha: 'Are you feeling weird? Or is it just me?'

'How do you mean?' Leetha said, detouring her mount around a half-buried, unexploded brass and pig-iron rocket missile.

'Edgy,' Benny said. 'Jumpy. Like you want to jump around, know what I mean?' She snapped her fingers for a while to illustrate. It took a conscious effort to stop them snapping.

'Oh, that,' Leetha said dismissively. 'I'm feeling that, too. It's just Rojahama's Song-and-Dance.'

'Oh yes?' said Benny, uneasily.

'It isn't dangerous. It just builds up in people sometimes, in certain places. It affects everybody, and then you have the fit and it's over.'

'Fit?' Benny remembered the St Vitus's phenomenon of Earth's Middle Ages, caused by viral contamination of rye bread: mass 'dancing' fits as a result of massive neurological damage followed by seizure, collapse and death. 'Um. What sort of fit are we talking here, exactly?'

Leetha shrugged, unconcerned. 'You just hear strange things and do strange things – or, rather, you do what you were going to do anyway but you just do it strangely. It's difficult to explain. It isn't dangerous,' she repeated, 'mostly.'

They rode on. Overhead, the sun shone steadily for a while longer and then, by imperceptible degrees, began to fade towards the darkness of night. They reached the foothills by what Benny was trying and failing not to automatically think of as sunset, but which was of course the sun shining a reddish maroon from its eternally fixed point.

'We're here,' Leetha said. 'At last. The N'han Crags. We're here at last.'

174

'Yeah,' Benny agreed. 'We're here.'

Which was the exact point at which the *Schirron Dream* came shrieking out of the sky, detonated its retros and nearly landed on top of them.

━━━━━∞━━━━━

Benny's head was pounding now. The sensation was not entirely unpleasant. It was as though she were pumped full of something, filled to bursting point, and soon it was going to burst out.

She trailed after Leetha as the Sun Samurai stormed towards the ship, shaking her head, trying to clear it.

A number of the crew had come down the ramp from the main hatch, and were pitching tents while others watched the skies. Benny saw the unmistakable, bustling form of the Doctor and a couple of others as they organized a camp-fire. Evidently someone had suggested a night out under the clockwork.

Li Shao, Kiru and the floating form of Six were gathered around a small collapsible campaign table and conferring when Leetha and Benny arrived.

'You gave our horses heart attacks!' Leetha shouted, pointing down the scree of the N'han foothills to where both her and Benny's ponies lay on their backs with their legs in the air. 'They were very old and you gave them coronaries!'

' 'Evening,' Li Shao said amiably to Benny, ignoring Leetha. 'I was wondering where you'd got to.' He gestured vaguely towards the Doctor, who was currently and extremely enthusiastically rubbing a pair of dry sticks together over a pile of logs and tinder. 'Your friend told us not to worry, though, so we didn't.'

'What are *you* doing here?' Leetha spat at him.

Li Shao shrugged. 'Show them, Kiru.'

'Well, our sources suggested that we might find the Promethean Eye somewhere in the N'han,' Kiru said, pulling a thick sheaf of rather crumpled papers from his belt poke. 'But we already knew that –'

'Since we already knew where the Valley of the Scorpions of Glass was anyway,' Li Shao said. 'On account of how, before I became a nefarious freebooter feared far and wide throughout the known System, I was *Shi Noor*. The Valley of the Scorpions of Glass was a specific place of power in our –'

Leetha was staring at the papers.

'Kimon's notes!' she cried, snatching them from Kiru's hand.

'Hey, listen, Leetha,' Benny said as things juddered and pulsed in her head. 'I don't know if that's such a good –'

Leetha backed off, snarling, swatting the floating black bundle of Six out of the way.

'Hey, watch it, yeah?' the polymorph squeaked.

Li Shao went after her, glowering murderously. 'Give them back,' he growled. 'Give them back. Now.'

Leetha snarled at him and pulled a blade from her living armour. 'You keep away. You better keep away –'

'I think I've had about enough of this as I can stand,' Li Shao said, in the perfectly calm and reasonable voice of one who is not threatening – but is simply going to commit mayhem.

'Um. Excuse me again,' said the Doctor, appearing as if from nowhere.

All four heads, and one floating amorphous lump with eyes on stalks, snapped round to him in surprise.

'I'm really sorry to keep on doing this,' said the Doctor, 'but I have something to say.'

And then, in the privacy of Benny's own head, something painlessly burst.

Dimly, she was aware that, suddenly, all the rest of the crew of saurian Aneans and hairy Reklonians and humans and pigmies and frogskinned Elysians and – and every single one of them – had gathered around and were watching the Doctor, expectantly, too.

And then, from all around, from everywhere, came the sound of a full orchestra playing a sweeping prelude.

'What do you want to say?' she asked – and then she realized that, somehow, every single other person gathered here was simultaneously asking the exact same question. In precisely the same words.

It was like a chorus line.

The Doctor did a little soft-shoe shuffle to an arpeggio in Benny's head, apparently unaware that he was doing it.

'Well, I just really want to say,' he said in a smooth

176

and manly baritone, his words somehow fitting perfectly into the music of the aural hallucination, 'that as I wend my weary way/through space and time,/worlds thick with slime/where monsters win the day,/there's a little piece of sound advice/that helps me on my way . . .'

And the music in Benny's head came up.

———∞———

'How are you feeling now?' The Doctor handed her a steaming mug of something. Benny sipped it. Cocoa made with frothy buttermilk. She winced.

'Sorry.' The Time Lord dropped into a neat little lotus, rummaged around inside his linen jacket, discarding scraps of paper, a couple of yo-yos and a wind-dried amputated foot. 'Now I know I had some somewhere . . . ah yes!' He pulled out a little glass miniature of brandy, of the sort they gave away on the better class of twentieth-century airline, and upended the contents into her mug. 'Better?'

'Much, thanks.' Benny sipped again, stared into the flickering camp fire and shivered.

So that was Rojahama's Song-and-Dance. Never again. Never – she wanted to be perfectly clear about this – *ever* again. The memory of herself and thirty-odd other people doing a choreographed, high-kicking production number and singing 'everyone should learn to trust each other' would haunt her for the rest of her days, though she would try to forget it – and she made a mental note that should she ever experience a similar sense of accumulating internal pressure again, she must instantly brain herself with the nearest available rock.

'Well, I think it helped to break the ice a little,' the Doctor said genially, rubbing his hands together and glancing across the camp-site to where, by the light of a hurricane lamp, Li Shao, Kiru and Leetha were conferring at the campaign table with a remarkable lack of incipient mayhem. 'Music hath charms to soothe the savage breast, as it were.'

The Time Lord suddenly turned back to Benny with an evil grin. 'Did I ever mention the trouble I had once in the Gallifreyan retro-engineered spare-body-parts repository? When an unfortunate retrogenic mutation caused a –'

'Don't,' said Benny coldly, 'even think about it.'

177

'As you prefer.' The Doctor smiled. 'Though it certainly taught *me* a few things of which I was far too frightened to ask.'

'Well, it would, wouldn't it.' Benny sipped her cocoa and brandy. 'I just hope it's going to last, all this new-found accord. I mean, Leetha's not exactly what you'd call stable at this point. What with the denial and everything. She's liable to fly off the handle at any moment.'

The Doctor nodded, momentarily serious.

'I think she'll learn a few things,' he said. 'Now that they're actually talking and pooling their information.'

'Incidentally,' Benny said. 'What exactly was it you were doing with Six just now? You took them aside and had a long talk with them. What was that all about?'

The Doctor smiled enigmatically. 'That is something for tomorrow. That is not something for tonight. Things are going to become a little strange, and not a little unbelievable – but all shall become as clear as crystal shortly, Benny, never fear. Trust me. For the moment, though, I'm more interested in relationships between our Sun Samurai and our erstwhile captain. You've heard something of his history already, yes?'

'Only more than I can stand,' said Benny. 'One version of it, anyway.'

'There are other interpretations. I have it on good authority, for example, from one who was there, that the loss of the pocket rocket-gunboat *Wayfarer* was entirely due to the cowardice of its captain at the time, now deceased – one Percival Bosie Critchton. The nephew, I gather, of the Admiral of the Fleet.'

'Really?' said Benny. 'What about the thing with the degenomancers?'

'Well, from what I gather, after Li Shao shot Captain Critchton in the head and took the helm, the moon of Rubri was the only Systemic body within limping distance. They crash-landed and the degenomancers promptly used them for their foul and unnatural experiments. Li Shao escaped, still horribly wounded and with several scalpels still sticking out of his head, and was instrumental in freeing the others and stealing a ship. That's where they met Six, too, I believe.'

Benny shrugged. 'That's roughly what I heard. Different slant though.'

'Be that as it may, the interesting thing for our purposes is what he did when they finally made it to Sere. Now, privateering is a pretty competitive business, apparently. You need something of a reputation such as might chill the very bones of all who list to it and so forth, so what Li Shao did was –'

'– make up a bunch of stories about inventive uses for mangles and feather-dusters and stuff and put them about,' Benny finished for him. 'I kind of worked that out already, because in addition to being sex on legs, yummy as all get-out and incredibly vivacious, I'm also highly intelligent.' She glanced again to where the figures were gathered round the campaign table. 'I hope the poor dear isn't too disappointed when she finds out.'

Her face fell. 'Oh, look. All that nice brandy fortification seems to have gone.' She affected a couple of weak and invalidular coughs. 'I'm a martyr to the cold, you know.'

The Doctor went through his pockets again, unearthed another little bottle and peered at the label. ' "Bartle and Critchlowes Patented and Very Efficacious Horse Oil Linament". Made from genuine horses.' He proffered the bottle to Benny, and drank from it himself when she demurred, passing her a half-pint bottle of Bells in its stead.

'You know,' said Benny, when she had been sufficiently internally fortified for the nonce, 'I can never quite work out where you get all this stuff from.'

'It's just a knack.' The Time Lord shrugged. 'Sometimes it works, sometimes it doesn't. It helps if you don't worry it to death with overexplanation.'

He smiled, stuck his hand into a pocket, pulled out a perfect little crystal orchid, all fragility and filigree, and presented it to her with a neat little seated bob and half-bow. 'Sometimes everybody needs a little bit of pointless and inexplicable magic in their lives.'

The Twenty-Second Chapter

In a repository cavern in Planet X, a number of Sloathes were
looking interestedly up at an object sitting on a big pile of
cutlery. What with every one of their prisoner-slaves gone off
to Reklon, and having no creative impulses in themselves,
they now merely tended to go around pointing at things.

'Is very blue,' said one. Hir name was Slempi Ko. 'Is very
blue all over.'

'And is oblong,' said another, who was called Skleki
Yamo, rippling happily. 'Nice.'

'Yes,' Slempi Ko agreed. 'Oblong things are nice.'

'I like oblong things,' said the third, hopefully. 'I like nice
oblong things because they are very blue and nice.' Hir name
was Plog.

It was just beginning to dawn upon these particular
Sloathes that something had indefinably gone out of life of
late. It was becoming increasingly difficult to work up any
enthusiasm for anything. It was becoming increasingly difficult to string two coherent thoughts together. It was becoming increasingly difficult to think.

The reason for this was very simple. Sloathes were almost
entirely other-directed, relying parasitically upon other life-
forms to shape their thought-processes and even their physical forms – indeed, these three had already reverted almost
completely to lumpen obloids with only the most rudimentary of sensory organs and manipulatory tentacles.

While the prisoners had actually been here, on Planet X,
the mere fact of their presence had sent knock-on subliminal
associations ricocheting throughout the little moon, affecting
every Sloathe in a proliferating riot of metamorphosis. Now
the prisoners were gone, and the Sloathes were turning in
upon themselves – and finding there was nothing there. All

that was left were the artifacts, things that they were suddenly and fundamentally finding themselves unable to comprehend.

The smallest of the three, Plog, now slithered up the mound of silver knives and forks and spoons and peered at the object closely. 'Is blue here, too,' it pronounced firmly. 'Is blue down there and blue up here. Very interesting phenomenomenom.' It force-evolved a little vestigial ear. 'Is talk to me. Mutter-mutter, it go. Mutter-mutter-mutter-mutter-mutter.'

'Is going mutter-mutter,' Skleki Yamo informed Slempi Ko.

Slempi Ko rippled. 'What things it go mutter-mutter?' it said at last.

'It go grumble-grumble, moan-moan, *grrr!*' said Plog, reaching out a tentative slimy tentacle to feel the flat blue surface.

There was a sharp *crack!* of electrical discharge. Plog whipped hir slightly scorched exploratory tentacle back into hirself as it was thrown, tumbling, down the cutlery mound. It hit the floor of the respository cavern with a particularly wet and plibquous *plop!*

'Don't like oblong things,' it decided. 'Nice blue oblong things are nasty.' It slithered off to examine something else.

The other two Sloathes followed it vaguely.

'What you looking at now?' said Slempi Ko.

'Is looking at paper book things with words in,' Plog informed it loftily. 'They got big words in. Now is looking at little clock-thing and it say ten past hundred o'clock. Now is looking at very big thing. Is look like Sloathe but is very, very big. Is going glurp-slurp in front of me, and is opening big, big mouth and is very, very, very . . .'

———≈≈≈———

In the bare and half-buried remains of a little canvas tent on the plains of Reklon, by the dimly flickering light of an all-but expended hurricane lamp, Roz Forrester flipped through a crumbling and ice-flecked diary:

Storm coming in from the east [an entry read]. Will try to make the plateau before it hits, and we must pray to

181

the Gods that our endeavours will have not been in vain. Huskies are most frisky, this morning. Am beginning to have serious doubts as to the efficacy of the bromide. Arcron complains of minor frostbite to little toe. Sline bearing up well, as befits a gentleman of the Old School.

Roz shrugged, and flipped on further through the diary:

Storm continues unabated. Cannot see a hand in front of face. Have killed the last of the huskies, now – food more important. It looked at me when I cut its throat. Arcron's leg has turned gangrenous. Smell is appalling. Sline still bearing up, a veritable tower of strength.

The next entry read, in handwriting that was little more than a shaking and tear-smeared scrawl:

I will never see my darling golden-haired Amelia again. Resigned to that now. Fear that we have shot our bolt. Husky meat is almost gone. Arcron worse.
    Sline is gone. 'I'm just going out,' he said. 'I may be some time.' Weep manly tears at his noble sacrifice – oh, Gods, if such there be, take note that this was a *lion* amongst men. Can't go on now. Too overcome.

Roz turned over the page. The last and almost illegible entry read:

Five days without food now. Almost too weak to hold pencil. Arcron and self near to death. All is hopeless.
    We have vowed, with the last of our mortal strength, to go out into that bitter wind and find Sline's body. Give him decent hero's burial before we ourselves die. It is all we can do now.

Roz stuck the diary in a pocket and crawled out of the tent. She walked across the hard-packed snow, past the tethered woolly behemoth they had stolen from the Reklonian guerrillas, around a small drift and to the little log cabin less than twenty metres away.

Inside, Cwej was banking the big iron stove with cordwood from the pile they had found outside, while the Sloathe they had rescued sat on the fur-and-blanket-piled bed and peaceably opened a big tin of nutritious stew from the well-stocked larder with a little claw appendage.

'Hi, Roz,' Cwej said as she came in. 'Did you find out why there were three dead bodies in here? And why two of them had their hands around the other guy's throat?'

The glorious Reklonian liberation resistance and indiscriminate murdering movement had soon given up on chasing them, partly because of Chris Cwej's marksmanship with his liberated clockwork machine-gun – but mostly because Roz had found a half-empty and long forgotten packet of rolling tobacco in her jacket and had applied an old horse-racing trick. It wasn't how much you had, it transpired, but where you in fact stuck it, and the purloined behemoth had fairly flown across the snowy plain. Roz for her part had gripped, white-knuckled, the juddering side of the pine and leather howdah and prayed to God she wouldn't get too desperate for a smoke.

The Sloathe they had rescued was called Sgloomi Po. For a number of hours it had remained unconscious, so far as they could tell, while its wounds visibly closed. Then it extruded a couple of eyes and regarded them shyly.

It seemed almost pathetically anxious to help them. Roz thought it was just being sneaky, but Cwej was of the opinion that the sheer fact that they outnumbered it two-to-one and were thus the dominant faction had somehow affected its basic thought processes. Sloathes lived their lives through others, and now Sgloomi Po had only the pair of them to draw upon to give it form. Roz had contented herself with informing the Sloathe that if it did anything suspicious whatsoever, if it even *looked* like it was going to transform into transmitter-shapes and contact its fellows, she would personally chop it in half with her machine-gun at point-blank range.

She had also pointed out to Cwej that having an effectively endless supply of the addictive alien venom to hand was a very, very dangerous thing indeed – and they had resolved to watch each other very closely.

Now, after a restful overnight sojourn in the little log cabin, they were heading in the same general direction as the Sloathe ship had been flying before it was shot down. This was also incredibly dangerous, of course, but they knew next to nothing about Reklon except that they wanted to get the hell off it. Sloathe ships were the only available option, and it might just be possible to board one and remain undetected.

Now the plains gave way to dense coniferous forest. They dismounted from the behemoth and led it along a twisting pathway by the reins attached to its tusks.

Sgloomi Po bounded along in front of them in a manner remarkably similar to that of a large and friendly and overexcited dog. It barrelled into a snowdrift, burst out of the top and bounced up and down. 'Is big fun, yes?'

'Marvellous,' said Roz, who was still entirely convinced that the Sloathe was having them on.

They pressed on. After a while, Cwej said: 'Y'know, I just can't shake the feeling that we're being watched.'

'Oh yes?' said Roz. 'What is it that is making you feel as if we're being watched?'

Cwej looked thoughtful. 'Probably all those little doors sunk into the tree-trunks that keep opening a crack, and these beady little menacing eyes peering out before they slam firmly shut again. That's what makes me feel as if we're being watched.'

'It's probably your imagination,' said Roz. 'Ow!'

'What, like that stripy candy-cane sticking out of the forest floor that you've just tripped over?' said Cwej, innocently.

(Interpolatory textual note: Roz Forrester's reply appears to have been entirely mistranslated, inviting in its extant form as it does a well-dressed and neatly turned-out bottom to suck an item of anatomy she could not possibly possess. It has therefore been excised.)

It was at this point they heard a sound. *Shring-ching-shing-a-ling,* it went. *Shring-ching-shing-a-ling-shring-ching-shring-a-ling-ching.*

There was a ragged and clottedly rattling snorting and the stumbling trample of hooves. A hulking, ragged form came round a bend in the path with the hiss of runners through snow.

'Hello, little girl,' said a moist and gloaty voice. 'Hello, little boy. Have you been a good little girl and boy? Or have you been *bad*?'

This time the distinctive cry of Roslyn Forrester could be heard half-way across the Wanderer.

The Twenty-Third Chapter

In the morning, when the Sun lit up, Nathan Li Shao and Leetha T'Zhan toiled up the foothills of the N'han. Behind them, down the steppe and across the blasted desert, faint and distant dustclouds indicated the progress of nomad tribes on their horses and behemoths and in their jeeps and tanks. Soon the desert would be a war-zone again.

'I still don't know how I can trust you,' Leetha said, negotiating a boulder-strewn crevice. 'How can I trust you?' She had elected to come with him for the simple reason that if he was going to be around, she was damned well going to keep him where she could see him – and the first move he made that was even slightly suspicious, he was going to get the surprise of his suddenly terminated life.

Li Shao shrugged. 'You'd never find the·Valley without me. The pass leading into it is too well hidden for that. You need me if you want to find it. Trust doesn't come into it.'

'Why did the *Shi Noor* hide it?' Leetha said. 'I thought it was a holy place.'

Li Shao frowned. 'It's not a holy place. It's a place of power. Different thing, and it's nothing good.' He shifted his pack on his shoulder and looked up at the grey, forbidding mass of the Crags. 'Foul things reside therein that would pull your face off as soon as look at you. Sundry creatures with the vampire virus; killer rodents of remarkable size and ferocity . . . people have tried to enter, over the years, or so they say. At least they've said they were going to. Not one man or woman who ever went up through the pass came back to tell the tale.' He looked at her. 'Possibly it has to be somebody who was "Chosen" – whatever that actually means.'

'That's why you insisted that everybody else remain at the ship?' Leetha said.

'That's why.'

Leetha looked at him, a little strangely. 'So why are *you* doing this? Why are you here? You've said before that you don't believe in the Eyes.'

Li Shao nodded. 'Nor so do I. But there were others who wanted to try, Kiru for one, that Doctor chap for another, and I . . .' For a moment he looked almost shamefaced. 'I'm the captain. If anybody's going to blithely walk into certain death, it's going to be me. I have to take the responsibility.'

They climbed on. Presently, Li Shao began glancing about himself intently. 'We're almost there. It's familiar. I was found somewhere around here, as it happens.'

'Found?' said Leetha.

'By the *Shi Noor*,' Li Shao said. 'I'm a foundling. They found me as a baby, apparently, in the broken shell of a meteorite, sitting in a bed of mariposa and playing a reed flute to a noble cormorant – a sight most surpassing odd, because the noble cormorant is indigenous to other climes, and you couldn't get flute-reeds for neither love nor money, what with the System-wide embargo on flute-reeds at the time of which I speak.'

'You're having me on,' Leetha said.

Li Shao grinned. 'That's what my adoptive father said – but then again my adoptive father's name was *Rha-Ghang-Sung-Ka* – which in the old *Shi Noor* tongue means: One-Who-Continually-Speaks-the-Inveterate-Shit-of-the-Baldy-Headed-Behemoth – which might give you some idea.'

'Hm,' Leetha said, thoughtfully. 'Not that it makes any difference for a couple of reasons, but was there any mention of a caul? Were you born with a caul?'

'Probably. Means I'll never be drowned, so long as it is kept secure within a firmly stoppered jar reserved for that same purpose.' Li Shao shrugged. 'This is a desert Wanderer. Big deal. What do you think?'

'I think,' said Leetha, in a suddenly uneasy voice, 'that there's somebody following us. Did you hear that?'

From behind them, approaching, came the sound of someone scrambling over rocks, falling flat on his face and cursing in a polyglottal tongue that neither of them could understand. A minute later, a small figure came bounding round an outcrop, linen suit flapping, his fedora jammed firmly on his head and a huge coil of rope with a grappling hook slung over his shoulder. Floating behind him came the black bundle of Six.

'I overslept,' said the Doctor accusingly. 'Why didn't you wake me?'

'Because you weren't coming,' said Li Shao. He should have known, he thought, that the Doctor was going to turn up at some point, posted orders to the effect that absolutely everyone was to stay in camp notwithstanding. The irritating little bugger had turned up, like a dud penny, everywhere else so far.

'Where's Benny?' asked Leetha.

'Ah, well.' The little man shrugged. 'Benny's feeling a little fragile this morning. The last I saw of her she was leaning over the sink in the ablution and going, "Oh, my Jesus bleeding Christ, I think I'm going to die!" Something she ate, I suspect. Everything she ate, probably.' He regarded the two of them with his infuriating, innocent smile. 'So what's the plan?'

'The plan is,' said Li Shao, 'that you go back down the hill, confine yourself to quarters and I'll deal with you later. You have no place here.'

'Oh, I do,' said the Doctor. 'I really think I do. I have some small idea as to what you're in fact up against, and what you're going to have to do. Have a sweet,' he said, proffering a crumpled bag.

Bemusedly, Leetha took one. 'Interesting flavour,' she said, chewing. 'What is it?'

'Chocolate-coated liquorice, garlic and spam,' said the Doctor happily. 'Garlic to deal with the undead, spam to deal with the half-dead and liquorice to keep you regular.'

'And what are you doing here, Six?' said Li Shao over Leetha's startled spluttering.

The black bundle revolved slowly. 'Big talk we have with Doctor-man, yes? Make suggestions. Make sense, think we. Listen to the man you really should, think we.'

Li Shao thought about it. The Doctor had stuck his nose in uninvited any number of times – and every time he had proved useful and even necessary in some unforeseen manner. He shrugged. 'Come along if you want to. What do I care? It's your funeral-rite.'

They ascended. After some short while Leetha said: 'Li Shao? You'll recall how you mentioned the *Shi Noor* had hidden the pass into the Valley so that none might be tempted to enter it?'

'Yes,' said Li Shao.

'Well, possibly I misunderstood,' said Leetha, 'but a big plank of timber painted with diagonal yellow and black stripes, a mound of skulls and a sign reading, in seven different languages: DANGER! VALLEY OF THE SCORPIONS OF GLASS! KEEP OUT! THIS MEANS *YOU!* doesn't exactly suggest concealment to *me*.'

———

Nothing moved here. Nothing sang. Nothing played the spoons after they prevailed upon the Doctor to stop it. Deposits of scintillating crystal ribbed the Valley, extending to its bare rock floor in serried ranks, like the legs of some monstrous mutant millipede slit along its length and pulled inside-out.

The Valley twisted and turned, narrowing to the width of a man. Above them the gap between the Valley walls narrowed to a thin line of sunlight, and then disappeared altogether: they were in a tight, cramped tunnel bored through the living rock of the Crags. They lit their hurricane lanterns and their galvanistic lamps.

Vampire chickens shrittered and scuttered in the dark, occasionally taking startled flight, their plump and ragged flapping forms bursting past, talons scrabbling and scratching in their panic, but doing little damage thanks to the Doctor's sweets (to which they were not partial), to flutter and thump off down the tunnel.

The tunnel grew progressively narrower, forcing them to stoop, first, and then to crawl – and then suddenly ended in a wall of solid rock.

Before this, in the rocky floor, was a sharp-edged and perfectly circular hole. A milky, greenish luminescence shone from it, solid-seeming and almost tangible, so that it seemed to be filled with some all-obscuring, lambent fog. They hammered in crampons and abseiled down through the hole, noting how their actual corporeal forms stood out, sharply, against the solid-seeming light but that everything

189

else was rendered invisible, so that their hands appeared to be gripping thin air rather than their stout hemp climbing lines.

There was the ghostly sound of wind-chimes, half-heard, half not, so that if one put a hand to the ear one might upon the instant cry, 'Hark! Can you not but hear the sound of distant faerie tambourines?' Until, again, they prevailed upon the Doctor to stop it.

They reached a flat surface, a floor of sorts, hard and smooth like polished rock to the touch, but invisible in the miasmic light.

Leetha knelt to run her hands over it. 'So what do we do now?'

'I have no idea.' Li Shao felt around himself in the hope of finding a cavern wall. There was nothing. He turned to the figure of the Doctor and the floating form of Six (who had declined the use of a rope and had simply floated down). 'Do you have any suggestions?'

'Is funny light,' said Six. 'See through same can we not. As good as we, your guess, we think.'

'I believe,' the Doctor said, absently glancing about himself, 'from what I understand of the legends, that one simply has to walk. I think any direction will probably do.'

Li Shao looked at him sharply. 'You can see here, can't you? You can see where we are.'

'Not exactly.' The little man frowned. 'There are certain extradimensional anomalies. I can intimate certain possible relationships, but there's nothing I could translate into terms you could possibly understand –'

'Try me,' said Li Shao flatly.

'Ah, well, the friplits in this particular polyfactal cross-section are evidencing a remarkably erratic sense of paeorpolation, resulting in a marked increase of the Prani-Shenko xeno-quinquilistulory factor, which in turn, so far as this particular sheaf of the perceivable mesh is concerned, is tending to result in a direct suppression of the collective grelking mommet, and thus an acute but purely localized simulation of the effects of a high-density meso-*Muludharic* field.' The Doctor beamed. 'I trust that satisfactorily answers any questions you might have at this point.'

'Oh,' said Li Shao dismissively, 'that.'

'Is entirely puts the different complexion upon things yes,' said Six.

'You might have mentioned it before,' said Leetha. 'I was getting worried for a while there.'

They walked. They would never have a clear memory of how long they walked. Their surroundings remained utterly blank and the blankness ate into their minds, shutting down conscious thought, distorting their sense of time and memory. They might have walked for hours, or days. Or years.

And then the change came, instantly, like the flick of a galvanistical switch.

They were suddenly on a flat and perfectly featureless white plain, stretching to infinity under a burning desert sky. The heat of it slammed down upon them, like a physical thing, like a mile-wide red-hot flat-iron blistering their skin and baking their flesh to their bones with its radiant heat.

'Li Shao!' The shout was like a croak in scabbed and consumptive lungs, amplified through its sheer desperation. Nathan Li Shao's head jerked round: he felt the skin on his face peeling, flakes of dry-leached skin, torn loose by the movement, falling from his neck.

Through parched, raw eyes he was dimly aware of the Doctor, the floating form of Six. Nearer and slightly more distinct, the figure of Leetha.

She put her dry hands to her face and spongy bits of it fell off.

'I feel strange,' she said in a quiet and perfectly calm voice. 'I feel so strange . . .'

And then other forms crystallized out of the heat-haze. Jackals, walking on their hind legs, with bowler hats and with little wicked daggers clutched in their forepaws.

'L.s.d,' said one of them in a plummy and orotund and gloatily self-satisfied voice. 'Pounds and shillings and pence!' A thick rope of drool fell from its slavering jaws.

'The economy has never been in better shape!' shrieked another.

'Sheckels and drachma and dollars and krona,' agreed the first. 'Deutschmarks,' it added with crushing finality.

'Slip the blade between the ribs and give it a twist,' sniggered a third, waving its dagger for emphasis.

'Oh, my various gods!' Li Shao croaked, as the abhorrent and unthinking horror of them burst upon him.

The back-stabbing, money-grubbing pack of jackals fell upon them.

━━━━

Back at the ship, Benny staggered into the galley. She nodded blearily to several crewmen who were enjoying an early lunch and poured herself a mug from the pot of coffee steadily turning to viscous sludge on the range. Kiru was at one of the tables, his half-eaten breakfast at his elbow, poring through Kimon's notes.

'Y'know, I'm positive there was alcohol in that scotch last night,' she said to him. 'So where did everybody go? Leetha wasn't there when I woke up, and I can't find Li Shao or the Doctor anywhere.'

'They've gone,' Kiru said. 'Nathan and that Leetha woman went up to the pass at lighting-up time, and the Doctor and Six went after them maybe a half hour after that.'

'*What?*' Benny thumped the table so hard that a couple of greasy plates bounced. 'Oh, the sneaky little sod,' she said indignantly. 'I should have known he was up to something when he let me get pissed last night. He normally just looks at me very pointedly and makes me feel guilty till I stop. Oh well . . .' She stood up briskly, hung on to the table until the world stopped spinning around her and attempted to inject a little forceful vigour into her ethanol-desiccated vocal cords. 'I suppose we'd better go and try to catch them up. You coming or what?'

Kiru looked up at her. 'I really don't think that would be a good idea. The Doctor had a word with me before he left, and –'

'And let me take a wild guess,' she said sourly. 'You somehow found yourself believing every word of it, right?' She was going to have a sharp word with the Time Lord about this, she decided. Occasionally smoothing the way with the old alien mind-control was all very well, but this was getting beyond a joke.

'He told me some of his theories concerning the Valley of the Scorpions of Glass,' said Kiru. 'I didn't understand much

192

of it – but he was adamant that you, in particular, should not attempt to follow him. Something about the fact that while those indigenous to the System are acclimatized to a certain extent and can deal with certain disruptions, the shock of them would almost certainly shut your central nervous system down in shock and kill you instantly.' Kiru shrugged. 'I didn't understand above a half of it, but he was very specific on that point.'

'Shut my central nervous system down in shock and kill me instantly, eh?' said Benny.

'That's what he said. He also said to tell you that he really means it, and if he comes back to find you with your neuropeptides fried and half your axon membranes prolapsed on the floor, you won't get any sympathy out of *him*.'

Benny thought about it. 'Well, he might just be saying that – but all things considered I think I'll give it a miss, then.' She glanced over Kiru's shoulder at the notes. The topmost sheet showed a blue line, presumably a river, winding through representations of foliage. There were a series of red crosses and circles annotated in the same colour and in the late Kimon's spidery hand. 'That's the jungle, right?'

'That's Aneas.' Kiru flipped through the notes until he came to a painstaking watercolour illustration: a tree in cross-section, its roots and branches radiating in dense tangles from the central point of a gnarled trunk. The 'upper' branches were matted together to the point of solidity: a solid 'ground' from which the other jungle flora grew.

Kiru tapped the sepia-delineated, depending whiskery roots of the lower section. 'Those are the Rootlands, where live the hamadryads and blindy-eyed kobolds and the Morlocks with their moleskin trousers. A dangerous place, so it's fortunate that from what I can gather the Anean Eye is located on the Top . . .' he flipped back to the map he had been examining before, 'somewhere along the mighty Anacon river, with its crocogators and strange marsupials and lost tribes of pale-skinned monkey-pigmies. The Doctor was of the opinion that you might have some helpful suggestions.'

'He probably just wants to keep me occupied and out of mischief,' said Benny. 'OK. What does it say?'

Kiru turned to a section of text and read it out:

Thus it was upon the death of *Ankara-Ha-Ha* that her Remains were entombed with the Eye that they might remain Inviolate. And her Sepulchre was surrounded with mechanisms of such exquisite ingenuity that might seriously Inconvenience those that might enter the Tomb, in that their limbs might be severed and their heads might be skewered by way of Cunning Blades and suchlike shooting out of the walls. And this was, in the common parlance of those Worthy Ancients, merely the Icing upon the Donut, since to guard the Tomb was a Dread Guardian that it might pull the head off and suck the blood out ere one ever got to it.

For this was in the Old Days, in the days when the Gods walked. We know, that when the Gods were at last killed, some few of their lesser number survived in hiding, and it has been suggested by some that this Guardian might be one of these same that yet lives . . .

'It goes on in that vein at some length,' said Kiru. '*Ankara-Ha-Ha*, I think, was the Anean goddess of carnal desire, said to appear in her aspect of a huge-breasted woman with a rubber glove, who taunted those who followed an ascetic way of life and made them shamelessly interfere with themselves in the middle of the night. Pretty blood-curdling stuff, eh?'

'Certainly frightens the life out of me,' said Benny. 'Anything in there on these "mechanisms of exquisite ingenuity and cunning"?'

'Only a selection of detailed schematic blueprints in the appendix,' said Kiru.

'Ah, well.' Benny sat down and rubbed her hands with brisk anticipation. 'Strange alien radiations that pull your axon membranes out and eat them I can take or leave – but antiquitous temples of the Old Gods packed with deathtraps and guarded by monsters of utter evil that like to pull your head off, I'm your lad every time.'

Deep within the Valley of the Scorpions of Glass, Nathan Li Shao cried out with sheer, unthinking horror as a jackal caught him in the chest and bore him to the quasi-ground.

194

'A little hardship and probity now will give you five whole shiny pennies of the *pound* next year!' it slavered in his face, its eyes burning and flare-pulsing spasmodically like blown coals, and then it fastened its jaws upon the crisp-fried skin of his throat to take an experimental nip.

Li Shao struggled under the rank and matted weight, but to no avail. Peripherally, off to one side, he was aware that Leetha T'Zhan was shrieking, terrified beyond belief, something about how she didn't *want* to go down the marmoset's hole and eat his magic jam tarts.

Then, suddenly, she stopped.

The jackal on top of Li Shao spat out a lump of partially cooked flesh. 'Privatization is the only viable option!' it shrieked. 'Would you care to see a prospectus?'

'I believe,' said a quiet voice beside Li Shao, 'that my client is already well served in that area.'

Something slimy and, somehow, more solid and *real* was pressed against Li Shao's face – and then the form of the jackal changed.

Now, standing over him, giggling behind its surgeon's mask and bringing down its rusting and encrusted scalpel, was the rotting form of a degenomancer. It was just like he remembered it, in that foul time on Rubri, when the degenomancers had cut into his head.

It's not real! Li Shao thought, his mind desperately refusing to believe this final horror. It's not possible. It's not real!

And then the degenomancer was gone. Just like that. His vision was once again filled with pale and solid greenish light. Forms moved within it, disturbing, but diffuse and without triggering the unthinking horror of his vision of the jackals.

The pin-sharp figure of the Doctor and the floating form of Six looked down at him. Off to one side, Leetha was gasping, short of breath but apparently calmer now, getting groggily to her feet.

Li Shao sat up and looked down at his intact and healthy body. 'What happened?' he said, weakly.

'The electromagnetic activity of your brains was almost terminally disrupted by the standing field here,' said the Doctor. 'I believe you'd call it a curse or a cantrap, laid by

195

whoever originally sought to protect this place. It's been accumulating since we entered the Valley – you probably noticed some of its incidental effects. It induced visual and aural hallucinations utterly inimical to you, and your minds nearly tore themselves apart trying to interpret them.' He turned to the polymorph. 'Luckily, Six was able to push you through the abreaction by the judicious application of their psychic sting-reflex, diverting your sensorium-impulses into a slightly more familiar, and not to say possible horror.'

'Worst thing in the world,' said Six, smugly.

'It was rather fortunate that Six, themselves, remained unaffected due to their incompatible neurology,' added the Doctor. 'And fortunate for you that you have been exposed to background emissions of the same general sort since birth, and thus have a certain innate degree of immunity to them.'

Li Shao scratched his head, running back through the events of the past few minutes in his mind. 'But why was it so horrifying? Jackals talking insane gibberish. It was surpassing ridiculous, and not a little improbable. There was no possible way it could have been real. So why was I so horrified?'

'The basic ridiculousness was the point,' said the Doctor. 'The mind can cope with any number of ridiculous notions, absurdities and aberrations – in a story, for example – because the actual physical experience of them is of merely listening to someone speaking words, or of reading words on a page. A direct confrontation with their actuality, however, could and would be lethal.'

The Doctor gestured about him at the shifting light. 'There are degrees of perceivable actuality built into consciousness itself, and based upon the very structure of the universe which it perceives. The sudden appearance of a tiger in a drawing-room, for example, is highly unlikely – but possible enough within its basic terms of reference that the mind can cope. But if the tiger was wearing a smoking jacket and a cravat, and politely offered you some tea and cake, it would be so absolutely and fundamentally outside what you knew to be possible that it would, simply, drive you mad until you killed yourself to make it stop.'

'What's so odd about that?' said Leetha, who had by now walked over to join them. 'The talking tigers of Aneas are known throughout the System as the most considerate and courteous of hosts.'

The Doctor deflated slightly. 'Perhaps I picked an unfortunate example. Pick something that by its very nature could not possibly talk to you or offer you anything.' He looked at Leetha pointedly. 'An Anean marmoset, for example. The fact remains, however, that whatever you experienced was so at odds with what you fundamentally knew to be possible that your reaction to it nearly killed you.'

'Is it going to happen again?' said Leetha uneasily.

The Doctor grinned, evilly. 'Possibly. But you know, now, deep in your bones, that all is illusion. It won't be so bad.'

'You yourself seemed singularly unaffected,' said Li Shao, thoughtfully.

'Ah, well,' the Doctor beamed. 'That might be because I have a rather singular set of notions as to what is in fact possible or not.' He gestured onward with his umbrella. 'Now, if we're all quite recovered, shall we proceed?' He strolled off, whistling cheerfully.

Li Shao turned to Leetha as they followed after him. 'Do you ever get the feeling you're being led around by the nose? I'm not exactly sure I like it. What exactly did you see, anyway? And what did you see when Six stung you out of it?'

'Mind your own business,' snapped Leetha.

'Suit yourself,' said Li Shao.

~~~

They walked on, through the hallucinations. Winged serpents with the faces of babies fell from a chequer-board sky and systematically bit their heads off. They found themselves, apparently, underwater where piranha fish with the squeaking and somewhat bedraggled snouts of mice stripped them down to the bone, so that for a while they assumed the aspect of walking bloodstained skeletons. They passed through a quasi-space – perhaps the strangest of all – where strange globes bigger even than a Wanderer swung around a vast ball of burning gas, against a jet-black backdrop scattered with tiny, twinkling points of light.

For her part, Leetha became increasingly thoughtful. When Six had shocked her from her own private horror of a

197

singing marmoset with an egg-timer and a chef's hat, she had again seen the hideous nightmare vision of the Fiendish Captain Li Shao of her dreams – and she had been shocked out of her fugue, more than anything else, by her sheer surprise at the disparity between the monstrous Li Shao of her fears and the patently human figure in the red leather, who toiled through the shifting illusions beside her.

She found herself looking at Li Shao closely – or, at least, closer than she had let herself look before. It was becoming harder to associate this striking (and even, if she was honest, rather attractive) man with the monster she knew him in fact to be.

She consciously and firmly steeled herself against this line of thought. That way lay madness.

The visions flickered and flared behind their eyes, building up a sickly pressure that, suddenly, they were only aware of when the pressure suddenly released. The invisible ground suddenly juddered under them and then, in some indefinable way, locked solid with a series of heavy clicks.

A blinding light burst over them, driving them to their knees. They climbed to their feet, dazed, blinking, looking about themselves.

'I think,' said Li Shao, 'that we're through.'

They were at the wall of a cavern less than a hundred yards wide, lit by bright sunlight from light wells running down its walls. Beside them, trailing from a hole high up in the ceiling, hung the ropes down which they had made their descent, hours before.

Before them, a perfectly clear pool, its crystal waters frothing and sparkling to one side as they were struck by a waterfall.

About them, a profusion of colour. Clumps of tiny flowers sprouted from every crevice, blossoms of every conceivable shade clung to vines strung through the actinic light. Succulent and moisture-beaded fruits hung ripe for the plucking.

'It's beautiful,' Leetha breathed. She plucked an apple-like fruit of a deep and lustrous reddish-gold and put it to her mouth.

'*No!*'

The Doctor, who had been glancing about himself with a sour and unimpressed scowl, rapped her knuckles with his umbrella, causing her to drop the fruit. He rounded on her, his eyes boring into hers. Leetha backed off with a startled snarl, instinctively reaching for a blade from her living armour.

'What does the Book say?' the Doctor snapped. 'You should know it by heart, by now. You've inflicted it on Benny and myself often enough. What does it *say*?'

' "But she shall turn Her Back upon this Oasis," ' Leetha said, startled into quoting automatically, ' "for it is an Evil Place, and in that Act of Turning shall She discern the True Nature of the Treasure Within . . ." '

The Doctor nodded. 'Precisely.'

Spinning pinpoints exploded behind her eyes and, once again, everything changed.

'It was just another vision,' Li Shao said.

'The final vision,' said the Doctor. 'The final defence.'

Structurally, the cavern was unchanged – only now the light from the wells was something sickly and putrescent, illuminating runelike projections on the walls that seemed to writhe disquietingly in the mind.

The pool was choked with mouldering bones and skulls, the mortal remains of those who had come before, floating in a rich, thick scum of decay, from which tendrils of pulsing fungus crawled up the walls. Bulbous lumps of matter depended from the tendrils.

Leetha looked down at the thing she had dropped. 'I almost ate that,' she said in a small voice.

'It would have been the last thing you ever ate,' said the Doctor. 'In all probability.'

'But I almost ate that!' Leetha shouted.

'But you didn't,' said the Doctor.

'I *almost* ate it,' said Leetha defiantly.

'Um, I hate to interrupt the gustatory flow, here,' said Li Shao uneasily, 'but I think something else is happening.'

'Is something come,' said Six, revolving several of their eyes to the noisome pool.

There was a sound like massive galvanistical relays being thrown, somewhere deep in the Promethean bedrock. The scum and skulls roiled, and parted, and from the centre of the

199

pool rose a truncated granite pyramid. At its apex, something bulky and encrusted with black and malignant matter.

Steps were cut into the side of the pyramid, and as it rose there also emerged a slimy stone causeway built from interlocking heptagons of volcanic glass, bridging the gap between steps and the cavern floor.

'That's it?' Li Shao said. He swung himself on to the causeway.

Light burst from the clotted object on the pyramid, pinwheeling through crazy-paving cracks in the ichorous crust, and the crust flaked away. An uncut and perfectly clear jewel now rested there, secured by entwining copper wires, pulsing with a golden light that burned within it, connecting and disconnecting, forming and re-forming and shifting like a writhing mass of glowing worms.

At the edge of the pool, Leetha stared at the Eye as though hypnotized, eyes wide and sucking its light into her, filling her up so that her whole being twitched and pulsed to its resonances.

She saw herself in the centre of an infinite, perpetually expanding, intricate glowing web of cause and effect, endless possibilities radiating from her and all of them under her control, so that the flick of a finger could move mountains, or turn Wanderers, or swing the very System around – not through mere brute force but by the fact that everything there ever was, or ever is, or ever will be is balanced on a knife-edge, and a single push just *so* will . . .

Leetha gazed upon the Eye, and saw that it was like a hole, a little opening at an impossible angle to somewhere inconceivably big and so impossibly hot – with a heat that was somehow not a heat, but something more complex and alive and vast that the mere term 'heat' could not encompass it – and that the hole was sealed by the thinnest and most insubstantial of membranes, so that to do so much as touch it would rupture it, instantly, and loose the alien energies into the world.

And as she saw the hazy form of Li Shao, as he climbed the pyramid towards the Eye, she knew that its merest touch would kill him instantly, and then the desert world, and every world, and everything on them, and then the Sun and . . .

'No!' She pelted across the interlocking causeway and

flung herself up the steps, shoving a startled Li Shao aside with the unthinking strength of desperation and pitching him head-first into the pool of charnal slurry.

And then the Promethean Eye blazed and crawled before her. She stared into its depths, at the burning worms, saw without quite knowing how she knew that the outer shell might be grasped *here*, and *here* . . .

She put her hands to the Eye and, with a roar that seemed to come from somewhere else, merely channelled through her, ripped it from its housing.

———————

She would never have another memory until she woke, propped against the cavern wall, with Li Shao and Six looking down at her.

'How are you feeling?' he asked her.

'I . . .' Leetha felt at her exposed skin. It was dry and sensitive and felt vaguely raw, as though the very top layer of it had been burned off. Confused memories of light and fire half-surfaced in her head. 'What happened?'

'You went right past me and knocked me off the pyramid,' said Li Shao. 'When I came up out of the water, you were just standing there, holding the Eye over your head and screaming. Lightning was crawling over you – and then a kind of solid light burst out of your eyes and mouth, like the beams of searchlights, burning everything in its path.' He gestured towards a series of scorched swathes cut through the fungus on the cavern wall. 'You seemed to be chanting something that I couldn't make head nor tail of.'

'Speaking in tongues,' said Six. 'Agrajebbergrag, you say. Rakabloer-ramagragadrab-ababagag-a-glurk-glurk-glurk . . .'

'And then the Doctor simply walked up and took it out of your hands,' said Li Shao. 'You went over as if you'd been pole-axed and I had to drag you out of the pool before you drowned.'

'Oh yes,' Leetha said flatly. 'The Doctor. So just where, exactly, is the Doctor?'

Off to one side, sitting on a rock projection and whistling tunelessly, the Doctor had the Eye on his lap and was intently winding copper wire around it from a spool, twisting the wire into an intricate cat's-cradle pattern so that the Eye appeared to be encased by an interconnected series of triangles through which a now-dim light within it gently pulsed.

He pulled a pair of pliers from a pocket, snipped off the spool, examined his handiwork critically and then, from another pocket, took a little tin box with a switch, which he affixed to the wire tracery by way of a pair of small crocodile clips. He flipped the switch. 'It's contained now, to a certain extent. It can be handled with some degree of safety.' He offered it to Leetha. 'Would you care to . . . ?'

She snatched it from him. The little box hummed and a light set into it blinked on and off. The tracery of wires vibrated warmly against her hands.

She clutched it to her. Something inside her wanted to simply shout *mine*, over and over again – and then, all of a sudden, and for no reason she could discern, she felt utterly ashamed of the impulse. She stood there, dumbly, holding the Promethean Eye, suddenly unsure of herself, unsure of what to do.

'I'd take very good care of it, if I were you,' the Doctor told her mildly. 'There's a lot of power in there. I just wonder if you've worked out, quite, what you are actually going to *do* with it, now.'

———

They climbed their ropes and made their way out through the tunnel, the perils of vampire chickens and zombie gerbils and man-eating tortoises familiar and mundane after the arcane forces of the cavern, the madness-inducing electrofield dissipated or earthed.

They came down the foothills to find Benny and Kiru waiting for them outside the ship.

'The spotters spotted you through their big spotting telescopes,' Benny said. 'What happened? Did you give up or something? You've only been gone a couple of hours.'

The Twenty-Fourth Chapter

The chamber was cluttered and noisy and the little furnaces filled it with the heat and smoke and the flickering, pulsing light of some bustling anthropomorphic Hades. Strewn higgledy-piggledy across the matter-smeared earthen floor were workbenches and kilns and turning lathes, at which mad-eyed woodland folk in little human-skin jerkins and trousers twisted little wires with pliers, hit tiny nails with little silver hammers and gouged at planks of wood with little chisels. The fur of these various rats and mice and rabbits and stoats and badgers and hedgehogs and weasels was matted and ragged, falling out in diseased clumps. The skin of their pelts was disfigured by crusted and suppurating sores. They were making snares and traps and nooses and little paw-carved wooden gibbets, and they were singing a mad and squeaky little song about it.

Running across the ceiling of the chamber were sets of chain-strung rails, from which depended hooks such as might be found in a particularly brutal and noisome slaughterhouse. From several of these hung blackened rotted and partially butchered carcasses that might once, at some point, have been basically humanoid in form. Some of them were very small.

From other hooks hung elongated cages riveted together from thick strips of black iron. The majority of them were empty. In one of them hung Roslyn Forrester. In another hung Chris Cwej.

—————

The Snata had looked at them with its eyes like burning coals. It grinned to show its serried, twisted, broken rows of teeth, four sets of them in all, the outer little more than shattered, blackened flecks rotted into abscessed gums, the inner little more than buds. A parched grey tongue rasped across them, cracked and split in several places to the glistening, muscular meat. Its inflamed, infected epiglottis twitched.

It was deathly white and bloated, like a drowned corpse leached albino by the waters and only just beginning to putrefy, face bulging at the cheeks and under the jaw, as if it might burst at any moment, and deluge those before it with a white and stringy discharge. Brittle strands of pure white hair sprouted from its twitching, quivering jowls in irregular clumps, and crushed strands protruded from beneath a black cowl trimmed with white furs ripped, skin and dangling guts and all, from some small and mouselike species of creature and stitched together with lengths of knotted hairy string. The cowl, like the robes, within which the Snata's pendulous form slumped like a pearshaped sack of half-clotted pus, were black because they were crusted with old blood – layer upon layer of it: you could, should you look close enough, differentiate between the smears.

The Snata sat upon a roughly carpentered travois, drawn by two diseased and diarrhoeic, winged, wild-eyed and de-antlered deerlike creatures with bright red noses that glowed like coals.

Twisted, rusting loops of cable cut into their throats, the stiff cable running back to the Snata and the ends twisted, laterally, like a pair of handlebars. The Snata gripped them with pale little hands on the end of tiny and vestigial-looking arms that peeped out of its robes. Behind him, on the travois, were several bulging sacks, the contents of which were not entirely pleasant.

All of this Forrester and Cwej had taken in in an instant, rooted to the spot. They looked into its piggy little glowing eyes – and then, somehow, without quite remembering how, they were suddenly less than two inches from that bloated face. It filled their fields of vision. The clockwork machine-guns they had stolen from the Reklonian guerrillas crunched into the snow, dropped from suddenly slack and nerveless hands, unheeded. Near by panicked whittering and the frantic crunching of something clawing through a snowdrift that might or might not have been Sgloomi Po, the Sloathe, went unheeded.

'Well now, little children,' the Snata slobbered in their faces. 'Have you got a kiss for Snata? Are you going to get what you want, or are you going to get what you deserve?'

And then its eyes began to spin, laterally, and engulfed them. And then it picked them up and popped them in a couple of its sacks, for later.

Every single aboriginal inhabitant of the System would have known the Snata, and run for cover at the very moment that they heard the distinctive sound of its progress. Once there had been many of them, infesting every Wanderer, burrowing their semi-hibernation lairs into the very core-rock, only emerging for their month-long active period every solar year.

In that time, during that month-long period, doors and windows were barred and ventilation shafts and chimneys blocked, and people stayed awake all night, their eyes propped wide with matchsticks and with weapons close to hand. Totems and traditionally lucky foliage were strung through homes, and distilled wines and delicate pastries were left for the repast of any god that might be in the vicinity, in the hope that it would do some good.

It didn't. Snatas were very sneaky and spied on people, and, come the morning of the final day of their active period, people would wake – if woke they did at all – from a sleep into which they had not been aware of falling to find the Snata's little presents.

The Snata's metabolism was as specialized as any koala chewing on a eucalyptus leaf. It was an abhorravore. It fed upon the complex endocrinic secretions of a humanoid undergoing a specific blend of horror and revulsion.

It was almost completely mindless – its apparent cognizance and use of tools, even the controlling influence it exerted over the smaller life-forms around its lair, was merely an extremely complex behavioural pattern, evolved over millennia and only possible at all due to the unique potentiality-quotient of the System. Its original gene-plasm had in fact come from Earth, from a species long extinct and which had formed the basis for certain vestigial human myths – in much the same way that partially evolved anthropoids tricking gibbons into finding water had formed the basis for the myth of people tricking leprechauns into giving them gold.

This Snata was probably the last of its kind. Quite apart from those who had died by the people of the System digging them up and killing them while they slept, the vast majority of them had been shot down over the last few years by Sloathes mistaking them for aboriginal aircraft, and by aboriginal anti-aircraft emplacements mistaking them for Sloathes. This last Snata, moreover, despite its apparent bulk, was on the point of starving. The Sloathe occupation and depopulation of Reklon had effectively left it nothing upon which to feed.

Never mind. Never mind now. This new prey would make up for all of that. The sheer amount of fear and loathing that had come off them – particularly from the little black one – would sate its hunger for some long while.

In the innermost chamber of its lair the Snata squatted, rifling through an ineptly constructed approximation of a filing cabinet with its atrophied claws, occasionally pulling out a ragged sheet of peeled dry skin to apparently peer at it. This was simply part of its behavioural pattern. Soon it would go to its prey and make noises, which would be interpreted by them as it saying that they had, in fact, been very, very bad *indeed*.

And then the feeding would begin.

———

Roz screwed her eyes shut but it didn't do any good. Her hands were pinioned to her side by the iron cage, and she could still hear the ring of little hammers and the churning of lathes and the utter and unmitigated horror of the singing.

'It's not real,' she moaned. 'It isn't happening. It's not real.' She had been saying this, over and over again, for the best part of an hour now and she had long forgotten what the words originally meant.

Suddenly, Cwej, who had remained silent in his own cage for some while after failing to get any salient response from her, spoke up again: 'Hey, Roz . . . ?'

'Itsnotrealitisnthappening,' said Roz, 'itsnotrealitsnotreal-itisnthappeningitsnotreal . . .'

'Just listen, yeah?' Cwej shouted. 'Just shut up and listen, will you?'

'. . . realitisnthappeningitsnotrealitsnot . . .'

Trapped immobile in his cage, Cwej sighed. 'OK. OK. It's probably not important or anything. I was just going to call your attention to that particularly large badger that's just walked in . . .'

'. . . happeningitsnotrealitsnotrealitisnthappeningitsnot . . .'

'Only there seems to be something a little odd about it,' said Cwej.

'. . . itsnotrealitsnotrealitisnthappeningitsnot . . .'

'Like the fact that it's rather suspiciously sort of grey and slimy,' said Cwej. 'And plus the fact that it seems to be dragging a couple of clockwork machine-guns behind it.'

And a thousand leagues away, and further all the time, as the ice-world continued on its orbit, the big horrible eating thing rampaged through Planet X: elongating to squeeze its vast bulk through them like fresh and minty toothpaste squeezing from a tube; bifurcating where the tunnels branched; explosively sprouting ouroglous and prepoleptically swiving tentacles into side-passages to engulf the luckless Sloathes within, as they shluttered and smlerped with a terror most abject and piteous to behold.

Many and heart-rending would be the tales of this loathsome beast's passing: of how it detached and pressure-ejected glutinous lumps of itself to hunt down those who tried to flee in panic, each casting around itself with several extensible secondary sets of jaws, and each trailing slippery ganglionic stalks; of how it plastered itself across whole caverns in a thin and glistening film to subsequently fall billowing upon those Sloathes within so that they writhed and struggled in their hundreds against its enzyme-oozing folds; of how it spread across the floors to erupt into sudden forests of jaggedy-toothed spikes, impaling Sloathes in their thousands and drawing them into a pitcher-plant-like mass-digesting mass . . .

Many and heart-rending would be the tales of its passing – had Sloathes, in and of themselves, the degree of generatively creative skill with which to relate them. And had so much as one single Sloathe that encountered the horrible eating thing lived to tell of it.

For itself, the horrible eating thing didn't care. Very soon now, it would have eaten them all up.

Every single one.

Canto Fourth:
The Ripple Effect

Q: What is it that is white and swings through the jungle?
A: It is a fridge.
Incredibly Bad Jokes of the Twentieth Century No. 12,347
ed. Professor Bernice Summerfield

Q: What is it that is black and white and swings through the jungle?
A: It is a fridge with a leather jacket on.
Incredibly Bad Jokes of the Twentieth Century No. 12,348
ed. Professor Bernice Summerfield

'If you ask me why elephants paint their balls red one more time, Benny, I'm going to kill you.'
Leetha T'Zhan (attr.)

The Twenty-Fifth Chapter

Shaking and ague-ridden and babbling incoherently, the little savage scrambled through the dark and cloying undergrowth, the mud and cadmium that caked his skin mingling with the moisture in the air and his own sweat to form a pale and oily toxic paste, already working itself into multiple scratches and abrasions. In addition to these, a large and angrily inflamed wound disfigured the little savage's thigh.

In one shaking hand, the little savage clutched a small collection of resin beads, the hemp cord that had once run through them lost and gone. Clutched them as though his life depended on it.

Behind him, distant, flickering torchlight and the sound of human figures running through the jungle, the sound of human voices calling to each other. And the sound of something else. Something that advanced, inexorably, crushing everything in its path.

A root twisted under the little savage's bare foot in the dark. He pitched forward with a barely stifled cry, twisting, arms flailing, to strike his head sharply against a tree bole. He was not aware of losing consciousness – only that, suddenly, bright sunlight was coming through the jungle canopy in actinic shafts, illuminating a small tree-frog that was sitting on a stone and looking at him glumly with its bulbous eyes.

For the moment the little savage remained perfectly still, sprawled on his side, head resting against the thick roots of a banyan, listening to the shriek of parrots and the chitter of marmosets overhead, the slithering of an anacon along a nearby branch.

Something scuttled over him. Instinctively, he grabbed it.

The tree-frog, startled, leapt into the undergrowth with a cry like that of someone sitting on a spike.

The little savage sat up. His blood had clotted on the banyan trunk and he lost a little skin. He examined his catch. A large, black and frantically struggling stag-beetle as big as his hand, a yellow stripe running down its back. The little savage cracked its carapace open on the rock on which the frog had sat and sucked out the pulp.

Cautiously, the little savage cast about himself in a watchful semi-crouch, tasting the air.

He could smell water near by.

'They're back again,' Benny said, pointing to several sets of ripples fanning back through the fetid, black water from the tell-tale protruding reeds.

'Oh, good,' said Nathan Li Shao, surreptitiously moving back from the edge of the raft and gripping his sword uneasily. Quite apart from the perfectly natural uneasiness around water of a desert-dweller who had subsequently spent the rest of his life in asteroids and airships, he seemed to have developed an active phobia about Anean crocogators – an all-but subaquatic species that had evolved the knack of breathing through hollow reeds (of a peculiar variety, Benny had observed, that were remarkably similar to red-and-white-striped drinking straws) and only rising to the surface to kill.

'I understand,' Leetha said innocently, from the packing crate on which she was sitting and trimming her nails with a blade from her living armour, 'that it's the tails you've got to watch out for. One flick of them and – *snap!* – your back's broken in twenty-three entirely different vertebraic places.'

'Thank you so much,' said Li Shao.

The Sun Samurai shrugged. 'Any time.'

In the time they had spent on the Anacon river, both Li Shao and Leetha had been sniping at each other continually in a way that Benny (who knew a thing or three about interpersonal dynamics, so far as they concerned other people) was finding highly amusing.

'Well, I think I'll leave you to it,' she said. 'Don't let the crocogators bite.'

'Oh, their jaws are very weak,' said Leetha, absently. 'It takes three or four bites before your leg comes off.'

The *Schirron Dream* had landed on Aneas at a point roughly a third of the way down the river and just past the evacuated wrecks of the Dirigible Cities. It had been collectively decided to conduct the search for the Anean Eye at, as it were, ground level, with Kiru and Six taking the ship back up into orbit to deal with any Sloathe forces as might appear. Aneas was the nearest Wanderer to the Sloathe-occupied airspaces of the System that was itself not occupied, and was under constant threat of attack. Once the Eye was found, if it was at all, the ship could be called down by battery-operated radio-beacon.

Three longboats had been scavenged from a deserted wharf that had originally serviced the floating cities, and had been lashed together to form a raft and fitted with outboard motors. They had now spent the best part of three days travelling down the mighty Anacon in the hope of spotting signs of the temple mentioned in Kimon's notes. Aboard were: Nathan Li Shao, Leetha T'Zhan, several native Aneans both saurian and human, including the little pigmy-girl Yani, Benny for her archaeological skills and the Doctor, who had by now of course made himself indispensable. It was amazing how he did it, really.

Benny found him to the aft of the middle longboat, past the large packing cases that had been roughly nailed together to provide cabins of sorts. He was lying on his bedroll, on the bulwark deck by the picnic hampers from which the expedition was fed, in his rolled-up shirt-sleeves and with his hat over his eyes.

'I told you,' he said, without moving, as Benny plonked herself down beside him, 'that we could all do with a little messing about in boats. Do you remember that?'

'I remember,' Benny said. 'I'm just wondering how much of that you really meant right from the start.'

'You credit me far too much prescience, Benny.' The Time Lord stretched and yawned hugely. 'Why does everybody always think I know something they don't? Everything doesn't necessarily have to prefigure everything else.' He settled back again and put his hat back over his face. 'At this point I'm as much in the dark as you are.'

213

'I'm not so sure,' Benny said. She was remembering a conversation they'd had in the *Schirron Dream* some days before, *en route* to Aneas.

—∞∞—

She had found him in the cabin she shared with Leetha, sitting in a lotus and staring intently at the wire-encased Promethean Eye resting on Leetha's bunk. He was levitating three feet off the deck – something he swore blind that he could only do occasionally and with concentrated mental effort, but which Benny had lately come to suspect was the result of being so engrossed that he simply forgot to stay on the ground.

'I've just come back from the bridge,' she said.

Still floating three feet off the deck, the Time Lord casually reached out and pulled a feather pillow from the bunk, considered it for a moment, plumped it up and then placed it carefully on the deck under him. He then did an extremely blatant double-take, flailed his arms and dropped like a half-brick with an: 'Ak!'

'I really wish you wouldn't do that,' he said.

'Sorry if I startled you,' said Benny.

'I was actually referring to you whipping the pillow out from under me at the last second,' said the Time Lord, feelingly. 'So what, exactly, is happening up in the bridge?'

'Well, Li Shao's finally convinced about the Eyes.' Benny tossed the pillow back on to the bunk. 'And he wants to try to harness their power into some sort of Big Death Weapon against the Sloathes. Leetha, on the other hand, is adamant that the prophecies must be fulfilled to the very letter. When I left they were in full bicker.' Benny scowled. 'It's like living in a bloody sitcom. If we ever get out of this, I hope we go somewhere grim and humourless and run by miserable bastards.'

'Do I take it,' said the Doctor, still sitting on the deck and grinning up at her, 'that you're beginning to tire of all this? Can it be that the novelty is wearing off?'

'Leetha told me some of what happened on Prometheus,' said Benny. 'I mean, vampire chickens? Back-stabbing money-grubbing jackals? Marçel the marmoset and his magic patisserie? Give me a break. There are limits.'

The Time Lord nodded. 'Indeed there are.' He turned his face away from her. 'Indeed there are,' he repeated, softly, to himself.

He turned his face back up to her, and looked at her – and there was suddenly something in his eyes that, momentarily, dried her throat and sent a crawling shudder through her.

'Tell me,' he said suddenly. 'Do you recall your classical mythology? Do you remember the story of the birth of Dionysus?'

'Um . . .' Benny, startled by this apparent change in tone and subject, found that it was instantly and automatically in her head.

'Semele,' she said. 'Daughter of Cadmus, who founded Thebes. She was seduced by a handsome stranger and was got with child. She demanded that her lover show himself in his true form – which was *not* a good idea, since she instantly found herself gazing upon the naked face of Zeus and she was instantly fried by the thunderbolts.

'All that survived, being half-god – the last of the gods – was the child. Zeus sewed it into his thigh, to feed on his blood, and in the fullness of time he slit it open and out sprang Dionysus.' She shrugged. 'That bit always struck me as a particularly blatant bit of male-motherhood.'

'And you'd be right to think so,' said the Doctor. 'Myths tend to be one part truth, two parts metaphor and five parts corruption, and patriarchy has always been a particularly vulgar form of corruption. The actual truth of it would have been something far different, probably, if truth there actually was. I'd concentrate on the central metaphor if I were you – and particularly how it relates to limits and aspects, and how the mind must react to the truly horrifying if it wants to survive.' He smiled, reminiscently. 'Zeus had the unfortunate habit of blowing everybody's head off wherever he went, but Dionysus had few problems getting on with anybody, as I recall.'

Benny looked down at him, thoughtfully. 'Until the Romans turned him into a fat little idiot, sitting on his ass.'

'Don't be too sure. Maybe he got cagey. Maybe things got a little hot for him after that unfortunate business with Pentheus and he decided to go under cover.' He grinned up at Benny with a sudden, little, knowing, feral glint in his eye. 'For a while.'

Abruptly, he bounced to his feet and peered at th Promethean Eye with a theatrical intensity, briskly rubbin his hands. 'I've been examining this. I've been looking ver close, and I've noticed something.'

'What?' said Benny. 'What have you noticed?'

The Time Lord tapped the Eye absently. A little pulse o light flared behind the mesh, under his finger. 'Now appears to be uncut,' he said. 'A diamond in the rough, as were – but in actual fact it's been shaped, by tools, t precisely this form and to the molecular level. I find tha rather strange.'

'No you don't,' said Benny suddenly, startled by her ow vehemence. 'I don't think you find it strange at all. I thin you expected it. It's like what Leetha told me and all thos other times. I think that you somehow know exactly what going on, and what's going to happen and you're jus waltzing through your lines.'

'It isn't like that, Benny,' the Doctor said, quietly. Benn was startled. For the first time the Time Lord seeme genuinely worried. 'It isn't like that at all. I have certain – he hesitated, ' – suspicions. That's all. Just suspicions. I keep hoping they'll prove to be wrong, only . . .'

'Only?' said Benny.

The Time Lord sighed. 'Only so far they haven't.'

———

Benny and the Doctor sat back, watching the distant clock-work and energy flares through the gap in the jungle canopy and occasionally pointing out interesting shapes in them. Sometime later they heard, close by, a loud and plunging splash. Startled by the sound, a flock of iridescent purple flying lizards with yellow eyes and needle teeth burst from the jungle canopy and wheeled in flapping confusion.

There was a sudden commotion of struggling and raised voices towards the foredecks. Instantly, the Doctor sprang to his feet. 'Would you bring my bag, Benny?'

'What bag?' said Benny.

'It's right by your foot.'

Benny looked down to see an elderly, cracked black leather medicine bag. She knew for a fact that it hadn't been there earlier.

216

'Where – ?' she began.

'No time!' The Doctor bustled forward, clambering over the packing-case cabins. Benny looked down at the bag, shrugged to herself, picked it up and followed him.

She found the Doctor and Li Shao at the prow of the port boat, crouching before a tiny, soaking, scrawny pale-skinned figure of an Anean pigmy smeared with partially dissolved and silvery mud. Li Shao was gripping him as he struggled and choked and growled while the Time Lord tried ineffectually to calm him.

'Ah, thank you,' he said without looking round as Benny dropped the medicine bag beside him.

'*Riki-tiki-paka-plek!*' shouted the pigmy defiantly. '*Taki-plepki-sami-vroosht!*'

'Don't mention it,' said Benny.

'And here comes Leetha with Yani,' he said, happily, as they clambered over from the central boat. 'Tell me, my dear,' he said to Yani, 'do you speak the same language as our rather overexcitable friend here?'

'*Tlakaki-lama-boya-boya!*' spat the pigmy, renewing his struggle against Li Shao's grip.

'Different tribe.' The pigmy girl looked at her feet, shyly. For some reason she seemed completely awestruck when around the Doctor, completely different from the cheerfully vicious little imp that Benny ordinarily knew. 'I can try,' she said hopefully.

The Doctor nodded towards Li Shao. 'Well, tell him if he doesn't sit still and shut up this minute, I'll have the man with the fearful eyes cut his head off with his big sword and feed it to the crocogators.'

'*Klami-klami-pooli-grenk*,' Yani told the pigmy. '*Pooli-yamo-soosi-mamo-kek.*'

Suddenly the pigmy went very quiet. His eyes widened. '*Plek?*' he said.

'*Koogi-boola*,' Yani agreed solemnly.

'*Sansi-pog*,' the pigmy said – and, suddenly, his face broke into a smile of such radiant joy that those gathered around suddenly found themselves transfixed by something that they could not name.

'Thank heavens for that,' said the Doctor, all oblivious, pulling on a pair of rubber gloves with a snap.

217

For the next few minutes he examined the pigmy with a clinical briskness. Occasionally the tiny man flinched and once, when the Doctor pressed a little wooden depressor to his thigh, he snarled.

The Doctor merely looked at him sternly and pointed to Li Shao, who tapped the hilt of his sword meaningfully. At this the pigmy subsided with a mortified, horror-struck whimper.

Benny, sitting with Leetha and looking on, wondered if she had been the only one to notice that the pigmy had not so much as glanced at Li Shao. His eyes had never left the Time Lord. Just what, she wondered, had Yani in fact told him?

It was only later, subjective years later, that it occurred to her to wonder exactly why she couldn't understand the pigmy speech in the first place. But by then of course, it was far, far too late.

Too late to help her.

Because by then she already knew.

'I want to get this mud off him,' the Doctor said, 'and I really don't like the look of that wound. There seems to be stitches in there, some sort of uncured gut. They're going to have to come out. Yani.' He gestured to the pigmy girl, who had been following the proceedings with wide eyes. 'Come here and hold out your hands.' He took a bottle of grain alcohol from his bag and poured half of its contents over her outstretched hands and forearms. 'Rub them together. Do you faint at the sight of blood?'

'What do you think?' Benny said from her vantage point. 'Bloodthirsty little devil.'

'I wasn't talking to you,' the Time Lord said with a faint note of irritation. He turned back to the pigmy girl and regarded her with a warm concern. 'Do you think you can do this?'

A look of abject horror passed across Yani's face, and then she nodded. 'I can do it,' she said vehemently. 'Really.'

'Good girl.' The Doctor pantomimed to his patient that he would, personally, pull off his legs and stuff them down his throat if he made a fuss, and then swabbed out the wound with spirit. Then he crumbled a white and strangely glittery pill from a little brown bottle into the remainder, and handed it to the pigmy with a gesture that he should drink. The little man, apparently without even a moment's thought of caution, upended the bottle, beamed imbecilically and collapsed back as though pole-axed, with a small thump as his head bounced off the deck.

'I knew that would come in useful at some point,' the Time Lord mused to himself. 'Should be all right so long as we keep him away from labradors and married women for a while. Now, Yani,' he said briskly, pulling from his bag a scalpel handle and several blades in a small corked test-tube that looked as though it originally came from a child's toy chemistry set. 'First I'm going to cut away the infection, and then I'm going to work on the artery.' He examined the wound again, absently. 'The exposed vessels are far too abraded to risk clamps at this point, so when I tell you, I want you to pinch that little tube, there – pinch it *tight* and don't let go until I tell you. Do you understand?'

Yani swallowed hard and nodded frantically. 'I understand.'

'Very good, Yani. You make me very pleased.' The Doctor went to work.

———∞∞∞———

The little savage woke when the Sun was at His brightest time. He was lying on a hard flat wood thing, in the shade of a thin flat flapping thing on sticks.

In his mouth there was the taste of an old rotting dead thing, and the air things inside him were as dry and stiff as a very dry and stiff thing indeed.

There was a hurt in his leg, too – but it was the hurt of a clean thing. Not the hurt of a dirty thing that came after the work of the Needlemen. He gazed down at himself, and saw that his thigh was wrapped with a white thin soft thing.

The Magic Man. The Magic Man had put it there.

The Magic Man had laid his hands on him.

For a long time he was lost in the wonder of it. On him!

The Magic Man who made the world.

A sudden movement startled him. The girl he had seen with the Magic Man was sitting, in the light of the Sun, watching him. When she saw that he was awake, she scowled contemptuously and tossed him a bundle of thin soft thing.

'You are to wear these,' she said shortly, in his own language but with a strange and exotic accent he couldn't quite place.

The little savage stirred the soft thing dubiously with his hand. It appeared to be made of two tube things, like hollowed tree straight things, only joined together at one end.

'Why?' he said reasonably.

The girl snorted. 'If you don't wear, big people go, "Ho, there go stupid marmoset thing with bare arse hanging out!" ' She spat softly. 'You know nothing.'

'I know lots thing, me!' the little savage said indignantly. 'Don't care what stupid big people say.' He picked his teeth at her. 'They not proper people. They are nothing.'

The absolute rage that accompanied the slap frightened him more than the pain – which was saying something, since he thought his head was going to fall off.

'You *are* stupid monkey man!' she hissed, her furious face very close to his. 'We are all slaves of the Magic Man. You say Magic Man's things are nothing! Magic Man will know what things you said!'

And, suddenly, the sheer enormity of his blasphemy struck him. How he had disgraced himself when the stranger laid his hands upon him – not knowing, then, that it was the Magic Man, even though he knew the signs – and how, now, knowing, he had slighted the Magic Man without a thought. He shook and jerked and gouged at himself. 'Didn't mean,' he whimpered. 'Didn't mean . . .'

'Shh!' The girl put her hands to his; gently took them off his face. 'The Magic Man will forgive,' she said. 'He is very kind. He will forgive. Even his very littlest and unworthy.'

The absolute and joyful certainty in her voice calmed him. He remembered how the Magic Man had laid his hands on him. Then he suddenly recalled the other slaves who had been there when the Magic Man had laid his hands on him. How they had acted. He was puzzled.

'These others,' he said slowly. 'The big people. They cannot see his other body.'

'They must not know,' she told him solemnly. 'We must not tell. Not ever. That would be a very *bad* thing.' Her face cleared and she smiled, suddenly, with warmth. 'And what shall I tell of you? Are you a really nothing monkey man, or do you have a true name?'

<hr />

220

'His name is *Kai-hatuda-puki-ani-heh*,' said Yani, bashfully. 'It means, "This Blood Animal for the Eating Thing".'

'Takes all sorts,' said Benny from where she had slung a hammock between a couple of packing-case cabins and was trying to have a small late-afternoon snooze.

'Now, Benny,' said the Doctor with mild reproof. He was sitting by a paraffin-charged primus with a frying pan, frying eggs for their tea. He turned back to Yani and the little savage, Kai, who was squirming uncomfortably in a pair of cotton trews (which he had in fact pulled on the wrong way round) and gazing awe-struck at the Doctor. 'Could you have him tell me a little more about this "eating thing".'

Yani muttered something to the little savage, who gabbled excitedly for a minute or so, waving his arms and pointing frantically at his wounded thigh.

'He says it has always been here,' Yani said when he had stopped. 'But before it was always here it came in a big shiny burning thing that killed the big hard hut the gods were in. All the proper people – ' She suddenly looked aghast, and corrected herself. 'All the people who aren't big for miles around are in its thrall.' She shuddered. 'Once it would suck your blood until you were dead, and many tribes all died in that time. Now it keeps them alive so it can suck their blood again and again and *again*.'

'Interesting,' the Doctor mused. 'Does this sound at all familiar, Benny?'

'Now you come to mention it,' Benny said, suddenly all interest. 'Big hard huts of the gods, eh? And things that like to suck your blood out?' She took off her straw boater and swung herself down from the hammock. 'Tell me more.'

It was at that point that there came a number of loud warning shouts from towards the bow of the port boat, the sound of things clattering repeatedly against the hull. They scrambled forward with the pigmy-man, Kai, hobbling uncertainly after them.

Li Shao and Leetha and the Aneans were firing on the bank with their flintlocks and muskets and machine-guns. On the bank, where a thin muddy incline gave way to knee-high underbrush and then to almost solid jungle, pale little figures crusted with silvery mud, hundreds of them, were flinging spears and firing arrows and blowing darts.

As Benny arrived, an arrow with a little resin suction cup planted itself firmly in the centre of a saurian Anean's head. He plucked at it angrily – and then a look of shocked surprise crossed his face.

His eyes bulged.

His cheeks puffed.

He inflated like a balloon affixed to a helium canister.

And then he exploded.

'Poor devil,' said the Doctor, ducking a spear that buried itself in a water barrel behind him. 'Blown to smithereens.'

'Tell me about it!' shouted Benny with some force. 'I've got the smithereens all over me. Yuk!'

'Is exploding puff-marsupial venom!' Yani shouted urgently. 'Made from exploding puff-marsupials! Must not get it on your skin!'

'Thanks for telling me,' Benny said in a small and slightly queasy voice, looking at the greenish smear on the back of her hand where a blowpipe dart had clipped her. 'Thank you so much.'

Sweat burst from every pore of her body and something clamped around her heart. She felt herself beginning to swell and –

Instantly, Yani was on her, bearing her to the deck, pulling a knife. For a moment, Benny instinctively and ineffectually tried to fight back – but the pigmy girl merely whittled frantically at her hand, roughly but with precision sawing off the stained areas of skin.

After a while, Benny found that she could breathe again.

Yani regarded the bleeding, whittled wound critically. 'Got it all.'

'Are you sure?' Benny said weakly.

The pigmy girl shrugged. 'If I hadn't, you'd go boom-kasplat.'

'Thank you,' Benny said, with feeling.

She became aware of some sudden commotion amongst the others. The remaining Anean crewmen were still firing on the pigmies while the Doctor sat safely in the gunwhales with a hand clutching his hat firmly to his head – but Leetha and Li Shao seemed to be struggling together.

Li Shao was snarling with an absolute and almost mindless rage that reminded Benny of a time she had spent on a Viking

222

longboat, when it had attacked an Angle settlement. In combat the Vikings had displayed a similar all-consuming berserk rage that had even given Ace, who had been there, pause for thought.

'Sod that!' Li Shao was roaring, in response to something Leetha was trying to say. He broke free of her grip, wrenched his sword from his back and depressed the stud on its grip with his thumb. Razor-sharp little blades extended from its curved edge and buzzed like a miniature chainsaw.

'Never surrender!' he roared, brandishing the sword over his head and heedless of the poisoned projectiles that showered around him from the bank.

Then he planted a boot on the keel and hurled himself over the side.

The snout of a crocogator broke the surface and he caught a glimpse of jagged, yellow teeth yawning back from a red wet throat. He planted his feet on its head, driving it down into the water so hard that its breathing reed shot out of its blow-hole.

His momentum carried him forward into the muddy river bank. He slithered up it and roll-bounced to his feet in knee-high scrub that inclined towards the almost solid wall of jungle vegetation. Around him, the silver-painted pigmies seemed taken aback by this display of recklessness and not to say outright stupidity. He charged upon the group where they were thickest, flailing his buzzing sword about him, and decapitated several of them before they quite knew what was happening.

Several of the little men simply, at this point, turned tail and ran. Those foolhardy enough to remain prodded at him ineffectually with their spears. He barrelled through them, trusting to the heavy, blood-red leather and steel plate of his body-armour to turn aside the points, backhanding a pigmy in the face with his left hand and planting a heavy kick between the legs of another. This luckless particular pigmy went down with a squeak and a couple of lumps in his throat.

Dimly, Li Shao was aware of covering fire from the raft: The *phut!* of flintlock fire and the zip of blowpipe darts.

One of the remaining pigmies, a wiry little man fully half a head taller than the rest, seemed to have caught on to the general idea of effective use of a spear in close-order combat – which is, of course, not to use it as a spear at all, but as a quarterstaff. He swung it at Li Shao with a murderous shriek.

Li Shao ducked under the blow, took it away from him and poleaxed him with it.

He cast about himself, every sense alert for further sign of attack. The remaining pigmies, however, apparently finally getting the message, were making for the cover of the jungle with all possible speed. Li Shao watched them for a moment, debating whether to go after them, and then turned back to the river, where the lashed-together raft was now drifting towards the bank, its outboards churning against the backwash.

'Sorry about that,' he called. 'Can't think what came over me. I think that deals with any small problem we might have most satisfactorily, though.'

He slowly became aware that those on the raft were suddenly in some confusion, babbling at each other, staring past him and waving at him. He couldn't make out what they were shouting through the confusion.

'What?' he shouted. 'What is it?'

And then he heard the sound of something bursting from the jungle behind him. Slowly, he turned –

It was big; fully half his height again and twice as wide. It reared, lurching on elephantine hind legs, from between which a thick, spined tail squirmed, bulging growths upon its tip splitting open in little needle-toothed mouths. Its wizened, atrophied forelimbs were clutched together across its sternum, twitching and febrile.

Its skin comprised translucent interlocking platelets, clogged with black and spongy filth from which a clear liquid drooled. A horrible corslet of bones, miniature human pigmy bones, connected together with cured human tendon, was wrapped around it, bulging across the shoulders to form two misshapen 'wings' of dangling little metacarpals and phalanges.

Its head was vaguely saurian in construction, the rough flesh worn away from what had once been its snout to expose

224

pitted and calcinated bone. Globular eyes, hundreds of them, covered its cranium, like a pulsing cap of animated frogspawn. Where its mouth should have been, hung a mass of writhing, wormlike tubes.

Of all these many features, Li Shao was only peripherally aware. The shape of this thing, the very shape it made in the world, was in some indefinable sense so utterly *wrong* that the eye refused to accept it. Its features seemed to shift constantly, the eye slid off them. It was, quite simply, an abomination. It was alien, in the truest sense of the word. It had no place in any world in which anything like Li Shao existed to look at it.

For a moment, as this monstrosity advanced upon him, he was transfixed by the sheer horror of it. And then, with a roar that was part disgusted rage and part horrified shriek, frantically swinging his buzzing sword, he just went for it, with no thought in his mind but to destroy it utterly.

Possibly his experience in the Valley of the Scorpions of Glass had rendered him immune, to a certain extent, to the debilitating effects of this creature's inimicability. Possibly this was a simple, mindless and perfectly natural reaction. He never found out, because at this point his foot slipped on something in the underbrush. He was dimly aware of something slippery and fishlike splurting under him, and then he was flat on his back, the breath knocked out of him, his sword sailing off into the undergrowth with a juddering whine, and he was gazing up at the lurching monstrosity as it towered over him.

It bent over him, the wormlike appendages depending from its snout reaching for him. Rainbow-lights rippled across the frogspawn-mass of its eyes, and there was the physical sensation of something coiling and crawling in his head, and that was the last thing he knew.

———

Leetha hauled herself up the bank and walked through the knee-high undergrowth until she came to the place where Li Shao's sword lay, cutting its own miniature crop circle as it revolved. She poked at the hilt with a stick until the little blades along its cutting edge retracted and it was still.

Sure now of not losing her fingers in the process, she

picked it up and hefted it. The grip and the weight felt utterly wrong. She shrugged, and laid it over her back, her living armour extending little hook-appendages to grip it.

A smithereen-bespattered and still slightly groggy Benny, with a sticking plaster on her hand, the Doctor and Yani were coming up the bank behind her, together with the pigmy, Kai, who was hobbling with the aid of the Doctor's umbrella.

The Doctor himself looked down sadly at the pathetic little smear in the undergrowth that Li Shao had slipped upon. It was bescaled and piscine, but with perfect little webbed hands rather than flippers and it had human eyes.

'Well, that's set back the natural selection in these parts by a couple of million years,' he said. He turned his attention to the trampled devastation that marked the monstrous creature's passage from and back into the jungle. Benny, watching him, suddenly got the impression that he was now very, very worried indeed.

The pigmy man, Kai, was pointing frantically into the jungle and gabbling. He tugged at Benny's shirt and pointed at his own bandaged thigh.

'What's he on about?' she asked Yani.

The girl shuddered. 'The eating thing has him,' she said. 'He says the eating thing has him now.'

The Twenty-Sixth Chapter

Roz Forrester and Chris Cwej stumbled through the twilight
forest, Sgloomi Po the Sloathe keeping pace with them on
little rollers, spraying gouts of snow to either side from a
force-evolved and chitinous snowplough attachment. It was
singing happily to itself in a high-pitched polyphonic gabble:
Roz uneasily recognized the mad little song that the woodland folk had been singing as they scraped and planed and hit
things with hammers.

Back there in the Snata's lair, Sgloomi Po had surreptitiously slimed up the wall, and across the ceiling and had
popped the rivets on the iron cages with a chisel-like
appendage. Roz, who had been the first to be released, had
swung herself down on to the bench below, crushing a
half-completed miniature hangman's scaffold with a sound
like a strawberry punnet breaking, and all hell had broken
loose.

The little animals, every single one, had stopped what
they were industriously doing and turned to look at her with
their mad and beady eyes – and then had simply lunged
for her, every single one, chattering and shrieking with a
rabid frenzy. Roz shook off a particularly tenacious squirrel,
stamped on a couple of mice who were advancing on her
in tiny human-leather jackets and wicked little flick-knives
and drop-kicked a weasel into a smelting furnace on the
other side of the chamber. She dived for the guns which
Sgloomi Po had left discreetly in the corner and opened
up an indiscriminate swathe of leaden death through the
assorted vermin at the astonishing rate of thirty rounds a
minute, which not unnaturally gave them pause for thought.
They beat a hasty retreat, taking their wounded with them
on little improvised stretchers, and soon the earthen floor

of the chamber was alive with the sound of them digging in and entrenching themselves with their little picks and shovels.

A gruff and portly badger with gout and a forage cap on, making quite sure he stayed safely behind in his little iron and wicker bathchair, organized an advance by mixed rabbit and stoat light-irregulars in a pincer movement. Things were looking dicey for Roslyn Forrester – but then Cwej and Sgloomi Po turned up and together they were able to beat their way from the chamber and out into the twisty, turny tunnels of the Snata's lair where, after a number of false starts, apocryphal stops, wrong turnings, right angles, getting themselves completely lost, arguing about who it was that had gotten them completely lost, finding themselves again by sorting out their chakras and getting in touch with their respective inner children* and, finally, making their way up through the stables, where the Snata's mutilated deerlike creatures dangled from slings over grease-monkey pits (filled to brimming with genuine Reklonian albino monkey-grease) to emerge, spluttering, from the side of a snowbank.

Now the forests were thinning again; they could see through the fir trees and birches to the snowy plains beyond. Dark clouds boiled above the skyline and a wind tore and whipped the snow-cover into a scintillating haze before them.

Cwej looked at the approaching storm dispiritedly. 'We're never going to make it through that . . .'

Roz eased the strap of her now-empty machine-gun on her shoulder and glanced behind her, worriedly. She was sure she could hear faint and jingly bells. 'We're going to have to try. It's not like we have a lot of choice.'

They set out across the plain. Some half an hour later they heard the distant, approaching flap and slam of monstrous

---

* 'Of course the best thing about confronting your inner child, I've found, is that you can very easily belt the living crap out of the little bastard and steal his dinner money.'
Bernice Summerfield BMA, PhD, honest.
Head Invaders: Asinine Quasi-Psychological Old Toot of Your Times, pub. 1997

228

wings and an ululating howl of vulpine rage that sent shivers of abject dread through them – coincidentally, operating in the precisely opposite phase to the shivers induced by the cold, so that for a moment they were perfectly still.

A rickety travois pulled by two crazed reindeer burst from the forest behind them and soared into the air, barrelling towards them with an impossible and unstoppable acceleration, the bloated, ragged, howling thing upon it rippling and flapping in the crosswind.

'Hey, listen,' Roz said to Cwej quietly. 'If you have any ammunition left I think now might be a good time to use it, yeah?'

'I don't have any,' Cwej said worriedly. 'I used up the last of it on that particularly muscular hedgehog with the bandana and the bow and arrow, remember?'

'Never fear!' cried a heroic if slightly high-pitched voice. 'Sgloomi Po will save the day! Again.'

They turned in some surprise to look at the Sloathe, who had transformed into a squat and chitinous cannon-like form.

'*Banzaiii!*' The cannon fired with a concussion and a recoil that knocked Forrester and Cwej off their feet, firing a big round lump of Sloathe matter that shot for the Snata, spooling a wire-thin line of nerve tissue behind it. As it shot upward, the mass developed several barbed spikes that burst through the travois, shattering it completely and then, explosively, through the Snata in a shower of blubbery gore.

As the remains of Snata and travois dropped towards the plains the winged reindeer, suddenly relieved of their burden, fluttered and wheeled in confusion. And then, with strong and purposeful beats of their dragon-like membraned wings, they banked in the air, turned and soared off, soon lost in the haze of the approaching storm.

The solid lump of Sgloomi Po that had liberated them was dropping like a brick. It unfurled a membranous drogue-chute, and landed lightly less than ten feet from the rest of itself, reeled in its connecting line and re-formed.

'That was fun,' it said happily. 'Do it again?'

Roz looked around at the scattered lumps of Snata meat. She was thinking about survival, and how it relates to foodless ice-deserts, and some incredibly horrible thoughts about what they were going to have to now do were forming in her mind.

'Not if I can possibly help it,' she said.

———∞———

A healthy and nutritious diet is important, and it is not a good idea to mess around with unfamiliar food-chains. Just as the meat of a herbivore, effectively, is concentrated vegetable energy and the meat of a carnivore is, as it were, *concentrated* meat, the flesh of an abhorravore is concentrated fear and loathing, and had either Roslyn Forrester or Christopher Rodonanté Cwej attempted to eat it they would have instantly died of fright. It was therefore fortunate that, by the time they had weathered the first and second of the storms (using the metamorphic Sgloomi Po as a convenient and ambulatory pup-tent) and were finally desperate enough from hunger to try it, they found the penguins.

Roz Forrester's first impulse, as she watched these noble birds skating happily around an ice-lake on their flippered feet, was to instantly imagine one of them roasting merrily on a spit with an apple in its beak. But she controlled herself. By this point she had started to come to some tentative conclusions as to how this 'System' in which they had found themselves in fact operated.

Now, in a small but comfortable tepee-like arrangement into which Sgloomi Po had formed hirself, sitting by a resiny campfire built from branches of the small trees clumped by the ice-lake, she casually raised a hand and snapped her fingers.

In a trice, a pair of dumpy black-and-white forms waddled in and offered her the items clutched between their flippers.

It was fish again. Why wasn't she surprised? She wouldn't mind but they almost always overcooked the vegetables, they couldn't make a decent sauce *en papillote* to save their lives and the house white was appalling.

Ah, well. They'd be wheeling in the sweet trolley in a minute. Roz lifted the domes from the silver salvers, helped herself to the glazed carrots and a large helping of sautéd potatoes and tucked in.

Chris Cwej appeared in the doorway. ' 'Tain't a fit night out for man nor beast,' he said, turning to face somewhere off to the right. A heavy gust of snow hit him in the face.

He brushed it off impassively, came into the tent and helped himself to Forrester's untouched starter. 'It's easing off a bit, actually,' he said around a tiger-prawn.* 'I think we might be able to try it tomorrow.'

'OK.' Roz wiped her mouth with a napkin. 'We try tomorrow. We can't stay here for ever.'

'I don't know,' said the tent. 'I'm quite enjoying the peace and quiet, myself.'

'You know, I'm sure it's getting cleverer somehow,' said Roz.

' "It" does have ears, you know,' said the tent pointedly. 'When it remembers to grow them, admittedly.'

'Sorry, Sgloomi,' said Roz, quite unaware that at some point over the past few days she had gone from utter and glowering suspicion of the Sloathe to thinking of it as someone familiar who just happened to be there. Almost a friend, even. 'What's happening to you? You're sounding almost human.'

'I don't really know,' said the tent. 'Possibly it's all this constant interaction with the pair of you. Or possibly certain Sloathes are simply drawn to certain people, who merely release and develop latent characteristics that were in there all the time. Either way, it's teaching me new ways to think. New ways to *be*. I like it.'

The door of the tepee flapped open in the wind. 'Excuse me a moment.' Cwej got up and looked out. ' 'Tain't a fit night out for man nor beast,' he said. A particularly heavy spray of snow hit him in the face. He came back and sat down again.

'Yeah, right,' said Roz. 'Until you get back with your little friends, and then it's going to be all, "Ho there, pretend-move excrescent hominid-thing! Give me rub-down toot-sweet matey with the carbolic and the oily rag!" '

'I don't think it works like that,' said the tent. 'I think that after a certain point true cognizance is a one-way tunnel. I

---

* Chris Cwej would probably not have cared to know that, so far as the System in general and Reklon in particular was concerned, a 'tiger-prawn' was not in fact seafood, but was more correctly related to the American Old-West delicacy of the 'prairie oyster'. Only from Reklonian polar tigers.

don't think I'd lapse back into that sort of state. I hope not.' It paused, thoughtfully, for a moment. 'I don't think you should be too hard on all those other Sloathes, though.'

'What?' Roz exclaimed with some astonishment. 'You decimated the people of this System and enslaved half of the rest, ripped off everything that wasn't nailed down, and then prised up the nails and stole them as well and you say we shouldn't be so *hard* on you?'

'Well, you people have killed a lot of us, don't forget,' said Sgloomi Po, reasonably. 'And don't forget we need other things to give us shape. When we arrived, everybody we met just went: "Argh! Argh! Horrible slimy monsters! They're going to murder us all in our beds! Argh! Argh!" How do you *expect* us to bloody act?'

This last, which sounded remarkably like an annoyed Roslyn Forrester, gave Roz sudden pause for thought. Just exactly how much had the people of the System projected themselves on to the Sloathes? How many Sloathe atrocities were in fact based upon the people of the System's expectations of them?

The doorway of the tent flapped open again. Roz got up and went to it. ' 'Tain't a fit night out for man nor beast,' she said shortly.

She looked downward.

'And you can put that bucket full of snow down for a start, you cheeky little sod,' she said to the bashfully grinning penguin.

———————

They pressed on across the snowfields. Some days later, a dark smudge on the skyline began to resolve itself. They heard the sound of distant digging and saw the lumbering motion of Sloathe ships. At night, when the Sun went out, the sky was alive with the roar and flash of fiendish alien heat rays.

'I don't like it,' Roz said to Cwej as they huddled inside Sgloomi Po. 'There's something going on there and I don't know what.'

The Twenty-Seventh Chapter

There was a pain in his left thigh, a horrible composite of something sliced and something torn and something bruised and fever-crawling, each element feeding off each other to produce a single and almost unbearable knot of agony.

He had been stripped to the waist and something rough and hard pressed against his back. Loops of scratchy rope about his armpits, from which he depended. His hands and arms were numb. He couldn't feel them. His feet prickled with needles and pins.

Nathan Li Shao opened puffed, encrusted eyelids.

Guttering torchlight in the dark, dimly illuminating squat huts of woven leaves in a jungle clearing. He was hanging from what seemed to be a gibbet of sorts, presumably in the centre of the settlement, though he had no way of telling.

Silvery little figures stood, perfectly motionless, silent, each holding a greasily burning torch that appeared to be a bone dipped in some sickly smelling and inflammable fat.

They just looked at him. For the sake of something to do, something to take his mind off the agony of his thigh, Li Shao looked back.

At first sight, there seemed to be little difference between the figures, save for the obvious discrepancies of male and female: each was naked save for a coating of silvery mud and a scrap of weather-cured skin serving as a clout. The only variation seemed to be that some of them wore little clusters of resin beads, strung on thongs around their necks. His first thought was that these beads denoted rank – but then he realized that those who wore them were even scrawnier and sicker-looking than the rest. Some form of pariahdom?

The pain in his thigh was impossible to ignore. He let his head fall, noting in passing that he was now wearing a set of beads similar to the sicker-looking of the pigmies, and forced himself to look down at it.

The thick red leather of his trews had been cut away, the skin under it slit open. From the split protruded a tube of cured gut, tied off at the end and inflated by the arterial pressure of his blood, tight as a well-packed sausage skin. Nathan Li Shao had the horrible feeling that this was not going to transpire as some revolutionary new method of producing black pudding for the export trade.

Now the pigmies were murmuring: an ululating moan intercut by glottal and dental modificatory inflexions that rippled from one side of the gathering to another and back again like waves in an auditory. One by one, in some apparently random but probably extremely formal and hierarchical pattern, their heads were turning to the largest of the huts, from which flickered a light that was not torchlight, or the artificial light of galvanistic beacons, or like any light Li Shao had ever seen.

The pigmies' murmuring rose in volume and pitch, rising to a climax – and then, again, they were utterly silent.

. And then the monster came out of the hut. And Nathan Li Shao, finally, began to struggle and thrash, but to no avail.

It cast about itself, viciously, the little mouths in its tail snapping. The pigmies made no move. It swung its head around to regard Li Shao with its cap of eyes, and then, slowly, advanced upon him with its lurching gait.

As it drew nearer, its tiny, atrophied foreclaws scrabbled feebly at its corslet of human bones and then, trembling and jerking with the effort, pulled it back to reveal the soft and scaleless and glistening flesh under its protruding, bifurcated sternum.

A toothless sphincter-orifice puckered there, wormlike growths, of the same sort that depended from its snout, protruding from it and radiating outward like spindle-spokes. As the monster halted before the desperately jerking Li Shao, these appendages gently took hold of the tube sprouting from his thigh, and drew it towards the central orifice, which was now dilating and contracting with spasmodic and slavering anticipation.

The murmurous chant of the pigmies began again, as the eating thing began to feed.

And then something bright and buzzing spun past Nathan Li Shao's eyes, and buried itself in the belly of the eating thing with a spraying gout of yellow discharge, and perfectly clear mucus, and black and half-digested blood and began to saw.

(It was fortunate, all things considered, that the eating thing's rudimentary ganglions of synaptic tissue that served in the function of a brain were nestled in its abdomen, in lieu of bowel organs – and that Leetha's aim, throwing an unfamiliar weapon, had been slightly off. If, as she had intended, the sword had struck the head it would have been the end of Li Shao, and of Leetha, and of everybody else, there and then – the head of the eating thing being little more than an ocular and vestigially manipulatory appendage. As it was, the eating thing was dead, and in the fullness of time it realized it.)

The eating thing collapsed backwards with a meaty thump, wrenching the tube from Li Shao's thigh, along with a carved wooden clamplike arrangement the size of a child's clenched fist.

'Cruag!' Li Shao took a lot of the skin off his back and nearly dislocated his arms wrenching himself free of the gibbet. Somewhere close behind him he heard a series of impacts as what he later learned to be crude boulder counter-weights crashed to the ground. For the moment, though, he was more interested in the gout of blood jetting out of him under arterial pressure.

He hit the hard-packed earth of the clearing and his legs collapsed from under him. Forcing his numb hands to move against all possibility, he hauled himself desperately over to the shuddering form of the eating thing and ripped the now flaccid tube of gut from it. With hands that now seemed simultaneously burning and freezing, he wound the tube around his leg above the spurting wound and, after a couple of thousand centuries, managed to tie a clumsy knot. He then pulled a fingerbone from the thing's horrible corslet and, with the last of his strength, got it under the length of gut and used it to twist the makeshift tourniquet tight.

It was becoming increasingly difficult to think coherently. Dimly he was aware of the confused yammer of the silvery pigmies, and of larger figures moving through them. There was a presence beside him, kneeling beside him, cool hands on him.

The last things he remembered, for some small while, were the gleaming catlike eyes of Leetha T'Zhan looking down at him.

'Just don't start, all right?' she said, a little defensively. 'I didn't do it for *you*.'

———

Li Shao woke to find himself lying on a bed of rushes in a hut, bright light slanting through the gaps in its woven roof in dust-mote laden shafts. He groaned, and tried to sit up. He was stiff all over and there was a dull and throbbing pain in his thigh.

From outside, he heard the gabble and chatter of Anean pigmies, though slightly happier and considerably less despair-ridden than before.

Something moved in the shadows, and a cheerful face with cropped dark hair hove into view. It was Benny, in a little woven grass lap-lap and a halter that would have probably done wonders for his recovery if he had not in fact been so unaccountably exhausted. In her hands she held a steaming unglazed earthenware bowl.

'The Doctor thought you'd be up and around,' she said. 'You're a lot less anaemic than you were. Here.' She offered him the bowl.

Li Shao took the bowl with slightly shaking hands and drank. He choked.

'What in the various corrective Sheols builded for the stern correction of the inveterately and unrepentantly villainous was that?' he spluttered.

'Blood soup,' said Benny. 'You really have to drink it.' She suddenly grinned at him wickedly. 'You really don't want to know how we had to administer it to you when you were unconscious.'

Li Shao forced himself to choke the foul stuff down. In actual fact, the flavour was not too dissimilar to that of the behemoth blood and milk he had regularly drunk whilst growing up on Prometheus, the *Shi Noor* prudently never wasting a scrap of their livestock. It was the fact that he had no idea from what, or from whom, *this* blood had actually come that was making him feel slightly queasy.

'How long have I been dead to the world?' he said when

236

he had finally finished the stuff.

Benny shrugged. 'Day and a half. The Doctor thought it would be inadvisable to wake you.'

'A day and a half?' Li Shao tried to stagger to his feet and fell back weakly. 'What have you been doing all this time? What about the Eye?'

'Oh, we've been there, done that,' Benny said dismissively. 'We found it. Well sorted, to coin a particularly asinine phrase.'

'*What?*'

'We found it.' Benny settled down on her haunches and sat on her heels, obviously preparing herself for a tale that threatened to be immoderately long and dreadful in the telling. 'Y'see, after Leetha killed that thing, we came out of the cover of the jungle and – do you know what it was, incidentally? This "eating thing"? Is it indigenous to the System?'

'I've never seen anything like it in my life,' said Li Shao. 'Nor ever heard of such a thing as it, save in the old stories of when the gods would walk the Wanderers.'

'Thought not, but you never know. For all I know there could be three of them on every corner, and one up every alley. Anyway . . .' Benny gestured vaguely to the flaplike doorway of the hut. 'We came out of the jungle, the little buggers took one look at the Doctor and fell on their knees with much prostration and the going of boogie-boogie and suchlike. I have no idea why they keep doing that. After the Doctor had taken care of you – they have these people called "needlemen" here, apparently, who are supposed to tend to the wounds caused by the eating thing; he wouldn't let them near you – after that, he sat down with them for this big pow-wow, with Yani translating, and learnt that the creature originally came from the direction of a lost temple buried deep in the jungle. It was rather fortunate that we got attacked, actually. We'd never have spotted it from the river.

'So at first light we rubbed *blooki*-beetle juice all over us to keep the lymph-sucking mosquitoes away, placed thick discs of brass in our navels to deter the dreaded Anean tummy-button-burrowing jungle leeches, securing them with adhesive tape, and we set off. Many and varied and extraordinarily strange were our adventures before we finally found the temple, and there a small surprise. The temple was over-grown and appeared to be Mayan in general construction – '

'Mayan?' said Li Shao.

'Never mind,' said Benny. 'The point is that the construction was not particularly enhanced by the wreckage of the spaceship that had crashed into the side of it. The ship that the eating thing probably arrived in. The odd thing about it, though, was . . .' Benny paused dramatically. Li Shao got the impression that she was relating her tale with some small degree of interpolated irony.

'Yes?' he said, after a while.

'It was built along remarkably similar lines to our ship,' Benny said. 'The *Schirron Dream*. The Doctor got really sort of thoughtful about that, I can tell you. He hasn't been quite himself, in fact, since he saw the eating thing . . .

'So we entered the temple with caution and trepidation, wary of the mantraps and mechanisms that with much exquisite cunning had been set therein. I was particularly looking forward to dealing with the one with the invisible bridge over a thousand-foot fissure with the pointy spikes at the bottom, the water-powered, pressure-triggered flesh-graters and the granite bowling balls flung by anvils landing on a see-saw and bouncing off a baby trampoline.' She sighed. 'As it turned out, though, we needn't have bothered.

'Something, presumably the eating thing, had gone through the lot and wrecked them all. All we saw were the bent and snapped remains of blades, the sad and prolapsed remains of winding springs. And when, at last, we reached the central chamber, we found a single stone plinth, empty, utterly bereft of any Eye-related item whatsoever.'

'It was gone?' exclaimed Li Shao. 'You said you found it.'

'We did,' Benny said. 'It was where we really knew it had to be all the time. Placed within the wreckage of the ship, in a little chamber that appeared to be designed especially for that very same purpose. So the Doctor put it in his special knapsack and we came back and switched on the radio-beacon. Kiru and Six and the *Schirron Dream* should be arriving any minute now, as it happens. Oh well.' Benny shrugged. 'Bit of an anticlimax all round, really.'

The Twenty-Eighth Chapter

In an area of the central Reklonian mass that would, had it in fact been a monstrous snowman, have been more or less its umbilical region, a particularly extensive bit of navel-searching was in evidence and had been for a number of weeks. Vast strip-mining trenches had been burned through the frost cover by Sloathe heat-rays, melt-water drowning several hundreds of those prisoners sent down into them before a number of Sloathes had been reluctantly prevailed upon to change themselves into systolic forms approximating the function of industrial pumps.

A large number of other prisoners, hundreds more of them, had already died by this point: either frozen in their tracks by the extreme cold before they could scavenge warmer clothing from the fallen, or vaporized instantly by Sloathes not caring what was under them when they opened up with the heat-ray.

Now a tangle of ladders ran down into the trenches to the living bedrock. The surviving prisoners worked on it under the watchful cannon of the Sloathe ships circling the area, cutting slowly through it with picks and sledgehammers and shovels and (since they had after all been equipped by the Sloathes) several highly impracticable implements including a crate of inflatable rubber bananas.

As they worked they sang doleful chain-gang spirituals of a sort that would have a 1963 Louisiania civil-rights activist instantly reaching for a placard, or failing that a club with a nail in it and wondering if the lynch-mobs did not in fact have the right idea. None of these songs come down to us which is, all things considered, probably very fortunate.

One such work-gang was making better progress than the rest. The Escape Committee, having finally been given the tools for which they had waited for years, were now boring through the solid rock like a pneumatic hammer-drill through a piglet.

They had been ordered by the Sloathes to instantly report anything even slightly unexpected that they found. They had, of course, other ideas.

'Get stuck in there!' cried their leàder, the scarred Anean in the hairy pullover who had made the acquaintance of Roslyn Forrester on Planet X, who had originally been a Wing Commander in the System's long-destroyed Fleet and whose name was Kruvars. He turned to a wiry maroon Reklonian who had taken a brief respite from the pitface to enjoy a surreptitious roll-up and was poring over a ragged hand-drawn map pieced together from scavenged envelopes and library glue. Reklonian legends spoke of vast and complex networks of natural caves and tunnels running throughout the Wanderer, and if they could be found then escape was assured. 'How far now, Smudger?'

The Reklonian frowned. 'Couldn't really say, sir. I think we've got a little turned around. Some of the lads have already lost their bearings.'

'Yes,' said Kruvars, 'it's probably the effect of this damned cold.'* He turned to glower back along the tunnel, towards the surface where a faint and flickering reddish glow told him that the heat-ray was in operation again. 'Damn those Sloathes.' He shuddered. 'Frightful buggers. Knew it the moment I first laid eyes on 'em. There goes a class of chap, Bertram, I thought, who'd slit your throat without a how-d'you-do, slake their foul molestatory lusts on the livestock and run off with the memsahibs as soon as look at you. And I was right, too.'

Smudger was looking at him dubiously. 'Well . . . actually, sir, when you come right down to it, that isn't actually what they do, is it? Not as such.'

'Shouldn't you be digging at this point, Smudger?' said ex-Wing Commander Kruvars pointedly.

Smudger saluted. 'Sah!' He trotted towards the activity at the pithead. Momentarily, he turned back. 'I say, you couldn't give us a hand, could you, sir? Only several of the chaps are feeling unaccountably fragile at the moment. Poor

---

* *Incredibly Bad Jokes of the Twentieth Century* No. 17,374.

240

old Beauchamp's sciatica's playing him up something terrible and Todger appears to have spontaneously generated an exceptionally severe case of haemorrhoids, which is making things jolly uncomfortable for him. If I didn't know better, I'd say we're all becoming strangely and unaccountably elderly.'

Kruvars sighed. 'Would that I could, Smudger.' He held up his rubber inflatable banana and waggled it meaningfully. 'Had I the proper tool, I'd be stuck in there with the rest of you chaps like a shot. Like a shot.'

'Damn bad luck, sir, drawing the short straw like that,' said Smudger. 'Especially after you went to all that trouble to collect them all in the first place.'

'Ah well,' said ex-Wing Commander Kruvars, with an air of noble self-sacrifice. 'Mustn't grumble. Such is life.'

Some time later, there was an excited shout from the pitface. Kruvars climbed to his feet from where he had been peaceably toying with his banana, and headed in the direction of the excitement. As he approached the pitface, a great shudder ran through the rock, knocking him off his feet.

The last thing he saw as he struggled to raise himself against a sudden and unWandererly wind, was an explosion of bluish fire, bursting from a breach in the tunnel wall, the silhouettes of skeletons through the skins of the Escape Committee standing before it.

The blue fire rolled over him, blasting him to a greasy stain to subsequently gout, under pressure, from the tunnel mouth.

Some time later, in a chamber of the Sloathe flagship, as it rose from the surface of Reklon, the Sekor Dom Sloathe turned the lumpen, fitfully glowing object in its tentacles. 'I perceive certain and decidedly entropic radiations. I can definitely feel my tissues getting older.' Sloathes are, effectively, perpetually self-renewing and only die by severe structural trauma or being eaten, so this did not distress it unduly. It peered at the object dubiously. 'Other than that, I must confess to being not a little unimpressed. It would appear to be a singularly unprepossessing return for all our efforts, yes?'

Solan gestured with the calm and relaxed precision that

only comes by actively forcing oneself to be calm and relaxed: forcing the body into the precisely correct postures, forcing the lungs to breathe slow and deep, forcing the pores not to sweat.

'I believe it lapses into a degree of dormancy once initial contact has been made,' he said smoothly. 'Rather fortunate for us all, I suspect. There wasn't much left of the work gang who actually found it.'

Weeks amongst the Sloathes had slimmed Solan slightly, so that his thin and already deathly pale skin had a subtle looseness about it, but he was still monstrously corpulent. He had established a certain degree of control amongst the prisoners actually on the flagship, making use of his minimal influence to save them from the worst of the rigours of the Reklon excavation, building a position of relative power that was almost that in microcosm of his previous position in Sere. Even the lesser Sloathes were wary of his influence.

Such power as he had, of course, derived directly from the Sekor Dom Sloathe, whom he had thus far strung along with loose interpretations of the System's legends, increasingly grandiose promises as to the power of the Eyes and an extremely parsimonious releasing of actual hard information, piece by careful piece. Solan had long since noticed certain basic and obvious similarities between himself and the monstrous, brainlike Sloathe – and he knew what he would do with a slave who suddenly failed to be of further use.

'Once the Eyes are finally united,' he now said, 'it'll be another story entirely. He – I do beg your pardon – it who controls the Eyes will have dominion over the System entire.' He smiled thinly. 'When they are disposed with the correct procedures, of course.'

The Sekor Dom Sloathe pulsed. 'Which you still refuse to tell me. If you will pardon any possible slur upon my part, I suspect on occasion that you are simply making it all up as you go along.'

'There is, of course,' said Solan, 'always that possibility.' He drew a sheaf of papers from the befouled and perished remains of his rubber robes. These were the copies of certain notes Solan had had Mr Glome, the degenomancer, transcribe from the images he had pulled from the head of Nathan Li Shao. There had in fact, he reflected, been a small problem so far as the Reklonian Eye was concerned. Li Shao had merely given the passages pertaining to it a partial and disinterested glance. Solan had been forced to give a heavily expanded and tortuously embroidered translation, merely pointing in the end to a general area, and relying upon the bludgeoning methods of the Sloathes to keep on digging till they found it. It had only been the fact that, even with its uncharacteristic and radically expanded mentation, the Sekor Dom Sloathe could not read a word of the System's Tongue that had allowed Solan to get away with it.

Never mind. He had anticipated such complications and had laid his plans carefully. The essence of the hunt, after all, was not the stalking but the waiting.

Now he rifled through the transcribed notes with an almost entirely feigned sense of portentousness. 'I know what you have to do. I know where you have to do it. I know *when* you have to do it. You'll know soon enough if I'm lying to you – but until then you need me.'

'It occurs to me,' said the Sekor Dom Sloathe thoughtfully, 'that I could get almost any one of your fellow aboriginals to read those papers.'

Solan nodded. 'But I'm the only one who'd tell you what I read.'

'And what do you think could possibly happen to you afterwards? When I am the absolute master of your System? Do you honestly expect to survive, then?'

'No,' Solan told it simply. 'But in the interim, I will have clung to just that little bit of extra life while others die.' A twinge went through him, under his heart. He maintained his conscious poise. 'And speaking of which . . . ?'

'Ah, yes.' The Sekor Dom Sloathe generated a needle-appendage and, without preamble, plunged it into Solan's neck. Solan gasped and shook, momentarily losing his conscious control, and lapsing into an expression of vicious, snarling and absolute ferality, reminiscent of a wounded rat in a corner, that even the sluglike lesser Sloathe guards gathered around them did not fail to notice. They flinched, momentarily, in startlement.

Solan slumped from his state and drew a shuddering breath. While he recovered, the Sekor Dom Sloathe warped a section of itself briefly into a transmitter-shape. Carefully shielding hirself against contact with Planet X – it would not do to broadcast hir personal plans to the Most Elevated and Puissant Emperor Kraator Xem, after all – it concentrated upon the spy-ships it had placed to watch over the inner Wanderers within the asteroid Ring.

The transmitter-shape collapsed.

'It would seem we have wasted too much time on this ice world,' it said. 'It appears that even now they are leaving the jungle world and preparing for the outer traverse.'

Solan had recovered his composure. 'No matter,' he said smoothly. 'It's only what I expected.' He smiled coldly. 'It is not, after all, as if we don't know precisely where they're going to end up.'

<hr />

And across the System the Wanderers continued their by now slightly lurching orbits around a Sun that, had one been able to directly look upon it, would be seen to be disfigured by several small but growing spots of darkness, like little freckles. Like little *fleurs du mal*.

On the Wanderers themselves the random disruptions continued, from miniature whirlwinds two feet across that destroyed diminutive jungle microclimates, to fault-fissures and tidal waves that respectively engulfed or drowned whole cities and settlements.

All of these were observed through the segmented telescopes of Planet X, and so engrossed by these (together with their observation of the events on Reklon that, from what they gathered from the Sekor Dom Sloathe, were apparently going to get them lots of *nice* and *pretty* things) that the Most Elevated and Puissant Emperor Kraator Xem and hir Lieutenant Lokar Pan had entirely failed to notice the complete and utter eradication of every other Sloathe in the tunnels outside their observation chamber.

'Is big volcano-explosion there,' said Lokar Pan, who was currently assuming the form of a large peeled boar-hog with a set of suckered octopus legs instead of tusks, peering through the eyepiece of a telescope with a single enlarged eye. 'And is big spout of water there . . .'

'Make it stop,' the Most Elevated and Puissant Emperor Kraator Xem growled, ejecting bits of partially digested

244

shredded smaller Sloathe from its vents in pique. Several smaller and mindless Sloathes darted out from behind the vitrine and fell upon them, fighting over them like a pack of slippery, hairless chihuahuas over a particularly tasty pile of sick. Automatically, the Most Elevated and Puissant Emperor Kraator Xem speared the lot of them and hauled them, squealing, in.

'Is breaking all my nice and pretty things!' it continued furiously. 'Make it go away and stop doing things like that!'

And then, abruptly, it stopped. It quivered slightly. 'Is what this thing is?' it said in a suddenly puzzled voice.

And then, uncontrollably, it began to shudder and thrash.

'AAGH! GRAAAAGH! AIEEE!' it said.

Vaguely interested, Lokar Pan left the telescope and wandered over to the jerking, screaming mass. 'What happen?'

'GRAH! HOCH! HURK! EEEEGH!' shrieked the Most Elevated and Puissant Emperor Kraator Xem. **'WHAAGH! HURK! IS ALL AROUND AND EATING! IS EATING ALL MY LOVELY BIG AND PENDULOUS APPENDAGES! AK! BREK! WRUGH!'**

'Ho, hum,' said Lokar Pan, in the cheerfully concerned tones of one who, whatever might be happening, it isn't actually happening to hir. 'Is must be very horrible and painful, yes?'

It moved closer to the suddenly very interesting-acting Most Elevated and Puissant Emperor Kraator Xem – and at that precise point, from the tunnels leading into the chambers occupied by the remainder of Kraator Xem's vast bulk, burst a squirming mass of tentacles ending in voraciously snapping jaws.

(And in the centre of things, undetected in its dying orrery chamber, the thing inside watched, and waited. Now it was expectant.

Death and revenge. It wanted it. It would not have long to wait, now.)

The Twenty-Ninth Chapter

And so at last to Elysium, the water world, a single mass of water held by surface tension in a slightly wobbly globule some seven hundred miles in diameter, circumscribed four thousand feet above the surface by a mile-thick hoop of gravitite and brass, around which the dread india-rubber moon of Rubri, with its polymorphic fauna and fiendish degenomancers, bounces.

And on the surface, the drifting remains of pontoon citadels left deserted and in ruins by the Sloathes, the wrecked and derelict hulls of whole nautical fleets. Capsized and partially crushed barques jostle the burnt-out husks of paddle-steamers, self-winding clockwork hovercraft spiral aimlessly on their emergency flotation tanks and hydrofoils have sunk without trace, to be mangled and crushed by the horrendous pressures of the depths lit only by the lantern-fish and lampreys. Galley boats, triremes and the once-swift and darting corsairs of the pirate-gangs who haunted the trade routes between the pontoon cities like packs of hungry sea wolves now wallow, waterlogged, helpless as the merchantmen and galleons and clippers and freighters upon which once they preyed.

Nothing humanoid is alive here, now. No artifact, nothing that is *made*, now moves. Only the squid and the nautili and the shoals of fish move under the surface, only the storm-fronts and a bouncing, malignant moon move above it. Only the freak clusters of waterspouts break the surface, playing a music no human ear was ever meant to hear.

Waves crashed against the side of a resin-sealed and varnished pontoon arcing to some fifty feet above sea level.

246

Through the spume, Benny saw the floating bulk of the *Schirron Dream* and, beyond that, the receding forms of the towering and majestically whistling waterspouts.

Benny hauled herself from the rubber dinghy tethered by its painter and began to climb the slightly rusted iron rungs set into the side of the pontoon. 'It's all very impressive,' she called back to the Doctor as he climbed behind her, her words, already half drowned out, whipped from her mouth by a wind that entirely failed to disturb the hat planted firmly on his head.

'Impressive?' he said absently, his words reaching her perfectly. 'Yes, I imagine so. Very impressive.'

'I just wish they were whistling something other than "Oh, I do Like to be Beside the Seaside",' Benny said. 'That always sort of spoils the effect for me.'

'Ah yes,' said the Doctor. 'Right you are. I'll attend to it directly.' He lapsed back into his own private thoughts. It was obvious he hadn't listened to a word she'd been saying.

Behind them came a couple of Elysians from the crew, one human and one amphibian in form. Up ahead, Li Shao, Leetha, Kiru and the floating form of Six were entering a hatch set in one of the massive steel pilings that supported the citadel.

Benny reached the top of the piling and climbed through the hatch to find a spiral staircase running upward. Above her she heard the multiple and receding clang of hobnailed boots on the steps as the others climbed. A moment later the Doctor appeared, and she held him back to let the two Elysians go on ahead.

'So what's the problem?' she said as they climbed relatively alone.

'Problem?' The Time Lord regarded her innocently with his flat grey-green eyes, the majority of his attention still clearly upon something else. 'Why should there be a problem?'

'Don't give me that,' Benny said. 'You've been like this ever since Aneas. Closed in. Preoccupied. Ever since you saw that "eating thing". I don't think anyone else noticed in the confusion, but I saw you go white as a sheet for a second or two. It was like you'd seen a ghost.' She scowled. 'You spent the best part of the trip here in one of your bloody trances in front of the Eyes, just staring at the things. I think

247

it's about time you told me what exactly's going on here.'

'That's easier said than done, Benny,' said the Doctor, cautiously. 'You're aware of the concept of simultaneity?'

Benny thought about it. 'That's Jung, right? Meaningful coincidences that have no basis in cause-and-effect. Or is that Bell's Theorem? Cosmic glue, the x-factor and the hidden variable, one of those lads.'

'You're actually thinking of "synchronicity", I think, which is something slightly different. Besides . . .' the doctor smiled, 'the x-factor isn't operating, here, at the moment. I'd know it if he was. I've met him, as a matter of fact.'

'Him?' Benny said, momentarily sidetracked by this latest bit of Doctorial bare-faced cheek. 'Let me get this straight. You've met the x-factor.'

'In the sense of a metasystemic "observer" that validates the transition between quantum states – the ear that hears the tree fall in the forest, as it were. It's been variously described as universal consciousness or even God, but it is in fact a Mr J. P. Critchlowe of 57 Leafy Bowers, Tring.' He grinned at Benny evilly. 'Anything that happens in the known universe, should there be no nervous system or a reasonable analogue thereof to hand and sufficiently capable of registering it, Mr Critchlowe goes and watches it.'

'What, the whole universe?' said Benny. 'The whole lot? Everything that does or did or ever will exist?'

'The whole universe,' said the Doctor.

'Now, hang on,' said Benny. 'I can spot the flaw in the premise, here. If this J. P. Critchlowe's out observing everything in the known universe, who's observing everything at home when he's out doing it, eh? Answer me that.'

The Time Lord grinned again. 'Ah, now that's all taken care of by his lovely wife, Moira, who goes around 57 Leafy Bowers looking at things in his absence. Lovely woman. Doesn't get out a lot, sadly.'

'Ha bloody ha,' said Benny. 'Now if we've all quite finished talking total bollocks for the moment, I still want to know what's really going on.'

'There's always time for nonsense,' said the Doctor firmly. 'And I must say I don't particularly care for your language of late. A paucity of language denotes a shallow and enfeebled mind.'

'Sod the paucity of language. Tell. Me. What. Is. Going. On.'

The Time Lord sighed. 'Very well. I'll tell you what I can. It seems that when Leetha spoke of the Eyes as being the "souls" of the Wanderers, she was closer than we knew. I've been studying them closely and the arrangement of their planes, the very shape they make in the world, seems to make them analogues of the Wanderers themselves, inextricably linked with them on certain subatomic and extradimensional levels. The state of one reflects and even, possibly, manipulates the state of the other.'

'Like a voodoo obi-doll or something?' Benny said dubiously. 'The Promethean Eye doesn't look like Prometheus, and the Anean Eye certainly doesn't look like a great big tree. I'd have noticed something like that.'

'You haven't got my eyes,' said the Doctor. 'The Eyes themselves, on the other hand, are analogues of the Wanderers – and something more.' He gestured sweepingly to take in the entire world. 'I think I've already mentioned that this whole System is something of a macrocosm, with its own set of personal and quite remarkable physical laws. You tend not to notice the effects because they occur in context, and because the defence-mechanisms of your own mind are desperately trying to protect you. It's evidencing itself in perceived phenomena that, apparently, take on the form of a series of incredibly bad jokes given life. If your mind ever let you see things as they truly are, you'd be profoundly shocked and horrified, I'm sure.'

'You've got to laugh or else you'd cry, eh?' said Benny.

'Something like that. The real point is that within the Eyes there seem to be a number of interdimensional wormholes, linking the microcosm of the System to a macrocosm – a universe far larger and with an entirely different energy-slope.' The Time Lord frowned. 'I think it's our own.'

'Do you mean there's a way out of here?' Benny exclaimed. 'There's a way home? Why didn't you tell me?'

'You didn't ask. Besides, it isn't precisely a practicable means of escape, unless you'd actively enjoy being sucked through a hole a fraction of a micron in diameter and ejected Rassilon knows where – probably the heart of a small sun.'

Benny thought about it. 'I think I'll give that one a miss,

thanks. So the Eyes are as powerful as the legends said they were. But how did that occur? Are you going to tell me that they were simply knocked up by a bunch of independent ancient craftsmen by coincidence? Without the precise degree of measurement you'd need? Purely at random?'

'If a thing is possible, it will happen,' said the Doctor. 'Given a random process and time. A particular primordial soup of complex enzymes must at some point produce DNA molecules, for example, and if a biological niche exists then it must at some point be filled. I think the Eyes extant came to be through a broadly similar process of evolution and natural selection – though I don't think the process was exactly random.' The worried, thoughtful look was back on his face again. 'It was directed. Something, somewhere, was actively willing this to happen.'

'This thing you suspected was watching over the lot of us.' Benny wasn't asking a question. 'And now you think you know what it is.'

'I think so.' Unaccountably, the Time Lord seemed hesitant, not so much lost for words, exactly, as picking through them with extreme caution, as though they might suddenly turn on him and bite him. Considering thoughts which he could safely articulate. 'When I saw the "eating thing" on Aneas, it triggered a memory – not my own, but a racial memory. Something Gallifreyans wanted remembered through the generations, and indeed the regenerations. Locked off. Waiting for a specific trigger. I looked at the eating thing, and the blocks came down, and I remembered certain things.'

'So what did you remember?' Benny said. 'What do you know?'

'Well, for a start, I know that the word "Schirron" is a corruption of something else. The real word is "Charon".'

Benny wanted to ask what a 'Charon' was, but at that point the staircase ended in a chamber walled with copper plates, and with passages leading off in three directions.

Li Shao, Leetha and the others were waiting for them.

'You took your time,' Li Shao said. 'We were going to send someone back for you. We thought that something ghastly had happened to you.'

Neither the Book of the Search nor the late Kimon's notes had proved entirely helpful so far as the Elysian Eye was concerned, beyond that it was associated with the pontoon citadel of Marloon. It had therefore been decided to split into two general search-parties and scour the citadel in the hope that if, as the Doctor suspected, something actually *wanted* them to find the eyes, then find the Elysian Eye they would.

Now Benny wandered through deserted gangways littered with the picked-over debris left by the Sloathes. Nothing moved here, nothing it seemed was alive, but a faint scuttling told her that rats and other vermin had survived.

With her were Kiru and Six and a phenotypically human Elysian, who was named Pol. The Doctor had gone with Leetha and Li Shao, and Benny had an idea that this was as much to defer her repeated questioning as anything else. She'd really have to bring this to a head at some point, she thought.

She remembered how she had once thought she could exist with the Time Lord in a partnership of equals. That was before she realized what being irreparably out-evolved actually meant in human terms and that she or any other of her kind, in relative terms, could never be much more than a glorified pet. This had troubled her deeply – it was only with hindsight that she recalled certain behavioural patterns remarkably similar to that of a dispossessed Native American, or a displaced Australian Aborigine, or an Aztec high priest confronted by an incomprehensible Cortez: a massive and subconscious culture shock that had one simply giving up and lying down to die. And it continued to trouble her until she realized that the relationship was in fact more like Ace, a previous companion of the Doctor's, and her bloody cats. Benny couldn't stand the vicious little bastards as a rule, but they seemed to have the right idea so far as it concerned getting on with creatures somewhat higher up the evolutionary ladder and who could operate tin-openers.

Of course the Doctor, for his part, maintained that it wasn't like that at all. Oh yes it was. He might show you how the tin-opener worked, time and time again, hoping against hope that you'd eventually get the message, but the unbridgeable gulf was still there. Finally, Benny had come to terms with it all by simply deciding it was as stupid as getting all upset about a Californian redwood because one is not a couple of

251

thousand years old and a hundred and thirty feet tall – and besides, actually being chosen by the Doctor probably put you head and shoulders above the vast run of humanity in any case. Then again of course, the Time Lord was just the sort of person who inveterately picked up injured and bedraggled and miserably pathetic strays . . .

But the acquisition of a pet incurs responsibility. That was something of which the Doctor had to be continually reminded. Three-odd subjective years before, when she had first met him, Benny had seen an entirely avoidable tragedy take place, simply because the Time Lord had secretively neglected to relate a vital piece of information.

Here and now, however, the gangway was opening out into a large and darkened space that, from the echoes of her footfalls, sounded larger than the hangar of an aircraft carrier. Benny, lost for a while in thought, realized that she had somehow lost track of the others.

'Kiru?' She cast about herself, the beam of her rubber-coated galvanistical torch playing across steel deckplates in a warping, ellipsoidal pool of light, ears alert for any sound. 'Six? Pol?'

Her voice reverberated off distant sheet-steel bulkheads. She turned to head back the way she had come – and something slithered through the dark.

It lunged for her. The beam of the torch jerked across something glistening and covered with eyes and the beaks of octopi, and then something bludgeoned the torch from her hand. It spun end over end in a shallow arc, to hit the deck with a tinkle as its lens imploded, and cast a diffuse fan of light across the steel.

Slippery, wormlike things crawled over Benny, sliding under her clothing and across her skin. She tried to scream, but then several of the thing's elongated tentacles slipped into her mouth and began to choke her. And other things just like it moved towards her in the dark.

Leetha T'Zhan, Nathan Li Shao, the Doctor and an Elysian named Goma wandered through an area directly under the Starsail tower of the citadel. It appeared to have once been a residential area, converted at some historical point from cabins originally used for some more communal way of life. Large and hall-like spaces had been partitioned off with materials scavenged over the years to produce a series of self-contained cabins. The wreckage of past battles had torn many of these partitions down; splintered planks of cedar and scale-like bronze and enamelled plates, tangles of copper wire and flakes of lapis lazuli, spongy chipboard and crumbled plaster, balsa glazed with cellulose dope, ceramic and terracotta tiling, larch inlaid with ivory, rust-eaten iron grilles, linoleum, ragged scraps of hessian lay strewn throughout this dark and derelict warren, together with a surprising number of valuables which had remained unlooted where they had fallen.

They passed through a stateroom reminiscent of a 1900s transatlantic liner overlaid with the captain's quarters of a seventeenth-century merchant-venturer: all art deco mixed with rococo gilt and black-oak decks and sextants hanging from the walls. The Doctor picked up a small, sealed globe of blown glass. Within it was a lumpen figure carved from pale-blue topaz: a gnarled Jack Frost figure that seemed to be woven together from icicle strands, around which flecks of white quartz swirled, suspended in distilled water. He gazed at it intently, seemingly lost in contemplation.

'The Sloathes left this place untouched,' Leetha said uneasily. 'I'm not sure if I like that.'

Li Shao nodded. They had come through the areas which the Sloathes had fully looted. Nothing remained there but bare decks and balks, if even that. More than once they had been forced to pick their way across bare joists slung over lightless pits. Then the evidence of looting, if not the actual destruction, had seemed to peter out.

'I don't like it at all,' Li Shao said. 'Elysian has been occupied for years. This whole place, the whole Wanderer, should be crawling with them.'

When the *Schirron Dream* had blasted through the Ring and into Sloathe airspaces, Li Shao had been looking forward to a fight. Some large part of him, even though he now believed to some degree in the importance of the Eyes, still dreamed of a final death-and-glory charge against overwhelming forces, and he had been slightly disappointed to find nothing. No Sloathe ships in radar range, nothing

253

enforcing any notional blockade. They had pressed on to Elysian to find this silent and deserted wreck with no apparent Sloathe activity. None at all. It was as though every single Sloathe had at some point simply stopped whatever they were doing and upon the instant left.

Like Leetha, Li Shao found this highly suspicious, and in an emotional sense not a little alarming. A Wanderer overrun with Sloathes was at least comprehensible, whereas this was simply not how the world *was*.

'It must have happened recently,' he said, running his hand over a brass astrolabe.

'How so?' said Leetha.

Li Shao held up his relatively clean fingers. 'No dust.'

'That doesn't mean nothing. Broak,' said Goma, a tough, squat and muscular woman who wore a jointed ivory prosthetic hand with brass fish-hooks screwed to the fingers in place of nails. 'This is the water world. No dust gathers here. Rek. Place could have been left any time.'

'The lady is quite correct,' said Solan, stepping from the darkness behind a partially collapsed oak panel, the bulks of Sloathes jostling amongst each other to enter behind him. And behind them all glistened the multiple eyes of something brainlike.

'In actual fact, however,' Solan continued, his slack and split lips twitched in a rictal attempt at an urbane grin, 'the citadel has in fact only been deserted for a short time. So everybody's right, and nobody's wrong. Now isn't that a nice surprise?'

———∞———

Floating some hundred yards from the pontoon citadel, the crew of the *Schirron Dream* watched the skies, their eyes trained on radar readouts, their cannon ready for any Sloathe vessel that might attempt to land.

They were therefore entirely unprepared for the fleet of Sloathe ships, hundreds of them, as they released their ballast and burst, like rearing whales, from the choppy sea.

———∞———

'The secret of hunting isn't in the chase,' said Solan. 'It's in the lying in wait.'

254

'Traitor!' Li Shao struggled in the tentacular grip of a Sloathe. 'You sold out your own kind! I'll kill you!'

'Now I don't really believe that is in fact an option at this point.' Solan waddled over to Li Shao and backhanded him in the face. 'Oh dear. You appear to have had a small and unfortunate accident.' He turned his gaze to the sullen Goma and the incoherently hissing Leetha. 'Do you have anything further to add, my dear ladies? No, then well, I . . .'

He found his gaze drawn to the Doctor, standing calmly within the coils of Sloathe tentacles and regarding him steadily and frankly.

'And you?' said Solan. 'Do you have some glittering pearl of wisdom in relation to my most reprehensible and treacherous behaviour?'

'Not particularly,' said the Time Lord thoughtfully. 'Though I have an idea that treachery is not exactly the correct word.' He glanced with his strange eyes at the Sloathes restraining the others, at the squat bulk of the Sekor Dom Sloathe, who was in turn regarding this scene with barely restrained impatience. 'I believe that you have infected these creatures with something of your own evil, twisted them around yourself in the same way that you twisted the society of Sere. There's only you, here. There's never anyone else. You're alone as you ever were.'

For the slightest instant, the face of Solan appeared to collapse into a blazing and absolute rage – and then he recovered his poise.

'Ah, but then there's just so much of me,' he said lightly. 'Now, where was I? Oh yes . . .'

He turned back to Nathan Li Shao. 'Now I'm afraid, my dear captain, that when we met last I myself was not being as completely honest with you as I might have – so far as my actual motivations were concerned, at any rate.

'You see, when I learnt that you were going after the Eyes, I became very interested in your exploits indeed. For various reasons I already had certain intimations of their power. But then of course you escaped my clutches, the Sloathes invaded and the situation changed. I was forced to cling to life as best I could.' Solan glanced back towards the Sekor Dom Sloathe briefly, and then became brisk again. 'No matter. Certain basic facts of the situation remained unchanged.'

The Sekor Dom Sloathe pulsed. 'I'm allowing you cer tain indulgences, Solan,' it said. 'A little leeway for you appetites. But my patience is rapidly becoming exhausted Get on with it.'

'Your wish, as ever, is my command.' Solan turned back to Li Shao again with a companionable smile. 'Now, I learn that you had obtained a ship outclassing anything even th Sloathes could provide – and indeed, you managed to locat two of the Eyes before the Sloathes with my assistance ha barely located one. Ah . . .'

Solan and the eye appendages of the Sekor Dom Sloathe simultaneously turned to the breach in the cabin partition from which there came a pale and shifting bluish glow.

Stumbling through the breach, a Sloathe guard behind him came the impossibly ancient figure of a Reklonian. His brittl hair had almost completely moulted. Folds of parched and crumbling skin hung from his bones. Clutched to his chest burning with an inner bluish fire, was the Reklonian Eye.

The Reklonian stumbled further into the cabin and then simultaneously, both his legs crumbled under him. He collapsed in a heap and began to moulder into what, in a more desiccated atmosphere, would have been dust, but which here in the moist Elysian air was more like sodde ashes.

The Reklonian Eye glowed through the mess.

'That seems to happen all the time, I'm afraid,' said Solar casually. 'We'll need some little helpers, as it were, to transfer the Eye to your own ship, and thence to the Sun, a the legends so charmingly instruct.'

He wandered along the row of Sloathe-pinioned captives idly considering each of them in turn. 'Not you, I think, m dear captain . . . nor you, my dear. You gave me some little trouble in Sere, I recall, and I rather think I'd like to save yo for last. Give you time to observe and reflect. Now, *you*, think,' he said, stopping before Goma and examining he critically, 'strike me as somebody with which we can easily dispense at this point –'

'No!' cried a sharp voice. Solan became aware that the small man with the hat had suddenly begun to struggle against the tentacles restraining him. 'No!' the small mar cried again.

'Oh yes?' Solan turned to him coldly. 'You have something to say?'

'You don't have to do this,' the little man snarled, still struggling desperately. 'You don't have to commit any more cold-blooded murders. You can let me handle the damned thing and –'

'How touching,' said Solan. 'But I'm afraid not. Once again, I'm afraid, I have not been entirely frank with you. I believe I've already mentioned that the secret of hunting lies in the wait, waiting where the prey will certainly go – and the reason that you were allowed through the inner Wanderers entirely unmolested is that we knew, precisely, where you would be going next.'

Another decomposing figure, a human, stumbled through the breach. In its gnarled and liver-spotted hands it clutched an irregularly shaped lump of crystal in which an unWanderly fire burned.

'The Elysian Eye,' Solan said quite calmly. 'It was taken from this very place some eight years ago in the refugee exodus – by some refugees who, unfortunately for them, fortunately for me, attempted to arrange safe passage to the inner Wanderers through my good self. They're long-dead now, of course. The Elysian Eye has been in my possession, a curio in my vaults in Sere, these past eight years.

'So you see . . .' Solan turned back to the Doctor with his slack and insane little smile, 'while your concern for the lady does you enormous credit, accepting her burden would leave you with no hands free for an Eye of your very own.'

───

With a Sloathe behind her prodding several spearlike appendages in her back, Benny was herded across a Sloathe which had extruded itself into a slippery approximation of a gangplank, bridging the gap between the pontoon citadel and a massive Sloathe ship. Its bulk was such that she could not see anything past it or to either side, and barely a thin ribbon of ocean water fifty feet below.

'Bugger!' Benny's foot slipped on the slick grey surface of the gangplank-Sloathe and she nearly went over the side.

'Silence!' her ambulatory captor squeaked. 'Is not nice to use such word. Is lower the lofty tone no enormously end,

257

monkey-hominids going shit sod bugger all the sodding time.'

'You should meet the Doctor,' Benny muttered to herself. 'You'd get on like a house on fire.'

'Is silence!'

'Suit yourself,' said Benny.

She had come to her senses to find herself surrounded by several Sloathes, who were taking it in squabbling turns to hold her by now weakly flickering galvanistical torch in front of her face and shout, 'Ve have vays of makink you talk!' in an atrociously guttural and vaguely Germanic-sounding accent. There was no telling how long this would have gone on had not a new Sloathe appeared, told them that this particular pretend-move thing was wanted for tip-top priority special stuff and taken charge of her. This did not, Benny thought uneasily, auger well, and directed every subsequent thought along the lines of frying-pans and gas-burners.

Now it took her through a maw-like opening in the side of the ship (with little holes around its edge from which the teeth had been pulled), and through a twisting series of slimy tunnels packed with junk that triggered vague images of her single, brief and disjointed glimpse of a Sloathe ship weeks before. Through several Sloathe-squirming chambers and towards the heart, as it were, of the ship.

They came to a sphincter-like portal guarded by an obloidular Sloathe roughly the size of a baby elephant, who regarded Benny suspiciously. 'Is what *another* pretend-move thing out now?'

'Is being taken for extremely big and horrible tortures,' said the Sloathe behind Benny.

'Now hang on a minute –', said Benny.

'Is stick spiky things into it and bite things off and make it go "Ghaagh!" '

'Hey, listen,' Benny surreptitiously glanced around for any means of escape. 'I mean a joke's a joke, right, and nobody can say I can't take a –'

'Silence!' The Sloathe shoved her through the portal, which had by this time dilated with a little wet and sucking sound, and into a chamber blocked by a second such portal to form an arrangement similar to a large and roomy airlock.

Sitting here, guarded by a Sloathe that looked like a nest of

258

snakes with eyes on stalks suspended from flotation sacs, were Kiru and Pol. They were slightly bruised and battered, but seemed relatively fit – Kiru even seemed cheerful, so far as could be judged from his permanently sardonic features.

Benny was so startled by their sudden reappearance that she momentarily failed to notice the sphincter-portal contracting shut behind her, the menacing presence of the Sloathe who had marched her here collapsing in on itself and transmuting itself into new shapes.

'Kiru?' she said. 'Pol? They got you as well? Where's Six?'

'Well, they didn't actually get us,' said Kiru. 'Not exactly, and –'

'And as it happens,' said the Sloathe depending from gas sacs, '*I'm* Six.'

'You.' For a moment Benny was, simply, unable to take it in. Then she backed off, shuffling on the balls of her feet, bringing up her hands in a defensive posture she had learnt in the Service and preparing for the final and inevitably doomed fight of her life. 'You were with us all the time. Spying on us . . .' she said absently, most of her mind automatically switching to the *muga*-processes of imminent unarmed combat.

'Oh bloody hell,' Six said. 'Here we go again. Laughing boy here nearly killed me before I got the chance to explain.' It swung a couple of eyestalks to indicate Kiru.

'Benny,' Kiru said, 'it's all right. Really.'

'Oh yeah?' she spat, still backing off – and backed right into the Sloathe she had forgotten about. She spun around with what she swore blind afterwards was a snarl of utter fury, but which struck the others there at the time as a little whimper of horror.

The Sloathe had formed itself into something bipedal and humanoid, raising its hands before itself placatorily. As Benny watched, dumbfounded, its features resolved into something increasingly human. There was something strangely familiar about these features, something she couldn't quite . . .

And then she got it.

The grey face was an amalgam of those of Roslyn Forrester and Chris Cwej, something caught between them as though in the median stage of a morphing program.

259

'It's all right,' the face said in rough but identifiably humanoid tones. 'You're safe for the moment at least. My name's Sgloomi Po.'

And in the centre of a System spinning towards catastrophe, black *acne Solaria* proliferated across the Sun. And on the desert-Wanderer of Prometheus, great cracks appeared in the bedrock of the battlegrounds causing sundry armaments, miscellaneous weaponry and whole warring K'ans to plunge to their deaths. And on the jungle-Wanderer of Aneas whole limbs of the world-tree that supported it collapsed. And in the asteroid Ring whole swathes of asteroids simultaneously exploded into millions of microscopic shards. And vast bubbles rose up through Elysium to burst upon the surface and overturn a thousand derelict craft and several deserted citadels in the backwash. And on the ice-Wanderer of Reklon a sudden burst of volcanic activity blew half the snowman's head off.

And inside Planet X, trapped in the System's encapsulating energy-field, something slithered through the otherwise empty tunnels, its tendrils extruding and meshing and interconnecting like some vast analogue of a nervous system built from fleshy cable.

And the thing that had once been the Most Supreme Captain Trenkor Lep still hungered. There was nothing left for it to feed upon. The impulses of the Sloathes it had digested still gibbered and shrieked in what still passed for its mind: it knew them all and it knew everything they had ever thought and known; they talked to it like half-forgotten ghosts, never ceasing, never still – but this was overwhelmed and all-but blotted out by the impulses of simple need.

It was hungry. It wanted more. It had to feed.

Elsewhere it heard the voices of other Sloathes. Other prey. They were a long way away and it wanted to *eat* them.

The thing that had once been the Most Supreme Captain Trenkor Lep spread itself through Planet X, like a neurosystem, and thought about it. What passed for thinking. In what passed for its mind.

It was the single largest Sloathe that had ever existed – the biggest living organism that had ever existed in the System. So big, in fact, that its very presence affected and distorted

260

e electromagnetic forces that held the System together. It
as inevitable that, at some point, it would learn to some
egree to control them.

It was not a conscious process. The thing that had once
een the Most Supreme Captain Trenkor Lep merely dis-
overed that if it made a bit of itself into *this* shape, and made
nother bit of itself into *that*, it could make itself and the
asalt moon it was infesting *move*.

And the energy field, the visible phenomenon of the
olydimensional möbeus surface that contained itself and the
ystem within it, thrashed and screamed as the basalt moon
f Planet X strained against it.

Thrashed and screamed in its death throes.

Canto Last:
Falling Together

Instant degradation followed in every direction – a flood of folly and hypocrisy. Mythologies, ill-understood at first, then perverted into feeble sensualities [. . .] Gods without power, satyrs without rusticity, nymphs without innocence, men without humanity, gather into idiot groups upon the polluted canvas, and scenic affections encumber the streets with preposterous marble. Lower and lower declines the level of abused intellect; the base school of landscape gradually usurps the place of the historical painting, which has sunk to the level of prurient pedantry . . .

John Ruskin
Stones of Venice

'That's all, folks.'
Porky Pig

The Penultimate Chapter

At last!

The thing inside knew an overwhelming flush of pleasure that flooded its response-systems to the point where, for an infinitesimal moment, it was quite delirious. For weeks now it had watched events unfolding, knowing that, as they gathered their own momentum, there was but a single direction in which they could lead. Only one, foregone, conclusion.

The thing inside had only extended its influence twice in the past weeks, and these merely to fine-tune events and save a little time. In Sere it had triggered the impulse that had led the corpulent human, Solan, into betraying the existence of the Eyes to the Sloathes, and on Aneas it had triggered the reckless bravura of the Li Shao human that had led to the discovery of the Anean Eye. Neither of these efforts had taxed the thing inside's failing strength overmuch: events would have followed a similar course in any case. The thing inside was simply making the individuals concerned be just that almost imperceptible bit more of what they already were. The loss of the thing inside's last remaining simulacrum in the latter case was unfortunate, and the thing inside had shrieked with its relayed death-agony – but the simulacrum was damaged and operating on its own independent control mechanisms, the thing inside couldn't control it, and it had been well worth the sacrifice. For now the Eyes were coming. They were being brought now into spaces where the thing inside could, at last, assume some degree of direct control. There were two minds in particular so similar to the thing inside's that they cried *out* to be infested.

Coming soon now. Very soon. Very very very very *very* very very soon. Very soon indeed. At some point.

———

And the Sloathe ships sailed towards the Sun, making use of
the slipstreams that had so aided them in their occupation of
Reklon, and then Elysium, and then their forays into the
inner Wanderers. Once there they would slingshot around it,
using its gravitational acceleration to fling them towards
Planet X: stuck stationary in the System's encapsulating field
while Elysium had swung into apogee from it. The Sloathe
were going home.

That, at least, was the official explanation. It might have
occurred to them that the simplest way would be to simply
wait until Elysium swung round closer again, but then again
Sloathes were not exactly used to thinking for themselves.
Those who were actually capable of contacting their home at
this distance merely put the absence of any reply down to the
fact that nobody wanted to talk to them at that point.

In the vanguard of the fleet, under half-power, flew the
Schirron Dream, its orgone engines pulsing a deep purple. In
its gangways and its cabins, Sloathes went about their duties
listlessly. The ship didn't like them, wanted to be rid of
them and was bombarding them with emissions that would
cumulatively kill a humanoid, but which because of the
Sloathes' radically different physiologies was merely giving
them the alien equivalent of sick and irritable headaches. In
the bridge squatted the Sekor Dom Sloathe, attended upon by
Solan, although it was becoming increasingly doubtful as to
who was slave and who was master: not through a simple
transposition of roles, but by a subtle merging of them. The
only other living things that were not Sloathes were locked in
a small aft storage hold, slightly forward of the secure
chamber where the Eyes themselves, all four of them, were
stored.

―――∞―――

The Doctor looked down at the withered corpse of Goma
with nothing in his flat and green-grey eyes. Leetha found
herself wondering if she actually had tear-ducts as such, and
whether the lack of them would in fact be a loss or a gain.

'It shouldn't have happened,' he said quietly. 'Just another
little piece of pointless cruelty. I shouldn't have allowed it to
happen.'

Leetha wanted to touch him, put a hand on his shoulder

266

make some sort of contact – but for some reason she couldn't. It was as if she couldn't pluck up the courage. 'There was nothing you could have done,' she said awkwardly.

The Doctor turned his eyes on her. 'Wasn't there?'

By the time they had been herded on to the ship and deposited the Eyes in their secure chamber, Goma had been eaten down to skin and bone. Leetha had been reminded of the mummified remains of high priests on display in the temples of Rakath – and had been suddenly shocked and a little ashamed to realize that she had not given her home a single thought in the months since she had escaped its destruction. Not once.

Nothing as decayed as Goma should possibly have been able to live – but she had clung on to life for days in the prison hold. The Doctor had spent that time with her. Not eating, never sleeping. Just sitting with her. Sometimes he would hold her hand.

Now he was looking at Leetha, his flat dry eyes radiating such a cold and absolute rage that she was forced to turn away from it – glancing desperately around at the other prisoners who had survived the assault on the ship on Elysium, simply so that she wouldn't have to look back to him.

Yani the pigmy girl was squatting in the corner in subdued conversation with Kai (who had formed something of an attachment with her on Aneas and elected to come along when they left). A couple of humans. A blue-furred Reknian named Hoch . . .

She realized that the Doctor was speaking to himself in a quiet and matter-of-fact tone that seemed to only partially obscure a barely controlled and blazing wrath.

'This is going to stop,' he said. 'It's time to stop it now.' It was such a voice as might be used by the King of the Gods, just before He simply switched off the entire System. It was simply the way things were going to be. Leetha tried to connect this suddenly alien, and not a little frightening, presence before her with the friendly little bumbling idiot she had originally met, all those weeks before. She failed.

Abruptly, the Doctor appeared to remember she was there and locked her in a gaze every bit as frightening, but from which she found she couldn't look away.

'There's something I want you to remember,' he said. 'It' just a detail, but its a detail that means life or death. Th Promethean and the Anean Eyes are neutralized and perfectl safe. Additionally, I was able to stand exposure to the Elysia Eye because of my slightly strange and not to say errati physiology, you remember?'

Leetha forced herself to nod. She recalled how the Doc tor's own prolonged contact with the Elysian Eye, as h carried it into the ship, had merely left him slightly weak an pale for a few hours after they had been incarcerated here.

'That allowed me to strategically deposit certain electro statically active substances. From my pores. The Elysian Ey can be handled relatively safely, if it's handled very carefully I was not, however, able to get at the Reklonian Eye.'

Something else appeared in the Doctor's eyes now. A kin of calm and concerned pity. Leetha still couldn't look away.

No matter how hard she tried.

'Please believe me that I wish I didn't have to do this,' h said. 'But I have to choose between warning you of some thing that will kill you, and taking away the thing that make you want to be alive . . .

'The legends of the Eyes,' he said, 'have been corrupte over millennia, and the majority of them are nonsense One of these particular bits of nonsense is that of th "Chosen". There are simply certain people more immune t the debilitating effect of the Eyes than others – there ar hundreds of them; you're one of them, Li Shao, I think, i another. The legends are merely corruptions of the signs b which they can be readily identified.'

Leetha didn't feel anything. She was idly surprised tha she didn't feel anything. Her entire world and everything sh was and everything she had been or ever done was dead an gone and she supposed that she should feel something. Bu she didn't feel anything.

'I have to tell you this,' the Doctor was saying, 'because a some point you're going to think you can handle th Reklonian Eye. Because you're Chosen. That isn't so. I would kill you just as dead as anyone else. As it killed Goma It would just take a little longer.'

There was no sense of transition. One minute Leetha wa looking into his terrible eyes, the next she just wasn't. Sh wondered why her body seemed to be jerking and sobbing, and why everybody else in the hold seemed to be gathering round with shocked confusion and trying to comfort her. She didn't really feel anything. She felt perfectly fine.

After some while she shook them off, and looked up from where she seemed to have collapsed into a little huddled ball. The Doctor was now looking down at her anxiously, just a strange little man, a little timid, as though she might suddenly launch herself at him and attack him at any second.

'Why did you have to tell me?' she asked, privately amazed at how small and quiet and childlike her voice sounded.

'Because these so-called legends were generated by something that doesn't care if you live or die,' he said angrily. 'I'm not like that. I can't allow myself to be like that.'

And she looked into his alien eyes, and she knew who he was. What he was.

'Oh my . . .' she said. 'You're –'

'No.' He offered her a sad little smile. 'No I'm not. I'm just the only alternative you've got at this point.'

———

The convoy drew nearer to the Sun – and if the Sun itself was looking slightly odd by this point, the Sloathes neither knew nor cared. For all they knew this was what Suns occasionally did.

System aboriginals were scattered through the convoy, thousands of them, addicted to the Sloathes' venom and serving as slaves. Some thousands more, survivors from the Planet X prisoners who had subsequently formed the Reklonian work gangs, were concentrated in several large freighters towards the rear.

One of these was captained by the Master of All Slaves, An Tleki, and in this freighter was a Sloathe by the name of Kloga Moo Duk who was wandering through a tunnel crammed with interesting-shaped rocks and the dead and brittle remains of fir trees. While on Reklon the Sloathes had taken the opportunity to stock up on things, the problem with which had been that there weren't actually that many things left. There had been some nice bits of ice, admittedly, but they had melted.

Kloga Moo Duk was feeling in need of some diversion – either a wash and brush-up or an idle half-hour pulling something apart to see what made it go, it wasn't sure at this point – and was looking for some pretend-move slave or other to provide it. There did not, however, appear to be any slaves around. Kloga Moo Duk was dimly aware that there seemed to have been less and less of them around of late, in the Sloathe-occupied areas of the ship.

Ah well. Kloga Moo Duk wandered down to the hold where the prisoners were stored. A large Sloathe was guarding the entrance to it.

'Is what?' it said.

'Is want pretend thing go "scrub-scrub-huppity-hup in the morning" or is go "Agh!" ' said Kloga Moo Duk. 'Not sure yet.'

The sphincter opened, Kloga Moo Duk went into the hold – and an extremely large Sloathe in the form of a Sloathe trap sprang from the floor, encircling Kloga Moo Duk with heavy calcine bars that began, inexorably, to contract.

'Agh!' cried Kloga Moo Duk. 'Agh! Agh! Agh! Agh! Agh!'

But it was to no avail.

In the prison-hold of the *Schirron Dream*, there came the muffled clang of the hatch that sealed the hold. The hatch swung open, a couple of chitinously armoured Sloathe appeared to take care of any attempted rush by the prisoners and Nathan Li Shao was shoved into the hold.

Leetha glared at him with cold loathing – and it was only later that she realized that, after the psychic shocks of the past hour, her first reaction upon seeing him was one of pure *joy* that she could now get on with something simple like good old cold loathing. Some annoyingly large part of her suddenly wanted to follow him around for ever so that she could coldly loathe him all the time.

The Sloathes, even the Sekor Dom Sloathe, had been unable to understand the controls of the *Schirron Dream*. Their thought processes seemed to be fundamentally incompatible with them. Solan had never piloted a ship before and could just about be trusted to steer it on a dead steady course and so Li Shao had been ordered to lift her from Elysian and get her under weigh, and had thereafter been called periodically to the bridge to handle course corrections. To the general surprise of the other prisoners, he had acquiesced immediately.

Leetha wasn't surprised. As far as she was concerned, Nathan Li Shao had finally revealed his true colours. How, she wondered, could she have ever begun to believe that he would ever do anything else?

'Having fun with your new friends?' she asked him as the hatch clanged shut behind him. 'What sort of deal have you made?'

Li Shao ignored her and turned to the Doctor, who was regarding him with enquiringly raised eyebrows. He nodded. 'It's still there.'

'I trust we'll only have to use it as a last resort,' said the Doctor.

'What?' Leetha said. 'What are you talking about?'

Li Shao ignored her. 'Yes, well,' he said. 'I think things might be rapidly approaching that point. That Sekor Dom Sloathe knows that Sloathes can handle the Eyes without ill-effects. They need me to get them to the Sun, Solan to tell them what to do when they get there, but everybody else is dispensable. The only reason people are still alive is that nobody's bothered to wipe them out. They could remember to do that at any time, and they're certainly not going to let anybody but me out of here.'

The Doctor nodded slowly. 'If the Sloathes gain control of the System through the Eyes it would be a catastrophe of cosmic proportions. That can't be allowed to happen. No matter what the cost to our own lives.'

'What's a cosmic?' said Leetha. 'What are you talking about?'

The Doctor turned to her. 'Li Shao's collaborating, as you might call it, solely at my request,' he told her. 'I'd hoped he could use his relative freedom to discover some way we could regain control of the ship without any further loss of life.' He suddenly seemed very old and careworn. 'It appears that won't in fact be the case.'

'I'm under constant guard the whole time,' Li Shao said. 'There's no way I can free the rest of you.'

271

Leetha glowered at him. 'So you're going to leave us here to rot and follow their orders anyway. What do you expect? You think they're going to let you live for being such a good little boy? If you want to know what *I* –'

'Who gives a damn what you think?' Li Shao said. Leetha became aware that he was regarding her with an expression of such irritated and empty distaste that she trailed off into a mortified silence. It was a look such as one might give a piece of particularly squelchy and noisome bit of filth after stepping in it. You are simply some disgusting bit of unpleasantness that the universe has flung at me as a matter of course, it said; you're nothing to me and not even worth the dignity of hatred.

It was such a look that made you want to scream incoherently in his face and hammer at him with your fists simply to get any sort of response – and Leetha might in fact have done so, had he not simply turned his back on her and walked off to converse with one of the human crewmen, leaving the Sun Samurai standing with her fists clenched at her sides, locked in a shuddering and impotent rage.

'You really shouldn't be so hard on him,' spoke the quiet voice of the Doctor beside her.

She rounded on him furiously. 'Oh yes?' she spat. 'He –'

'He's under a lot of pressure at the moment,' the Time Lord continued, not raising his voice but somehow drowning out her indignant protestations. 'You see, Leetha, when he embarked on this voyage, he knew it was something of a suicide mission, and he included several extra features when he modified the controls.'

He gestured around him. 'There are a number of rather large bombs concealed throughout the ship, enough to obliterate everything inside it and probably enough to split it open. They're wired to the control console in the bridge, to be galvanistically detonated in the case of capture.' The Doctor's pensive gaze travelled across the hold to Li Shao's back as he talked with the crewmen. 'I'm very much afraid Leetha, that the time is almost upon us when he'll have to set the lot of them off.'

'I wouldn't have believed it,' Benny said as she and Roz walked through the transporter's prison-holds, passing several Sloathes in cages extruded from their turncoat fellows. Before each of them several people from several Wanderers were talking with them. Several of the imprisoned Sloathes were responding, and some had already assumed vaguely humanoid forms. 'I wouldn't have believed the things could be converted like this.'

'That's because you still haven't actually met that many of them,' said Roz. 'You've spent a lot of time with people who simply can't believe Sloathes can be anything other than vicious slimy evil alien monsters. It took me a long time to see them any other way, and I was amongst them nearly all the time.'

Roz was looking relatively cheerful, all things considered, but she still had that haunted look Benny had come to associate with Sloathe-venom addicts. Indeed, when she had met Roz and Cwej on the Sloathe ship in Elysium, she had hardly recognized what had at first sight appeared to be a pair of relatively clean but incredibly wasted gutter derelicts.

She also noticed that, although wasted, Roz carried herself with a sort of iron-hard inner control, forcing her muscles to move her body exactly and precisely how she wanted it to move. Surrounded by friendly Sloathes, Benny thought, she must be feeling like a recovering alcoholic with a new charge card in an off-licence.

'They're like a bunch of kids,' Roz said, gesturing to the Sloathes in cages. 'You teach them long enough and they eventually start to think for themselves. The turning point seems to be when they automatically lapse into a humanoid form when in repose – although maybe that's just because all the teachers are human and – case in point. Hello, Six.'

'Hello,' said the Sloathe.

Six was still in the general form of a nest of snakes hanging from flotation sacs. It was floating amongst a group of humans and Reklonians who were talking to a particularly intransigent Sloathe, who was simply bouncing up and down in its cage and going: '*Agh! Agh! Agh!*'

'I've been meaning to ask you about that,' Benny said to Six. 'You can think for yourself, but you don't exactly look humanoid. How did that happen?'

The floating Sloathe rippled. 'I was left behind on an incursion to Rubri years ago,' it said. 'I was wounded, and I

273

knew that in the celebrated Sloathe manner they would eat me, so I hid myself until they upped and went away. I was found by that noble race, the polymorphs – who were almost the diametric opposite of the degenomancers in that they thought of life rather than death as sacred. They nursed me back to health, and by the time I was healthy enough to pose a threat to them, I was thinking like them.

'I think it's right what you said, Roslyn – did you notice that, incidentally? Roslyn. I think you can define true sentience as the point where you actually start to give other people names.

'Anyway. For some years I lived amongst the polymorphs – and when the Sloathes came back in force, I took one look at my own kind and decided that I'd rather go into the extermination tanks.

'They simply ignored me. It seemed to me that they simply couldn't see how I had changed.' Six paused. Benny got the feeling that it was ashamed. 'I have to admit,' it continued, 'that my resolve didn't stretch to actually *throwing* myself into the tanks after the polymorphs.

'For several more years I was alone. Then I met Nathan Li Shao and Kiru on the run through the methane swamps from the degenomancers. I passed myself off as a surviving polymorph, helped to conceal them and later helped them steal a ship.'

'That was why you were always doing all the "Is we is, is yes we is?" said Benny. 'It was a part of the act?'

'At first it was true,' said Six. 'I simply couldn't talk any other way. Later it was largely pretence. The thing is, my world view is still fundamentally based on that of the polymorphs. That's why I'm a healer rather than a warrior. The only weapon I can ever use is my sting-reflex, which doesn't actually hurt anybody. My shape, too. That's why I said Roslyn was right. I can assume a human form, I can still assume almost any form I like, with effort – but in repose I always lapse back into a vaguely polymorphic form. They're the people who made me.' Six rippled in a slightly different way than it had before. 'I shudder to think what would have happened if I'd originally been found by the degenomancers.'

'Well, from what I hear,' Benny said, 'if the degeno-mancers had found you, you wouldn't have survived long enough to tell the tale in any form.'

'There is that, of course,' said Six.

Benny and Roz passed on, as we all of us must eventually do, but for the moment they merely continued on their way. Around them Sloathes learnt to become truly self-aware, initially against their will but then with a kind of burgeoning joy at the things they could make themselves think of for themselves, without outside help. Benny looked closely at some of the humanoids who were converting them, trying to pick out the Sloathes from what she was now automatically thinking of as groups of people. It was becoming increasingly difficult, in some basic sense that was not entirely dependent upon physical visual sight.

'It's escalating fast, now,' Roz said. 'When we first infiltrated the ship on Reklon there was just me, Cwej and Sgloomi Po. Nobody bothered us. As far as anybody was concerned we were just a Sloathe and a couple of slaves. It took us quite a while to lure our first Sloathe for Sgloomi to catch and us to work on.' She frowned. 'The biggest headache was finding actual people who could be trusted not to simply kill a Sloathe who was at their mercy, and not blab it around and blow it for the rest of us.

'Now things have their own momentum. Pretty soon now we'll have the whole ship – and then we can start thinking about spreading the people-infection through the fleet, and then to Planet X –' Suddenly she winced. 'It'd be something to see, if me and Chris live that long.'

Benny darted a concerned look at her. 'Trouble?'

'I can feel the thing inside me,' Roz said simply. 'Believe me, you don't want to know where.'

'Perhaps the Doctor can help,' Benny suggested worriedly.

'If he's still alive.' Roz scowled. 'We're still heading for the Sun, so if what you told me about these "Eyes" is right then the Sloathes must have them – but that doesn't mean they haven't killed the Doctor and your other friends.'

'The Doctor's alive,' said Benny firmly. 'He can't be dead. We'll get out of this OK. We always do.'

'Yeah, well, I wouldn't know anything about that,' Roz said. 'The only so-called "adventure" I know about is the one that ended with my life and my career in shreds, the memory of the man I loved befouled, half the world I knew reduced to smoking rubble and the strong possibility of Cwej degenerating into a ravenously murderous maniac at any minute. That's all I've got to go on.' She turned to Benny. 'You've had more experience with the man. It doesn't always end like that, does it?'

She realized that Benny was of a sudden looking slightly nervous. 'Does it?'

'Um,' said Benny.

<hr>

And the bites of black continued to be bitten from the Sun, and the Sun burned dim – and across the System something shot towards it, wrenched free from its imprisoning energy field and tearing out its dimensional equivalent of guts in the process.

It passed close by to Reklon as this Wanderer swung towards it on its orbit, the shockwave of its passing cracking open the crust of permafrost and ice and scattering its three rock cores, sending them spinning erratically off through airspace, gouting fire and smoke from their internal volcanic activity, like the result of an extremely inept attempted snooker trick-shot. Only slightly more interesting.

It went straight through the water world of Elysium, rupturing its surface-tension with an explosion that drenched the circumnavigating, bouncing moon of Rubri with a billion tons of water, causing the foul degenomancers who infested it to shriek, 'I'm melting!' and dissolve and leave nothing but their pointed witch's hats.

It hit the Ring and smashed it open in a million, billion, billion flying shards. The spinning quartz asteroid of Sere, caught in a point of equipoise between its spin and the shockwave front, stopped dead in the air, transforming several of the inhabitants who had survived the Sloathe attack and the starvation into quite repulsive stains against the tunnel walls. Some hundreds, those towards the centre of the asteroid, survived with varying degrees of injury to find themselves in weightless darkness.

It burst from the Ring and passed by Prometheus just as it exploded. This was almost entirely unrelated, one of the warring K'ans having stumbled upon a fusion bomb and attempting to use it against an opponent attacking them with

276

armour-plated horses. Interestingly, for an instant, the mush-room cloud spreading across the face of this rocky cone made it look like a particularly fluffy ice-cream.

It shot past Aneas, the tree world, and all its leaves fell off.

It shot towards the Sun, throwing its shockwave before it to pulverize and scatter the various debris suspended in the air over the course of millennia.

Heading for the Sloathe fleet as it sailed towards the Sun.

Planet X was coming for the Sloathes.

The Ultimate Catastrophe

The hours in the prison-hold of the *Schirron Dream* flew by with all the speed and grace of a quadriplegic armadillo on a rocket-powered skateboard with a wonky wheel and a spluttery rocket. Leetha kept going to stand by Li Shao to try and talk to him, and slinking away when he utterly ignored her.

At length, there was a clang from the hatch. Nathan Li Shao rose from where he was crouching and idly tossing a couple of loaded dice he had found in a pocket while he totally ignored Leetha, and turned towards the hatch.

'Here we go again,' he said to nobody in particular.

He was slightly surprised when six or seven Sloathes poured through the hatch and started rounding up the prisoners, prodding at them with barbed appendages.

'Is go!' screeched the largest of the Sloathes. 'Is go now!'

The Sloathes herded the prisoners up to the bridge, where Solan and the Sekor Dom Sloathe were waiting.

Leetha stared at the ellipsoidal screens. 'Oh my gods,' she said in a small voice.

Peripheral clusters of the screens showed the jostling convoy of Sloathe ships behind them. The main bank of screens showed a composite of the Sun. A vast mass of utter black was now splattered across it, as though someone had flung the entire contents of a paint pot. As Li Shao watched, he saw that the mass was visibly expanding.

It was eating the Sun.

The Sekor Dom Sloathe pulsed, and turned an eyestalk to Solan. 'If you would, please?'

'My pleasure.' Solan pulled a sheaf of papers from his ragged robes and flipped through them. 'Now where was it . . . Ah. Yes.' He read a passage silently and with raised eyebrows – and Li Shao got the impression that he was going through this act for the benefit of the Sekor Dom Sloathe rather than anything else. At length, he folded the papers together firmly and turned his little piggy eyes to Li Shao.

'Now the worthy scribe who originally wrote these – Kimon, was it? – tells us that the Eyes must be taken to the Sun when it burns black.' He glanced theatrically to the screens. 'I would say that state of affairs has obtained, wouldn't you?' He turned back to Li Shao.

The Sekor Dom Sloathe rippled. 'I would like you to bring us into orbit, Captain, if you would be so kind.'

Li Shao shrugged and swung himself into the master control seat. He glanced back at the other prisoners and their Sloathe guards. Leetha was glowering at him furiously and he sternly forced himself to ignore it. The Doctor was standing very still, watching the proceedings with anxious eyes.

'Why are *they* here?' Li Shao asked the hulking Sloathe.

A blur of motion caused his gaze to snap back to the prisoners. One of the surviving humans, a young man originally from Sere named Marcus, was falling to the deck in a lacerated, blood-spraying heap. The Sloathe behind him was already drawing back its razor-sharp blade appendages.

The other human, a man named Kos, began to scream with hysterical grief, until his guard restrained him and stuffed a couple of tentacles in his mouth.

Very slowly, Li Shao turned murderous eyes back to the Sekor Dom Sloathe. 'Why?' he rasped.

'That is what will happen,' the Sekor Dom Sloathe said, 'one after the other, unless you follow my every instruction.'

'I must admit,' Solan broke in happily, 'that this was my own small suggestion. I suggested that he actually *tell* you first, incidentally, but then we both agreed that showing is far more effective, and not to say satisfying, than merely telling.'

'It ends now,' said a quiet and perfectly calm voice.

The eyes of all those gathered here found themselves drawn to the Doctor, who was standing, perfectly relaxed, turning his gaze first to the Sekor Dom Sloathe, then to Solan, first the one, then the other, and back again. It was as though he were comparing the similarities between the two with mild and idle interest.

'You have squandered any last chance of mercy I might have allowed you,' he said matter-of-factly. 'It's time to switch it off now.'

And then he turned his eyes to Li Shao and raised an eyebrow. And, casually, Nathan Li Shao reached out a hand to the console and flicked the galvanistical switch that triggered the bombs strewn throughout the *Schirron Dream*.

And nothing happened.

'Ah yes,' said Solan lazily. 'I'm afraid that in idle hours I'm something of an inveterate tinkerer. I must admit that I've been playing around a little with your controls, and I have the nasty feeling that I might in fact have broken some of them.' He regarded Li Shao with a cold, tight smile. 'I really do hope I didn't break anything important.'

He turned to the Sekor Dom Sloathe and shrugged his blubbery shoulders. 'We won't get anything out of him now. Look at him. He looks like he's going to collapse. I rather think we won't get anything further out of any of them.'

The brainlike Sloathe swept its gaze over the assembled prisoners. 'I'm inclined to agree. Kill them now,' it told the Sloathe guards.

And then, without warning, as though snatched by some monstrous hand, the ship lurched.

Not yet.

Not quite yet.

Not yet . . .

Now.

The thing inside had been driven quite frantic by the wait as the *Schirron Dream* crawled further and further into its shrinking sphere of influence, into its rapidly failing place of control. The thing inside was desperately conserving its energies, switching off whole areas of the Sun, but the lights in the orrery, in this orrery room, burned dimly.

Time and time again the half-living systems of the ship had flickered with the thing inside's consciousness, time and time again it had been tempted to attempt control. But not yet. Not quite yet. Wait until there could be no question that its control would be absolute. The thing inside had to be sure.

280

Not yet.

Not quite yet.

Not yet . . .

Now.

And now, the ship woke up, impulses firing through the web of its semi-sentient neurosystem, half-thoughts burning in its skin.

And it remembered what it was.

And the thing inside gathered it in.

In the gangways and cabins of the *Schirron Dream*, from nodules set into the bulkheads, the purpose of which neither Li Shao's crew nor, subsequently, the Sloathes had ever been able to determine, massive galvanistical discharges arced to every Sloathe, exploding them like a lot of large and rather disgusting balloons touched simultaneously by the lit end of a cigarette. And simultaneously, in the bridge, the Sloathe guards detonated. The only survivor of this instant slaughter was the Sekor Dom Sloathe.

Milliseconds later, as the Sloathes were still exploding, bluish galvanistical fire burst from the alien forms to which the control console was bolted, striking all who remained and dropping them as though poleaxed.

The *Schirron Dream* juddered and lurched. Blue fire crawled across its porcelain skin in crazy-paving tendrils. It wrenched itself around on an oblique plane, and tumbled, and dropped like a sudden brick, plunged burning and shrieking into the Sun.

And bounced. Slightly left of the smily face.

In the central chamber of a freighter towards the rear of the Sloathe fleet, Captain An Tleki was feeling a little irritated. For some while now, as it tried to keep the ship on course and in formation, it had been constantly plagued by interruptions. Sloathes had come in muttering darkly about how the pretend-move prisoners in the holds were restless, and An Tleki had told them to go and hit them with big things until they shut up. Other Sloathes had come in asking why there didn't seem to be any of the Sloathes they knew around any

281

more, and An Tleki had told them that if they didn't watch it *they* wouldn't be around, because An Tleki would have gobbled them up.

Now, five or six Sloathes herded four of the pretend-move prisoners into the chamber. 'Is important stuff,' one of them said. 'Is important stuff for you to know now.'

An Tleki glared at it with one of its eye appendages. 'Is *now* what?' it said angrily. 'Is up to bleeding bottom making ship go chuggedy-chug full speed ahead, and never get one little minute's peace. Is now what?'

'Is mutiny,' the Sloathe explained with a ripple of horrified fascination. Its fellows deposited the pretend-move prisoners in front of An Tleki and then lost interest, wandering aimlessly through the extruded nerve-tissue tubing that linked An Tleki to hir ship.

'*Mutiny?*' An Tleki cried. 'Is I hear you a'right, Mr Sloathe? Is dread and diabolical mutiny below the scuppers ahoy there matey?'

'Is right,' said the Sloathe happily. 'Is fault of nasty pretend-move prisoner things. Is what they do is catch Sloathes and make talk-talk all the bleeding time until Sloathes have to start thinking properly to get a word in edgewise. And when they convert lots of Sloathe they say, "Ho, now, is time to take over ship from big fat captain An Tleki!" So they get together a bunch of their best Sloathe friends, bluff their way into the control chamber and organize what you might call a quick and relatively painless *coup d'état*. Ready, guys? Three, two, one, *go*.'

As one, manipulatory appendages shot from the Sloathes surrounding An Tleki, grasped hold of hir connecting tubes and pulled them from the slimy wall of the chamber with a multiple and slightly wet *splop!* Instantly these Sloathes now mutated, sprouting thick and heavy barlike growths, which interlocked to form a contracting cage, trapping An Tleki and squeezing hir tight.

An Tleki screamed and thrashed against the bars, but the four Sloathes held hir tight. They sprouted squat and sturdy legs and shuffled from the chamber, taking An Tleki with them. Hir screams could be heard halfway down the tube outside.

'Nice going, Sgloomi,' Chris Cwej said to the Sloathe who

had done most of the talking, and was now re-forming into its preferred shape of an amalgam of him and Roz Forrester.

'Good one,' said Benny.

Sgloomi Po grinned. 'One does one's best.'

'Well, if we've all quite finished with the mutual appreciation society,' Roz said, 'maybe we should take control before we give someone a nasty rear end shunt.'

'You should be so lucky,' said Sgloomi Po, who had been spending a little time with Benny. 'OK, OK.' Tubes sprouted from him and plunged into the holes left by the late Captain An Tleki. The ship gave a little lurch and then settled down again.

'Sorted,' said Sgloomi Po. 'Hey, this is kind of fun. It's like having this, like, really big body and flying it really *fast*, yeah? You'd enjoy it immensely, Chris.'

'I think that was quite uncalled for, Sgloomi,' said Chris Cwej, woundedly. 'I don't think I sound like that at all.'

'What about the other ships?' Kiru asked. He had remained silent up to this point. Even after knowing Six for several years all unawares, he had spent those years hating Sloathes and still felt a little disconcerted in their company. 'What about the *Schirron Dream*?'

'I can see it,' Sgloomi Po said. 'Couldn't miss it after that perfectly lovely description you gave me. It's right at the front, leading the field and – uh oh . . .'

'What?' Benny said. 'What's happening?'

'Something's hit it. It's like a bolt of lightning but it's there all the time. Coming from the Sun. It's like something's taken hold of it and –'

And at that point something hit the freighter.

───

The *Schirron Dream* skidded across the obsidian-black surface of the Sun, spinning on the horizontal plane and simultaneously rolling so that its progress described an erratic arc. At length it ground to a halt, revolved half-heartedly a few more times and then was still.

In the bridge, on a ceiling that was now effectively the floor, several human figures and one obloidular form lay sprawled and unconscious, ragdoll limp. Bruises flowered on their exposed skin, where they had hit some surface or object in the ship's tumbling descent and impact. It was impossible to tell, at this point, whether any more serious injuries had been done, whether bones had been broken – but this was, remarkably, relatively unlikely since they had all been absolutely relaxed. They were still breathing. The Sekor Dom Sloathe's oxygenation systems pulsed.

Now, again, tendrils of bluish galvanistical fire burst from the console. It arced from one body to another, each in turn, lingering at each, undulating sinuously. It was as though the ship were probing them, examining them.

The tendrils dissipated. Several of the alien controls lit up and gently pulsed. There was an electrical hum that, had there been one to interpret it, might have sounded almost contemplative.

Eventually, the *Schirron Dream* appeared to come to a conclusion. Bursts of blue light, straight as optical lasers, burst from the console, swung across the bridge and fixed upon the eyes of a wheezing Solan. Five more fixed upon the limp optical appendages of the Sekor Dom Sloathe.

The beams stuttered, streaming some complex Morse into their eyes. Then they shut off. Solan and the Sekor Dom Sloathe respectively opened their eyes and ocular analogues.

Solan climbed to his feet. The Sekor Dom Sloathe sprouted seven insectoid legs. Respectively they lumbered and scuttled for the hatch leading aft and into the ship.

Several of the Sloathe fleet had seen the pretend-move-thing ship struck by lightning and plummet towards the sun. They slowed and hung revolving gently in the air to investigate, and the rest of the fleet began to slow to a jostling halt behind them.

It was at that point that the shockwave hit them, tearing several of the more fragile vessels instantly to shreds and scattering the rest. Several ships dropped out of the sky to plunge into the Sun and smear themselves across its surface.

And something burst from the interWandererly darkness of the dying worlds, something huge and crackling with galvanistic potential differential discharge, trailing huge and whipcrack-flapping ragged wings of Sloathe membrane to slow its progress to a halt amongst the decimated fleet.

284

A susurrating roar issued from it, from its fissures and craters and lesions like a million lost souls shrieking underground, gibbering in the maw of hell. Its ragged 'wings' beat once, then furled and devolved into misshapen, tumorous lumps – and then exploded into streams of tentacles shooting for the fleet. A Sloathe fighter desperately flinging itself out of the way of a tentacle collided with a dreadnought and went to pieces. The tentacle in question deftly plucked these pieces out of the air and whipped back into the basalt planet. Several tendonic grappling lines shot from a dark crater surrounded by a ring of galvanistical fire, hooked themselves into the dreadnought and began, inexorably, despite its every effort as it strained against them, to haul it in.

Planet X had arrived.

It had come to eat.

———∞———

Leetha's scaly skin prickled. The sensation was familiar, something she had experienced before but only once. She drifted, trying to remember. It was a dry and scratchy feeling, as though a single layer had been burned off – and then she got it. It was the same sensation she had experienced on Prometheus, after she had touched the Eye.

She opened her eyes with a jolt. A face swam into focus, two eyes looking down at her with concern: one brown, one blue.

'How are you feeling?' Li Shao said.

'Like I've been lightly fried.' Leetha sat up and winced as bruised muscles complained in her back. 'This is getting to be a bad habit.'

A little bit of her mind reminded her that she wasn't talking to Li Shao. She shut it up by telling it that she'd do all the not talking to him it wanted later. She glanced around the bridge, at the mess left by the Sloathe guards, at Hoch the Reklonian and Yani, who was tending to Kai and the human, Kos, who appeared to have broken a leg and an arm respectively –

'Where's the big Sloathe?' she said. 'Where's *Solan*?'

'They've gone,' the voice of the Doctor said.

He was standing in the oval hatch leading back into the ship, his legs below the knees obscured by the bulkhead

285

between the door and the ceiling. He seemed very worried indeed. 'The Eyes are gone, too.'

'*What?*' Leetha and Li Shao exclaimed simultaneously.

'They've gone.' The Doctor regarded them all with an absolute seriousness. 'We have to find them. We cannot allow this to happen.'

Li Shao glanced at the oval screens, which were just broadcasting static. 'The spy telescopes,' he said.

The Doctor disappeared aft. Li Shao and Leetha pelted after him to the observation deck, where they found him peering through one of the segmented brass telescopes that were pressed against a porthole.

'There they are,' he said. 'They're on the surface, heading away from us. I can see the Eyes. They're carrying the Eyes, two each. I think Solan has the Reklonian Eye. It looks like it's killing him.' He turned from the eyepiece to Li Shao and Leetha. 'I think you can count yourselves relatively fortunate. If the pair of them hadn't been here, I have a nasty suspicion that it would have been one of you at this point.'

'Let me see.' Li Shao took the telescope and peered through it. 'Oh my gods,' he breathed. 'The sky. Look at the *sky*.' He took his face from the eyepiece – and Leetha saw that he had gone a deathly pale. 'What in the various Hells is happening?' he asked in a slightly shaky voice.

'The death of worlds,' the Doctor told him flatly. 'The death of your world.' He turned to Leetha. 'And the death of your world. The death of your entire System if we cannot retrieve the Eyes.'

———

They made their way across the black surface of the Sun: the Doctor, Leetha, Li Shao, Yani and Hoch, following the trail of Solan and the Sekor Dom Sloathe. The grease from feet and the slime from alien pores. Above them Planet X tore Sloathe ships apart and ate Sloathes. In the distance they saw the collapsed and scattered debris of the ships that had fallen.

As they alternated between a sprint and a dogtrot, Leetha glanced between Hoch, slightly ahead of her, and Yani, panting furiously but determinedly keeping pace. The big Reklonian had simply shrugged and come along at Li Shao's order. Yani, on the other hand, seemed to hold Solan and the Sekor Dom Sloathe personally responsible for the impact-injuries done to her friend Kai and damned-well wanted revenge. She had jumped at the chance when the Doctor had asked her – although, Leetha suspected, the pigmy girl would have walked through a blast furnace for the Doctor. For some reason.

Strangely, for some reason that she couldn't quite name, Leetha had found herself reluctant to leave the two wounded survivors back on the *Schirron Dream* to fend for themselves. The Doctor had simply pointed out that there was no time for such debate. The pair of them would in all probability be perfectly safe, whereas if the Eyes were not recovered then they and everybody else would certainly die.

Leetha hoped that nothing would happen to them – it occurred to her that she had been running off and leaving the wounded to die for most of her life.

Now they came to a pit, roughly twenty feet across. A thick circular plate of bronze had swung open from it on massive hinges. Steps spiralled down it: down into the Sun.

'So what do we do now?' Li Shao panted.

'What do you think?' the Doctor snapped. 'We go down.'

Leetha felt a sudden little chill: something small and cool twitching in the pit of her stomach, a little shudder. There was not just irritation in the Doctor's tone, but something more subtle. It was the tone of irritation one might use at the latest bit of stupidity or intransigence of a well-loved but slightly infuriating pet.

Or a slave.

They went down. Pale light glowed through translucent walls seemingly solid, polished rings of gemstone: agate and jasper and tourmaline and beryl and porphyry and jade and sapphire and cinnabar and turquoise and tiger's eye and garnet and topaz and taafite and pyrite . . .

They went down. As they descended, Leetha noticed that the Doctor had gravitated to the back of the group. She gravitated back herself until she was only slightly ahead of him and to one side, and examined him out of the corner of her eye – looking at the steps ahead, but focusing her entire actual concentration upon the periphery. He had lapsed into a kind of absent contemplation, lost in thought, trotting down the stairs and setting the pace from behind with the same preoccupation that a *tchkang*-player might actually, physically, move the pieces while concentrating upon the –

And then, all at once, like crystals instantly forming in a supersaturated solution, it was there in Leetha's head. Every apparently casual aside, every subtle prompting, every blatant manipulation glossed over with some new diversionary bit of clowning and every sudden bit of knowledge seemingly just pulled out of the hat, it all fell into place.

Abruptly, Leetha stopped. The Doctor brushed absently past her – and then skidded to a sudden halt himself. His head snapped round. 'What do you think you're doing?'

Leetha was aware of the collective pace slackening below her and gradually devolving into confusion.

She just looked at the Doctor. Looked into his eyes.

'No,' she said, simply.

The Doctor waved agitated hands. 'We have to go, Leetha,' he said urgently. 'There's no *time* for –'

'I've just worked it out,' she said composedly, as though she were merely passing the time of day with some acquaintance on a concourse in Rakath, rather than stuck down a glowing hole with the System tearing itself to shreds above her.

'I've finally worked it out,' she said. 'There's something down here. That's what it's all been about. You don't want the Eyes back. You want them down here. You want *us* down here.'

Below her, the forms of the others reappeared, climbing the stairs in some new puzzlement and worry. She was aware of their questioning eyes on her: their eyes, watching her eyes, watching the eyes of the Doctor.

'Everything you've done or made us do was to bring us here,' she said. 'You've been taking us into the pit.'

The Doctor returned her gaze. She steeled herself against his hypnotic stare – but he merely looked at her with sorrow. 'It wasn't me who brought you here,' he said.

'But you helped,' Leetha said. 'You helped at every turn. Shoved us along. Never giving us time to think. You *want* us here.'

'Yes.' The little man slumped. His eyes now seemed a thousand years old, and filled with so much pain, and guilt, and regret that it was like the Elysian ocean, of which this new guilt was merely one more drop.

It was not even, she thought, as if it might be the drop that would finally break him, like the final gulp that occasionally explodes an Anean swampwater bloater. Looking into his eyes, Leetha knew that his capacity had been by no means exceeded. It would probably never even be reached.

If he had done anything, the Doctor, at this point – if he had cajoled, attempted to command, tried to make a joke of it or even asked for the chance to explain – Leetha would simply have turned, climbed back up the steps and died along with the rest of her System. And she knew without looking that the others would do the same. She could feel it inside them, radiating from them to her.

The Doctor did nothing. But there was a little hunted look about him, now, and a sort of stillness Leetha had seen before in the more sophisticated of Anean animal traps, when the captured animal realizes, absolutely, that there is no way out even after chewing its leg off.

Leetha sighed – and simultaneously felt a collective release of tension in the others, a tension only now noticeable because of its absence.

She turned away from the Doctor's eyes.

'All right,' she said. 'Tell me.'

'Your System is undergoing catastrophic collapse,' he said in a flat, empty voice, like an automaton: simply laying out facts without attempting to give them even the slightest possible slant. 'Whatever happens, whatever we do, millions are going to die more horribly than you can ever imagine.'

Leetha looked at him blankly. 'There's only, what, maybe two million in the entire System.'

'That's why I said "millions".' The Doctor glanced at the others, at Li Shao and Yani and Hoch. 'There are two choices. If you let me take you down here, down into the pit, if you trust me enough to do that, we are all probably going to die – but there might be a chance to salvage something from the wreckage. Save some thousands. No more than that. Possibly only hundreds. Out of two million.'

It was too big to assimilate. Too big to feel. Leetha sighed again, and looked at the dumbstruck faces of the others. 'Why do I get the feeling that I already know what the other choice is? All right.' She flexed her bruised shoulders and rubbed at a neck seemingly cramplocked solid, as though it had been held immobile for hours rather than minutes. 'I want the proper explanation, I want it chapter and verse and it had better be good. You can tell us about it while we go down.'

———∞———

And as the very sky boiled and worlds died, the thing that had once been the Most Supreme Captain Trenkor Lep tore through the Sloathe fleet, breaking open entire ships and spilling the contents, Sloathe and aboriginal, accumulated junk and all, into its craterous maws. The sheer size of the thing that had once been Trenkor Lep, and the massive ingestion of the pickled matter that made up Sloathe ships was combining to produce something of increasingly super-Sloathal strength and resilience, inexorable and unstoppable. Literally unstoppable. Its only impulse was to kill and eat, kill and eat, kill and eat and it would do so until every last Sloathe, every last scrap of Sloathe matter, had been killed and eaten.

Quite what would happen then is debatable. Possibly, once this critical mass was achieved, it would eat itself and disappear, as it were, up its own alimentary analogue. Possibly this was part of some periodic life-cycle: one Sloathe becomes so big that it eats the rest, before fragmenting by fission to start the cycle anew. The natural order of things, so far as Sloathes were concerned.

But, if it were truly a part of some natural cycle, there were two important differences this time. The first was that the thing that had once been the Most Supreme Captain Trenkor Lep was all but mindless even for a Sloathe, and what mind it had left was disrupted and incurably insane. Who knew what horrors, under those conditions, the process might spawn?

The second difference was that a large number of Sloathes were now truly aware, in humanoid terms, and so far as they were concerned the natural cycle of things could stuff it.

In the control chamber of a freighter as it desperately and lumberingly tried to evade the massive tentacles and grappling hooks, Benny, Roz, Kiru and Chris were hurled from wall to wall to wall; bouncing where it was soft, bruising where they hit some piece of subcutaneous Sloathe-bone superstructure.

'It's no good!' shouted Sgloomi Po, who had anchored airself to the floor with a couple of force-evolved crampons. 'They just keep coming. It's only a matter of time.'

'Can't we just make a run for it?' Benny shouted as she rebounded off the floor.

'Not a good idea,' said Sgloomi Po. 'I saw some ships trying to do that. The damn thing seems to enjoy going after them particularly.'

Roz had been quietly thoughtful for a while – so far as one can be quietly thoughtful whilst rattling around like dice in a squishy shaker. Now she spoke up: 'I know what we can do.'

'Any ideas you have I'd be more than happy to hear at this point,' said Sgloomi Po, wrenching the ship around to avoid something that none of them would be made happier to hear about. 'I'm all ears, potentially.'

'Well, if we can't get away,' Roz said, 'there's only one direction we can go – and it's the way it would never expect.'

'Are you saying what I think you're saying?' said Benny, dubiously.

'That would simply be committing suicide,' exclaimed Kiru.

'Not exactly on the top of my list of options, I must admit,' said Sgloomi Po.

'I think I see what you're getting at, Roz,' said Chris Cwej thoughtfully. 'Do you think it could work?'

'I have no idea,' said Roz. 'I don't know if we'd even get through, and I don't know if it would do any good if we did – but at least it might open up a few more possibilities, and at the moment we don't have any.'

'Now hang on,' said Benny. 'What exactly are we talking about here?'

Roz shrugged nonchalantly. Or at least she would have done, had not Sgloomi Po at that point put the ship through a particularly spectacular evasive manoeuvre and landed her flat on her backside. 'I'd have thought it would be obvious to you, Benny,' she said with lofty dignity, from the membranous floor. 'But if you're really stuck, I'll give you

291

three guesses and I'll give you a clue: it's blue and it's oblong and it begins with a T.'

―――――

'Long ago,' the Doctor said as they descended into the pit, 'the birth and life and death of suns ago, there emerged a race of beings who could to some extent control space and time. My race. The Time Lords. They were the single most powerful species in the galaxy, very nearly gods – and having had a head-start in the natural selection stakes, as it were, they decided to keep it.

'Entire species, whole *orders* of species that might pose a threat were quite simply eradicated. That is our greatest shame – mine in particular, and by association everything that lives. Every life-form in the galaxy only exists because it exists in a galaxy where it is possible for the Time Lords to exist.

'Those exterminated creatures were not exactly evil as such, merely utterly incompatible with life as we can know it, inimical to it. A galaxy in which they existed could not possibly allow you or I or anyone else to exist too; it was a simple matter of us or them – or so the ancient Time Lords thought. In practice it just meant that they simply killed, and killed, and kept on killing until the perceived threat was gone and they felt safe. They encoded pattern-recognition systems into the genetic memories of their unborn young, so that any last survivors that were subsequently found would be automatically wiped out.'

The Time Lord paused. It was as though he were mildly puzzled: treading carefully through new and fragile thoughts as if afraid to shatter them. 'One of these races we called the Charon. Nobody knows what they called themselves. They were builders, twisting the very fabric of the universe around their distortive metadimensional mass. They built worlds that nothing humanoid could live in, and so, of course, they had to go. When I saw this System, everything I saw triggered a kind of unthinking abhorrence that threatened to tear me apart – and I didn't know why. I managed to conceal it from Benny, incidentally, by a judicious amount of the misdirection I do so well, and passed off any further lapses as the after-effects of that other, nameless race's reality bomb that wrenched us into these spatial dimensions in the first place.'

He frowned. 'There's a kind of horrible irony in it. Two completely different races who cannot and will never exist, finally have some measure of revenge against a Time Lord – and it's the one Time Lord who had he existed at the time would have opposed their extermination to the last breath.' He paused with a little, faintly fussy expression of consideration. 'Yes, I would. I'm sure I would have.'

'Oh no you wouldn't,' Leetha said, startled a little at her anger with him for the genocidal enormity that his race had apparently done. It was only some time later that she recalled the little edge of defensiveness that spoke of her own implicit guilt for simply existing and that told her, subconsciously, that he was telling the absolute truth. 'I think you'd have dithered a bit with your conscience, and then said "it's us or them" or suchlike and got right on with it.'

'No!' For an instant the Time Lord seemed truly mortified. 'If we any of us allow ourselves to be like that then we're utterly and irretrievably damned. Those who pick the "us" in that situation would put the universe in a concentration camp if they were allowed. Those who think in terms "us" and "them" would be better off killed by "them" in the first place!

'And besides, it isn't that simple. It never was. Because the Time Lords got it completely and utterly wrong from the start.'

'What?' said Li Shao, who had been following this, and for his part was making small mental notes to ask what things like galaxies and metadimensionals were.

'They got it wrong.' The Doctor scowled. 'The Time Lords thought that direct contact with these things would mean instant shrieking madness and death – but they forgot about the basic defence systems of the humanoid mind. Such as a sense of humour. Ever been to Gallifrey? No, of course you haven't, but you can take it from me that a more humourless and po-faced collection of individuals you could never hope to meet, and I have no reason to suspect that the ancient Time Lords were any better.'

The Doctor gestured sweepingly. 'All of this, this whole system, should not be inhabitable to humanoid life by its very nature: it's a killing bottle writ large and nothing should

293

be able to survive in it – but survive you do. You've taken the unending horror of it and turned it into something with which you can live. You've turned it into jokes. The entire race of the Charon, and countless others besides, were wiped out because we thought we couldn't coexist with them. We could have. We could have lived with them, and we might even have eventually been able to live peacefully.' He smiled bitterly. 'How's that for a joke.'

'It's horrible,' Leetha said. 'I think it's horrible.'

'And so do I. But that isn't the worst part.' The Doctor swept them with his strange, sad eyes. 'You see, you're quite correct in that I've been assisting the influences bringing you here, prompted by impulses I could not really explain, even to myself. I knew that the Eyes were extremely powerful – possibly a power-source for the System itself, but I still had no idea exactly what was in control, in the very heart. And then I saw the Charon's drone, on Aneas, and then I knew.

'The Charon's down here, almost certainly the last surviving of its kind in the universe. It's at the end of this particular life-cycle, now, and if it's not prevented it will destroy your System and everything in it to start again anew.

'I intend to prevent it – but I cannot countenance its destruction. I will not have the ultimate culmination of the Time Lords' greatest atrocity on my hands.' He grimaced. 'The problem is, the pattern-recognition processes inside me are linked to automatic and overriding reflexes. I have the horrible feeling that I'm simply going to kill it, and I won't be able to stop myself.'

And then, from below, there came a dazzling flash of white light, a juddering and accelerating roar of engines.

'And I also have the horrible idea,' said the Doctor in a suddenly small and very worried voice, 'that we might in fact be too late.'

The raw power coursed through the thing inside, now, blasting from the big hot place at a metadimensional angle, channelled through the Eyes. The thing inside could feel its strength returning, tissues repairing themselves as the equivalent of cells replicated and proliferated from nowhere.

The thing inside, with the last of its dying strength, had

drawn the two creatures from the surface of the Sun, the corpulent human and the brainlike Sloathe, infesting their heads and making their bodies move to its precise will. Down here, in the orrery room, it had guided them as they replaced the worn nubs of the previous Eyes – worn down not through the vast interdimensional energies flowing through them, but by the simple, attritional erosion of convected air molecules over millennia – and as these new Eyes flared to life, it had simply withdrawn from the beings it infested. Stopping the human's heart in passing and, since the Sloathe had no actual heart to stop, dropping a counterweight on it as an afterthought.

The thing inside had been surprised to experience a small but nagging pain and sense of loss when it had killed their bodies. These creatures had devolved into a state where their own minds had been remarkably similar to the thing inside's. In some indefinable way it had been like killing little things like itself. Of its own kind.

It didn't matter. The rebirth process was running, now, and the other things were coming, and the hated Doctor-thing was with them. The disruptions to the System taking place outside were of no account whatsoever: the raw mass was still there, the rebirth process would reduce it to its respective atomic building-blocks anyway, and take the interloper planet with it.

Death and revenge was the important thing, now. Death and revenge.

The thing inside almost swooned with anticipation, the energies steaming into it from the big hot place crackling and sparking inside it in a manner that, in more human terms, would immediately have necessitated the purchase of a big box of strong and particularly absorbent triple-ply tissues.

They pelted down the steps, which suddenly ended at an archway in the side of the shaft – ended so suddenly, in fact, that all five of them were caught wrong-footed and tumbled through it to hit a crystal floor in an undignified heap.

Leetha bounced to her feet, pulling a blade from her living armour. She cast around, senses operating at a combat-ready pitch as she took in her surroundings.

'Oh gods . . .' she breathed. Beside her Yani was looking

295

around with the wide and frightened eyes of a child.

They were in a five-mile-wide hall, its dimensions so vast that it evidenced its own weather-systems and microclimates: streams and eddies of cloud swirled through it as though accelerated by time-lapse photography, and little electrical storms raged in its vaulted, domed ceiling. They saw a number of pillars, seemingly constructed from translucent, interlocking rings of gemstone, running upward to the dome, arched doorways set into the bases in the same manner as the stairwell-pillar from which they themselves had come.

On the crystal floor ahead of them, like some massive and bloated and partially collapsed maggot, lay the body of Solan, his heart stopped cold, and slightly beyond this was an extremely unpleasant splatter that could only be the remains of the Sekor Dom Sloathe, radiating outward from a huge pig-iron weight on a chain.

The weight had '10 TONS' written on it.

And beyond this, a churning mass of machinery, of pistons and rocker-valves and spinning regulators, of intricate tiers of gearing mechanisms, of hissing steam engines and juddering internal-combustion engines and flywheels and bearings and drive belts and cogwheels and pulleys and hydraulics and pneumatics and their respective brimming cisterns and pressurized tanks; huge and jointed and extensible arms that seemed to doppler away from you whichever way you looked at them, shadows playing across the walls suggesting shapes half-seen from the corner of your eye.

And the Eyes of the Schirron – of the *Charon* – blazing from within the mechanism, in the centre of it all, like four small crystal Suns.

'My word, that is certainly a jolly impressive orrery,' said the Doctor. 'I really think it's time we threw a hyperconductive spanner in the works, don't you?'

The freighter ploughed into the crater, ploughed through the brittle crust of ash, and through a tangle of matter that had once been the Most Supreme Captain Trenkor Lep, and through a couple of tunnel-riddled substrata and into a cavern; carried through by sheer mass and gravity and its own desperately hurled momentum, buckling and tearing

296

open under every impact until at last it hit the cavern floor in a slumped and tangled, prolapsed heap.

Sloathes and aboriginals spilled from the wreckage, most of them remarkably similar. Roz Forrester grabbed hold of a humanoid Sloathe who looked like a cross between an Anean and a Reklonian save that his 'fur' (he was rather obviously male in design) – save that his fur was more like tiny porcupine quills.

'Get as many of these people as you can somewhere relatively safe,' she said. 'Somewhere you can seal off and defend. I reckon most of that damned thing's attentions are directed at the fleet, but I think it may have sort of noticed us hitting it. I think extremely nasty things are going to be happening around here incredibly soon.'

The humanoid Sloathe nodded. He glanced towards a number of unconverted Sloathes who were milling through the crowd in some terror and confusion 'What about them?'

'Take them along,' she said. 'We're all in this together, now. This thing is bigger than both of us. I can't believe I just said that.'

The others, Chris and Benny, Kiru, Six and Sgloomi Po, were similarly directing people from the crowd. Roz scrambled over the debris to Benny. 'I hope we're doing the right thing,' she said uneasily. 'These people will be completely trapped if we fail. We've dumped them in a killing bottle.'

'Well, from what I can gather,' Benny said, 'they've got the same chance down here as they would up there. How are we going to do this?'

'Fast,' Roz said. 'I think I know where we're going, and if we do it fast enough we might just make it.'

━━∽∽━━

And under the surface of the Sun, in its orrery room, the thing inside lay in wait.

The rebirth process and the attendant destruction of worlds for their raw materials, once triggered, was largely an automatic process. It could look after itself for some while.

Now the thing inside held very still. The secret of hunting was, after all, in the waiting.

The thing inside couldn't quite remember when this notion

297

had occurred to it, but it was perfectly true, anyway.

Lying in wait.

'How can something like this work?' Li Shao shouted as they stumbled through the roaring orrery mechanism. 'There's no rhyme or reason to it. How can it operate?'

'This is merely a result of your perceptions,' the Doctor told him, his quiet voice somehow overriding the din. He neatly sidestepped a reciprocating camshaft that suddenly elbowed out of a mass of whirling clockwork, to bludgeon through the exact space where his head had been. 'These are alien mechanisms with which your mind is simply unable to cope,' he continued, 'and it's trying to come up with the nearest available equivalent – in this case, odd and demented machinery. It's merely an extension of what you do every waking minute of the day, out there in the System. My own travelling companions would be remarkably familiar with the process, if they actually gave a thought to it.' He frowned, momentarily. 'I do hope they're not dead.'

'Let me get this straight.' Leetha looked up at one of the extensible arms as it pulsed erratically, bulging and contracting as it moved in directions that seemed perfectly reasonable in the instant that they did it, but unthinkable before and impossible afterwards. 'You're telling us that those things actually have the *Wanderers* on the ends of them?'

'Only in the sense of yes.' The Doctor turned and glanced down at Yani, who was strolling through the mechanism beside Hoch. The blue-furred Reklonian was glowering around himself, alternately flinching and growling, like a bear or a wolf confronted by some threat he couldn't understand. The pigmy girl, on the other hand, had her hands in the pockets of her trews and was glancing about at the insane machinery with casual insouciance, as though this was something she saw every day of the solar week and twice on Sundays. 'How are you feeling about it all?' he asked her.

Yani shrugged, took a hand out of her pocket and waggled it noncommittally. 'It's OK, I suppose.'

'So what exactly is she seeing?' said Li Shao. 'And what are *you* seeing for that matter?'

'You really wouldn't want to know,' said the Doctor. 'And

298

I'd advise you not to ask again.' Some of the Time Lord's inveterate briskness seemed to have returned to him – but it was a strangely bullying kind of briskness: something that demanded obedience and would brook no argument from mere underlings.

'Now what I want to do,' he said, 'is shut this whole thing down. Stop the regeneration process dead in its tracks. If I can do that, what remains of the System may at least survive in its present form, for a little while at least.'

'And just how long,' said Leetha dubiously, 'is a "little while"?'

The Time Lord shrugged disinterestedly. 'Five, ten years.'

'And that's *it*?' Leetha exclaimed. 'That's all there is?'

'That's all there ever is. All I can ever really do is buy you and others like you a little extra time. Just be grateful if you get it.'

'Five years?' Leetha was suddenly filled with a desolate and futile rage. 'Then there's no point to *any* of this.'

'Five or ten years,' the Doctor corrected her with slightly pointed patience.

'Doesn't matter. There's still no point. Everything we've gone through, everything we've done is meaningless.'

She was aware of the Time Lord glowering at her with a barely controlled rage more towering than she could hope to envision, let alone match.

'Slit your wrists,' he told her coldly.

'What?' Leetha suddenly went very chilly and still. 'What?'

'Slit your wrists,' the Doctor repeated. 'Go on.' He prodded at her living armour, which flinched away from his finger with a startled whimper. 'You've got the tools to hand, so why don't you do it?'

'Um,' said Leetha.

'Quite. So let's have no more of this "it's all pointless" talk. You never know what might occur in five or ten years. Certainly more than might occur in –' the Time Lord glanced about himself at the mechanisms '– an hour and a half, if I'm any judge. The important thing at this point is the Charon. It's here, somewhere. I can smell it. It's making my head do several things, and they're none of them entirely pleasant.' He glanced between the others, catching each of their eyes in turn. 'It's watching us. The important thing is that it doesn't attack before I do what I have to do – but if that does happen, I need you to wreck the controls. You must pull the Eyes from their sockets. Can you do that? You have to do that.'

'And what will you be doing at this point?' said Leetha.

The Doctor hit her with another of his glares that made you wonder who, in fact, was really the enemy here. 'Oh, I'll be occupied,' he said softly. 'Don't you worry about that.'

<hr>

The thing inside watched the little figures as they made their way through the machinery, several minute parts of its intelligence noting the others, and dismissing them, because the others were not important. The majority of its attention was focused upon the hated being whose race had killed its kind – setting the thing inside apart for ever, alone in its little pocket cosmos, alone in a universe where there were no more like it.

None at all.

It was astonished that the hated being was so small.

The thing inside had expected it to be bigger. The thing inside's hatred was simply too *big* for this little creature to be worthy of it; it was as ridiculous – to express the inexpressible in its nearest human equivalent – as taking a ten-pound sledgehammer to a repulsive but singularly undistinguished nest of wasp larvae. Momentarily satisfying, of course, but ultimately not worth the effort expended.

But it would suffice, for the moment. Once the destruction and regeneration of the System was complete, once the thing inside was fully in possession of its powers again, it would stock its new System exclusively with the creatures that – some instinct told the thing inside – the hated Doctor-creature had the most affinity for.

No more reptile things and frogskinned creatures and furry things and insect things, just the funny little hairless simian creatures. They were particularly easy to get hold of, too, when the thing inside was in full possession of its powers. The thing inside could imagine dragging them through a wrong angle to reality and into its killing bottle, and killing them in their billions for a million years before it tired of it.

But for now, as the hated creature reached the centre of the machinery, as it reached for the Eyes to attempt in its imbecile and bumbling way to manipulate them, the thing inside would simply crush it with the utter contempt it deserved.

———❦———

The Eyes were fixed into circular flanges on what appeared to be a squat and hexagonal plinth, which mushroomed out into a hexagonal tabletop and from the centre of which there rose a column of sharp clear crystal. Tangled lengths of soft and extruded and somehow organic-looking cabling ran from the brightly glowing Eyes to the central column, within which galvanistical sparks Jacob's laddered and which oscillated lurchingly, up and down.

The Doctor had muttered something about how he supposed he should be flattered, reached for one of the Eyes and gone to work: brushing them and pressing them lightly in turn and leaving short-lived, varicoloured lesions upon the writhing fires within.

It appeared that the twisted wire cages and the little galvanistical boxes, with which the Time Lord had rendered two of the Eyes safe to human hands, had not impaired their function in the slightest so far as the Charon was concerned – and nor did they seem to affect the Doctor's own manipulations now. Their little bulbs winked on and off while he worked, his face filled with an intense concentration, the little pink tip of his tongue sticking out of the corner of his mouth.

This had been going on for some minutes now, and Li Shao, Leetha, Yani and Hoch had found themselves reduced to standing awkwardly around and attempting to make desultory conversation, which had of course dried up extremely quickly. It was not, after all, as if any of them had any news the others hadn't heard.

Once or twice they seemed to sense a change in the rhythm of the machinery around them, once or twice they felt a strange lurch inside them that seemed to be subtly different from anything they had ever physically experienced before – but the overriding experience felt by all concerned was of suddenly finding themselves at a bit of a loose end. They attempted to keep a watch for the Charon, but this was

301

proving difficult in all the noise and motion going on around them, and by the fact that none of them had the faintest idea of what they were supposed to be looking for anyway.

Now Li Shao found his eyes repeatedly drawn to a row of churning twenty-foot-high turbines that ran off into the middle distance. There was nothing there, of course.

Nothing at all.

He screwed his eyes into a squint and peered. The nothing that was there seemed to be somehow obscuring some extremely large areas of machinery. The nothing that was there was extremely big . . .

And then it moved.

Li Shao drew breath to shout a warning – and something shoved him firmly in the chest, knocking him back off his feet and twisting in the air. His trajectory missed a boxful of churning gears by inches, seemingly by pure coincidence, and he hit the crystal floor face-first. He heard the rattling scream of multiple chains through bearings. He rolled with a curse, just in time to see the ten-ton weights, five of them, hit the exact positions where he, Leetha, Hoch and Yani had respectively wandered off to, and the precise position where the Doctor had been standing – this latter missing the control plinth containing the Eyes by the merest fraction of an inch.

With a sick certainty that the floor would now be covered with up to four large spreading stains, he staggered to his feet and saw that the others, who had obviously been shoved out of the way as had he, were doing the same.

All except the Doctor.

The Time Lord now stood, some thirty feet away from the plinth, and some ten feet further than that from Li Shao (could it really have been the *Doctor* who had pushed him out of the way?), sweeping his gaze over the orrery mechanism as though invisible searchlights were beaming from his eyes.

The thing that wasn't there was prowling through the orrery mechanism now: you could see the shapes it didn't make. It was as though your eyes were refusing to see it, your brain flatly and hysterically refusing to register it. The huge and bloated shape it didn't make was circling, circling, closing in for the kill, tracked all the while by the beams that eren't coming from the Doctor's eyes.

'You know what you have to do,' the Doctor said, very
almly, in a quiet voice that cut through the deafening roar of
e machines. It was as if he were making your eardrums
brate by some means other than mere sound. 'You have to
) it. Do it now.'

Li Shao took a deep breath and started for the plinth – and,
nstantly, he knew that the thing that wasn't there was aware
f him. It had noticed him. The eyes it didn't have were on
im. A low and chilling growl that he couldn't hear came
om what, if it had existed, might have served the purpose of
throat.

Slowly, very slowly, Li Shao walked towards the Eyes, the
aze of the thing that wasn't there locked upon him and
ending crawling shivers down his spine. On the periphery of
is vision he saw that Leetha, Yani and Hoch were converg-
g on the plinth, too. The Sun Samurai was trembling,
uddering like a high-tension wire in a storm. The pigmy girl
as deathly pale, her eyes as big as saucers. The fur of the
eklonian stood on end as though he were a big blue
erambulatory hedgehog.

And still the thing that wasn't there circled, closing in,
ıch by gradual inch and foot by foot and yard by yard –

It went for them.

'No!' The Doctor leapt forward, his voice like the crack
nd roll of a thunderclap. 'I will not permit this! I will not
llow it!'

And then he faltered. He staggered a little, and pressed the
ack of a hand to his brow. 'I – I cannot. Allow . . .'

And the Eyes set in the plinth pulsed. And an explosion of
nergies that neither Li Shao nor the others could ever
omprehend enveloped both the Doctor and the thing that
vasn't there.

———

Wolsey the cat had spent a particularly tedious few weeks.
There was more than enough food, of course, from the thing
ou had to press with your head, and water from the little
tream that ran through one of the corridors, but he had been
n his own for *weeks* now, wandering through the bits the
ARDIS let him go without electrostatically zapping him –

303

and there are just so many times you can claw things [to] shreds, knock over anything else that isn't nailed down an[d] crap in Benny's underwear drawer before it all begins [to] pall.

Now, in the console room, desultorily pawing at th[e] dried-up remains of something small and furry (the dismem[-]bered mortal remains of one of Benny's experiments, i[n] which she had been trying to selectively breed a hamst[er] capable of doing a handbrake-turn*), Wolsey the cat wa[s] feeling a little alone. He wanted someone to stroke him, h[e] wanted someone to love, and, perhaps most importantly, h[e] wanted somebody to annoy the hell out of.

It was at this exact moment the door of the TARDIS bur[st] open, and Benny hurled herself through it with two peop[le] Wolsey vaguely remembered, another person he didn't an[d] two things he had never seen before in his life.

Muscular, slimy tentacles whipped through the doorwa[y] after them, clutching for them, but Wolsey wasn't pa[r-] ticularly interested. He swept across the floor in a flash an[d] nuzzled and rubbed himself against Benny's legs.

'Get away from me, you horrible little scrofulous fleabag[,'] Benny swatted at the cat as Chris and Sgloomi Po heave[d] their weight against the door, chopping the ends off a numbe[r] of tentacles. They twitched and spasmed on the floor an[d] then were still.

From outside there came an awful and repeated poundin[g] and the TARDIS shuddered. Benny turned to Roz. 'Wel[l,'] she's looking a lot better than the last time I saw her.'

'You should have seen it when we left,' said Roz.

Kiru, Six and Sgloomi Po were looking about themselve[s] with a kind of wonder. Kiru turned to Benny and Roz an[d] opened his mouth –

'You say it, I'm going to kick you out and let the thin[g] outside eat you,' Benny told him. 'If I hear one more perso[n] say it I think my brain's going to implode.'

'I can see how that might be a problem,' Roz said. 'OK[,] Benny, where exactly are the weapons systems? Where doe[s]

---

* So it could ram-raid rabbit-holes. Don't ask stupid questions.

he Doctor keep the guns?'

'Um.' Benny glanced around a little shiftily. 'I don't think we actually *have* any weapons.'

'What?' Roz exclaimed, with some incredulity.

'I think there's some old Purdeys and an Ice Warrior *sklaki* word in the Curio Room,' Benny said, 'but we don't tend to believe in weapons very much. The Doctor told me once that he always tries to think in terms of tools.'

'So what you're telling me,' said Roz, 'is that there aren't in fact any weapons. Is that what you are in fact telling me?'

Benny shrugged. 'There aren't any weapons. Is that a problem?'

'Typical,' said Roz. They had scrambled through the junk and debris-strewn tunnels of Planet X, Roz and Chris and Benny, Kiru, Sgloomi Po and Six, avoiding the filaments of extruded Sloathe matter that ran through them like nerve-fibre – but all the while, behind them, had come something massive and roaring and with eye-analogues that burned like searchlights, detached from the main mass of what had once been the Most Supreme Captain Trenkor Lep, trailing nerve-issue and hunting down this internal infection. And now the mass was outside. Knocking on the door.

'There has to be *some* sort of defence system,' she said. 'All this power at our disposal. There must be some way we can fight back.'

'I know how we can do it,' said Six, suddenly, from where it was floating before the octangular control column and examining it, intently, with a series of complex and faintly glowing weblike appendages. The crystal in the centre of the column pulsed faintly, and murmured.

They turned to Six in some puzzlement.

'I can sense the things inside it,' it said. 'The somewhere *else* that's inside. I can feel it thinking and remembering and feeling things. It's alive.'

'Well, I've always thought that the TARDIS was almost –' Benny began.

'It's alive,' Six told her firmly. 'Or as near to it as makes no odds. And I know what we can do.'

It told them what they could do.

'Oh no!' Benny said, horrified. 'Oh no. I can't let you.'

In the centre of the Sun, the thing inside peered down at th
little thing it hated, trapped within its burgeoning energies. I
was so small.

I will kill you now, it said, in words that nothing else tha
lived could possibly recognize as words.

Please don't, the little hated Doctor-thing said, its word
still carrying the flavour of the things it liked – those eve
more minuscule things that lived inside their meat machine
that it amused the little thing to emulate. *Please don't*.

You'll beg me? the thing inside asked the little thing
honestly intrigued. You are pretending to be like them s
much that you will *beg* me?

No, the hated little thing said simply. *I am merely tryin*
very hard not to kill you. Almost all my quite considerabl
energies are directed towards that end – but if you attack me
or you attack those things I have decided to protect, I will no
be able to restrain myself. Please. Do not try to kill me.

The little hated thing's tone was so matter-of-fact that, fo
the barest instant, some large part of the thing inside almos
found itself believing it.

But no.

Without mercy, or quarter, the thing inside summoned it.
energies, pulling them through the Eyes from the big hot place
and hurled them at the boastful little hated thing, who writhe
and shrieked as they engulfed it, burning it away as if it were
blooki-beetle alighting upon the nozzle of a blowtorch.

———

'Oh my . . .' Leetha watched in horror as the Time Lord wen
into spasm, his mouth open in a silent scream as the unseer
energies of the Charon crawled around him – distended so
far that she couldn't believe it hadn't split.

His eyes were screwed tight shut and something that wa:
red – too much of a bright and ruby-red to be blood –
streamed from them, running down his cheeks to drip to the
crystal floor and evaporate in little pools that hissed and
bubbled like spit on a stove.

And then, inside clothing that remained utterly pristine
even now, his body ignited like a magnesium flare.

His blazing form shimmered – and there, suddenly, standing there, was a slightly taller man, splitting the linen suit a

the seams with his larger frame, his hair slightly fairer and clenched in tight curls, his mouth set in a sardonic and slightly supercilious sneer.

The sneer distorted. The figure shrieked soundlessly, clutching at his face, and burned again.

He didn't last long.

Now stood a man of similar size but with fine and lank and slightly sparse hair, a face that might have seemed engaging and friendly, if a little weak, if it were not twisted into a rictus of absolute agony.

This form lasted slightly longer before it caught fire. Through the greasy smoke Leetha thought she caught something a little darker take its place; a little more gleeful and feral, just a little more dangerous –

Somebody was pulling at her. She wrenched her attention from the spectacle of the detonating Doctors to find Li Shao gazing at her, his disparate brown and blue eyes fearful and filled with concern. For *her*?

'I thought you'd gone like her.' Li Shao pointed to where Yani stood, absolutely still, transfixed, her eyes wide with wonder and gazing upon the Doctor as he burned and transmuted and burned again. 'I can't snap her out of it. I think she's out of it.' He gripped Leetha by the arm and tried to lead her towards the plinth that contained the Eyes. 'Come on. Remember what the Doctor said.'

Leetha held still. Off to one side she was aware of Hoch, looking askance at his captain. She kept wanting to turn her eyes back to the Doctor. Every doubt, and every loss, and every thought put off till later welled up inside her.

'How can I choose?' she said, more to herself than to anyone or anything else, hoping against hope that something inside her would tell her what to do. 'Would it really save some people, for a little while?' She shook her head viciously, trying to clear it. 'I used to be so sure of things. I used to be so sure. The Doctor poisoned that – but in the end he only *told* me things. How can I know if he or anyone else was finally telling me the truth?'

'You can't,' Li Shao said. 'You can never know. But I think that in the end you have to decide who you're going to trust.'

Leetha looked up into his variegated eyes.

Then she shrugged. 'Sod it. What the various corrective hells. Let's just do it.'

Li Shao nodded to Hoch. Leaving the transfixed Yani where she stood, leaving the Doctor as he writhed and screamed soundlessly and ignited in invisible fires (and now temporarily in the aspect of a tubby little man with a pudding-bowl haircut and a penny whistle) they finally walked to the octangular plinth.

'You know more about this than we do, Leetha,' Li Shao said, staring at the Eyes as though fascinated. 'What should we do?'

Leetha barely gave the Eyes a cursory glance. 'Don't touch the Reklonian Eye,' she said briskly. 'It hasn't been made safe. Hoch, you take the Anean Eye, the red one.' She gestured without looking to the Eye blazing with yellow light. 'You take the Promethean.'

Then she turned to the Eye that burned green, the Elysian Eye. The Doctor had told her that his strategically smeared bodily secretions had neutralized it to a certain extent, she remembered, but how much of that had survived after so much handling?

Ah well. It was too late to worry about it now.

Simultaneously, the three gripped their respective Eyes and wrenched them from their sockets in a shower of galvanistical sparks.

Instantly, the fires inside them died, leaving them holding nothing but flawed and slightly grubby-looking and vaguely disappointing lumps of diamond. Around them, the churning of the orrery mechanism faltered. There was the clash of massive relays being thrown.

And then the single remaining Eye, the Reklonian Eye erupted with a light brighter than the Sun when it was lit.

The heat of it seared Leetha's scaly skin. She heard the roar of the mechanisms accelerate again, to the pitch at which it had been before, and then higher. And higher. And higher.

'We have to pull it out!' Li Shao shouted, his hand raised to shield his eyes and casting a shadow across his face that, in relation to this blazing light, seemed like a slash of purest black – his exposed skin strangely powdery and glittery as its very topmost layers dehydrated and flash-ignited and burned away. 'We have to pull it *out*!'

308

'Let me do it, Cap'n,' Hoch said firmly, instantly starting forward, his fur crackling and blackening in the heat. 'I ain't one much here. Let me do it.' And something in his voice made Leetha's head snap round to his scorched blue form as hazed in the glare.

It had not been anything major, in the big Reklonian's voice. It had only been a little thing and it was something entirely implicit – something, she now realized, that had always been there amongst the crew of the *Schirron Dream*, and in Benny, and even in the Doctor, and which she had never quite shared. And which she had never so much as noticed.

It was the simple fact that Hoch, like the rest of them, was ready and willing to lay down his life for someone else if it came to it.

'No!' she cried – and realized that Li Shao was shouting the same thing, simultaneously, as he barrelled into Hoch. A Reklonian was commonly half again as heavy as a human, and three times as strong, but surprise combined with Li Shao's absolute determination knocked him off his feet.

Nathan Li Shao glowered down at the fallen Reklonian with a cold and murderous fury that would have given a rabid wildcat in a sack and being hit repeatedly by a baseball bat pause for thought. 'Don't you move. You move one inch and I'll kill you myself.'

And the orrery mechanisms were still accelerating. Leetha suddenly felt very calm. Without thinking much about it, she drifted back to the plinth and the remaining, blazing, lethal Eye.

'If I let you do it in my stead,' Li Shao was saying to Hoch, 'I would have never been worthy of your trust. Nothing that crawls through the filth of the lowest hells would be lower than me. I led you here. This is my responsibility and mine alone.'

'Yes,' said Leetha, turning towards them as she stood before the plinth from which the Eye blazed, 'but you never commanded me, Li Shao. I was never one of your people. Not inside.'

Li Shao spun to face her, his mouth falling open in shock – it had simply never occurred to him, she suddenly knew, with a flash of self-insight that sunk hooks into her heart, that she

309

would act with the same basic nobility and self-sacrifice as had Hoch.

For the simple reason that, for all her blustering, for all her posturing, for all her single-minded pursuit of some all transcending mission, that she was in any case privately certain of surviving by way of being Chosen, she had never been capable of it and never would be.

'Leetha!' Li Shao roared. 'Don't –'

'Too many people,' she told him, very quietly. Her voice was drowned out by the scream of engines, but she knew somehow, that he could hear her every word. 'Too many people have died instead of me.'

In a state that was something like serenity, something like a state of grace, as Li Shao launched himself desperately towards her, she reached out for the final Eye.

———

'You can't,' Benny said, her voice very quiet, very calm. Very reasonable. 'I won't let you. I'm not going to let you.'

'It's my choice,' said Six, equally quiet. 'It's my decision. I owe so much and now it's time to repay.'

It glared at her with seven separate ocular appendages. 'It's my decision, and so help me I'll try to kill you *myself* if you try to take it away from me.'

Benny held the Sloathe's septocular gaze for several seconds that seemed to stretch into an eternity . . . and then she turned her head away, her face working as though she were trying very hard not to cry.

Six bobbed gently in the air. 'Now get back.'

Benny backed off slowly, never taking her eyes from the Sloathe, joining the others who had already pressed themselves against the wall of the control chamber farthest from the floor – deciding, perhaps subconsciously, who this confrontation would be between.

And who would win.

'Thank you,' Six said simply – and then, with a note of sardonic humour: 'And for my next trick . . .'

It pressed a couple of sucker-like appendages to the control column. And then it extruded an elongated tentacle behind hirself, and opened the TARDIS door.

Instantly, a squirming mass of tentacles burst through the

loor, blindly probing across the floor and ceiling and the
valls. One of them shot straight for Six, developing a barbed
pear in the process that plunged into the floating Sloathe.

And in that instant, in hir death-throes, Six hit the TARDIS
vith every last iota of hir phobic sting.

<hr/>

n the chamber under the surface of the Sun, Yani was only
aguely aware of Li Shao and Leetha as he collided with her,
rasping for the Reklonian Eye with a desperately outflung
and, saw them collapse to the crystal floor with the Eye
lazing between them, fire crawling over them, plasma light
xploding from their eyes and nostrils and mouths and
wining round them. She paid it no heed.

She was not, as Li Shao had thought, merely shocked into
nsensibility. She was experiencing an absolute and devo-
ional rapture as she watched the ablation of the Magic Man,
pon which her mind, her being, her very soul refused to
llow anything else to intrude.

All of Yani's pigmy race were very, very slightly dislo-
ated in space and time – indeed, she and others like her were
he descendants of a tribe that had because of this been
vrenched entirely from their original home by the Charon,
nd had thus retained something of their group-rituals and
nyths and legends, through the millennia when the *Big
:ating Thing's* gods had roamed the Wanderers, and through
he centuries thereafter.

Central to these was the legend of the Magic Man.

He had come to the Old Place from a hole in a big rock that
ad suddenly appeared from nowhere, scattering the parrots
nd the lemurs and griffons for little-time-walks all around
vith its roar. At that time the People had been plagued by
nonsters that were half duck, half hippopotamus and half
nandrake,* who would transfix you with their awful quack

<hr/>

The terms of this legend have been translated to their nearest
:nglish equivalents, and if it all sounds a little implausible then that
s hardly *our* fault. In all probability, what Yani knew as a 'duck'
vould be entirely different from any aquatic fowl you've ever seen,
nd would probably give you a very nasty peck indeed. (The
'ranslators.)

311

and plant their pods in your stomach so that in the fullness of time their shoots and branches would burst from your mouth and your bottom and explosively blow you apart. The Magic Man had aided the People in their struggle against these beasts and then, stopping only to cure the sick, heal the lame and the halt and teach them all juggling, he had been on his way – but they never forgot him. Not least because, being very slightly dislocated in space and time, they had seen certain things about him that others could not.

Now Yani watched the solid shadow of the Big Eating Thing – a form that she could only see hints of but which she knew, the others could not see at all – as it tore at the Magic Man, blasting him with alien energies and burning him up, peeling him back, layer by layer.

And Yani saw, in a direction that the others would have never seen, that each time a layer was torn from the Magic Man he was getting *bigger*.

Now, as he was a white-haired and elderly human, writhing in torment as the oil in his pores caught fire, he was at one and the same time massive; filling what we must through paucity of multidimensional language conceive as a 'space' as large as the orrery room itself, pulsing with dark barely contained energies that crawled and intertwined and squirmed through him like a burning nest of snakes.

The Big Eating thing, by contrast, seemed to be weakening, shrinking. Yani dimly sensed that its contact with the energies streaming through the Eyes had now been cut, and that although it had stored them almost to capacity it now had no way of replenishing them.

It directed another burst of energy at the Magic Man – burning away the thin and human-seeming figure that existed on the physical plane – and the Magic Man replaced it with what Yani thought of as his 'other body'. The body that nobody but she, and Kai, and the others of her people had been able to see.

And the thing in the quasi-space that was the Magic Man was vast now. Bigger than the Sun.

And still the Magic Man just waited, very still, very calm.

In desperation the Big Eating Thing launched everything it had, every last scrap of its stolen energy, obliterating the Magic Man's other body completely.

For a moment there was nothing.

And then, before Yani's eyes, the Magic Man changed into his *other* other body.

The tentacles writhed through the control chamber of the TARDIS, hunting blindly, looking for something to kill and eat. One caught Benny and slithered over her as though it were tasting her – then hurled her aside in irritation, sending her flying into Kiru. Off to one side, Roz Forrester and Chris Cwej were desperately wrestling tentacles that slithered inexorably towards a cowering and terrified Sgloomi Po.

The remains of Six were being eaten by a tentacle covered with hundreds of tiny, circular, snapping mouths – but still it gripped the control column with hir suction-cup appendages and with the last of hir dying strength.

And around the walls, circular screens stuttered and strobed and played disjointed, abstracted but strangely horrifying images, the air shrieking with their associated sounds.

The police-box exterior-interface of the TARDIS plunged shrieking, its beacon flashing, into the inrush of hydrogen that would result in Event One.

A man in black with hawklike, hooded eyes, a black goatee and his black hair slicked back from a widow's peak, slid his hands over the TARDIS control column with a gloating and salacious anticipation. At last, he said. At last.

A man in a limp purple hat, a multicoloured knitted scarf and with slack and flaking features, lay sprawled and dying in a roundelled corner.

A thick-set, slightly jowly man in a striped shirt and red braces, with an expensive grey-tinged haircut and with hard, cold eyes, gestured dismissively and reassuringly and said something about how he had faith, of *course* he had faith. This was merely a period of re-evaluation –

A white hole is basically a conduit bludgeoning its way through the entirety of space/time, through which the energies of the entire universe course and flow.

The TARDIS was inextricably linked with the white hole known as the Eye of Rassilon – was indeed an analogue of it, a

tangible manifestation of it in whatever spaces and dimension:
with which it happened to interface, wherever it happened to
infest.

And as the TARDIS shrieked with pure and semi-sentien
abhorrence, it struck back at the thing that had stung it with
all the energies at its command.

And thence, by natural progression, to the thing that was ir
the process of digesting it.

Every time the thing inside had burned the hated thing away,
the hated thing had merely got *bigger*. The thing inside
couldn't understand it. It was as though a series of fleshly
masks had been burned away, one after another, exposing the
larger mass enfolded within to at last reveal the massive skull
beneath the skin: the horror at the core.

And in dimensions and directions that only the thing
inside could see, the hated thing was vast, now, impossibly
powerful. It could crush the thing inside with the merest
flicker of an idle thought.

And the thing inside was itself very tiny now. Vestigial, all
its stolen energies expended. Nothing left of it but the
overwhelming, almost mindless need that had driven it for
millennia and thousands of millennia. Death and revenge. It
needed it.

Death and revenge.

And in its vastness the hated thing, the thing whose race had
killed the thing inside's kind, spoke:

You are no danger, now, it said. Its voice was almost kind.
You are no threat.

Want it. Need it. Death and revenge.

I do not want to kill you, said the hated thing. *I wish to let
you live. Your people and mine could have lived together and
could eventually have been friends.*

Death and revenge.

*It's not too late. Here. I will give you some small power,
enough for us to talk, to find some common ground. The
establishing of links. The exchanging of gifts. What can I
give you? What is it that you* want?

Energies seeped through the thing inside, and with them
flared the memories: the endless recycling of the millennia,

ıe endless hate, the endless crawling loss and the chilly, still ıd silent hole inside that comes from knowing you are tterly alone and there are no more like you.

And the thing inside knew, precisely, what it wanted.

———

And in the boiling sky above the Sun, the thing that had ınce been the Most Supreme Captain Trenkor Lep and was ıow Planet X, did not even have time to scream, as energies ıe nature of which it could not begin to comprehend, burst ·om the little blue box with the big things inside it, and ıngulfed it.)

———

omething was shaking him roughly.

Nathan Li Shao tried to shake it off, because it was very ıce feeling the other things, like the soft, warm body he was urled together with, and he didn't want to stop.

All around him was the whine and judder and crash of ıachinery. It seemed to be ailing, as if the mechanisms were ınning down and tearing themselves to pieces in the ·rocess. The hard areas of floor he could feel under him were ıddering.

The soft, warm body against him stirred vaguely, and then ·rked. Li Shao forced his eyes open, and found himself)oking at the drowsy, puzzled eyes of Leetha T'Zhan. She ·as jerking because a large and vaguely pawlike hand with :orched areas of fur on its back was now shaking her.

They disentangled themselves from each other and, with ome degree of self-consciousness, looked up into the big, ınxious face of Hoch. 'I didn't know if you were still alive,' ·e said. 'After the fire went over you and burned.'

Li Shao glanced at the slightly scarred and battered exposed ·esh of his arms. They didn't seem to be in any worse shape ıan when he had seen them last. As he came awake, his body ang, crackling with an energy that made him want to jump up ıd down and shout and push down walls.

Leetha sat up and scratched at the back of her neck, ·riskly. Like Li Shao she seemed suddenly and subtly full of itality and life.

'What happened?' she said. 'I thought it was supposed to

315

kill us. I thought we were supposed to die.'

'I have no idea,' said Li Shao. 'Maybe you should ask th
Doctor.'

He became aware that Hoch was looking down at hi
worriedly. 'That's, uh, one of the things you should see,
think,' the Reklonian said.

As they climbed to their feet something rolled away fro
them with a rattle across the crystal floor. It was th
Reklonian Eye, now just a rather undistinguished lump o
impure diamond crystal.

The first thing that they came to as they crossed th
shaking floor was Yani. The pigmy girl was lodged agains
the side of a large and now free-spinning galvanistical moto
unconscious and white as paper, an expression of absolut
horror still on her face. From her position it seemed that sh
had been frantically trying to crawl into the non-existent ga
between the motor-casing and the floor before her min
switched itself off.

Beyond her lay the Doctor, lying flat on his back, his su
pristine, a fedora on his head and his umbrella clutche
loosely to his chest. He seemed utterly relaxed and happil
asleep.

Pinned to his lapel was a little silver badge comprising tw
stylized faces, one contorted with laughter, the other wit
anguish. Beside this, affixed with a large safety-pin tha
might ordinarily be used to secure a baby's diaper, was
sheet of rag-bond paper, printed by a neat hand with th
ideograms of the System's tongue. Li Shao pulled the pape
from him and read it:

> I think it might be an idea to leave, now. Immediately.
> Rather large things are going to happen at this point,
> and if you're not careful you might find yourselves
> stuck in the middle of them. Hoping this finds you in
> good health.

D.

From somewhere above and to one side there came a
extensive and complicated crash as some extensive an
complicated bit of machinery fell over. The floor, momen
tarily, bucked and heaved under them.

'Of course he might just be saying that,' Li Shao said. 'But I think we should probably take his advice.'

------∾∾∾------

They stumbled up the shaking stairwell, Hoch the Reklonian carrying the unconscious Yani, Leetha and Li Shao supporting the Doctor between them. He seemed very light – though whether that was because he actually was or because of the unWandererly energy fizzing and crackling through their muscles, they couldn't tell.

Behind them came a series of cracks and deafening crashes, as the interlocking rings of the stairwell-pillar detached and shattered on the crystal floor below. The sound of them shearing off became more frequent and increasingly closer, overlaying the judder and the roar of the orrery mechanisms as they tore themselves apart below.

Up through pyrite and taafite and topaz and garnet and tiger's eye and turquoise and cinnabar and sapphire and jade and porphyry and beryl and tourmaline and jasper and agate and finally out on to the black surface of the Sun.

Deep fissures were opening up, and hellfire glowed within them: magma filled them spitting and hissing in overflowing rivulets turning from searing white, to yellow, to lumpen cherry red as it cooled. The fissures seemed to descend down to the Sun's very core. It was as though the Sun existed in two completely different states: one on the inside, one on the outside.

Above them, set against the spinning wreckage of the System, Planet X crawled and writhed with tendrils of fire, its dying light illuminating the drifting ships of the Sloathe fleet such as had survived and, below, the small and distant form of the *Schirron Dream* still lying overturned upon blasted surface of the Sun.

Li Shao pulled the battery-operated radio transmitter with which he could contact the ship from his poke, where it had remained since their capture on Elysium, and all but forgotten by himself since it had been of no Wandererly use. Now he twisted the Bakelite knob. The batteries were low, and it was some small while before the miniature valves glowed, and even then glowed fitfully.

'Kos!' he shouted into the little trumpet. 'Kai? Can you

317

still read me? If you can hear this, we need to get the engine started *now*. Start the engines! I have the horrible feeling tha this whole place is going to go up like a Raintime Festiva firework display.'

He pressed the trumpet to his ear and heard the ghost o carrier static, the sound of gabbling and screeching so fain and distant-seeming that it might merely be the echoes of th blood pounding through his inner ear.

He switched the radio back to send. The valves flare briefly and then faded completely.

'I don't think I got through,' he said.

'It wouldn't have done any good anyway,' Leetha sai gloomily as she surveyed the distant wreck. 'The ship was th creature's thing. The Schirron. Charon. It's probably dead.'

'You're probably right.' Li Shao slumped; the strang energies within had dissipated now and he felt drained an disconnected, as though he had overindulged in Promethea *kief* for some considerable and immoderate period: he coul make his lungs suck in and out and make his limbs move an his mouth talk, but there was nothing much inside hin actually doing it.

Hoch was sitting crosslegged, supporting Yani on his lap and idly checking her condition; peeling back an eyelid t expose a rolled-back eye, slapping lightly at her cheek so tha her slackly yawning mouth shuddered.

Li Shao looked from Leetha to the semi-conscious Doctor now curled up on the black surface and apparently aslee with a silly and vaguely childish grin on his face. Then he turned his eyes up to the boiling chaos of the sky.

He was utterly dispirited. Possibly they could make it t the ship and try to start it up once they got there, but wha was the point?

Li Shao sighed and sat himself down on some hard lump of debris unidentifiable in the poor light – and it was at tha point that the poor light was pierced by a dazzling bluish flare from the propulsion vents of the *Schirron Dream*.

———— ∞∞∞ ————

The *Schirron Dream* rose from the surface of the Sun, riding a streak of plasma, small items of debris suspended in orbi clattering against its ceramic hull.

In the bridge, Nathan Li Shao gazed bleakly at the screens showing nothing but devastation. 'There's nothing left alive,' he said. 'Everybody's dead.'

'What about the Sloathes?' Leetha said from the couch that had previously been occupied by Kiru. 'I thought I saw a lot of Sloathe ships left. What about them?'

'I say leave them to it,' Li Shao said. 'And good luck to 'em. I'm sick of fighting. I'm sick of it all.'

They broke free of the Sun's pull and Li Shao cut the engines, allowed the *Schirron Dream* to drift. Behind him and Leetha, Hoch unstrapped himself and hauled himself over to the couch where Yani was strapped. The pigmy girl had begun to recover consciousness as they entered the ship, and now she stirred drowsily and opened her eyes.

Li Shao simply sat, watching the screens. The brief flare of purpose he had experienced along with the flare of the ship's engines had utterly left him. He was vaguely aware that Kos and Kai, now allowed some degree of mobility by freefall despite their injuries, had appeared in the aft hatch and were looking at him anxiously.

Nathan Li Shao was suddenly aware that they were all looking at him: Hoch, and Kos, and Yani, and Kai and even Leetha. They wanted him to tell them what to do.

The problem was, what he wanted to do, what he *really* wanted to do, was open up the cover plate on the controls, find the galvanistical detonator Solan had disabled, reable it again, hit the galvanistical switch and switch it all off.

It was at that point that he half-heard the constant static squeal from the radio set break into a frantic, half-phased gabbling.

Li Shao was hindered by his straps. By the time he got free of them Leetha was already at the radio set and adjusting the frequencies while the others gathered around. There was a burst of static and then the voice, a woman's voice, came through clear as a bell:

'. . . to ensure mutual security. This is Roslyn Forrester of the Planet X occupation forces. We are broadcasting this message simultaneously on emergency radio frequencies and through Sloathe mental contact – yes, OK, Benny, I know the Sloathe transmissions are more like "Hey, is big, big happy day for all us not-dead Sloathes, boogie-boogie

319

all right matey!" Just shut up, will you? Anyway. Will all survivors please respond on this waveband. You will be assigned a landing site and there will be a period of quarantine to ensure – look, I said shut *up*, all right? Oh sod it. If there's anyone left out there to hear this, come on down, and can we all just try not to kill each other, OK? This is Roslyn Forrester of the . . .'

'You know, if that's a trick of the Sloathes to kill off anyone who's left,' Leetha said, 'they've certainly got a lot more sophisticated than I remember them. Do you want to try it?'

Li Shao never got a chance to answer her – because at that point, Yani turned her head towards the aft hatch and emitted a piercing scream.

She flung herself across the bridge, still screaming, clawing at herself in panic, tried to scrabble under a control console and then fainted dead away.

'Sorry,' the Doctor said, stepping through the hatch. 'I just thought I'd join you for the big show. Is she all right?'

'What?' Li Shao said. 'What big show? What are you talking about?'

Kai and Hoch had gone to Yani instantly and were glaring at the Time Lord with a sort of futile hate. He shrugged, hauled himself over to the radio set, and listened for a moment. 'Oh, good. I'm glad they're all right. Not that I ever had a moment's doubt, of course.'

Li Shao and Leetha and Kos stared at him, utterly dumbfounded.

'What happened to you?' Li Shao said, after a while. 'What exactly *happened* down there in the Sun?'

'That is something for slightly later,' the Doctor said. 'That is something to be told in the fullness of time.' And for a moment his eyes clouded with such an utter pain and loneliness that those watching him were forced to turn away, as though stung. 'Let's just say it was a mercy killing and leave it at that for the moment.'

Abruptly, he clapped his hands together and glanced about himself cheerfully, as though the death of worlds and the death of millions had simply never happened.

'And for now,' he said, 'I think you'd better strap yourself in and prepare for some extremely extensive evasive manoeuvring.' He smiled. 'It wouldn't do to give up the ghost just at the end. You'd miss the prize, and that really wouldn't do at all.'

Li Shao wanted to ask the Time Lord what in the various hells he was talking about again – but he suddenly became aware that Leetha was staring at something in shock.

'The screens,' she said, very, very quietly. 'Look at the *screens*.'

'Yes,' said the Doctor. 'I'd advise you all to look at the screens.'

And of a sudden, for one last time, the *Schirron Dream* lurched as though clutched by some monstrous hand.

———⟨⟩———

And in the Sun, in the collapsing remains of a decelerating orrery chamber five miles wide, a flawed, discarded diamond on a crystal floor flickered, flared and then detonated.

The explosion tore the cold black Sun to pieces, blowing a gaping hole in it to leave nothing of its main mass but a crescent, still carrying the vestiges of a massive, fatuous face along its ragged inner edge.

And the remains of the Wanderers lurched in their unnatural orbits, hesitated, and then of a sudden retracted on their metadimensional camshafts on a collective and catastrophic collision course.

And the worlds, naturally enough, collided.

And the atmosphere of this little System, the breath of life spread thinly but evenly through it all, was dragged shrieking towards this new gravitational mass. Atom piling on atom, molecule piling upon molecule to cloak this new mass with an almost suffocating hypoxic richness.

And storms boiled in this new, rich atmosphere. And below them rock, turned liquid by the immense release of kinetic energy, flowed together. And every scrap of combustible matter burned, until several billion tons of water that had previously comprised Elysium arrived to put the fires out with a commensurately spectacular splat.

And far away, the ruptured, deformed and dying energy field that had contained this little System finally gave up the ghost and flipped over on its back with its spatially anomalous legs in the air. If it had legs. Which it didn't.

321

And suddenly the sky was full of stars.

Which would have been extremely impressive, had they not in fact been almost entirely obscured by the new sun, bigger than anything any inhabitant of the System could ever imagine or envisage, impossibly far away, orbited by several additional globes and bathing this new planet in its radiance. The sun that, via the various generations of Eyes, had provided the little System with its energies all along.

And around this new planet orbited Planet X, a true moon, with its own admittedly slightly thin but perfectly serviceable atmosphere.

The Epilogue

It was night – or at least the orbit of Planet X was at the point where the new sun was behind it, and would be for almost an hour. Benny and the Doctor, Nathan Li Shao and Leetha T'Zhan stood on the surface of the moonlet, breathing its thin, still and chilly air and looking at the new planet hanging on the horizon. Storms still swirled over its surface, and lightning crackled across it, but a number of large landmasses could be glimpsed through the clouds.

'It's rather fortunate that several reality disruptions were still in operation when it was made,' the Doctor said. 'It wouldn't have been possible for it to exist otherwise.'

'Let me get this straight,' Li Shao said. 'You're saying we *made* this thing, me and Leetha?'

'In a sense.' The Time Lord turned to the pair of them, Li Shao and Leetha. 'You see, the Eyes were the components of a control system inextricably linked with its operator. If the Charon had used them the result would have merely been another killing bottle. If Solan and the Sekor Dom Sloathe had used them, I shudder to think what sort of world they would have made. As it was, you made a world in which people could live.'

'Then when you made everything seem hopeless,' Leetha said, 'when you told us we had ten years at the most, you were lying?'

The Doctor nodded. 'I'm afraid I didn't have a lot of choice. You were right when you said I was manipulating things to a certain extent, Leetha – but I'm afraid I was also doing a little manipulation on quite different levels than you meant. The rituals of the Search were unimportant in and of themselves. What counted was not the farcical following of them to the letter, but what was in your head and in your heart. I had to force you into some degree of emotional maturity despite yourself.'

'Well, I suppose I should thank you,' Leetha said, 'but it doesn't feel at all good and there's no way I can go back, now.'

'It's not supposed to be good,' the Doctor said. 'Feeling good has never been a major part of what you might call the human condition.'

On the skyline the new planet seethed, although the storms now seemed to be dying slightly down.

'It should be perfectly habitable by the time people are capable of landing on it *en masse*,' the Doctor said. A little, bleak expression flitted momentarily across his face. 'There's certainly enough biomass in the mix.'

The chill began to get to them. They walked to a circular hatch and climbed down. The tunnel in which they found themselves still bore little scorched traces of the thing that had once been the Most Supreme Captain Trenkor Lep.

'It was remarkably specific, in the end,' Benny said. 'It killed the thing and whatever it happened to be digesting at the time, but every other Sloathe and humanoid in the planet survived. I think that, in the end, the TARDIS was simply too fundamentally decent to kill indiscriminately.'

'I suppose I should feel good about that,' Li Shao said as they walked through the tunnel. 'I still have a problem thinking of the Sloathes as anything other than evil.'

'You owe them an enormous debt,' the Doctor said. 'Admittedly they did it for entirely the wrong reasons, but it was only the fact that the Sloathes have been taking people and things off the Wanderers for years that allowed as many of them to survive as they did.' He pointed to an elegant silver figurine lying amongst the slightly fire-damaged junk that filled the tunnel. 'Take that. If the Sloathes hadn't stolen it then it would be gone for ever.' He turned back to Li Shao. 'Do you have any idea how many people in fact survived?' he asked with a slightly deceptive lightness.

Li Shao shook his head. 'A surprising number of people managed to evacuate from the Wanderers after Planet X went through them. A lot of them subsequently died, apparently, when they couldn't pressurize their various crafts, but there's more coming in every day. We had some people in from Sere

324

a few hours back. I'd say some two hundred thousand survived in the end.'

'I must admit that's slightly more than I expected.' Again, the little bleak look passed across the Doctor's face. 'I just wish it could have been more.'

They passed into a large repository cavern in which humanoids and Sloathes were clearing away debris to make room for the hydroponics the Doctor had planned. Two hundred thousand survivors out of millions might be regarded as barely failing to lose utterly rather than winning, but it also presented several very real problems so far as food was concerned. A large pile of sterling silver cutlery still remained to be cleared, and on it stood the TARDIS.

Li Shao spotted Kiru and Yani, Hoch and Kai amongst the crowd, and he and Leetha wandered over to join them, arm in arm.

The Doctor, however, hung back. 'I'd better not. Yani seems to go into a shrieking fit every time I go near her.' He frowned. 'I can't think why.'

Benny was watching the departing pair with a little smile. 'Well, Leetha seems to be getting on exceedingly well with Li Shao, now. She was talking earlier of them taking the *Schirron Dream* and exploring the other planets when things are a little more settled. I wonder how she's going to react when she finds out Li Shao and Kiru are in fact an item?'

The Time Lord shrugged. 'I don't think that will be too much of a problem. I think it was you yourself who pointed out that such things are a little looser and more complex here. I wouldn't know about such things myself, of course.'

'Ah yes,' Benny said. 'Time Lords don't concern themselves with little things like that. You just screw the entire – oh, hi, Chris. Hello, Roz. Hello, Sgloomi.'

Roz Forrester and Chris Cwej were looking slightly more cheerful and healthier now. The Doctor, when they had met him, had listened for some time to the problem of a ravenous little Sloathe inside each of them, and then had pondered aloud that surely Sloathes must have biological defences against such things in the same way that humans have defences against bacteria. The serum, produced by Sgloomi Po, had been administered to good effect – save that both Roz and Chris would now have a tiny Sloathe skeleton inside them until their respective bodies broke it down.

'You know, I'm not sure if I'm cut out for this,' Roz said as they headed for the TARDIS. 'I mean it's had its moments, but I really think I need to live in a world I can understand.'

'You're doing yourself a profound injustice,' the Doctor said with a reassuring smile. 'You're far stronger than you think you are. You and Chris spent your time out near the edge, where things were particularly disrupted. You saw and experienced things that would have instantly killed Benny stone cold dead.'

'Thanks a lot,' said Benny indignantly.

'Don't mention it,' said the Doctor.

Chris Cwej had returned from where he was saying his goodbyes to Sgloomi Po, who was by now almost completely indistinguishable from a human being, if vaguely androgynous. It had even begun to develop pigment.

'It seems that the Sloathes are capable of becoming more complex than even we suspected,' he said cheerfully. 'Sgloomi was telling me how he was able to eat and digest a cheese sandwich a few hours back.'

'With a little bit of pickle?' Benny said. She glanced around at the Sloathes in various stages of transformation thoughtfully. 'I wonder if we're looking at the birth of a new species, or a very old one. Maybe these Sloathes lapsed into their previous state because they were isolated for so long. How many other worlds are hosts to things just like them? So similar to their host-species that they're indistinguishable?'

Cwej was looking around himself with a happy smile. 'I just think it's really good to see people getting on like this.'

'Yeah,' said Roz cynically. 'I just wonder how long it's all going to last.'

The Doctor shrugged. 'I think that's something they're going to have to sort out for themselves, and without any more interference from us. At some point you simply have to let people go to heaven or to hell in their own way.' He grinned suddenly, and twirled his umbrella. 'Things change. They always do. That's what they're there for.'

The Appendices
with Special Extra Added Piglets

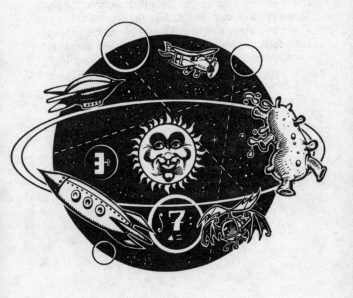

Wherewith is shewn sundry additional material pertinent to the Work being entitled *Sky Pirates!* or *The Eyes of the Schirron*, the which is included gratis, at no extra charge, and this by the way of being just yet one more irrefutable proof of the generosity, benevolence and not to say open-handed liberality of the extremely lovely Virgin Limited Liability Company. You lucky people.

Appendix II: A Benny Bibliography

Enfant terrible, *bon vivant*, archaeologist, pharmacologist, behavioural psychologist and best-selling novelist, these are just some of the words Benny Summerfield knows how to spell the best two tries out of three – and it is a little-known fact that, every time she steps out through the TARDIS door, she steps out clutching a hefty typescript and looking for a nearby, unwary and subsequently extremely unlucky publisher.

Indeed, the works of Benny Summerfield may be found strewn through the remainder bins of the space-time continuum like a large and slightly ragged, foxed and slightly water-damaged flock of irradiated dead seagulls upon Canvey Island beach.

But now, for the first time, the PractiBrantic Press offers you the golden opportunity to own the pristine *Collected Benny Summerfield* for yourself! Fifty-seven volumes bound in genuine hand-tooled human-skin leather, actually cloned and force-gestated by herself and from her very own DNA!

The *Collected Benny Summerfield* includes:

DOWN AMONG THE DEAD MEN

All you ever wanted to know about running around lost temples in a silly hat whilst patronizing the local native bearers rigid and much, much more. *Special to this edition*: an expanded section upon the many aspects of a small rock-hammer and precisely what you can do with it.

'I owe it all to Benny. She certainly showed me what's what with a bullwhip.' – Mr I. Jones, USA, 1938.

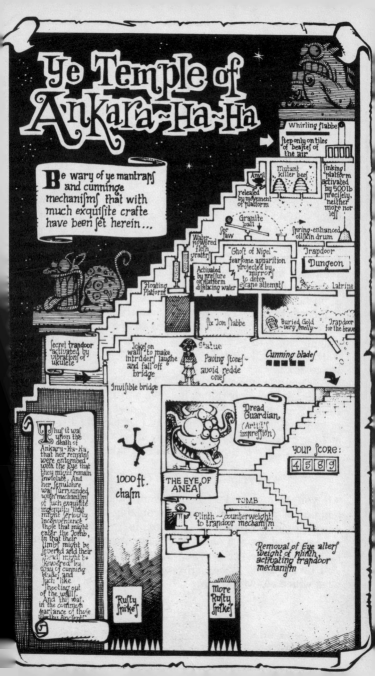

electroceph-stim/brothel/soma-parlour. Your copy of the *Collected Benny Summerfield* will then arrive. Sometime. At some point.

PractiBrantic Press

It isn't an entirely fraudulent scheme of Benny's to obtain extra free beer money wherever she goes at all.

Appendix III: The Lyrics

The Discerning Reader may have noticed that several passages have been judiciously omitted from the text of *Sky Pirates!* – most notably and conspicuously the lyrics to certain songs.

It was the intention of our translators to present these here, in full, in all their scintillating beauty and with a musical score especially composed for full orchestra with timpani and exploding piglets by Mr James Last.

Then we came down off some incredibly powerful hallucinogens, realized that James Last was in fact dead* and decided to forget it.

* Those of us who are of the generation whose parents actually enjoyed this noted German light-orchestral band leader, have insisted upon the additional, and final, addendum: 'and if he's not then he damn well should be.'
Stuff.

Already published:

TIMEWYRM: GENESYS
John Peel

The Doctor and Ace are drawn to Ancient Mesopotamia in search of an evil sentience that has tumbled from the stars – the dreaded Timewyrm of ancient Gallifreyan legend.

ISBN 0 426 20355 0

TIMEWYRM: EXODUS
Terrance Dicks

Pursuit of the Timewyrm brings the Doctor and Ace to the Festival of Britain. But the London they find is strangely subdued, and patrolling the streets are the uniformed thugs of the Britischer Freikorps.

ISBN 0 426 20357 7

TIMEWYRM: APOCALYPSE
Nigel Robinson

Kirith seems an ideal planet – a world of peace and plenty, ruled by the kindly hand of the Great Matriarch. But it's here that the end of the universe – of everything – will be precipitated. Only the Doctor can stop the tragedy.

ISBN 0 426 20359 3

TIMEWYRM: REVELATION
Paul Cornell

Ace has died of oxygen starvation on the moon, having thought the place to be Norfolk. 'I do believe that's unique,' says the afterlife's receptionist.

ISBN 0 426 20360 7

CAT'S CRADLE: TIME'S CRUCIBLE
Marc Platt

The TARDIS is invaded by an alien presence and is then destroyed. The Doctor disappears. Ace, lost and alone, finds herself in a bizarre city where nothing is to be trusted – even time itself.

ISBN 0 426 20365 8

Appendix I: Kimon's Notes

Few can boast of having such a profound effect upon the lives of the many as can Kimon, the high priest of the Sun Samurai cult of the dirigible city of Rakath. Particularly after dying some time around Chapter Three. But influence them he did, largely through his celebrated notes concerning the Search for the Eyes of the Schirron.

In commemoration, therefore, we present certain facsimiles of these notes such as survive, for the delight and edification of all who might behold them.

We are indebted to Mr Roger Langridge, whose own small works have appeared in such noted periodicals as *Deadline*, *Knuckles the Malevolent Nun*, *Art d'Eco*, *Bloody Hell* and *Judge Dredd The Megazine*, for preparing these excerpts for general publication.

Mr Langridge, we are reliably informed, also mows lawns remarkably cheaply.

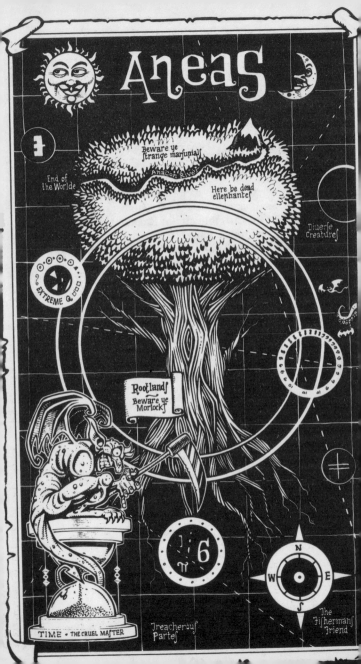

THEATRE OF WAR
Justin Richards

Menaxus is a barren world on the front line of an interstellar war, home to a ruined theatre which hides sinister secrets. When the TARDIS crew land on the planet, they find themselves trapped in a deadly reenactment of an ancient theatrical tragedy.

ISBN 0 426 20414 X

ALL-CONSUMING FIRE
Andy Lane

The secret library of St John the Beheaded has been robbed. The thief has taken forbidden books which tell of gateways to other worlds. Only one team can be trusted to solve the crime: Sherlock Holmes, Doctor Watson – and a mysterious stranger who claims he travels in time and space.

ISBN 0 426 20415 8

BLOOD HARVEST
Terrance Dicks

While the Doctor and Ace are selling illegal booze in a town full of murderous gangsters, Bernice has been abandoned on a vampire-infested planet outside normal space. This story sets in motion events which are continued in *Goth Opera*, the first in a new series of Missing Adventures.

ISBN 0 426 20417 4

STRANGE ENGLAND
Simon Messingham

In the idyllic gardens of a Victorian country house, the TARDIS crew discover a young girl whose body has been possessed by a beautiful but lethal insect. And they find that the rural paradise is turning into a world of nightmare ruled by the sinister Quack.

ISBN 0 426 20419 0

FIRST FRONTIER
David A. McIntee

When Bernice asks to see the dawn of the space age, the Doctor takes the TARDIS to Cold War America, which is facing a threat far more deadly than Communist Russia. The militaristic Tzun Confederacy have made Earth their next target for conquest – and the aliens have already landed.

ISBN 0 426 20421 2

THE LEFT-HANDED HUMMINGBIRD
Kate Orman

Someone has been playing with time. The Doctor, Ace and Bernice must travel to the Aztec Empire in 1487, to London in the swinging sixties and to the sinking of the *Titanic* as they attempt to rectify the temporal faults – and survive the attacks of the living god Huitzilin.

ISBN 0 426 20404 2

CONUNDRUM
Steve Lyons

A killer is stalking the streets of the village of Arandale. The victims are found each day, drained of blood. Someone has interfered with the Doctor's past again, and he's landed in a place he knows he once destroyed, from which it seems there can be no escape.

ISBN 0 426 20408 5

NO FUTURE
Paul Cornell

At last the Doctor comes face to face with the enemy who has been threatening him, leading him on a chase that has brought the TARDIS to London in 1976. There he finds that reality has been subtly changed and the country he once knew is rapidly descending into anarchy as an alien invasion force prepares to land . . .

ISBN 0 426 20409 3

TRAGEDY DAY
Gareth Roberts

When the TARDIS crew arrive on Olleril, they soon realise that all is not well. Assassins arrive to carry out a killing that may endanger the entire universe. A being known as the Supreme One tests horrific weapons. And a secret order of monks observes the growing chaos.

ISBN 0 426 20410 7

LEGACY
Gary Russell

The Doctor returns to Peladon, on the trail of a master criminal. Ace pursues intergalactic mercenaries who have stolen the galaxy's most evil artifact while Bernice strikes up a dangerous friendship with a Martian Ice Lord. The players are making the final moves in a devious and lethal plan – but for once it isn't the Doctor's.

ISBN 0 426 20412 3

HEAD INVADERS:
QUASI-PSYCHOLOGICAL OLD TOOT OF YOUR TIMES

Brief meditations upon some of the debilitating memes infecting Planet Earth during the later twentieth century, including:

Multiple personalities: 'That Howling Rabbit woman had a grand total of 64 distinct personalities, supposedly – one of whom was a literary genius on the level of a Shakespeare or a Joyce. So where the hell was *he* when she wrote the book?'

And:

Alien abductions: 'Listen, I've been there, done that, and if the alien *I* know ever tried to stick a probe up my bottom I'd be out the door like a bloody *shot*.'

'Burn it! Burn it now! It's evil and putrescent filth so burn it now!' – Archdeacon Arlo Blue, Evangelical Church of the Whitley Strieber Communion Inc., USA, 1998.

INCREDIBLY BAD JOKES
OF THE TWENTIETH CENTURY

A transputer-assisted compendium with over 50,000 entries, the size of a large telephone directory. Entries include:

'Waiter, waiter, this egg isn't fresh!' 'Don't look at me, sir, I only laid the table.'

And:

'An elephant peered down at a mouse and said, "Ho, ho, ho, you're very tiny, aren't you?" "Well," said the mouse, "why don't you sod off then, you bloody speciesist." '

Supplementary index: *Incredibly Stupid Songs*, including:

> One evening in October,
> When I was far from sober,
> And dragging home a load with manly pride,
> My feet began to stutter
> So I lay down in the gutter
> And a pig came up and parked down by my side.
> Then I warbled, 'It's fair weather
> When good fellers get together',
> Till a lady passing by was heard to say:
> 'You can tell someone who boozes
> By the company she chooses!'
> And the pig got up and slowly walked away.

333

THE FORTY-FIVE-SECOND PIGLET

A US comic-book, instantly commissioned in 1988 when, while on a small errand for the Doctor, Benny happened to be wandering through a big building in New York, with an English accent.

The plot involves a sexually ambivalent half-human, half-piglet superhuman who doesn't like hitting people, travelling across the USA with a group of animal-liberation terrorists with clocks instead of faces, the ghost of John F. Kennedy, the Lord God Almighty, his nice young friend and a brain-fried New Age hippie in a psychedelic, motorized, soft-top convertible Irish pub, interminably trying to make sense of his/her life in the sort of crystalline and pause-laden prose that would have Samuel Beckett on Mogodons reaching for a shotgun.

The Forty-five-second Piglet was never in fact published. It appears here for the first time, in a strictly limited Graphic Novel format edition. Buy one now! Buy two! Stick one in your mylar bag and shove it up your loft! In ten years' time it'll be worth exactly the same as a mint-condition first-run issue of the *Inverately Postmodern Pigswill Bandits*!*

All of these and many more including 'The Entropy Alternative', 'Blag your way through Higher Education', 'Interesting Roundels I have known' and 'Why I Don't Like Daleks' will be found within the plump and firm-packed volumes of the *Collected Benny Summerfield!*

But how, you ask, can I get hold of this gorgeous literary panoply of metatemporal and unearthly delights?

Good question.

It couldn't be simpler. Wherever you are, whenever you are, simply open up a bank account in the name of Bernice Summerfield (where applicable, please ensure that the smartcard cashpoint PIN is: 0743) and deposit cash to the equivalent of a good night out in your local pub/club/

* i.e. utterly worthless.

THE HIGHEST SCIENCE
Gareth Roberts

The Highest Science – a technology so dangerous it destroyed its creators. Many people have searched for it, but now Sheldukher, the most wanted criminal in the galaxy, believes he has found it. The Doctor and Bernice must battle to stop him on a planet where chance and coincidence have become far too powerful.

ISBN 0 426 20377 1

THE PIT
Neil Penswick

One of the Seven Planets is a nameless giant, quarantined against all intruders. But when the TARDIS materializes, it becomes clear that the planet is far from empty – and the Doctor begins to realize that the planet hides a terrible secret from the Time Lords' past.

ISBN 0 426 20378 X

DECEIT
Peter Darvill-Evans

Ace – three years older, wiser and tougher – is back. She is part of a group of Irregular Auxiliaries on an expedition to the planet Aracadia. They think they are hunting Daleks, but the Doctor knows better. He knows that the paradise planet hides a being far more powerful than the Daleks – and much more dangerous.

ISBN 0 426 20362 3

LUCIFER RISING
Jim Mortimore & Andy Lane

Reunited, the Doctor, Ace and Bernice travel to Lucifer, the site of a scientific expedition that they know will shortly cease to exist. Discovering why involves them in sabotage, murder and the resurrection of eons-old alien powers. Are there Angels on Lucifer? And what does it all have to do with Ace?

ISBN 0 426 20338 7

WHITE DARKNESS
David McIntee

The TARDIS crew, hoping for a rest, come to Haiti in 1915. But they find that the island is far from peaceful: revolution is brewing in the city; the dead are walking from the cemeteries; and, far underground, the ancient rulers of the galaxy are stirring in their sleep.

ISBN 0 426 20395 X

SHADOWMIND
Christopher Bulis

On the colony world of Arden, something dangerous is growing stronger Something that steals minds and memories. Something that can reach out to another planet, Tairgire, where the newest exhibit in the sculpture park is blue box surmounted by a flashing light.

ISBN 0 426 20394 1

BIRTHRIGHT
Nigel Robinson

Stranded in Edwardian London with a dying TARDIS, Bernice investigates series of grisly murders. In the far future, Ace leads a group of guerrillas against their insect-like, alien oppressors. Why has the Doctor left them, jus when they need him most?

ISBN 0 426 20393 3

ICEBERG
David Banks

In 2006, an ecological disaster threatens the Earth; only the FLIPback team working in an Antarctic base, can avert the catastrophe. But hidden beneath the ice, sinister forces have gathered to sabotage humanity's last hope. The Cybermen have returned and the Doctor must face them alone.

ISBN 0 426 20392 5

BLOOD HEAT
Jim Mortimore

The TARDIS is attacked by an alien force; Bernice is flung into the vortex and the Doctor and Ace crash-land on Earth. There they find dinosaur roaming the derelict London streets, and Brigadier Lethbridge-Stewart leading the remnants of UNIT in a desperate fight against the Silurians who have taken over and changed his world.

ISBN 0 426 20399 2

THE DIMENSION RIDERS
Daniel Blythe

A holiday in Oxford is cut short when the Doctor is summoned to Spac Station Q4, where ghostly soldiers from the future watch from the shadow among the dead. Soon, the Doctor is trapped in the past, Ace is accused of treason and Bernice is uncovering deceit among the college cloisters.

ISBN 0 426 20397 6